THIS
VICIOUS
GRACE

THIS
VICIOUS
GRACE

EMILY
THIEDE

HODDER &
STOUGHTON

Some of the thematic material in This Vicious Grace includes death, violence, and war, with references to child abuse. For more information regarding potentially sensitive content, please visit http://ekthiede.com/.

First published in Great Britain in 2022 by Hodder & Stoughton
An Hachette UK company

1

A CIP catalogue record for this title is available from the British Library

Hardback ISBN 978 1 399 70011 5
Trade Paperback ISBN 978 1 399 70012 2
eBook ISBN 978 1 399 70013 9

Printed and bound by Clays Ltd, Elcograf S.p.A

Hodder & Stoughton policy is to use papers that are natural, renewable and recyclable products and made from wood grown in sustainable forests. The logging and manufacturing processes are expected to conform to the environmental regulations of the country of origin.

Hodder & Stoughton Ltd
Carmelite House
50 Victoria Embankment
London EC4Y 0DZ

www.hodder.co.uk

For the little girls who talk "too much" and feel "too intensely."
Never change.

And in loving memory of one very special girl. We miss you.

CITY of SAVERIO

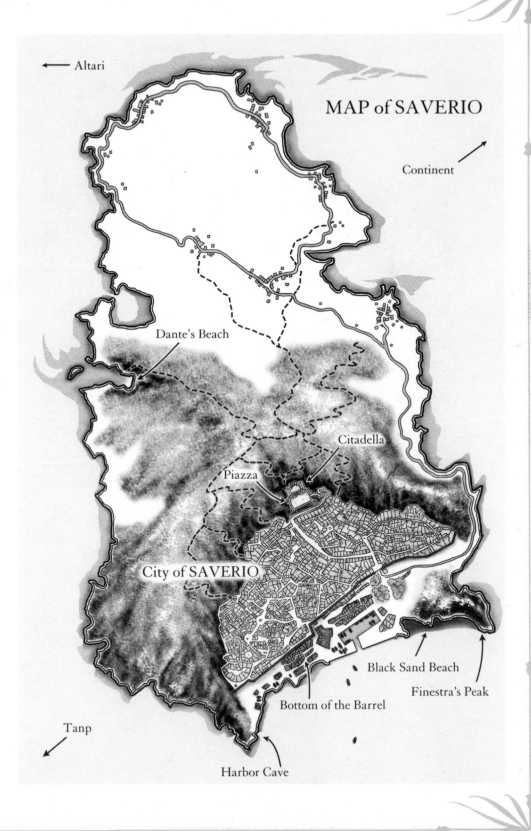

← Altari

MAP of SAVERIO

Continent

Dante's Beach

Citadella

Piazza

City of SAVERIO

Black Sand Beach

Finestra's Peak

Bottom of the Barrel

Tanp

Harbor Cave

Benedizioni Della Dea

(L'ORIGINALE)

Alla fine dell'inizio,
la Dea creò isole santuario per i fedeli,
Benedicendo ciascuno con tre doni:
Alcuni nacquero con la magia.
Un salvatore, per migliorarlo.
E quando arrivo il momento della battaglia, i combattenti
  sarebbero stati forti,
poiché ha dato loro una fonte di guarigione.

Dea's Blessings

(TRANSLATION)

At the end of the beginning,
the goddess created sanctuary islands for the faithful,
She blessed them with three gifts:
Some, born with magic.
One savior, to enhance it.
And when it came time for battle,
The fighters would be strong,
for she gave them a healing fountain.

—TRANSLATED IN 242 D.I., SCRIBE UNKNOWN

One

Attraverso la Finestra Divina, la luce riduce i demoni in cenere.
Through the Divine Window, light burns demons to ashes.

Three weddings.

Three funerals.

A better person would have been devastated, but Alessa bowed her head to hide dry eyes as she knelt before the jewel-encrusted coffin on the altar. The temple beneath the Cittadella smelled of mildew and death, the air thick with dust motes drifting like the ghosts of fireflies.

She *would* cry. Later. She always did. Being widowed at eighteen was tragic, after all, and none of her partners had deserved to die. Still, it was difficult to muster tears for yet a third time.

Hugo, her third Fonte and the unfortunate body before her, had insisted it was only nerves when his hand trembled in hers. She should have known better. She *had* known better. But the gods had chosen her, and she'd chosen him. So, even knowing her touch might be his last, she'd reached for him a second time.

Alessa Paladino, divine weapon of the gods.

Her latest wedding dress was packed away, traded for a mourning gown and knee-high boots, with a black mantilla over her hair. And gloves, of course. Always gloves. Still, the dank chill reached for her bones. Even on a sunbaked island, the sun couldn't warm what it never touched.

Cupping her hands as though in prayer, Alessa brewed a minuscule wind funnel between her palms. The faint echo of Hugo's gift only lasted a moment, but she offered it back to him anyway. The empty space it left behind felt like penance.

Her knees ached, but she didn't stand until the last stragglers found their seats. It wasn't easy. Every minute spent mourning was one she didn't get to spend choosing her next Fonte, and she didn't have time to spare. Or Fontes, for that matter.

On one side of the aisle, the twelve members of the Consiglio watched her with inscrutable eyes. Always watching. Always waiting. First, for her to be old enough to choose a partner. And then, for her to choose another. And another after that. Soon, they'd summon her next victim.

Partner. Her next *partner.*

She had to get it right this time. The Consiglio would have her next choice dragged to the Cittadella at sword-point if needed, but she wanted someone *willing.*

On her way to her seat, Alessa paused to curtsy before Renata Ortiz, the previous Finestra, whose power had winked out the day Alessa's blossomed five years ago. Renata nodded, cool and aloof, while her Fonte, Tomohiro Miyamoto, offered a sympathetic smile. They were a good pairing. A great pairing. Exactly what Finestra and Fonte should be.

A familiar pull of envy threatened to drag Alessa under as they laced their hands together.

She'd give anything for a hand to hold. Or a hug.

She would *kill* for a hug.

Literally.

Alessa took her seat, pressing a fist to her mouth before a sharp inhalation became a giggle, or worse, a sob. Stiff, black fabric pulled across her chest as she steadied her breathing. If she'd known how often she'd need one, she would have asked for a new mourning gown after the first wear.

Adrick slid in beside her, tugging his lapels and doing his best to look forlorn. "No weeping for good old Hugo, little sister?" he murmured, barely moving his lips. "Lucky for me, there was an open seat beside you."

"There's *always* an open seat beside me." Alessa squeezed her gloved hands together in a vain attempt to warm her fingers.

Renata shot Alessa a look of warning from across the aisle.

It wasn't *her* fault Adrick didn't respect rules. He might even be willing to hug her, but she'd never ask. A Finestra wasn't supposed to touch anyone but their chosen Fonte until after Divorando. And it was too dangerous to chance. The thought of her twin brother laid out on the altar turned her stomach.

He should've sat somewhere else. The Finestra was expected to sever all ties from her previous life. Above and apart. Always. She wasn't even supposed to *think* of him as her twin anymore, and she definitely wasn't supposed to speak to him.

"Picked the next one yet?" Adrick signed as the choir began rustling in place. Sort of. Their Nonno was Deaf, so they were fluent in Sign language, but the "whispered" half-signs he'd shaped in his lap were a bastardization of language only she could interpret. Papa would be mortified. But Papa wasn't there. And he wasn't her papa anymore.

"Still deciding," she signed back.

"Better hurry," he said, switching to a hoarse whisper. "A dozen fled Saverio in the past month."

Dread pooled in her stomach. She'd lost track of how many eligible Fontes remained on the island, but she couldn't afford to scare off more. She resisted the urge to turn and see who was left.

All Fontes were blessed at birth with defensive magic—fire, wind, water, earth, electricity, and so forth—and thus they were respected and revered, considered a precious resource whether they were chosen to serve or not. Each Fonte received a generous annual stipend, was exempted from military duty, and was protected from harm.

Until they weren't.

"Good riddance," Alessa hissed. Anger was safer than panic, and she knew her duty, which meant not falling apart where someone might see. "Anyone who'd abandon their people isn't worthy of being my Fonte."

Without a Finestra to absorb and magnify their power, a Fonte's gift was fairly weak, but at least they *had* useful powers. Not like hers, which was basically worthless without a partner to draw from.

So she couldn't argue with Adrick's response of "Better an unworthy Fonte than none at all."

She risked a quick glare. Aside from his eyes—green on a good day, hazel on most—her brother was nothing like her. Tall and lanky, with tanned skin and golden curls, Adrick strolled through life with an easy charm, while she had their mother's dark waves and creamy skin that burned easily, and her ease and charm had been snuffed out by years of rules and isolation.

"You could be more encouraging," she whispered.

Adrick appeared to consider the possibility. "Someone has to laugh about it."

"It isn't funny."

"Of course it isn't." There was a slight tremble to his voice. "But if I think about it too seriously, I'd never get out of bed."

Alessa swallowed. When her first Fonte, Emer, died, Adrick had stood outside the Cittadella's walls belting out bawdy sea chanteys in his best pirate voice for hours until her sobs became hiccups of laughter. Adrick was never serious, no matter how dire things became, but after years of wishing he'd take her situation seriously, she wasn't sure she could handle it if he did.

A soloist began the Canto della Dea in the common tongue, soon joined by another in the ancient language, then others, until a dozen languages wove a harmony as intricate as the community.

Together, we protect. Divided, we falter.

Wizened old Padre Calabrese shuffled up the stairs as the last note died, clearing his throat repeatedly even though no one was speaking.

"The gods are cruel but merciful," he began.

Easy for him to say.

"In the beginning, Dea created humankind, but Crollo insisted we were too flawed, too selfish, to endure. When Crollo sent fire, Dea made water to quench it. He brewed storms, and she granted shelter. And when Crollo vowed to cleanse the earth and begin anew, Dea challenged him, because she had faith in us. 'Alone,' she said, 'a person is a thread easily snipped. Intertwined, we are strong enough to survive.'"

Alessa squirmed on the unyielding bench. It would be her luck to lose feeling below the waist and topple over when she stood to leave. Dea really should have sweetened the deal by throwing in some tolerance for discomfort with the great and deadly power.

Sensing Padre Calabrese's attention shift her way, Alessa sat up straighter.

"And so, Dea and Crollo made a wager: Crollo could send his devouring minions, but Dea would raise sanctuary islands from the sea where the faithful could strive to live in harmony, proving their worthiness and defying Crollo's cynicism. And because she loves us, she armed her children with gifts . . ."

Alessa tried to look as gift-like as possible as furtive glances flicked her way.

While it was all *true*, and obviously they owed Dea a debt, the goddess *could* have chosen a simpler solution. An impenetrable shield, perhaps. Or made the islands invisible. Maybe she could have negotiated Crollo down to *one* planetwide scourge, and they would've been done with this nonsense a half a century ago. But *oh, no*, in her infinite wisdom, Dea decided to teach her children about community and partnership by creating saviors who couldn't save alone.

The divine pairing existed as a constant reminder that shared strength was their path to salvation. Hence, a Finestra could only magnify someone *else's* gift.

Hand in hand with an opera singer, a Finestra could bring the harshest music critic to his knees. For a few minutes after touching an archer, a Finestra could hit every bull's-eye. And paired with a Fonte, a Finestra could defeat an army of demons sent by the God of Chaos.

At least, that's how it was *supposed* to work.

When Alessa first stood before the Consiglio, the row of wizened elders had made it sound as easy as one, two, three.

1. Choose a Fonte.
2. Do *not* kill them.
3. Amplify their magic to save everyone and everything on Saverio—or become the first to die.

Alessa's gaze slipped to the glittering coffin.

Well, not the *first*.

Even now, some insisted the deaths were a good omen. Terribly sad, of course, but reassuring. A Finestra so powerful she accidentally killed her first Fonte? They would be well-protected in the siege. And her second? Well, accidents happened. Besides, she was young, and these things took time. Surely, she'd be more careful with the next. But after three funerals, Alessa's strength didn't feel like a promise of victory anymore, and time was running out.

The service concluded with, "Per nozze e lutto, si lascia tutto, però chi vive sperando, muore cantando." *In weddings and mourning, one lets go, but he who lives with hope dies singing.* It might have been the saddest thing she'd ever heard. Hugo certainly hadn't left the world mid-note.

As the pallbearers made their way down the aisle, guests reached out to brush the glossy surface of the coffin.

Alessa did not. Spirit or ghost, surely whatever was left of Hugo would prefer she kept her distance.

As the casket passed beneath an archway of carved stone gods, the crowd murmured, "Rest in the company of heroes," and he was gone.

Hero was perhaps a *bit* of a stretch—all he'd done was die—but she had no right to talk.

People stood, straightening jackets and gathering skirts with slow hands, brushing invisible dust from their clothing.

Alessa recoiled at Adrick's elbow jab to her ribs, her heart racing at the rare sensation of physical contact.

Oh. Everyone was stalling. And she wasn't taking the hint.

She flashed a rude gesture at him behind her back, then rose and made her way toward Dea's shrine in the front of the temple. Everyone could flee while she pretended to pray.

Such a dutiful Finestra. *So* devout. *So* obedient.

Shielded from curious eyes within the alcove, Alessa sat beside the stone Dea on the altar and rested her cheek against one cold, marble shoulder. Her chest ached, hollow with everything she didn't have.

Family, forsaken.

Friends, none.

Even the fortress carved into the bedrock of the island wasn't for her. When Divorando came, other people—people who *had* families and friends—would huddle together in the darkness, thanking the gods they weren't her.

When the nave rang hollow, she climbed the wide stairs alone to the piazza above, straining to breathe past the constriction of her gown. The temperature rose with every step, and the fabric clung to her skin, damp with perspiration. At least the Consiglio had finally let her remove her veil during private events after a brush with heatstroke at the last Midsummer's Gala, and the current fashion of cape skirts—full and long in the back but with overlapping panels that crossed at knee-height in front—saved her from falling on her face daily in Saverio's capital, the City of a Thousand Stairs.

Alessa stepped out, blinking in the light, to take her place beside Tomo and Renata. The red-faced guards lining the wide steps to the Cittadella saluted, sweating through their uniforms, and the waiting crowd hushed to bow and curtsy.

From her usual vantage point—a balcony off the fourth floor of the Cittadella—the stylish young women of Saverio often looked like flocks of peacocks strutting around the city in jewel-toned skirts. Now, clad in shades of black and gray, they huddled like dirty pigeons around the margins of the piazza.

No one looked directly at her, as if she was too horrible to view with the naked eye, yet, somehow, the weight of their stares pressed in from all sides.

Go ahead. Bow before the blessed savior who keeps killing your friends and family.

At Renata's pointed look, Alessa flushed, as though she'd spoken aloud the blasphemy in her head. Despite the two decades between them, Renata looked young enough to be Alessa's sister, with an amber complexion, golden hair, and rich, brown eyes, but to Renata, Alessa was a duty, not family or even a friend. It was painfully clear in moments like this.

Tomo's expression warmed with encouragement. "Remember, frightened people crave certainty."

"You are *confident*," Renata said under her breath. "You have matters *under control*."

Alessa bared her teeth in a "confident" smile that made one guard flinch. She eased it down a bit.

Honestly. If she were to rank every *possible* description of herself, "confident and under control" wouldn't make the list.

When she'd first been presented in this piazza, everyone had crowded close, eyes sparkling with hope, smiles heavy with promises.

One day, she was an ordinary girl. The next, Dea's chosen savior. Beloved, important, and so popular she hadn't known where to look first.

Not anymore. Now no one vied to become her Fonte. No one wanted to share their gift with her. Although it wasn't *really* sharing, was it? Sharing implied they'd get something back. That they'd both be alive at the end of the transaction. That was a promise she couldn't make.

But she'd try. She always tried.

Even in such a restless crowd, it was easy to find the Fontes, draped in a visible miasma of gloom. She'd met them dozens of times, but they were still nothing more than strangers with familiar names:

Kaleb Toporovsky, whose eyes slid away a bit too fast as he smoothed his burnished copper hair with a look of perpetual boredom.

Josef Benheim, impeccably clad in midnight black, his gaze so steady she could almost hear him reminding himself not to blink. He looked so much like his older sister that Alessa's heart caught in her throat. Families rarely had more than one Fonte, but when they did, it was seen as a sign of strength, of the gods' favor. He should have been one of Alessa's top candidates, but she'd already cost his parents one child.

Other Fontes reluctantly met her searching eyes: Nina Faughn, Saida Farid, Kamaria and Shomari Achebe.

Most tried to blend in with the crowd. She couldn't blame them. While she'd barely known the people she'd killed, they'd all grown up together.

Now they were expected to act like they were desperate to be chosen by a girl whose power was useless without theirs.

Dea, give me a sign.

What she really needed was a push. Hours upon hours watching from high above the city, longing to be amongst the people, but every time she escaped her golden cage, her wings forgot how to fly.

She only made it three steps before a sudden commotion in the crowd stopped her.

A woman shoved her way through the tightly packed wall of people to burst into the clearing.

In stark white robes, she stood out like a star on a moonless night. What kind of person started a shoving match at a funeral?

The woman's gaze landed on Alessa, and her eyes blazed.

For a bizarre moment, Alessa was embarrassed. It had been a few years since anyone had been overcome with religious fervor at her presence, and it was an awkward time for a fit of rapture.

The woman's face twisted, the gleam in her eyes turning dark, and she broke into a run.

Alessa's pulse raced to the beat of footsteps against the stone.

The robed woman didn't slow, didn't flinch, heedless of the guards rushing at her from all sides. Without breaking her stride, she drew her arm back.

And threw.

Something whistled past Alessa's head with a whine so high-pitched it was painful.

Guards tackled the woman, wrestling her to the ground, their bodies muffling the words she tried to scream.

Alessa reached a hand to her neck, and the fingertips of her glove grew warm and wet with blood.

"*Dea,*" she breathed. Not *that* kind of sign.

Two

Chi cerca trova.

Seek and you shall find.

lessa's breath came fast and shallow as she wiped the hot trickle from her neck. Blood wouldn't show on her gloves, and fear wouldn't show on her face. It couldn't.

Her eyes followed the trail of crimson droplets on the stone to a flash of sunlight glinting off a dagger. If she'd been one step to the left, the blade that had notched her ear would be lodged in her skull.

The Captain of the Guard barked orders, and his soldiers formed a protective wall around her. For the first time in her life, she yearned for the protection of the Cittadella's high walls.

"Wait," Renata said. "They need to see she's unharmed."

Alessa clenched her fists. Hiding wasn't an option. Not for her. *Never* for her. Duty called, a little blood be damned.

"Chin up, Finestra," Renata muttered. "Show them you are *not* afraid."

Alessa fought the horrific impulse to laugh as she lifted her head so high, no one could see the tears burning behind her eyes.

At her reassuring wave, a ripple of relief—at least she hoped it was relief—rolled through the crowd, and Renata gestured for them to retreat at last.

"How bad is it?" Renata asked as soon as the gates clanged shut behind them.

"Could have been worse." Alessa winced, probing her injury. "Why would someone do that?"

It made no sense. A Finestra dying before Divorando was unimaginable. Or, at least, she'd thought it was. A number had been wounded *during* battle, but they'd all lived long enough to climb Finestra's Peak. Without a Finestra and Fonte, Saverio would be entirely defenseless against the demons.

"Who can explain the choices of an unhinged person?" Tomo said, holding out his elbow for Renata. They exchanged a tense look.

"If you know something, tell me." Alessa followed them through the arched corridor to the interior courtyard. Tomo, tall and still athletically built despite his health struggles, made Renata look even more petite by comparison.

"You can't protect her forever, Tomo."

"Renata," Tomo pleaded, his tan skin going a bit gray. "We don't even know if he's connected."

He? The knife-thrower had been a woman.

"Who?" Alessa asked. They didn't answer. In moments like these, she became invisible.

"I told you, we should have him arrested." Renata's voice crackled with fury. "Lash him to the peak and leave him to die."

Tomo sighed as if he'd made the argument countless times before. "For talking on street corners?"

"For inciting violence!"

"*Who?*" Alessa said, louder, and they turned to look at her as though she'd blinked back into existence. "*Who* isn't connected? *Who* should be left to die? Tell me. I'm the Finestra, not a scared child." If she said it firmly enough, she might even convince herself.

Tomo waved his hand as if shooing a fly. "Some ridiculous street preacher calling himself Padre Ivini. He's just fanning fears to line his pockets."

"And which fears are those?" Alessa hugged her sides, suddenly cold. She knew what *she* feared—swarms of demonic insects descending from the sky, everyone counting on *her* to stop them. But braving terror so others didn't have to was the Finestra's burden.

"Foolish prattle. Everyone with sense is ignoring him." Tomo looked to Renata for support, but she shrugged.

Alessa gestured at her ear. "*Everyone?*"

"Everyone but a few desperate souls looking for certainty in an uncertain world. Enough about that." Tomo's smile was kind but pointed. "We have more important matters to deal with."

Than her life? Alessa frowned. She might have managed to pry one answer from them, but that didn't mean she'd asked the right questions.

Renata sighed. "It won't happen again. Put it from your mind."

Right. The many things Alessa was *supposed* to remember had a tendency to slip away like sand through her fingers, but she wasn't likely to forget a dagger flying at her head.

Renata rubbed her temples. "The sooner she chooses a Fonte, the better."

"I didn't even get to speak to anyone," Alessa said. "I have to make an informed choice. I *need* it to work this time. Please."

Please don't make me kill again. She might as well have said it aloud. They knew what she meant.

Tomo moved as though to clasp her arm, awkwardly brushing at his sleeve instead. "How about a performance? A gala, where every eligible Fonte can demonstrate their gifts, and you'd have a chance to speak with each of them."

Anticipation fluttered beneath Alessa's breastbone. She'd expected to spend the next few days in isolation, begging Dea for a sign before choosing whom to shackle herself to, but a demonstration might be exactly what she needed to choose the right Fonte, for once.

"Tomorrow." Renata nodded. "And she needs to look transcendent. The more jewels the better. I want her dripping with proof of Dea's favor."

Inwardly, Alessa rolled her eyes. Once, she might have equated wealth and jewels with a person's worthiness, but now she knew the truth: The gods gave and took for their own incomprehensible reasons, and only fools tried to make sense of it.

Her. *She* was the fool. Because she still wanted to understand.

"Perfect," Tomo said. "Our guests will leave here raving about our blessed savior, prepared to choose her final, *true* partner. That will silence the naysayers."

Alessa still didn't know what, exactly, needed silencing, but she'd slipped back into invisibility, so she left them to their plans and climbed the stairs on leaden feet.

Adrick would know what this Ivini person was saying—he collected gossip like children hoarded pretty rocks—but she had no idea when she'd see him next.

From outside, the Cittadella looked like a massive stone block, but within the austere facade, the building blended a military stronghold and an elegant estate, with an exquisite atrium in the center and lavish gardens out back. The first two levels were all business, with a mess hall, barracks, an armory, and training spaces, while the second floor served as military command center.

The upper levels, however, served as a private residence for the Duo Divino, the divine pairing. *Pairings*, plural, as the previous Finestra and Fonte were expected to return to the Cittadella when a new Finestra rose and remain for the duration of the five years Dea gave them to train their successors.

Dea must have ignored the fine print of whatever divine contract she'd signed with Crollo, however, because instead of sending Divorando on the fifth *anniversary* of the new Finestra's rise, Crollo chose a month at random *in* the fifth year, and no one knew precisely when he would strike until the First Warning arrived.

Seven months into her fifth and final year, Alessa was no closer to finding her battle partner than she had been the day the Consiglio confirmed her.

The formal banquet hall on the third floor was empty and dark, and Tomo and Renata had not yet returned to their suite, so Alessa didn't see another soul until she reached the fourth floor, which was all hers and would remain so until she found someone to fill the rest of it. The largest library on Saverio, a private chapel, and two suites for one lonely girl.

When she reached the top of the stairs, Lorenzo, the young soldier assigned to guard her rooms, blanched beneath his olive complexion. He was supposed to open the door *for* her and complete a thorough inspection before she entered, but he, like the string of guards before him, refused to touch anything of hers.

She opened her own doors now.

She'd never say it aloud, but it stung like ice water on bare skin every time someone cringed away from her. Especially soldiers. They'd volunteered to face a swarm of demons but acted like she was something even worse.

Lorenzo deigned to cast a cursory look around and retreated to his post, muttering something under his breath that sounded suspiciously like *ghiotte*.

Greedy one.

Alessa kicked the door closed.

"Don't be a ghiotte," her parents used to chide her whenever she'd asked for more than her fair share of sweets. They'd softened the word, so it sounded almost endearing, but visions of Crollo's thieves took residence in her head. Even now, she often dreamt of growing claws and horns.

Every child on Saverio grew up hearing tales of the ghiotte. How Crollo sent demons disguised as humans to find Dea's third gift before the first Divorando. When the ghiotte found La Fonte di Guarigione—the healing fountain created for the soldiers—they stole its power, becoming nearly impossible to kill and leaving nothing behind for the troops. Caught and damned for their sin, they were hunted or driven into the sea, their only remaining legacy a warning about the consequences of greed and selfishness.

Some skeptics believed the story was a metaphor, a morality tale to keep people in line, but the church elders insisted that every word in the holy Verità was history dictated by Dea herself.

The Finestra was Dea's first blessing.

The ghiotte had stolen the third.

And Alessa kept killing the second.

She stripped off her gloves and tossed them with the others piled by her bedside.

A warm, citrus-sharp breeze from the balcony blew dark curls into her eyes as she padded barefoot to a small table set with a selection of breads, cheeses, and fruits. The cheese shone with grease in the waning sunlight, and the bread was stale. Not a feast worthy of a Finestra, but she could hardly blame anyone else for underperforming.

The sunset reflected off the ocean below, painting shades of rose-gold across the city cascading down the hillside in a jumble of sun-bleached pastel buildings. It looked as if the city walls were holding everything in check so they wouldn't collide with Finestra's Peak, looming over the black sand beach where she and her chosen partner would take their place at the head of Saverio's army.

At least her prison had a great view.

She should bathe, wash off the blood and anxious sweat, but she curled up in an armchair instead, pulling a throw blanket up to her chin. It was too warm, but the texture coursed over her bare arms and neck, sparking her nerves awake after a long day of slumber. Not a human touch, but a touch at least. Anything was better than the static half-sensation of being covered from head to toe.

After a childhood littered with forgotten schoolwork, burnt loaves, and waste bins she'd never remembered to empty, Alessa had finally made her mother proud the day she became the Finestra and had to stop calling her "Mama." But even ordained by the gods, she disappointed everyone. Sure, she was determined, always trying to please. She *meant to* complete her chores, to remember the shopping list or check on the bread, and now she *meant* to control her gods-given power. Her failures didn't mean an extra trip to the market anymore, but dead Fontes and dried blood crackling on her skin.

Papa always said any problem looked better in daylight, but it would take a wickedly bright sunrise to improve hers.

She closed her eyes and plucked at the underside of the blanket, pinching the knots, running her fingertips over the stitching.

You are not alone. You are alive. You were chosen.

You are lonely. You will die. Maybe Dea chose wrong.

This was hopeless. She couldn't afford to get trapped in a never-ending spiral of worries, and the only way out was to get answers.

Alessa sat up, letting the blanket slide to the floor.

If no one inside the Cittadella would tell her what was going on, she'd find someone who would.

Three

Dio mi guardi da chi studia un libro solo.
Never trust a man who only studies one book.

S he hadn't had many opportunities for rebellion since leaving home, but Alessa was making up for lost time. With a lightweight cloak under her arm, boots clutched in one hand, and a rough sketch of the tunnels going soft with sweat in the other, she crept past the kitchens where Lorenzo was attempting to flirt with unimpressed kitchen maids.

She stopped before the banquet hall, listening for the rise and fall of conversation within. She was only a *semi*-prisoner, with free rein inside the Cittadella, but she'd blow her cover if Renata saw the guilt scrawled across her face. At the scrape of silver on ceramic, she held her breath and dashed past on the balls of her feet.

"Where"—Alessa tensed at Renata's words—"do we even begin tomorrow?"

Alessa sagged against the wall until her wobbly knees got their act together, then tiptoed on. Through an archway off the court-

yard, a spiral staircase connected the Cittadella above to the Fortezza below it. Narrow and dim, the ancient stone stairs dipped
in the middle, worn down by countless feet over centuries.

The Cittadella was formidable, but it was nothing compared to
the stronghold beneath. The maze of tunnels and caves carved into
the island dated back to the original settlers who'd expanded the
natural volcanic tunnels to make the entire island into a fortress.

A Finestra did not, by nature, explore. Under normal circumstances, Alessa only entered the Fortezza to attend Temple
with Tomo and Renata, but the master key she'd never used slid
easily into the lock.

Shivering from nerves rather than cold, she pulled on her
cloak and let herself out the first gate beyond the line marking
the border of the Cittadella above.

Outside, the warm, thick air carried the wafting sweetness of
roses from the Cittadella's gardens, but she turned away from the
high walls to follow the humble scents of home. The sun set over
quiet avenues and shops closed for the evening.

Each terrace bloomed with sounds and smells so distinct she
could have navigated the city with her eyes closed. In an area ripe
with peppers and cumin, nimble fingers tripped out a melody on
a guitar as heels clicked the tempo. In the next, garlic and green-
onion dumplings sizzled in hot oil while a voice so tender it must
belong to a mother sang a lullaby that sounded like spring rain
on a rooftop.

Nearly every house had a lemon tree, often standing alone on
a tiny island of soil amongst the stone, and dried boughs hung
over thresholds, marring otherwise pristine windowsills with
sticky drips of dried juice. The gesture was rumored to ward
off Crollo's demons—named "scarabeo" for their resemblance to

horned beetles—but if it actually worked, Saverio wouldn't need a Finestra.

Urging herself to keep walking, to pretend it was a stranger's home, she paused by a blue-shuttered window.

Inside the small kitchen, her mother tended to a pot on the stove. She reached for the salt, resting her hand on it, as though she'd forgotten what she'd meant to do. The small table in the middle of the room was only set for two. Maybe Adrick refused to eat meals with them anymore. Maybe family suppers didn't feel right without her.

Wishful thinking. He was probably just working late.

Supper smelled like something hearty, simmered for hours, with lamb and red wine. Memories tangled around her. A crowded table, stories repeated so many times they lost all meaning, becoming poetry, children falling asleep in soft laps—

Alessa swiped at her eyes and moved on.

She might never be a normal girl who clipped rosemary for supper again, but they had to survive.

The alleys narrowed as she descended, until buildings butted into each other, and the island made its presence known with wildflowers pushing through cracks in the cobblestones and vines creeping up walls.

Alessa pulled up her hood as she passed the guards who manned the city gates, but they paid her no mind. They were there to watch for incoming threats, not girls running off to the docks, where folk stayed up late getting into trouble.

On Saverio, criminals were marked for their crimes, and those who'd committed irredeemable offenses were banished to the continent, where they'd perish in the next Divorando without any protection from the Duo Divino and their army. The rest were merely forced to wear their shame, but when Saverians barricaded themselves inside the Fortezza, those with marks were left outside to fend for themselves. Past curfew, no one marked was permitted inside the city walls without an official pass from the Cittadella.

There was no one else on the dirt road to the docks, but the night sounds expanded to fill the emptiness, with tiny creatures scurrying and invisible wings thrumming in the grass.

The whine of insects succumbed to the creak of ships as the road widened and became clogged with people and vendor tents. If the city was a four-course meal for the senses, the docks were a hearty stew. The din of myriad languages was intoxicating, and the crush of bodies made one girl in a cloak practically invisible.

As the largest of the four original sanctuary islands, Saverio had drawn the widest array of people from nearby regions before the first Divorando, and even now, almost a millenium after Crollo's first siege had stripped the continents to bones and dirt, Saverians boasted of being the entire world in miniature. An exaggeration, to be sure, but there was no one left to dispute the claim.

Alessa slowed at the sound of chanting as a dozen cloaked figures emerged from an alley, their white robes stark against a backdrop that was dark and grimy. She squinted to make out the crimson words embroidered on their backs. *Fratellanza della Verità.*

Passersby gathered, captivated by the spectacle. It wasn't hard to see why. The group's barely audible humming raised the hair on Alessa's arms, and the hoods shadowing their faces lent an air of unearthly anonymity.

Fear tightened her scalp as one figure disengaged from the

rest, pushing his hood back to reveal a striking face and prematurely silver hair. He smiled benevolently and a few people began clapping, though he hadn't said a word.

Strategically veiled in the glow of a streetlamp, he held a large book aloft. Not an official copy of the Holy Verità—she of all people could spot the difference between the genuine article and a fake—but the glyphs on the cover bore a close enough resemblance to fool most people.

Women at the front of the crowd jostled for position, gazing at him with rapt devotion, and Alessa finally caught the whispered name. Ivini.

"Our gods tell us to have faith," he said in a low, hypnotic voice. "That we are blessed with holy saviors."

A savior you nearly got killed today.

"But we've grown complacent. Trusting. Naive." His features softened with carefully crafted sadness, but his sharp eyes gauged the crowd's response. "I ask you, are you sure our *esteemed* Finestra will save us, or do you, too, wonder if the gods are testing us?"

A child in a stained dress worked her way through the growing crowd. She held out a beggar's hat, but most ignored her, clutching their purses and avoiding eye contact.

Ivini dropped to an ominous monotone, and the crowd went silent. "The lost texts warn of a day when a false Finestra shall rise. One whom the faithful shall recognize on sight."

His eyes raked across the crowd, but his all-knowing gaze spent no more time on Alessa's face than anyone else's. So much for that theory. He was a convincing liar, though. Shaking his head as if regretting what he had to say next, he pressed a hand over his heart. "There she sits, in *our* Cittadella, slaughtering *our* precious Fontes, coddled despite her wickedness. Sent by Dea?

So they tell us. But would Dea send a murderer to save us? I think not. No, this bears the mark of Crollo."

A young man with tousled dark hair and sun-bronzed skin shot a disdainful glance at the crowd as he strode past, and Alessa's shoulders relaxed. At least *someone* wasn't buying what the holy man was selling.

"I ask you," Ivini said, his gaze sharpening, "when the demons descend to devour every living thing on Saverio, will our *dear* Finestra even pretend to fight or will she simply laugh while our brave soldiers are massacred? Will she cheer for the creatures as they gnaw at the gates of the Fortezza, or will she open them herself? And who will die first? Who will suffer most, but those of you who will be locked outside?"

The beggar girl tripped, spilling her coins across the ground. Her high cry cut through Ivini's speech, and he stopped with a loud sigh, motioning one of his robed minions toward the girl.

Alessa couldn't push through to help the poor child, but at least someone was going to.

The robed man bent to grab the girl's tunic, forcing her to stand. "Blessed be the wretched, for they know not what they do. You'd need no coin if you had the sense to listen to your betters."

Frowning, Alessa took an involuntary step forward.

"Let her go." The crowd parted like butter to a hot knife as the young man stepped through, his sneer darker, frightening. He couldn't be but a few years older than Alessa, but he walked with the authority of one who expected others to move aside.

Ivini's disciple straightened until the girl's toes barely touched the cobblestones, his grip firm. "Is she with you? If so, you need to teach her some manners. The gods don't appreciate—"

"Drop her, or I'll send you to meet your gods right now." The young man's movement was slight, his broad shoulders shifting in the merest threat of a lunge, but Ivini's minion stumbled back, inadvertently dragging the girl with him.

He didn't make it far. The young man seized his wrist and gave it a brutal twist that splayed his fingers.

The girl broke free, darting behind her rescuer to use him as a barrier. With wide eyes, the child watched her bully forced to his knees, whimpering in pain.

The young man let go and wiped his hands on his pants with a look of disgust.

The disciple glanced around, clutching his injured arm, but no one leapt to his defense, not even his leader. It seemed the Fratellanza's religious fervor didn't extend to putting their bodies on the line.

"Brother," Ivini said in a cold voice, fury burning in his eyes. "Let us show grace. Even the most wicked may come to see the light. Eventually."

The dark-haired stranger knelt to help the child gather her scattered coins, adding a few from his own pocket before he stood and continued on his way, strolling past empty storefronts to where the street narrowed to little more than an alley. He stopped beneath a worn placard reading *The Bottom of the Barrel* and pulled the door open, releasing a burst of raucous voices. As if he could feel her eyes on him, he glanced back and met Alessa's gaze, raising an eyebrow in silent challenge.

She looked away, blushing.

Ivini resumed his sermon, funneling his anger into it, and the crowd responded like a bonfire to dry kindling, flaring hot and fast.

Cold sweat dewed Alessa's forehead. Renata and Tomo had

made it sound like a few lone dissidents, but this was a revolt in the making.

"*Who* has the courage?" Ivini demanded. "*Who* is brave enough to smite the false prophet?"

"I'd do it," a woman shouted, and the crowd roared their approval.

Alessa inched back into the shadows.

Death was creeping closer, but this wasn't where she intended to meet it.

Four

Chi ha fatto il male, faccia la penitenza.
As you make your bed, so you must lie.

A bell tinkled above the door as Alessa entered the apothecary. Luckily, Adrick was the only worker on the floor. He looked up, his mop of curls bouncing as he fumbled the jar he was handing to an elderly woman.

Alessa signed that she needed to speak to him.

Hiding his movements, he signed back, "Trying to get me banished?"

"Knife. My head," she signed, pulling her hair back to reveal the bandage.

His nostrils flared, and he signed a curt "Outside, ten minutes" before turning back to the customer and saying aloud, "That one's infused with dried herbs, but if you ask me . . ."

Alessa pretended to peruse the store's offerings, uncorking a small bottle and coughing at the rank contents.

Adrick looked pointedly at the open door to the storeroom, and she left to wait for him outside.

When he emerged from the darkened building a quarter-hour later, Adrick held up a hand to stop her from speaking and jerked his head toward the main road, setting off without checking to see if she followed. His legs were considerably longer than hers, and he made no effort to adjust his stride.

"Did you know?" she said, trotting to keep up. "About this Ivini person claiming I'm a false Finestra?"

Adrick's silence was answer enough.

"Adrick! Why didn't you tell me?"

"I knew it would worry you."

"Strangers are throwing knives at me. I *should* be worried."

"Then why are you here?" he shot back. "One knife to the head wasn't enough excitement for the day?"

She blanched. "I only stopped wearing the veil recently. Hardly anyone knows what I look like."

"Signor Arguelles does."

"Well, he didn't see me."

As children, they'd spent countless hours crushing herbs for their neighbor before Adrick became his apprentice, and while she couldn't imagine the kindly older man betraying her, it wouldn't be the most shocking recent event.

"Tell me what you've heard." Alessa stopped short, forcing her brother to turn back.

"Look." Adrick blew out a breath. "It's been a long day. The apothecary has been mobbed with people looking for tinctures to remove their tattoos—impossible, of course—and medics needing supplies to treat people who tried to burn or cut theirs out. People are panicking, thinking . . ."

"That I can't protect them." She'd thought she was the only one who lay awake at night, afraid she'd let everyone down. Instead, her deepest fears were being shouted from every street corner.

He tugged his ear. "Well, can you?"

"Can you *please* believe in me?"

"I do. It's just—" Adrick cast a wary glance ahead at a group gathering around a robed woman. "People are saying all kinds of things, like Crollo has cursed you, or you're some new kind of ghiotte sent to steal the Fontes' magic. Some even think you're proof Dea's forsaken us and Crollo's finally going to end it this time. Hell, there's a whole cult of people who think we all deserve to die and Dea should never have defied him in the first place."

For hundreds of years, Saverians had survived against the odds, trusting their saviors to protect them when wicked wings descended. And now, the people were giving up. Because of her.

She'd never asked if any of the rare trading ships had offered news from the other islands about her counterparts—whatever they were called—so it was possible she might not be alone on this sinking ship. Maybe, somewhere across the sea, someone else was railing at their own inability to perform their duty. It wouldn't change the fact that if Alessa failed, she'd be the one responsible for the deaths of every living thing on Saverio. If the other islands fared better, their survivors would someday arrive on Saverio to find barren shores and empty ruins, and if any records remained, Alessa would live on in their history as a cautionary tale:

Alessa, the last Finestra.

Dea's greatest mistake.

She swallowed, throat tight. "Do *you* believe I'm a . . . a new kind of ghiotte?"

Adrick smirked. "I've seen you bedridden with cramps. Ghiotte would be tougher than that."

She bared her teeth. "Adrianus Crescente Paladino, you'd cry like a baby if *you* got cramps."

Adrick made a gagging face at his full name. "I know, I know. You're the divine warrior and I'm the worthless brother you left behind. Why do you care what I think? You're the one with the direct line to Dea. Ask *her*." His lips twisted with a hint of bitterness.

"It doesn't work like that." She flicked a glance at the dusky sky.

"You!" a robed woman called out.

Alessa flinched, but the woman looked past her.

Adrick broke into a jog. "Keep your head down and hurry up."

"Do you know her?"

"'Course not. They're all pushy like that."

She frowned. It had sounded like the woman was speaking to someone she recognized. Alessa glanced over her shoulder. The woman wasn't following. No angry mob giving chase. Not yet.

"Adrick, what do I do?"

"Prove them wrong. Get a Fonte and keep them alive for once."

"I'm *trying*."

"I know." He gave her a sidelong glance. "You always do."

The twinkling lights of the city grew closer as they walked in silence.

She ducked her head, baring her unmarked wrists for the drowsy guards manning the city walls. Adrick bid them a hearty good night and they traded some sort of manly handshake.

After checking that the surrounding area was clear, Alessa unlocked the first tunnel entrance they passed and stepped inside. "I still can't believe you didn't tell me about Ivini."

"I *said* I'm sorry." Adrick's moonlit silhouette was fragmented by the bars. "Lock it."

Alessa turned the lock with a click. "Satisfied?"

"Never. I should take your keys."

"Stealing keys to the Fortezza is a banishable offense."

"Oh *no*, not *banishable*. I would *never* do something *banishable*, like defying the church's edicts by fraternizing with you."

"They wouldn't *banish* you. Only lock you up for a few days."

"Much better. Now that I've risked my freedom, tell me who you're going to pick so I can make some bets."

"I haven't decided yet, and I wouldn't tell you if I had. In fact, I hope you're the last person on Saverio to find out this *very important* information."

He snorted. "Fine. I deserve that. But everyone's been asking."

"Why do they expect you to know? I'm not your sister anymore, remember?" She couldn't hide her resentment. "You handed me over to the gods."

"Now, now," he said, gaze flicking upward. "The Verità says *parents* must relinquish a chosen child to the community. It doesn't specifically say anything about siblings."

"Oh, so that's why you still talk to me, huh? A brotherly loophole?"

"I'm just saying, in Dea's eyes, *I'm* not doing anything wrong here."

Unlike Alessa, who *was* violating the holy rules. How fitting for Adrick to skate by on a divine technicality and leave her with the guilt. He always had known how to charm his way out of trouble. "Well, loophole or no, Mama would swat your bottom raw if she knew you'd tainted her holy sacrifice by staying in touch."

"Aw, Lessa, that's not fair. She loves you, but she loves Dea, too, and she knows her duty. Once you finish saving Saverio and they release you from your golden cage, she'll be the first one running to hug you." His gaze roamed across everything but his sister. "Well, maybe not *hug* you."

"If you say so." Alessa's voice was too high, too light.

"You'd better not cry. Goddesses can't go around weeping in public."

"I'm not a goddess. And I'm not crying."

"Good. Now, scurry back to your palace and order a few strapping young guards to fan you while you eat bonbons or whatever it is you do all day."

Alessa snorted. "Oh, yes, it's all luxury, all the time. If you're volunteering to take my place, go right ahead."

Adrick laughed drily. "Would if I could, lil sister. Maybe Dea's aim was off on choosing day, eh?"

"Now, there's a thought. Bring a batch of Mama's macarons the morning after the gala, and *maybe* I'll tell you who I'm going to choose. For half your winnings."

"Half?" Adrick's grin returned. "Not a chance. I brought you two dozen last week. What mere mortal could finish that many so fast?" He slid into a sardonic drawl. "Ah right, but you *are* no mere mortal, are you."

"You're terrible."

"And you love me. Hope Dea picked the right twin."

She snorted. "How can you doubt, when it's going so well?"

"Hey!" A masculine voice called out. "You, get away from there."

"Until next time, little sister." Adrick trailed off as he fled. "Try not to kill anyone before then."

Five

Chi sta alle scolte, sente le sue colpe.
Eavesdroppers hear no good about themselves.

The following evening, Alessa unwrapped layers of tissue-thin paper to reveal the most beautiful gown she'd ever seen.

The tiny buttons down the back were meant to be fastened by someone else, but she made do, turning the gown backward halfway up to fasten the buttons, then rotating it and squeezing her arms through the neckline.

Her breath caught as she looked in the mirror, and only partly from the constriction around her ribs.

She glittered like a sea of diamonds. The structured bodice was cream-colored silk studded with gems, and it swooped into a low neckline that exposed her shoulders and dipped in the middle. Below, layered cape-skirts flashed silver and gold silk with her every movement. She hadn't shown this much skin in public since—well, ever.

When she'd first entered the Cittadella, she'd expected parties every day and a wardrobe full of gowns like this. Then she'd come to learn her days would be spent studying, training with weaponry, and analyzing battle strategies, and she realized most of her clothing would serve one important function—to cover every possible bit of her lethal skin.

This dress, though. *This* was a dress fit for a fairy-tale princess. It hadn't been made for a Finestra at all, but commandeered from the city's most illustrious seamstress, and somewhere in the city, a very wealthy woman must be justifiably furious.

With a sad sigh, Alessa found her longest silk gloves to cover her arms up to the cap sleeves, and tights that looked suitable beneath the overlapping panels of the cape skirt. She couldn't decide whether a long chain of pearls or a heavy diamond necklace went better with blue topaz earrings. Mama used to say the trick to looking tasteful was removing one piece of jewelry before going out, but Renata's goal for Alessa's look was obnoxiously garish, so, with a shrug, she put them both on.

Tipping her head to one side, Alessa studied her cosmetics. Did she want to look intimidating? Nonthreatening? Pretty? It wasn't easy to find a look that said, *Welcome, suitors. Please perform for the right to marry me, and I will try not to kill you.*

She settled on a thin stroke of eyeliner, pink lips, and bronze eye shadow. Sparkly, but approachable.

It took an ungodly number of jeweled pins to corral her curls, but she was proud of the final results, which hopefully looked more "deliberately tousled" than messy. Another fistful of pins, and a fall of curls hid her injured ear. It would always have a funny shape at the top, but with the blood washed away, it wasn't too gruesome. If there was an award for evading a public assassination unscathed, she'd get an honorable mention at *least*.

The delicate heels she unearthed from a pile of shoes in the back of her closet threatened twisted ankles and pinched toes, but she'd suffer in style. Besides, it wasn't like she'd be dancing.

Someday after Divorando, when she'd wrestled her power into submission or Dea had passed it on to the next poor Finestra, she would throw a bigger, better party, with a full orchestra, diamond glasses, a prosecco fountain. She'd stay up until dawn, laughing with her Fonte and dancing all night in shoes that were stylish *and* comfortable. It was a fantasy; she might as well dream big.

She was radiant with an hour to spare, more than enough time for Tomo and Renata's scheduled pep talk before she wooed her next Fonte. She descended slowly, heels wobbling, dress trying to suffocate her, clutching the railing so her grand entrance didn't culminate in a tumble of silk and sequins.

The front gates were open, and a stream of deliveries, soldiers, and staff flowed in and out, carrying chairs and stacks of linens down to the piazza. Two grungy-looking men rolled a runaway keg back into place, flicking a rude gesture at the soldiers who did nothing to help. As Alessa neared the bottom, people turned to stare, appreciation joining the fear in their awestruck gazes. Her cheeks warmed. Apparently the Angel of Death looked more angelic than deadly, for once.

Two transfixed young servers collided, dropping their trays in a clatter of broken china, and the Captain's furious voice rose above the ruckus. "What in Dea's name—"

"It was my fault, Captain Papatonis," Alessa called out. "All these jewels must have blinded them."

Captain Papatonis scowled, but he couldn't scold her. Or dispute that she was very sparkly.

Alessa left the chaotic noise of the atrium for the quiet labyrinth of darkened corridors, wishing it wasn't gauche to kick off her shoes for the walk.

As she made her way, cursing silently at every twinge that promised blisters, she caught a flicker of movement at the end of a long corridor leading to the barracks.

A man. And he wasn't in uniform.

"Excuse me," Alessa called out. "Guests aren't permitted down there."

He stepped into the light, shadow taking the form of dark curls, a sharp jawline, heavy-lidded eyes, and a familiar challenging expression.

"You," she said, accusingly. "You aren't a guest." Young men who fought with cultists by the docks weren't the sort of people who got invited to a glittering gala at the Cittadella.

"Nope." His scorn-filled gaze raked down her, from the diamond-studded pins in her hair to her gold-slippered toes. "Barrel sent me to deliver spirits."

She fired back a haughty glare. "That doesn't explain what you're doing back here."

He sauntered closer as though he had all the time in the world. "Got lost."

A pack of soldiers erupted from the barracks at the end of the hall in a riot of boisterous laughter and shoulder-punching, helmets tucked under their arms. Their laughter fizzled at the sight of Alessa and the stranger, but for reasons she couldn't begin to fathom, she didn't order them to escort the interloper out.

Swapping looks, the soldiers continued, veering around the stranger like a stream diverted by a boulder.

Alessa pressed herself against the side of the corridor to let them pass.

Brow furrowing, the stranger studied her.

"What?" she demanded.

"You trying to burrow into the wall?"

Her cheeks burned. Fine, so she wasn't brave, she wasn't strong, and she wasn't up to being a savior, but he didn't have to look at her like he *knew*. "I was getting out of the way."

His eyes narrowed. "Why?"

"It's *polite*. A concept you're clearly not familiar with. They've seen the damage I can do." Bitterness singed the edges of her words. "I can't blame anyone for keeping their distance."

He gave her a level stare. "Then let them walk around you."

She hadn't even told him which way to go, but the aggravating stranger strode away, leaving Alessa alone in the hallway. She stood there, silent, in the half-light.

Let them walk around you.

As though it were that simple.

"Ah, Finestra." Tomo stood, adjusting the hem of his emerald jacket as Alessa entered the military records room. "Our blessed vessel."

Alessa forced a strained smile. The damned vessel again. Once, she'd been a person. Now she was a tunnel. A basin. A lens. Or whichever metaphor Tomo came up with to help her understand her role. But *understanding* wasn't the problem. She simply had no idea how to *do* it.

He and Renata had years to practice together before their battle, while she'd give her right hand for a few months. Well, maybe not a hand. She'd need both to hold on to her Fonte and a weapon at the same time. Maybe a foot. Or an ear. She'd already nearly lost one that afternoon, and with the right hairstyle, no one would even know.

Renata glanced up from the table-sized book in front of her. "We've told her a thousand times, dear. I doubt another meta-phor will make the difference."

Tomo deflated. "The bridge to understanding is constructed of words."

"Thank you for trying, Tomo," Alessa said, easing into a chair. "You do have a beautiful way with words."

Tomo rapped his pen on the table. "The only visual aid I can think of is a prism, and it fractures light, while a Fines-tra does the opposite, merging the colors . . ." He wandered off, muttering about wavelengths.

Alessa's book might have held history's greatest secrets, but it was written in the old language, so she'd never know. It was too heavy for her to slam shut, and her dramatic gesture became a wrestling match as the pages flipped back in the opposite di-rection.

Renata closed the ancient tome in front of her, sending up a puff of dust. "Pages of flowery prose, but no *actual* advice. Bunch of would-be poets. I swear, if I could meet the Finestre of old, I'd slap some sense into them."

"Ooh, let me do it." Alessa ventured a smile. "It would hurt more."

Renata strode across the room, midnight blue skirts parting to reveal green tights. After Ilsi's death, people had begun eying

Alessa's delicate lace gloves and sandaled feet like they were venomous snakes, so she'd covered up. Renata had added tights beneath her own skirts soon after, insisting she simply loved colors too much to settle on one.

"Tell me again," Alessa said, trying to sound upbeat. "What should it feel like?"

Renata left a chair between them, dark eyebrows drawing together as she propped her chin in her hands. "To sustain a note, a singer gathers the precise amount of breath, then carefully modulates their volume."

"But how do I know how much? Singers don't learn to sing by being silent."

Tomo dropped a prism on the table. "Oh, Renata, let me try. She needs to practice with *someone*, and I haven't had an episode in months."

Renata's expression shuttered. "Absolutely not."

Alessa traced invisible circles on the table. Sometimes their love shone so brightly it hurt to look at them.

"A Fonte exists to serve." Tomo massaged Renata's shoulders.

"To serve *his* Finestra. You've done your duty." Renata squeezed her eyes shut. "We won't take it off the table forever, but please, Tomo, not yet."

Renata was right—Tomo had fulfilled his duty before Alessa was born, and years of training followed by a drawn-out battle had damaged his heart, often leaving him confined to bed for days. He deserved an easy retirement, not getting thrown back into the fray to train a new Finestra with a reputation for draining the life from everyone she touched.

"No," Alessa said firmly. "I need you both alive. I can't do this without you."

"Fine, fine," Tomo said. "Finestra, why don't you get some air before the guests arrive?"

Renata still hadn't opened her eyes.

Alessa slipped out, settling the door on its frame, and she waited, listening. There'd been a strange undercurrent to Renata's words.

After a long silence, Renata spoke. "What if the next one doesn't work out either?"

"It will."

"We're running out of time. If they're right, and she truly can't—"

"Have faith, Renata. The gods wouldn't abandon us." For someone who enjoyed a spirited debate, Tomo sounded almost angry. "Don't speak of it again."

Renata sighed. "I'm not *suggesting* it, but we have to discuss our options."

"Five hundred years of tradition cannot be dismissed."

"Oh, so abandoning precedent to risk your health is fine but—"

"It's one thing to bend the rules," Tomo said. "Another to *kill* a Finestra."

Six

Dai nemici mi guardo io, dagli amici mi guardi Iddio.
A man's worst enemies are those in his own house.

Days before her fourteenth birthday, Alessa had won a race and became Finestra. The two events weren't related, but she'd often wondered if she could have avoided it all by reading a book instead.

After a classmate, tall for his age and built like a baby ox, convinced the girls to chase him around the schoolyard instead of the other way around, packs of schoolgirls had become military strategists. Some plotting to steal a kiss, most simply tagging along for fun.

Alessa wasn't the fastest or the most determined, but she'd turned the right corner at the right moment. Or the wrong corner at the wrong moment.

Caught off guard, her target hadn't stood a chance, and seconds later she was sitting on his chest, flush with victory, realizing she had no idea what she was supposed to do with him.

So, she'd touched his forehead and declared, "You lose."

And he died.

Or at least, she'd thought he had. Tendons taut as bowstrings, blood-flecked foam between clenched teeth, he'd spasmed beneath her. He'd nearly bitten his tongue off and still talked with a lisp. Not to *her*, of course. He'd screamed so loudly when the Cittadella guards escorted her past his house later that day, they'd stopped to lecture his parents. That was when guards were still offended by things like disrespecting the Finestra.

Adrick had wheedled his way into the convoy, insisting he had to carry a few "priceless family heirlooms," and gleefully rehashed every second during the walk to her new home, tossing her case from hand to hand.

Tomo and Renata had been waiting on the stairs out front as he wrapped up his impression, and Alessa had forced herself to laugh despite a current of unease. Maybe she'd already sensed it wouldn't be the last time her touch brought pain, or that Dea's gift would become a curse.

Alessa needed her fury to stay red hot, to solder herself together, but as she waited in the archway to the courtyard, it fled, leaving behind an aching hurt.

Tomo and Renata were already seated at the head table, with no trace of doubt or fear in their proud expressions.

She'd always known they were loyal to the island, not to *her*, but even if it wasn't her death up for discussion—and it was difficult to put *that* aside—their sworn duty was to train the next Finestra, not kill her.

And she'd thought, maybe, they even cared about her. A little.

She pulled the tattered shreds of anger around her like a cloak against the cold as trumpets announced her arrival. A bass drum or out-of-tune violin would have been more appropriate.

The carefully curated guest list of influential citizens took to their feet around tables groaning beneath so many candles it was a miracle no one had caught on fire yet.

No daggers flew. No one shouted their allegiance to Ivini. No one gave any sign at all they were losing faith in her.

Like a dutiful show pony, Alessa promenaded past pillars wrapped with flowered vines, beneath strings of twinkling fairy lights that burnished everyone and everything with a warm, romantic glow. A true storybook wonderland for everyone's least favorite ice princess.

Renata looked proud and Tomo smiled as Alessa took her place between them at the head table.

She didn't return it. Maybe someday, after she'd wed her next Fonte, and the battle was over, her mentors would completely forget they'd ever considered killing her. She never would.

Discreetly, she adjusted herself as every ragged breath shifted her low-cut bodice a fraction lower. While a wardrobe malfunction might tempt some candidates, she'd burst into tears if anything else went awry.

"Rolls?" Tomo said, gesturing to a basket of steaming bread.

How nice of him. How considerate. Perhaps *Make sure the Finestra eats a well-balanced diet* was listed right below *Discourage your life partner from murdering her* in the mentor handbook.

According to the stories, Renata had faced her own army of scarabeo without breaking a sweat, but Alessa's monumental failures had her so shaken she was contemplating heresy *and* murder. It was almost impressive, really.

Maybe it wasn't fair to hold it against them. Dea only knew

she had plenty of thoughts that wouldn't land well if she spoke them aloud. Lucky for her, she had no one to talk to.

If her life depended on it—and maybe it did—Alessa couldn't have recited the dinner menu when the tables were cleared, but her stomach wasn't empty, so she must've eaten something.

Now she was supposed to *say* something. If only she could split her mind in two and let one half obsess about her predicament while the other kept chugging along.

Liveried servers circulated with trays of a bitter digestivo in tiny crystal goblets. It scorched a trail down her throat but did nothing to settle her stomach.

Not all Finestra/Fonte pairings were romantic, so it wasn't like she needed to find someone who was *perfect* for her. Many took lovers or life partners after Divorando, and it didn't diminish the divine bond. After all, hearts were meant to love in more than one way. Her daydreams might feature a Fonte who was a partner in *every* sense of the word, but in real life, she'd settle for a friend.

Or anyone, really, at this point.

Everyone turned to watch as she stood, and she realized she was still holding her napkin, twisting it until it curled on itself. She bent her legs slightly until her hands were below the level of the table and dropped it. Saved by a tablecloth.

"Um. Hello," Alessa said. Oratory genius. "I'm delighted to welcome you to our glorious Cittadella, the pinnacle of Saverio's stronghold and home of our armory, where we keep our greatest weapons." Oh drat, *she* was supposed to be the greatest weapon. "That is, our greatest weapon aside from the *people* of Saverio. Like me." This was falling apart. "And our Fontes! Our miraculous Fontes, blessed by Dea to serve and protect. And by protecting, serve."

Why did anyone let her speak? "So, with no further ado"—and no more talking—"we will now be treated to demonstrations by those noble Fontes." She nodded, smiled, nodded again, and sat with a thump.

Tomo, bless him, began to clap, and it only took a thousand years before others joined in a wan round of applause.

The Fontes stood from their respective tables and made their way toward her, reluctant boats being towed against the current.

Let the games begin.

Seven

A conti vecchi contese nuove.
Old reckonings, new disputes.

O ur first performer tonight will be Josef Benheim," Tomo said, kicking off another round of applause.

Lanky and long-limbed, with deep brown skin and serious eyes, Josef had always been a solemn boy. Nicknamed "little man" by their teachers, his rare smiles had become even more rare since he'd lost his sister. Or, rather, since Alessa *took* his sister from him.

Josef's entrance was hindered by Nina Faughn clinging to his hand. They were the closest to Alessa's age, so she knew them better than the other Fontes. It looked as though their longtime friendship had taken a new direction in recent months.

After extricating himself from Nina's grasp, Josef strode to the center of the performance space. The light glittered on the silver trim of his royal blue tunic as he bowed, his attire a subtle tribute to Ilsi, who'd worn the same colors the day Alessa had selected her. Josef wasn't spiteful, so she knew it wasn't meant as a jab, but pain lanced through her anyway.

Like Tomo, Josef's power was to create cold, or rather, to remove heat, as Tomo always made a point to remind her. *Cold is merely a lack of heat, therefore one can remove heat but not create cold.* Unsmiling, Josef froze the contents of a few waiting glasses. In addition to supplying his family's year-round gelateria, Joseph's gift made his family the primary supplier for the iceboxes of Saverio, and their home was one of the finest on the island. Not that his family only used his gift for their own enrichment—that would be shameful—but distributing ice to the poor wasn't what gilded their home in luxury and thus didn't come up in conversation quite as often. Of all the Fonte powers, his was fairly straightforward— aim, freeze, watch scarabeo fall and shatter—but it had a narrow range, and that could mean a long, drawn-out battle.

After Josef, Nina minced across the floor in a simple white gown. Her pale skin was nearly translucent beneath a constellation of freckles, but her cheeks went pink at the first polite smattering of applause. She'd come with props—a collection of small objects like spoons and rocks—and used them to demonstrate how she could warp matter, turning solids malleable and changing their shapes. It was a crowd-pleaser, but the more people clapped, the redder she grew, until her face clashed with her strawberry-blonde hair.

The next performer missed his cue.

Tomo checked his notes and scanned the shadows for whoever was up next, and Alessa let her gaze wander to the dark walkways above the glittering party.

Her eyes narrowed at a flash of movement. Soldiers wore blue, and servants wore black, so no one in white should be on the third floor, especially at this time of night.

"Kaleb Toporovsky?" Tomo called out, louder this time, and Alessa pulled her attention back to the matter at hand.

Visibly peeved, Kaleb looked up from his conversation with a handsome boy at the nearest table.

Alessa wrinkled her nose.

Auburn-haired and blue-eyed, with perfectly tanned skin, Kaleb was almost absurdly handsome—if you were into arrogant pricks—but she'd been thirteen to his fifteen the first time they'd met, and while eighteen and twenty didn't feel nearly as far apart, she could never shake the feeling that Kaleb saw her as an annoying child he was forced to interact with. Granted, he looked at most people like that, so it might not be personal.

Kaleb took his time getting to the front of the stage. "Finestra, Fonte . . . new Finestra," he drawled. "An honor, I'm sure."

An honor for him? Or was he saying they were honored to have him? She tried to give him the benefit of the doubt, but couldn't.

Bolts of lightning danced above his palm as he plowed through a dry explanation of his powers, seeming annoyed that his gift made him eligible for anything but lazing about town. And yet, judging from his finery, he didn't turn down the perks of being god-touched.

Next up were Kamaria and Shomari, copper-skinned twins wearing matching expressions of grim determination. Shomari's eyes were flat when they met Alessa's, while Kamaria's glittered with something Alessa couldn't interpret. Despite them being the only other set of boy/girl twins she'd ever met, she didn't really know them. They'd gone to school together before she became Finestra, but Shomari and Kamaria were a year older, popular, and Fontes, while Alessa had been nobody back then. She'd admired them from afar but never tried to talk to them. And now they *had* to talk to her, which didn't count.

Shomari lifted the water from a drinking goblet and swirled droplets through the air in intricate maneuvers. Kamaria, holding a candle, used her control over fire to turn the droplets into puffs of steam, occasionally winking at the crowd. Alessa hid a smile behind her glass. Some people, like Kamaria and Adrick, were born with too much charm to contain, and it poured forth no matter the circumstances.

Next up, Saida checked the gold headband holding her thick curls off her face before creating a wind funnel that made all the napkins on the head table twirl. She was also a year older than Alessa, but when she smiled at the applause, her round cheeks dimpled, and she appeared much younger.

Thanks to Hugo, Alessa had a bit of experience with wind power, but not enough to make Saida an automatic front-runner.

The next two performers were strangers who must have traveled from outside the city. One girl controlled fire, like Kamaria, and the other manipulated matter, like Nina, but not very well.

There was a long pause before the next performer. A skinny boy with glossy black hair, hovering slightly apart from the rest of the group, stepped up, his arms held stiffly at his sides and a look of determined courage on his face.

Alessa felt ill.

"Jun Cheong?" she whispered to Renata. "Really?"

"His parents weren't thrilled, but he's old enough."

"*Is* he, though?"

Jun couldn't be more than thirteen, and while the bonding of a Finestra and Fonte wasn't a *regular* sort of marriage, Alessa didn't want a *child groom.*

"No. Absolutely not. I used to babysit for him."

Renata protested, as Alessa knew she would, but Tomo agreed, as she knew *he* would. And soon, they had one fewer prospect on their list. Alessa tried to give Jun's parents a reassuring smile, but they didn't know that Alessa was arguing for their son's elimination and only looked more nervous.

When the last performance was over, Renata heaped effusive praise on the Fontes, so out of character for her that it made Alessa squirm, then invited the guests to enjoy the rest of the evening, with a pointed look at Alessa.

Alessa took a last, fortifying sip of water before stepping down from the dais, scanning the Fontes for a promising place to start. A smile was too much to hope for, but maybe someone would look her way without flinching.

Kaleb and his handsome friend were perusing a table of desserts, and a Fonte with pastries was more appealing than one without, so Alessa headed there first. Brushing a stray hair from his forehead, Kaleb met Alessa's gaze, and her heart leapt. His power over electricity could make him a powerful Fonte, especially if he was willing and not compelled. She could deal with a poor personality if he was strong enough to endure her touch. And, who knew, maybe he was one of those people who *looked* angry but would warm up once she got to know him.

His lip curled as she neared, and he leaned in to say something to the other boy that made them snicker.

Face hot, Alessa bent to fix an imaginary problem with her shoe.

Fine. Not Kaleb, then.

She found another target. Their huddle tightened as she neared, but Kamaria, Shomari, Nina, and Josef held their ground.

At Alessa's tentative hello, Kamaria and Shomari glanced at each other, a brief look loaded with words unspoken. Kamaria uncrossed her arms. Shomari did not.

Silence fell after a round of strained greetings. The others nursed their drinks, but Alessa had nothing to hold, so she wedged her hands inside the deep pockets of her skirt, picking at a loose thread. If Saverio's morale depended on her talent for small talk, the outlook was bleak.

Nina tugged on her long reddish braid. "Do any of the books in the Citadella say when, exactly, Divorando will arrive?"

"No," Alessa said. "We won't know the date until the First Warning."

The gods' idea of a countdown clock to the final invasion was a month of blights, floods and storms and locusts, so people didn't forget that something much worse was coming.

Nina didn't seem reassured. "But it will be *sometime* this year. Aren't you worried?"

"Of course, she isn't," said Josef. "That's why Dea sends the First Warning, so we know to begin preparing, and that hasn't happened yet, so we still have plenty of time."

"Exactly," Alessa said. "She won't let us miss it."

"Right," Nina said. "How big, exactly, are the scarabeo?"

Apparently, Nina hadn't outgrown her tendency to blurt out uncomfortable topics. Kamaria sighed. "Nina, most people will never even see one. Including you. Right, Finestra?"

"Not from inside the Fortezza," Alessa said. "You can leave the scarabeo to me. And my Fonte, of course."

The scarabeo were the last thing Alessa wanted to talk about.

Joseph cleared his throat. "Have you chosen, then?"

Fine. *Second* to last.

"Not yet." Alessa's smile pulled tight as a violin string about to snap.

As the silence stretched from uncomfortable to painful, Alessa caught the eye of a passing server, who extended his tray as far as his arms would reach so Alessa could snag a sweet.

"You should try one," Alessa said to the others, smiling too brightly. "They're absolutely to die for."

The words stuck in her throat as everyone flinched. Where was a scarabeo when you *wanted* to be torn to bits?

She cast up a silent apology. *Dea, I didn't mean that. Please give me as much time as possible.*

The paving stones didn't open up and swallow her as she requested, so she pinned on a smile and excused herself from the group.

Saida Farid sat alone, scribbling what appeared to be a recipe in a small notebook.

Alessa cleared her throat so she didn't startle the girl. "What are you writing?"

Saida flushed and put the notebook in her lap. "It's just a pet project. I like to analyze food, try to figure out the ingredients of dishes so I can recreate them. My goal is to write a culinary history of Saverio, to memorialize our ancestors' respective cultures through food."

"That's ambitious."

"It started as a school assignment, but it got me thinking about how most families have special dishes they've passed down for generations that aren't written down anywhere else. I want to make sure they're recorded, just in case . . ." She trailed off. "How's your . . ." She gestured at Alessa's ear.

Self-consciously, Alessa checked to be sure her hairstyle was still covering it and took an empty seat. "It's fine. Really. Barely a scratch."

"Still. Must have been scary."

At the other girl's sympathy, tears pricked Alessa's eyes. She smiled harder to force them back. "Knives are the least of my problems, right?"

Saida's tawny complexion went ashen. "But you've been working to get that, um, sorted out, right?"

Damn. She'd been referring to the scarabeo, not her Fonte-killing problem.

"Absolutely." Alessa stood quickly. "I am *confident*, and I have everything *under control.*"

Whoops. She hadn't meant to say the last part out loud. It seemed to reassure Saida, though, so for once, her tendency to say the quiet part out loud hadn't made things noticeably worse.

It was past midnight when Alessa returned to the relative peace of her rooms. Sleep offered the only escape from the hum of anxious energy twitching through her body, but her bed loomed rather than beckoned. Insomnia never felt more inevitable than when she settled herself in the middle of the massive four-poster monstrosity, acres of cold emptiness on either side.

Alessa flopped onto the couch instead.

She still didn't know who to choose. The strongest? The person whose gift was most practical? If her chosen Fonte didn't live long enough to fight, what difference did it make? She needed a Fonte who would *live.*

Choosing Emer, her first Fonte, had been so easy. His funeral, unbearable.

At first, she'd been so angry when people insisted he was a bit *too* gentle, but the thought became a lifeline. It was still her fault for choosing him, but maybe not entirely her fault he'd died.

Her naive, selfish heart had wanted the golden boy with a sweet smile, and the gods had not approved. Message heard.

She'd chosen more wisely the next time.

Ilsi, Josef's older sister, had been so confident, beautiful, and powerful she might have stepped out of the Cittadella's mosaics. Everyone knew *she'd* be strong enough to withstand Alessa's power, including Alessa, who'd been awestruck by the older girl, and for one brief day, Ilsi illuminated the Cittadella with her charismatic presence and sly sense of humor. Alessa hadn't even decided whether she *wanted* Ilsi or wanted to *be* Ilsi before Ilsi was dead, too.

Once, she'd followed her heart. And Emer died.

Then she'd listened to her brain. And Ilsi died.

So she'd thrown the rules out the window and picked someone entirely different.

Poor Hugo.

It had been worth a shot.

She could put all their names in a bucket and ask Dea to guide her hand. Or read another dozen historical texts in search of hints that didn't exist. Maybe rearrange their names to see if she could spell anything fun with the letters.

If only she could extinguish her thoughts like blowing out a candle. Her family used to affectionately joke about her "busy brain" but it wasn't amusing when her thoughts refused to quiet themselves so she could rest.

She'd heard of people who struggled to sleep because of tingling in their legs, but the restlessness that plagued her nights went deeper than muscles. It was a nagging need, like her skin had shrunk in the wash and would never fit again.

In daytime, she could stay busy enough to ignore it, but when the night grew quiet and still, the clamoring returned.

Movement was her only remedy, so she spent most evenings pacing. Even when she wasn't especially anxious—rare, but it happened—she'd walk her room for hours. But she'd already been on her feet all night socializing, if one was generous enough to call hours of stilted small talk "socializing," so she closed her eyes and guided her thoughts to a sandy beach. Hot sand between her toes, waiting for someone special to row back to shore with fresh-caught fish for dinner. The sun, blindingly bright behind a tiny rowboat, erased the rower's features, but imaginary Alessa knew exactly who it was, and her heart swelled . . .

Darkness descended, but before she'd fully sunk beneath, she jerked awake.

She couldn't breathe.

Her eyes snapped open.

Couldn't see.

Something—someone—had her pinned, trapped, crushing her windpipe. Thrashing, she fought to free herself. Her fingers scrabbled against leather. Hands, encased in thick gloves, tightening around her neck.

She wasn't strong enough.

Alessa forced her fingers to reach, touching coarse fabric, a hard chest, thick arms—a sliver of bare skin between his collar and some sort of mask over his head.

The man's grip faltered. She sucked in a desperate breath before he extended his arms to keep his vulnerability out of reach.

"Go easy, will you?" he growled in a coarse whisper as his hands tightened. "I'm trying to be respectful about it. Just let go and it'll be over soon."

Stars burst in her vision, colorful flashes in the darkness, like fireworks celebrating her impending death.

Eight

Di buone intenzioni è lastricato l'inferno.
The road to hell is paved with good intentions.

No. She refused to die like this.

Arching her back, she strained until she caught the man's collar, yanking it down.

She didn't need to overpower him. Only one touch.

Her finger pressed into his flesh, and he screamed. The stifling weight vanished, and she heard thrashing over the rasp of her labored breathing. She dragged herself up to sitting as the door flew open.

"I-intruder," she croaked, pointing a shaky hand. "Attacked me."

Her eyes adjusted enough to see Lorenzo's eyes widen as he glanced from her to the man and back. He wasn't the bravest guard, but at least he was there.

She coughed, wincing as the pain flared brighter.

Lorenzo examined her attacker, his face flickering with thoughts she couldn't decipher, and one she could—recognition.

He hauled the man to his feet, his expression stone, looking every inch the soldier, and she forgave him all the times he'd been a terrible guard.

Until he drew the man's arm across his shoulder and said, "Stop your moaning until we get out of here."

"Didn't you hear me?" Alessa stumbled off the couch. "He tried to kill me."

Lorenzo spit on the ground. "You should have let him."

She couldn't do anything but stare as her personal guard half-dragged, half-carried her would-be assassin out the door, and two pairs of identical boots disappeared around the corner.

The walls bowed as though straining to crush her, and Alessa found herself in the hallway, searching for safety that didn't exist.

The reasonable part of her wanted to scream for help, to demand her advisors and Captain Papatonis assemble a battalion of guards at her door. But they might not rally to protect her at all. Maybe they'd given the order to take her out. Would they be shocked to hear what had happened ... or disappointed to see her alive?

How deep did the betrayal go?

She yearned to run, to hide, to become so small no one would ever find her. But she couldn't run, and the only place to hide was the tiny chapel off the hall, set aside for the Finestra's daily prayer. Inside, she locked the door and sank to the floor, laying her hot cheek on cold stone. With her eyes squeezed shut, she didn't have to look at the murals of her predecessors in all their victorious glory.

No one came for her.

Alessa opened gritty eyes to glare at a life-sized mosaic of an idealized Finestra. Angelic. Perfect. Serene. Aggravating on the best of days.

It was too dim to read the ornate script haloing the Finestra's blessed head, but Alessa knew the words by heart.

Benedetti siano coloro per cui la finestra sul divino è uno specchio.

Blessed are those for whom the window to the divine is a mirror.

If she had a mirror, she'd smash it and use the jagged shards to carve out every opalescent tooth.

Blessed. Oh, yes, she was the *luckiest* girl in the world, fending off murderers on a daily basis for the right to live long enough to fight a swarm of demons slavering to chew on her bones.

The walls, floor, and ceiling of the tiny chapel were adorned with glass tiles and precious stones, but in the gloom, they might as well have been slate. Ages ago some poor artist had spent years crafting the mosaics that told the story of Saverio, a massive effort for an audience of one, and it was too dark for her to see more than outlines.

Saverio's power system had grown unreliable over the centuries as the wires from the water mill to the city were gnawed on by vermin, and Saverians couldn't produce the same materials the ancients once had, so she hadn't bothered to tell anyone when the light bulbs around the perimeter of the room failed, blinking out one by one. It seemed only fitting for the lights to die during her reign.

The ruby eyes of onyx *scarabeo* leered at her from the upper corners of the chapel, along with silhouettes of monstrous *ghiotte* lurking amidst skeletal trees. The artist responsible either had some bizarre ideas about the sort of art that motivated a person or a sadistic sense of humor.

She dragged herself to a sitting position, and her elbow crunched the dried leaves of a bouquet on the altar. *That* tribute hadn't done her any good.

"If you prefer a different flower, there are easier ways to drop a hint." Plucking a shriveled blossom from its wrinkled stem, she shredded the petals between her fingers. It didn't deserve the punishment, but when had *deserving* ever protected anyone?

If she had died, another Finestra might be rising to take her place. Either that, or Saverians would've woken to find themselves completely defenseless. Her family would have lost their daughter *and* their last hope of survival in one moment.

Below her bare feet were depictions of the three remaining sanctuary islands.

The fourth wasn't shown. The lost island had been wiped from the maps, forsaken to fade into obscurity after it fell during the first Divorando.

It was up to Alessa whether Saverio would survive the next.

She pushed to her feet, grimacing against the pain, and crept around the statue to the pane of glass set into the wall. She needed to face her enemies head on, and of the entrants on her rapidly growing list of foes, at least this one was dead.

The husk of a scarabeo, shriveled and dusty from centuries in its airless tomb, peered back at her with unseeing eyes. Like some enormous, warped nightmare of an Atlas beetle, it had three curved horns and a glossy carapace that appeared midnight black at first glance but was actually mottled with all the colors of the rainbow, like a spill of grease on dark water. The desiccated specimen, a souvenir from the first Divorando meant to be a testament to Saverio's survival, taunted her.

The girl and the monster, face to face. The girl, a killer. The monster, dead. Or perhaps, the girl a monster, soon to be dead.

She curled her fingers against the glass, nails scraping against the surface.

Thousands of these . . . *things* . . . were coming. For her. For Saverio.

And now she had to deal with knives flying at her head and hands itching to wring her neck.

Frightened people crave certainty.

She was frightened, but even worse, beneath the fear and grief and anger was a whiff of relief. For years, she'd clung to her parents' faith. Then she'd become the blessed Finestra, and it had been easy enough to have faith at first. But now, with everyone else's certainty stripped away, it turned out she had none of her own.

If Ivini was right, she'd wasted the final years of her life. She couldn't bear that.

If he was wrong, her death would doom them all. She couldn't risk that.

Papa always told her not to trust fear, but fear was all she had.

Fear. Stubbornness. And the simmering anger she'd been tamping down since that knife drew her blood.

Every swallow brought tears to her eyes, but the burn in her throat threatened to ignite a fire in her chest that would spread, take over, scorch her from within until she was nothing but a pile of ash.

And she was going to let it.

If she failed again, she'd have her answer, the sign she'd been waiting for. If her hands killed once more, she'd sacrifice herself for the greater good.

But first, one last try.

Back in her room, Alessa stood before the mirror on trembling legs. The dark shadows below her eyes echoed the bruises around her neck, but her eyes sparked with determination.

She dressed at quarter speed, inching a loose dress up her torso and gently knotting a shawl around her neck to hide the evidence. If anyone reacted when they saw her, she needed to know it was because they didn't expect her to be alive, not because they were shocked by her injuries.

She chose the two sharpest of the small knives in her kitchenette and carefully slid one inside each of her tall boots.

As she reached the ground floor, a regiment marched past. Boots. So many boots. Each identical to the pair he'd been wearing.

Alessa froze, her muscles seizing in terror. She hadn't seen her attacker's face. He could be one of them, still moving through the Cittadella with impunity.

One soldier flicked a quick glance her way and frowned. Alessa couldn't tell if the woman's reaction was pity or distaste, but it was enough to snap her out of her trance.

Alessa ran through her plan before opening the door. If Tomo and Renata showed any sign of shock or disappointment when she entered, she would know.

She stepped inside, waiting as the door closed behind her.

Renata gave a little wave and yawned into her espresso.

"Good morning, Finestra." Tomo pushed his chair back and bowed. "You're early today."

"No time to waste." Forced detachment cooled Alessa's voice, making her sound abnormally calm.

They didn't notice. Renata drained her cup, oblivious, and Tomo turned back to his news sheet.

Alessa fought the urge to exhale. To trust. She couldn't forget. Even if they hadn't ordered last night's assassination, they might order the next. Her fortress had always been a cage, but now it felt like a trap about to spring. She'd be a fool to trust anyone in the Cittadella.

She needed someone to watch her back. Someone who defended the weak and didn't buy into Ivini's theory. Someone who might be desperate for something only she could offer. Someone who didn't back down—or step aside—from anyone, especially the Cittadella's soldiers.

Hope flared, bright enough to burn.

She needed to visit the Bottom of the Barrel.

Nine

Chi ha più bisogno, e più s'arrenda.
Beggars can't be choosers.

The Bottom of the Barrel wasn't just a clever name after all.

This part of Saverio—Alessa discreetly covered her nose as she entered the fine establishment—was a breeding ground for unsavory characters. "Fodder," they were often dubbed. As in, fodder for the scarabeo. Even if she could ignore the stink of fear and sweat—and she couldn't—the dingy tavern didn't even have a tone-deaf musician for entertainment. Instead, a crowd surrounded a cage large enough to fit a dozen men.

It held only one.

People shoved their faces against the bars, jeering at the lone figure inside, but he didn't seem to notice. Bronze, barefoot, and stripped to his waist, he stood facing away from her, lazily gripping the bars. Dark hair, wet with sweat, curled at the nape of his neck, and his muscles were streaked with blood.

Fights to the death were illegal, but betting on fights was common entertainment on the docks. According to Adrick, as long as both combatants were alive when the fight ended, it didn't count as murder. If grievous injuries caused one fighter to die *later* . . . well, that was bad luck.

The crowd roiled and Alessa curled inward, using her cloak like a shield against the jostling bodies. These people didn't recognize her, didn't know to fear her touch. It was exhilarating and terrifying.

She was so busy studying the crowd that she stumbled as a wiry, grizzled man shoved his way through, leading a hulking brute. Their eyes were fixed on the cage.

The man inside it rolled his neck, revealing his profile, and Alessa muttered a distinctly un-Finestra-like word. She'd found who she was looking for, but judging from the bloodthirsty roar of the crowd, he was about to get beaten to a pulp.

The uneven lighting cast his features in stark relief. Sharp cheekbones, a strong jawline, and lips a braver person might have described as pouty. He didn't seem the type to pout, though. Or appreciate the compliment. He appeared utterly disinterested, but his eyes glittered. The older man entered the cage, growling and snapping at him, and he merely cocked an eyebrow as though faintly amused.

She, on the other hand, couldn't breathe.

His lean, bronzed muscles were nice enough to look at, but his opponent's arms were thick as tree trunks, gnarled with scars and burn marks, and his massive hands could've smashed Alessa's skull. Well, not *hers*, but anyone else's.

No one with such smooth, unmarred skin and graceful movements could possibly stand a chance against this massive, battle-scarred brute.

It was going to be a massacre.

The announcer made a dramatic show of ordering the barking hulk to stay back, and turned to the crowd. "We have a challenger! Will the Wolf's fourth match be his last, or can he bring down the Bear? Who will walk away and who will be carried out?"

The crowd surged forward, waving their bets in the air. There was no escape from the tide, and Alessa didn't try. She didn't want to see such a beautiful man reduced to a pile of bloody bones, but she couldn't look away.

The bell startled her. Stretching onto her toes, she strained to see over the shoulders partially blocking her view.

The big man lunged, leapt back, and lunged again, taunting the young man. The Wolf, they'd called him. It fit almost too well. Poised but motionless, he resembled the shadowy creatures who lurked in the forests on the far side of the island. His lip curled, exposing sharp canines. A wolf, cornered by a bear, refusing to show weakness before a stronger, deadlier opponent.

The Bear lowered his head to ram.

The Wolf glanced down to study his fingernails.

Alessa pressed her tongue between her teeth so she didn't cry out.

At the last moment, the Wolf stepped aside, and the other man barely avoided crashing into the bars.

Their dance continued until the Bear landed his first blow, his fist smashing into the Wolf's jaw.

The Wolf dragged a hand across his chin and shook it, splattering blood across the floor, then landed a punch to the big man's gut, but the next blow he took sounded like it cracked a few ribs. Alessa bit down on her knuckles.

The Wolf slammed a fist into the big man's cheek and looked

about to land a second hit when someone smashed a glass against the bars, sending glittering shards over him. The Wolf flinched and turned away, one hand to his eye. The crowd booed, and the announcer called for a time-out.

The Bear ignored the call. His opponent's back was turned, and he slammed his fist into the Wolf's lower back.

He dropped.

Alessa wasn't the only one who gasped. The room seemed to hold its collective breath as the Bear stalked over to nudge the Wolf with his foot.

Alessa squeezed her eyes shut. She shouldn't have stayed. She didn't need another death to remember.

The crowd cheered, and she opened her eyes to see the Wolf struggling to his feet, shaking his head to clear it.

The Bear glowered at having his victory lap cut short. "Hit me, pup!"

"Hit him," Alessa whispered, the plea echoed by others as they realigned their loyalties, exchanged new bets.

The Wolf cocked his head as if he'd forgotten why he was there, and the Bear launched himself again, only to meet an uppercut that snapped his head back. Stumbling, unsteady, the Bear shook himself, but the Wolf's next punch came too fast. Another. And another. The big man spun, upright but bent, his back vulnerable.

"Hit him!" the crowd screamed, vibrating with anticipation for the moment the Wolf would take his revenge and deliver the type of blow that had felled him. Instead, the Wolf stepped back, arms loose at his side.

The Bear took a few halting steps and dropped to his knees.

The Wolf lifted his head.

The Bear bowed his.

Alessa remembered how to breathe.

The crowd roared, equal parts elation and disappointment, but the Wolf didn't preen or savor his victory. He accepted a towel and used it to clean his face, blood staining the grungy fabric.

The gate opened, and he disappeared into the crowd.

It took an age to make it across the room, and she'd almost given up on finding him when she spotted the Wolf.

"—fifteen, not twelve." He slapped a bloody hand on the bar. "Four matches, plus a bonus for being undefeated."

The barkeeper glared, pausing his efforts to polish the scarred surface with a rag even dirtier than the wood. "Minus three for last night's room and board."

"For sleeping on the floor of the pantry? You can't be serious."

"Minus—"

The Wolf cursed. "At least give me a whiskey before you empty my pockets."

"Sure, if you want to sleep in the alley." The barkeeper looked over at Alessa as she settled herself on a stool. "What'll it be?"

"Whiskey, please."

"Good, decent, or cheap?" The man's covetous smile revealed a graveyard of gray teeth.

"Good, please."

His gaze lingered on her gloves as she counted out the price, and she grimaced inwardly.

In the city, covering your wrists implied you had something to hide. But here by the wharf, where so many bore the marks of exile, some preferred to keep the specifics of their crimes a secret.

For once, wearing gloves didn't automatically mark her as different, just another stranger ashamed of her past. But black leather as thin and smooth as satin didn't belong in a place like this.

After carefully measuring a finger's worth of amber liquid into a glass, he slid it her way, not bothering to hide the tattooed coins on his left wrist. *Thief.*

Alessa swirled the glass, watching the whiskey hug the sides, and inhaled the sweet heat before she took a sip. It wasn't the best she'd sampled, but it wasn't the worst. She snuck a glance from under her hood as the Wolf took the stool beside her. He'd pulled on a shirt but not buttoned it, and he was no less intimidating than before, scowling as the barkeeper served everyone but him. He smelled of fresh sweat, which should have been revolting, but wasn't.

"I'll buy his drink." Alessa pulled two shiny coins from her pocket. "Your finest, please."

The Wolf's dark eyes flicked to her face. He accepted the glass, downed his drink in one swallow, and slammed the empty glass on the counter with a grunt she assumed was thanks. He, too, made no attempt to hide his mark.

Crossed knives circled by the seal of Saverio. *Killer.*

She shivered.

"You shouldn't be here," he said, eyes forward.

"Why is that?"

"If *I* figured out who you are, someone else will, too. And most people in here want to see what happens if you die."

"And you?" She held her breath. "What do *you* want?"

He stood. "I don't care either way." Throwing a threadbare satchel over one shoulder, he strode away.

She closed her eyes.

In a city full of people who feared or plotted against her, ambivalence might be the best she could hope for.

He knew how to defend himself, so he could defend her, too. Maybe not out of loyalty or devotion, but everyone had a price.

Alessa tossed a few more coins on the counter and abandoned her barely touched glass. The barkeeper would probably pour it back in the bottle as soon as she left, but that wasn't her problem.

He was already halfway down the street, thumbs hooked on his belt, when she made it outside.

The door slammed behind her, plunging the alley into silence. Without looking back, he pulled his hands free. Moonlight glinted off wicked blades held lightly, a warning to anyone who might think to follow him.

"I'd like to hire you," she called out from a safe distance behind him.

He sheathed his knives. "No."

"But I need your help."

"Sorry." His low refusal was just loud enough to carry back to her as he started walking again.

"You don't seem sorry." She tried to catch up to him.

"Fine. I'm not sorry. Not interested, either."

"I'm trying to save Saverio."

"Saverio can fall into the sea for all I care."

Her gut twisted. Because he'd sneered at a street preacher, she'd decided he was on her side. Assumed he'd care whether she lived or died because he defended a little girl. She was so naive.

She shook it off. "I need protection until I have my next—my final—Fonte." She wracked her brain for something, anything, to get him to stop walking. "I'll pay. And provide lodging and food."

He didn't even break his stride. "I'm good."

Alessa gaped. "Good? You're *good?* Fighting for scraps and drinking watered-down whiskey instead of food, shelter, money, and safety?"

"I don't want safety."

She jogged after him, too indignant to be cautious. "Everyone wants to be safe."

"Not me."

"If people are wrong and I'm killed, everyone will die."

"Quit wandering around here, then." He sounded entirely unconcerned.

Alessa's steps faltered, and the distance between them grew as he neared the end of the alley, taking her last shred of hope with him.

"Please," she said, her voice cracking.

He stopped and shook his head like he was annoyed at himself.

Alessa pushed her hood back, tugging the neckline down and lifting her chin. By now, her bruises had turned a sick greenish purple. "I need your help."

He turned, and his gaze dropped to her throat, lingering.

"You have an army. You can—" He glanced around the quiet streets and strode toward her, lowering his voice to a rough growl. "You can kill with a touch. You don't need me."

"But I do." It was easy to let fear and helplessness well into her throat, to let her voice go thick with unshed tears. "A man tried to kill me last night, and my guard helped him escape."

In for a bite, in for a meal.

She clasped her hands below her chin and let hot tears rolls down her cheeks. They were an indulgence she couldn't afford in the Cittadella, but if wolves had a weakness for damsels in distress, she wasn't above playing the part.

If it even was a part.

"I don't know who to trust or who's working for whom anymore. I need someone who works *for me*. To watch my back. Temporarily. Just until I choose my next Fonte. I know I can do this," she lied, "but not if I'm dead.

The moonlight cast blue glints in his hair as he rubbed the back of his neck. "Temporary?"

"We may all be dead in a few weeks. Everything's temporary."

He cocked an eyebrow.

"Sorry. Gallows humor is all I have left. If you help me, I'll get you a spot in the Fortezza."

He pinched the bridge of his nose

"Please?"

He cast an exasperated look at the sky, and she knew she'd caught him.

Ten

Bella in vista, dentro è trista.
Fair face, foul heart.

The thrill of victory faded immediately.

He was marked. She couldn't walk him through the city gates without revealing her identity—and her unsanctioned trip—to the guards. She needed a plan, and there was only one entrance to the tunnels outside the city walls.

A woman stepped in front of them, carrying a swaddled baby. "Please, miss. Anything would help my baby stay safe during Divorando."

Alessa had no idea what money had to do with it, but she fumbled for her purse and dropped a few coins in the woman's hand.

Her new bodyguard was scowling when she turned around. "You going to help them all, or just that one?"

Alessa looked back at the woman, already hurrying down the street as though she feared Alessa would change her mind. "What do you mean? Children are always allowed in the Fortezza."

"And who's going to take them in and care for them if their parents die?" His voice was cold, his eyes colder.

"I—I don't know."

"That's why she's begging. So she can pay someone to take the child before the battle, knowing they might be stuck with the kid for life." The bite in his voice could have drawn blood. "Welcome to the real world, *Finestra*."

"It's not *my* fault. I don't want anyone to be kept out of the Fortezza. I don't *make* the rules, I just have to follow them."

"Yeah, well, it's a bit late to give a shit now."

Like *he* was some noble advocate for the poor. "I thought Saverio could fall into the sea?"

His mouth pulled up in a bitter smile. "Let the whole island burn or give everyone the same chances, that's all I'm saying."

Alessa led the Wolf past the ramshackle dockside buildings and onto a narrow footpath leading into the damp darkness of an immense cavern used to shelter the fleet during storms.

A scratch, and the Wolf's face was lit by the match he held up. "Walk faster."

She picked up her pace, searching the gloom for the glint of a metal gate.

There was only one ship in the enormous cave, but soon others would arrive, packed with passengers and cargo from the continental settlements. The lower caverns would become crowded with wine barrels, seeds, fabric, food supplies, and farm animals, all the supplies they'd need to rebuild what would be lost. The hearty souls who chose to move to the continent between invasions would be welcomed with warm beds in Saverian guest rooms until it came time for everyone to barricade themselves within the Fortezza.

She'd never been to the continent, but the paintings made it seem harsh and strange, all barren plains and jagged mountains. It must be incredible to watch the new life bloom between attacks. She'd read a book once about the ways some animals hid during the rise of the swarms, but Mama had taken it away when she couldn't stop crying about the creatures that didn't survive.

"You tell your handlers you were going on a hiring spree tonight?" the Wolf drawled.

"No," she said, even though it was none of his business. "I don't need permission to hire a guard."

"Oh, really?"

"Yes, really. Technically. I mean—" She steadied herself. "If anyone has a problem, I will take care of it."

He made a skeptical sound.

She pushed her hood back. If they ran into guards in the tunnels, her face was their only protection against a swift and deadly punishment.

"Do you need medical attention?" she asked.

He gave her an irritated look. "No."

Doubtful. But if men and wolves preferred to downplay their injuries, it was a waste of time to argue with either.

He moved so quietly he could have been hunting her. It made her want to run, like a scared rabbit.

Papa used to say fear began with the unknown, so maybe learning more about the man stalking behind her would quell the fear dancing over her skin.

"What's your name?" she said.

"They call me the Wolf."

"And they call me the Finestra, but it's not my name."

"I thought the Finestra didn't have a name."

"No, not until after Divorando, but at least you know what to call me. Shall I address you as The Wolf, then? Mr. Wolf? Or simply Wolf?"

She glanced over her shoulder and caught a glimmer of amusement in his eyes, quickly extinguished.

"Dante."

"Do you have a last name?" She had to turn back so she didn't run into a wall.

"Not anymore."

"Well, nice to meet you, Dante."

"Is it?"

Either her conversation skills were rusty from disuse, or he was exceptionally difficult to talk to. Or both. But while she might be lacking in some personality traits, persistence wasn't one of them. "Where are you from?"

"I don't know."

"If you don't want to tell me, you can say so."

"I'm not lying. I don't know."

"Too many fights knocked your memories loose?" She was treading on dangerous ground, but that seemed to be the theme of the evening.

"Do you remember *your* birth?" he asked.

"Obviously not, but my parents have mentioned it."

"Well, mine are dead," he said, his voice flat.

Dammit. She cringed.

"Where are *you* from?" He posed it like a challenge meant to deter her from asking more questions, but she answered as if he actually wanted to know.

"Here, in the city. One of the lower terraces, though, nowhere near the Cittadella."

Every gate seemed to clang louder and screech longer, and the final gate before they reached the Cittadella wailed loud enough to rouse the temple's dead. Alessa cringed. Escorting a marked man through the Fortezza—a crime punishable by death for anyone but the Finestra—at a time when so many sought to justify killing her felt a bit like handing over the final stone to throw, but miraculously, the corridor remained empty of ghosts and guards.

Dante's last match went out as they reached the entry to the stairs below the Cittadella.

Sometimes, when the world was quiet enough, she could find the echoes of stolen power, like the sparkle of Ilsi's lightning at her fingertips or Hugo's wind at his funeral. Maybe *echo* wasn't the correct term. More of an *imprint*. The dip left in a mattress by an occupant who'd left hours before. She turned her palm up and breathed a tiny blue flame into life above it. The illumination only lasted for a few seconds, but it was long enough for her to find the keyhole.

Dante stared. "What was *that?*"

She flushed. "An echo. Nothing to be alarmed about."

"A what?"

"A . . . remnant. I never had the chance to use the power I absorbed from my Fontes, so a bit lingers."

"Can you do it again?"

She reached into the recesses of her mind but found nothing. "No. That was the last bit."

The last of Emer. Her heart sank. She'd burned through his light, and it hadn't even been for something important.

"Why do you even need a Fonte, then? Touch them now and save it for the battle."

She shook her head. "A Finestra can only magnify a gift while in contact with a Fonte. At best, I'd only have enough power to delay the invasion for a few seconds. Probably not even that. Normally, a Finestra only holds on to another's power for a minute or so."

"It's been more than a minute."

She sighed and closed her eyes. "Because I killed him. Think of it as a final breath. I stole his last magical exhalation."

"But—"

"Believe me, we've tried. It doesn't work that way."

As Alessa led Dante up a spiral staircase, the vise gripping her chest eased, leaving space for a small rush of victory. She'd done it. She'd escaped the Cittadella, braved a tavern full of criminals and outcasts, and convinced a feral wolf to follow her home.

Around the moonlight-dappled stones of the courtyard, each staircase to the next level was on a different corner, forcing anyone bound for the upper levels to circle the entire structure, so the walk to the fourth floor would offer plenty of stilted silence.

The thought had barely crossed her mind when a form surged from a darkened doorway.

Eleven

L'uomo solitario è bestia o angelo.

A solitary man is either a brute or an angel.

"Watch out, Finestra." Captain Papatonis slammed Dante to the wall. "He's armed."

Dante's shirt hiked up, revealing a strip of skin and scabbards on either side of his waist. Even with his cheek pressed into the wall, he managed to look bored and irritated. Papatonis might have the upper hand, but only because Dante was letting him have it, and he clearly didn't plan on tolerating the rough handling much longer.

"At ease, Captain," Alessa said, drawing herself tall. "He's with me." She *was* technically the head of the military, and he'd better remember his place. "I have the right to choose my own personal security officer, and I have chosen him."

She'd never seen anyone look as profoundly offended as Captain Papatonis in that moment. Perhaps it wasn't fair to mistrust all the guards because of one traitor, but she was in too deep now.

A furious debate flashed across the older man's face before he released Dante and stepped aside.

Glaring at her, Dante straightened his clothing with a few rough tugs.

"With all due respect, Finestra." The grizzled older man bit her title short. "Do Signora Renata and Signor Miyamoto know about this?"

"Of course."

Captain Papatonis puffed his chest out. "He can't walk around looking like that."

"Then have someone send up something more suitable, Captain."

The man's dusky skin flushed beneath his beard, and he gave a jerky salute before storming off.

Alessa's hesitant smile only made Dante's scowl deepen.

When they reached her suite, she dropped her key, fumbled to pick it up, then couldn't get it out of the lock.

"Need help?" Dante said, his words clipped.

"No." She yanked, and the key popped free, sending her stumbling back into a wall of muscle. She jumped forward, grabbed the handle, and turned it with a vicious twist.

"Looks like you did."

What was she supposed to say? He made her nervous? She was still shaking from their confrontation with the Captain? That she'd broken more rules and told more lies in one day than she had in the previous five years and she wasn't sure whether to feel horrified or elated?

As soon as the door closed behind them, Dante locked it and eyed the metal brackets on either side. "These are meant for a barricade. Where is it?"

"I don't know."

He snatched a lace parasol from an umbrella stand and shoved it between the fixtures, glowering. "I'll find something better."

Alessa stared as he stalked the perimeter of her suite like a caged animal.

"What are you doing?" she finally asked.

"Assessing the security."

She didn't know much about bodyguard duties aside from "stand outside the door and look grumpy" which he seemed perfectly suited for, so Alessa bit her tongue as Dante examined everything she owned.

It wasn't *too* uncomfortable watching him investigate the main section, which held a cozy sitting area and a small kitchenette with a bistro table and glass-fronted cabinets, but she couldn't help squirming as he passed the doors to her closet and bathing room, or the standing privacy screen concealing the sleeping area.

Pulling open the balcony doors, he strode out and leaned over the side. She took a moment to admire his backside, not realizing until it was too late that he was about to massacre beauty. With no care for the orange and white roses climbing it, he grasped the top of the metal trellis and yanked the structure back and forth, loosening it until the bolts came free with a crumble of stone.

"Hey," Alessa said, hurrying to the balcony. "Those roses were planted by the first Finestra."

"Then they're hardy enough"—he pulled his lip between his teeth—"to survive"—a final tug—"the fall." The trellis parted from the wall with a scream of metal and clattered to the paving stones below.

Two guards ran around the side of the building, looked at the broken trellis on the ground, then up at her.

"Everything all right, Finestra?"

She gave them a small wave. "Sudden gust of wind!"

While Dante stalked around the room, she sat on the edge of her bed to pull off her boots, softly swearing at the laces slipping through her gloved fingers. She didn't hear his approach, so when he cleared his throat nearby, she nearly fell off the bed.

"Having trouble?"

Alessa calmed her breathing. "Everything's more difficult in gloves."

"So, take them off."

Bracing himself on her bed, he checked underneath it, his long fingers digging into the soft duvet.

She jumped up as though burned.

Satisfied that no one was hiding under there, he opened the small door in the corner and stared into the darkness. "What's through here?"

"The stairs to the salt baths."

He gave her an incredulous look.

"Not the *public* baths. The Cittadella has its own chambers, and the only other way in is through the Fonte suite. Which is empty. Obviously."

He scowled at the door to the baths as though it personally offended him, before giving the room one last scan. Passing the table, he paused to pick up a large, engraved envelope.

"For you." He held it out for a second, realized she wasn't going to take it from his hands, and tossed it back on the table.

She'd known the envelope was coming, but the sight stole her breath.

Alessa didn't want his keen eyes on her when she read it, but the letter refused to be ignored, like a persistent buzzing in her ears. She picked it up, turning it over a few times before breaking the seal and scanning the flowery script. When she finished, she crumpled the paper in her fist, squeezing until sharp corners jabbed her palm through her thin gloves.

Dante eyed the mangled paper in her grip. "Love letter?"

"A summons." Alessa dropped the crumpled ball into the trash. "The Consiglio is convening tomorrow."

He raised his eyebrows. "That was fast."

"Very." She swallowed hard. "I thought I'd have a few more days, but it seems they'll have the next poor soul trussed up and delivered by tomorrow evening."

Dante turned to her bookshelf, running a hand down the leather spines as if the books were precious or potentially dangerous.

"My guards usually stand outside the door at night," she said, walking toward the privacy screen. "But you can take a chair if you'd be more comfortable."

Studying the faded spine of one book, he gestured at the couch. "I'll sleep there."

Alessa cut off a yawn. "No, you won't."

"I didn't come to a castle to sleep in a chair."

"Then drag the cushions into the hall. You can't sleep in here."

"Why not?"

"These are *my* rooms." Her sanctuary, where she shed her layers and didn't have to worry about her every movement terrorizing others. But she couldn't say that. She refused to bare her pain to a rude stranger.

His biceps tested the linen fabric of his shirt as he crossed his arms. "How'd the guy who tried to kill you get in?"

She blinked. "The door?"

"Or the balcony."

"You think he scaled the side of a four-story building?"

"There was a trellis."

"Which is gone, thanks to your delicate handiwork. I can't have a *man* in my rooms. There are rules."

"You're the Finestra. If you can't change the rules, who can?"

"You don't understand how my position works."

"And you don't understand how bodyguards work. See, I"—he pointed to himself—"guard *your*"—he pointed to her, tracing curves in the air—"*body.*"

She half-scooted behind the screen. "*You* work for *me.* I give the orders."

"I don't half-ass any job. You want me to guard, this is how I do it."

If she had to close the balcony doors to get him in the hall, she'd spend the night tossing in a hot, stuffy bed, with visions of leather-clad hands squeezing her windpipe. "Fine. But I've killed three people already, and if you try to sneak up on me while I'm sleeping, you'll be the fourth."

Dante kicked off his shoes. "Same."

She squinted at him. Was he saying he'd killed three people? That he'd kill her if she sneaked up on him? Both?

Eyes locked on her like he knew exactly what she was thinking, Dante began unbuttoning his shirt. Panicked, she fled before she made an even bigger fool of herself.

How was she supposed to relax with only translucent panels between her and a half-dressed stranger?

"*Dea,*" she breathed. Surely he wasn't taking *everything* off.

Still trying to decipher his warning, Alessa determinedly steered her thoughts away from the brief glimpse of skin that was now branded into her memory and pulled on her most voluminous nightgown.

He was a criminal. He might be packing up her valuables already or waiting until she fell asleep to smash her head in. She should have shut her mouth in that alley the moment she realized he wasn't the hero she'd taken him for.

This was ridiculous.

She stepped around the screen with a firm "get out" perched on the tip of her tongue, but he was gone.

The main door was closed. The bathing room was dark. A neatly folded shirt on the end table was the only sign he'd been there at all.

Her gaze flicked to every corner, then the ceiling, as though he might have taken flight. Warmth tickled the back of her neck, and she whirled, but there was no one there.

The wind shifted, carrying the scents of Saverio farther inside.

The balcony.

Dante stood just outside the doors, pants riding low on narrow hips, knives still sheathed on either side. His thumbs found the hilts of his blades, then slid off, again and again, like he was checking to be sure they hadn't vanished. The broad shoulders and muscled back that had looked so golden and alive in the fighting ring looked like marble gilded silver in the moonlight.

He could have been a sculptor's masterpiece: *Man on Balcony.*

He tensed at some distant sound: *Man on Balcony Poised for Flight.*

Bit by bit, his shoulders lowered, and his hands unclenched, his chest rising as though he'd ordered himself to relax, one piece at a time. He stepped forward, but paused with a slight shake of his head, like he didn't trust the open sky before him, or feared freedom was a trap. Rubbing the back of his neck, he turned, looking back at the city over his shoulder.

Alessa ran away before he became *Man on Balcony Who Caught You Staring.*

He'd been sleeping on floors in tavern storage rooms. She could let him have one decent night's rest. Clearly, he had his own demons to slay, and she wasn't one of them.

Besides, it was only one night.

Twelve

Anche in paradiso non è bello essere soli.
There is no greater torment than being alone in paradise.

Alessa was in a coffin.

Not dead. Not yet.

Adrenaline flooded her veins, sharp and sour, as the air in her lungs went stale.

She woke with a start, swinging wildly. Fingers curled into claws, she struck something warm and hard.

A hiss of breath. In the anemic predawn light, Dante clutched his arm.

"What are you doing?" Alessa yanked the sheets up to her chin. "I told you not to come near me!"

He grimaced, shaking his hand as if scalded. "You were having a nightmare. I thought you were going to hurt yourself."

"Then you should have *let* me." Her words, so similar to Lorenzo's, struck like a blow. "Don't *ever* do that again."

He shot her a dark look. "Believe me, I won't."

At a sharp rap on the door, he motioned for her to stay back and strode around the screen. For all his initial reluctance, he took the job seriously. *Too* seriously.

Alessa pulled on a robe and followed.

Dante was glaring at the door, a stack of clothing in his arms. "She ran away. The maid, or whoever."

"Can you blame her?" Alessa asked, innocently. "You're a bit intimidating. You should smile more."

He gave her *a look.*

"If it makes you feel better, they run away from me, too." She waved toward the bathing room. "You can get cleaned up in there."

Dante bristled before skulking off.

She hadn't meant to imply he was dirty in *general*, but any attempt to clarify would only make it more awkward, so she bit her tongue. If he'd decided to take offense at every little thing she said, that was his problem. She covered her face with a pillow, but managed not to scream into it.

Fingers of dawn crept across the floor as she found the energy to face the day. The Consiglio was probably gathering below, waiting to hear her decision so they could summon her next Fonte, but she still had no idea who to choose. She'd give them a list of those she'd ruled out and let them decide. She was a coward, but at least she'd be a coward who wasn't responsible for making the wrong choice again.

Dante emerged a few minutes later in a crisp white shirt and military-grade trousers. They were a bit tight, but the Captain had done a fair job guessing his size, and she wasn't complaining about how they hugged his body. Hard to say whether Captain Papatonis would be satisfied with Dante's appearance, however. With his sleeves rolled to his elbows, the top button of his shirt undone, and the leather gloves shoved in his pocket, he looked alarmingly attractive, but barely respectable by Cittadella standards.

She gave him a bland smile. "Much better."

Dante scowled like she'd insulted him again.

The bathing room was humid when she stepped inside, and bits of fabric hung from every hook and rod. Intimates she'd left to dry after hand-washing them. Not silky, fine items, even, but practical, everyday underthings.

Nice work, Alessa.

He couldn't possibly fail to be impressed by her haughty Finestra-ness after bathing amidst her most boring underthings. She ripped everything down and stuffed it all into a drawer.

Strain had left her paler than usual, her eyes overly large, and her hair hung in limp tendrils instead of her usual flowing waves, curly on humid days. She looked nothing like a valiant savior, which felt about right, but was unacceptable.

Getting clean was a start, but Dante was on the other side of a door with no lock, and if for some reason he opened it, she'd be completely exposed. He couldn't touch her, with or without her consent, but *still. He'd see her.*

She grimaced at her reflection. Not like he'd have any interest in doing so.

After bathing, she picked through her cosmetics. Today called for extreme measures, so after dabbing sheer gloss on her lips, she slashed inky black across her lids, smudging until she resembled an avenging angel. No one would see her weakness beneath so much smoke and shadow. This look wasn't for impressing anyone else, but for herself alone. For courage.

After her face, she began concealing her neck's bruises, but every brush of her fingers hurt as she applied layers of cream and tinted powder.

At least the traditional white gown for meeting with the Consiglio was loose and flowing, so it would conceal her training clothes underneath, and she wouldn't have to return upstairs to change before her daily session.

To Renata, combat training was stress relief. To Alessa, state-sanctioned torture. The pain of getting dressed left her woozy; lifting a sword might break her.

The low neckline slid off her shoulders as she stood, fumbling to get the last satin button behind her neck through a loop that seemed intentionally too small, and a ragged sob of pain slipped out.

"You okay?" came Dante's voice.

It was one thing to cry in front of a stranger in an alley, but they were in the Cittadella, and she was the Finestra. Or at least, she was trying to be.

"I'm fine." Her voice cracked. Traitor.

"You don't sound fine."

"You're my bodyguard, not my nanny."

A lengthy pause, footsteps, and the stutter of chair legs against the floor.

She picked up a ribbon, wincing as the small movement sent a bolt of pain across her collarbone. What was wrong with her? Had she forgotten how to accept kindness?

She thought she'd sampled every flavor of loneliness, but this one was new. She should have felt *less* lonely, not more, but like a flame appears brighter in the darkness, her isolation cut even deeper with a stranger filling spaces usually left empty.

Gritting her teeth, she worked until a long plait lay down her back, but before she could tie it, the braid unraveled. Tradition be damned, the Consiglio could accept her hair down.

She stepped out, casually adjusting her position so it didn't look like she was holding a pose.

Expression blank, Dante was sitting at the table, flipping a knife into the air, over and over, so fast the blade blurred silver.

He raised his eyebrows at her transformation.

"I'm sorry," she said. "I didn't mean to snap at you. Some tasks are still painful."

Dante caught the knife and stood it on its tip. When he lifted his hand, it stayed upright, precisely balanced. "I could help."

"No. You can't." Gods only knew if there was anyone who could help her, but it wasn't him.

Alessa pulled on her gloves, pausing to straighten one twisted finger. "Keep the armband on at all times, especially when you aren't with me."

"Why wouldn't I be with you?"

"I won't need protection when I'm with my mentors."

Dante bit one end of the armband's fabric to tie it around his bicep, speaking through gritted teeth. "You trust them?"

Did she? She hadn't when she'd escaped to the city and begged a stranger to protect her.

"Of course," she said, well aware she'd taken too long to respond.

He plucked an apple from a fruit bowl, polishing it against his shirt, his expression inscrutable. "Got anything else to eat?"

Alessa worried her lip. She wasn't much of a breakfast person, usually just popping into the kitchens for an espresso and a biscotto in the morning. "There's bread and cheese. I could call for something more substantial if you'd prefer—"

"No. That's good." He glowered like she'd offered to hit him, not feed him. *Grumpy, grumpy.*

Dante rattled around the kitchenette, opening and closing cabinets as though he'd lived there for years. Despite being a stranger, an interloper, and a marked man, he didn't think twice about asserting himself and taking up space. Now that she thought about it, most men didn't. Some people stepped aside, and others stood their ground, as if they had every right to exist.

Maybe she deserved to claim her small patch of space too, not because of her title, or even because she'd earned it. Just because.

It shouldn't feel like a revelation.

Dante's knife clicked against the plate as he shaved off a slice of cheese, followed by the crunch of bread—the sounds were soothing, but disorienting after so many silent meals.

"So," Dante finally said, with the air of someone pulling a tooth. "How long's it been since you've touched anyone in a non-murdery way?"

"It's not *murder*. And I don't know."

He looked skeptical.

She fetched a glass of water and dropped into the seat across from him with a long sigh. "Four years, ten months. And a few weeks."

"Who's counting, right?" He nudged the plate toward the center of the table. "What's your plan this time?"

Alessa plucked a paper-thin slice of parmesan, which melted on her tongue in an exquisite rush of salt and fat. "Pray?"

"That's not a plan."

It also wasn't the truth. She hadn't prayed in years. Not since the gods first turned their back on her and let Emer die. Oh, she said the words, took to her knees in the Temple and cast her sights to the heavens. She even spoke to them at times. But she didn't *pray*. Prayer meant extending your soul like an open hand, trusting some invisible recipient to take hold. Whenever she extended her hand, death was placed in her grasp.

No, she didn't pray.

"Saving Saverio isn't like finding a new method for solving math problems," she said.

"Are there different methods?"

"Believe it or not, yes. My teachers were never impressed that I got all the right answers but couldn't explain how, but I *did* always get the right answers. This, however, isn't long division, and my *plan* is the same as every Finestra's before me." She raised her glass.

A smile tugged at his lips. "How's that working for you?"

An inappropriate laugh burst free, sending water splashing over the rim. "Obviously not great, or my Fonte would be sitting there, not you." She traced her fingers through the spill, drawing shallow rivers that dried faster than she could replace them.

"Maybe you should try something else, then."

"*Wonderful* advice. Thank you for that."

"You think it'll work this time?"

"It has to."

"Doesn't mean it will." He looked so matter-of-fact, like he wasn't tossing the possibility of Saverio's annihilation at her right before she had to make a life-or-death decision.

"Thank you for your vote of confidence." She pinched her lips together, inhaling through her nose. "I have faith."

"In what?"

"In . . . In the gods?" Divinely ordained warriors weren't permitted to doubt.

"If you're waiting for the gods to save you, you're doomed."

"That's blasphemy," she said, unable to put much feeling into it.

"Kill me, then. No one will miss me."

She gave him a long look. "I'd rather not. I like that carpet, and it would be a real nuisance to get your blood out of it."

An almost-smile softened his features. "You're a strange girl."

"I'm not a girl. I'm a Finestra."

As she rounded the final corner of the stairs, Alessa's heart plummeted at the sound of Tomo and Renata's voices echoing from the antechamber outside the temple.

She never went against them. Or anyone, for that matter. People gave directions and she took them. No exceptions. She didn't even know how to argue with them, much less win.

Tomo and Renata should have been mere backup by now, offering occasional advice to Alessa and her Fonte. But since Alessa was still alone, and the military was frightened rather than respectful of her, they took on more responsibility than they otherwise would, and her guilt deterred her from being more of a nuisance than she already was.

Not anymore.

"Finestra?" Tomo called out.

"I'll be right there." She unlocked the gate at quarter speed.

She could hand Dante some coins and send him toward the nearest exit. Tomo and Renata would never know, and everything would go back to how it was before.

When a woman threw a dagger at her head.

When Tomo and Renata casually discussed murdering her.

When a man tried to crush the life from her body. A man who might be walking the halls of the Cittadella right now.

She could send Dante away and accept her fate . . . or she could stall.

"Lock it behind me, then go," she whispered, tossing him the key.

Dante caught it in one hand. "Go where?"

"Anywhere. Just keep the armband on." She made shooing motions, but he merely tilted his head like a baffled dog. She'd assumed the wolf nickname was a compliment, but perhaps not. "I'll meet you upstairs when we're finished."

"What do I do until then?"

"I don't know. Whatever you want." She had no idea what guards did or didn't do. She nursed resentment when they shrank away from her, but rarely thought about them otherwise. Dozens of people who marched around the lower levels every day barely intruded in her thoughts. For someone who hated feeling invisible, it was an uncomfortable realization.

"Go make friends with the other guards or something," she said.

He curled his lip in disgust. "I'll sniff around for a bit and figure out who to watch out for."

"Good idea." Her stomach clenched at the memory of heavy boots and unforgiving hands.

"The Consiglio is *waiting*, Finestra," Renata called. "I hope you've made your decision."

If you can't change the rules, who can?

"I have," she said, then louder. "I *have* made a decision." She hoped they hadn't heard the waver in her voice.

Dante stared at her so intently she feared he could see right through her.

Thirteen

L'occasione fa l'uomo ladro.
Opportunity makes the man a thief.

W e gather today to ordain the holy partnership, complete the sacred circle..." Padre Calabrese would speak all day if they let him.

The temple was less solemn and crowded than it had been for Hugo's funeral, but Alessa was kneeling at the altar, again. The other council members stared down their noses at her, where she bowed like a supplicant rather than a savior.

She'd never bristled at the condescension etched on their faces before, but she was tired of being deferential, of feeling small and wrong and broken. No matter what happened in the weeks to come, she couldn't defeat it by cowering.

"I'd like a moment to speak," Alessa said, heart beating double time.

Renata and Tomo stole glances at each other behind the Padre's back.

She took a deep breath. "I'd like to train with *all* of the eligible Fontes."

Padre Calabrese shook his head. "Tradition demands a wedding before a Finestra lays hands on anyone."

"With all due respect, tradition died with Emer Goderick." The pain of speaking his name threatened to steal her breath. "But we adapted then, and we can do so again. After all, that pairing was meant to endure for a lifetime, but clearly, the gods had other plans. The First Warning could arrive any second. We've run out of time for rituals and rules."

Tomo shifted in his seat, his expression offering no hints whether his silence was a show of support or disapproval.

"Perhaps," Renata said, "if she trains with all of them, we'll discover who can withstand her gift *before* she chooses, and avoid another tragedy."

"No, no, no." Calabrese waved his hands to ward off the idea. "The people are already restless, they can't handle sudden changes to our most sacred traditions."

"Traditions won't save us from the scarabeo," Alessa said.

"The people *are* restless, Padre," Renata acceded. "And another dead Fonte could be the match that lights a wildfire."

"We can't abandon—"

"We won't *abandon* anything," Alessa said, clasping her hands in something akin to prayer. "Merely change the order of events a bit."

"The people don't need to know," Renata said. "We can tell everyone she's chosen her Fonte, but out of respect for her past Fontes, we're having a private ceremony, with a grand reveal to come."

"And how do you propose we keep them from noticing that none of the Fontes have left their homes?"

"Bring them all here," Alessa said, struggling to keep her elation from showing. "We can say they've been moved into safer quarters or are staying here to support the chosen Fonte."

Saverio's religious leaders and elected officials whispered amongst themselves, faces drawn. The church elders looked unconvinced, but a few of the politicians nodded thoughtfully.

Alessa rose. "I appreciate your support." Not permission. "As you know, it's critical we present a united front in such perilous times."

"Agreed," said Renata, but her eyes held a clear warning for her rebellious charge.

Tomo nodded. "We can't walk the same path again and again and lament arriving at the same destination."

"Padre Calabrese, esteemed councilors," Renata said. "We are, as ever, thankful for your guidance and support."

Tomo pressed a kiss to Renata's hand and stood. "I'll begin preparations immediately and instruct the escorts to wait on their doorsteps until they're packed and ready. We'll have everyone moved in this afternoon."

"Excellent, dear." Renata smiled up at him. "Finestra, shall we?"

Padre Calabrese seemed to realize a moment too late that the tide had turned on him. "Hold on. When will she make her final decision?"

Renata shrugged. "Carnevale. Side by side, our royal saviors will kick off the festivities from the Finestra's balcony."

Carnevale was perfect. Preparations for every Divorando involved gathering seeds, young plants, and animals. As long as *someone*, anyone, survived to open the gates afterward, Saverio would have a chance to rebuild and regrow. When those essentials were secured behind heavy locked doors on the lowest levels of the Fortezza, the people would have one night to cavort in the streets in the beautiful clothes they couldn't pack, gorge themselves on delicacies too perishable for the Fortezza, and drink themselves silly on wine and spirits. Carnevale was a collective taunting of the scarabeo, who might take lives and strip the world bare, but would *not* get their wine or chocolate.

"Brilliant, my dear," said Tomo. "Carnevale is a celebration of life's fleeting joys, after all, and what's more joyful than knowing your saviors will ensure there will be more joy to come? A quiet ceremony the following morning, on the Day of Rest and Repentance when there are no services, and the new Duo's first public outing can be the Blessing of the Troops the next day. Perfection."

Padre Calabrese blinked, but had no rebuttal.

Alessa dropped a low curtsy, her loose hair concealing the victorious smile spreading across her face. She'd won.

The temple doors had barely closed before Renata whirled on her. "Next time you decide to mutiny, Finestra, please remember to inform us ahead of time."

Alessa deserved a medal for the shortest-lived victory in history.

She caught sight of a shadow on the floor in the corridor beyond and bit back her automatic apology. "I thought you wanted me to be a leader. Doesn't leadership require making decisions?"

"It doesn't mean keeping secrets from *us.*"

"Oh?" Alessa said, lowering her voice. If the Consiglio wasn't debating the merits of killing her yet, she wouldn't give them any ideas.

Tomo frowned. "What's this about?"

"Do you believe in me, Renata?" Alessa tried to hold Renata's gaze, but her eyes kept slipping to the door.

"Of course," said Renata. "You're the Finestra."

"Am I? Or should we end my life and see if a better one rises?"

The older woman's cool expression barely changed, but a subtle play of thoughts tightened the skin around her eyes. "I've already told you to disregard that ridiculous man."

"And yet, *you* haven't."

Tomo sighed. "Renata. She heard us." It wasn't a question.

"Yes. I heard you." Alessa spoke directly to Renata. "I've heard the theories, too, and I don't blame you for discussing them. Your duty is to prepare for what's coming, and that means weighing every possibility, no matter how unpleasant. But next time, I should be a part of the conversation."

"I wasn't *seriously* considering it," Renata said, each word sharp enough to draw blood, "but Tomo and I have a responsibility to Saverio."

"I have a responsibility to this island, too. If you decide my death is the price we must pay—if you truly think it's our best chance—I'll accept your decision and do it myself. I will not, however, stand by and do nothing if I am attacked without warning."

Alessa had never been more thankful for the pockets to hide her shaking hands. She'd never stood up to her mentors before, but it was time. No more waiting to kill or be killed.

Renata reached for Tomo's arm, and they turned to leave, but the doorway was occupied.

Alessa nearly groaned aloud.

"Who are you?" Renata demanded of Dante.

"Someone who's *terrible* at following directions," Alessa muttered. She gathered a breath for strength. "He's my new guard."

Renata studied Dante the way a cat nudged a dead bird to see if it was fresh enough to eat. "Why is *this one* out of uniform?"

"*This one*," drawled Dante, "doesn't *like* uniforms."

"And who, exactly, are you?" Renata asked again.

Dante gave her a cold smile. "You heard her. I'm her new guard."

"And what happened to your previous guard, Finestra?" Renata asked, turning the title into a warning.

Alessa tried to speak, but the words seemed to be locked in a vault. "He . . . abdicated his duty."

"*What* did he *do?*" The lightning flash of rage in Renata's eyes did more to reassure Alessa than anything she'd said thus far.

Talking about what happened would make it too real. The terror had barely settled, and she couldn't bear to stir it up again. It must have shown on her face, though, because Renata inhaled sharply. "I'll have Lorenzo stripped of his rank immediately."

"Thank you."

"But honestly, did you throw a letter out the window and hire the first person who picked it up?"

"It doesn't matter how I found him."

"A stranger shows up at the Cittadella at the Finestra's side, and you don't want us to ask any questions?" Tomo scolded gently.

"The guidelines say a Finestra has the right to choose her own security personnel, as long as they're no relation." If relations *were* permitted, she would've begged Adrick on day one. Which was why the rule existed in the first place. Cutting ties with one's previous life didn't include dragging your twin brother along.

Tomo rubbed his temples. "The troops will be your only defense when Divorando comes, Finestra. If you're unsure of their fealty, we should take action."

She wasn't sure of *anyone's* fealty. The only person whose motivations she understood was standing right in front of her.

Dante had little chance of surviving Divorando without her, which meant that to him, her life was valuable.

"I will put my complete faith in our troops when it's time for battle," Alessa said, looking from Renata to Tomo. "But I'll focus on my duties better until then, knowing I have someone trustworthy watching my back."

For years, Alessa had been the figurehead of an army that treated her like a child at best, and an enemy at worst, but now she was in charge of someone. A strong young man who didn't take a knee for anyone, including the former Finestra and Fonte, and while he wasn't cowed by *her* authority either, he did follow her orders. Some of them. Regardless, he worked for *her*.

Renata sucked in a breath, and Alessa steeled her spine. "He's an experienced fighter, and I won't discuss this any further."

It was first time she'd ever seen Renata speechless.

Rebellion might prove addictive.

Fourteen

Senza tentazioni, senza onore.
Without struggle, there is no glory.

Alessa pinned Dante with a dark glare as Tomo and Renata left.

Leaning against the archway, Dante raised a bright green apple to his lips, entirely nonplussed by the staring war she'd initiated.

"I told you to wait upstairs."

He shrugged. "I was going to, but it turns out half this place wants you dead, so I figured you could use an escort."

The only sound was an occasional crunch as he casually chomped away, impervious to her goal of burning holes in his face through force of will.

"What was *that* all about?" he asked.

Cocking her head to be sure her mentors were out of earshot, Alessa pushed loose dark waves of hair behind her shoulders. "Renata is debating whether to kill me."

Dante froze, teeth sunk into the fruit's white flesh. He finished the bite and swallowed. "And?"

"*And?* That's all you have to say?"

"If I lay a hand on her, they'll hang me."

"Well, you're safe, because I told her if my death becomes necessary, I'll do it myself."

He stared into the distance. "Huh. Then how would I get paid?"

"I cannot believe I *am* paying you for this."

He tore another chunk from the apple, garbling his words. "If you wanted a *yes ma'am, no ma'am* kind of guard, you had plenty to choose from."

"Oh, I certainly don't expect *that.*" She rolled her eyes. "But a little sympathy wouldn't kill you."

"Not much can kill me," he said with a flinty smile. "And sympathy wasn't in the job description."

"Neither was talking back."

"I go above and beyond." Dante shrugged. "Pick your next victim?"

"No." She glowered, even though she'd had the same thought a hundred times. "As you suggested, I'm trying something new. Are you willing to stay on a bit longer?"

"How *much* longer?" Dante asked, squinting.

"I promised them a decision by Carnevale."

He threw his head back with a sigh. "This Fortezza pass better be written in gold."

"I'll sign it in blood. Now, come on. Renata's always tougher on me when she's in a bad mood. I don't need to be late, too."

Outside the training room, Alessa kicked off her shoes and began removing her temple finery while Dante peered through the open doors. Most of the room's surfaces were padded, and an array of weaponry, real and practice, hung from hooks and holsters on the far wall. Dante let out a soft sound of longing as he spotted the collection of ceremonial daggers.

Her Temple dress slipped down to her waist easily enough, but she had to squirm to get it over her hips. As the fabric slipped down to pool at her feet, Dante turned back, his eyes lit with desire—for *knives*, not *her*—and her knees went wobbly.

Jerking his head up, Dante stared at the wall above her. "What kind of training?"

She shouldn't have, but she blushed. Her thin, form-fitting training attire was crafted for freedom of movement, not modesty, but it covered everything it had to. "Fencing, I hope. I have a bo and sword, too, but they're much heavier."

At that, he looked at her with a curious half smile. "You know how to use a sword?"

In a perfect world, she'd whip a broadsword from its scabbard and prick his neck with a sardonic *Of course, don't you?* but even if she had one within reach, her arms would likely give out. Instead, she propped her hands on her hips. "I'm no master swordsman, but I know how to swing it around a bit."

Renata cleared her throat from inside the room. Her eyebrows flew up as Dante followed Alessa inside and found a corner to lurk in. Alessa had expected him to wait in the foyer, but she hadn't told him to, and now that he'd invited himself in, she'd be damned if she let Renata catch her surprise.

Renata picked up a practice bo, and Alessa's heart plummeted. Taller than she was, and almost too thick for her fingers to wrap around, there was a solid core beneath the cork coating. Practice weaponry might not inflict true damage, but it meant they were going to spar.

Renata wasn't being intentionally cruel. She didn't know about Alessa's injuries, but that wouldn't make the hits hurt any less. Ah, well. The scarabeo wouldn't take pity on her, so there was no point asking Renata to.

Alessa raised the bo, vividly aware of her audience. This was her chance to show Dante that she was more than a weepy girl. She wasn't *good*, really, but she had nowhere to go but up in his estimation. Not that she cared.

The lesson started with a warm-up, both women swinging and thrusting at open air. Each movement brought twinges of pain, but the steady flow warmed and stretched her tight muscles, so it wasn't all bad.

Renata spun, swinging at the back of Alessa's leg.

Her knee buckled, and she hit the mat with a yelp.

Spoke too soon. Still, she could get through this. She would. She had to.

Gritting her teeth, Alessa got a few hits in before Renata knocked her down again with a thump to the gut. Thankfully, the blow only knocked the wind out of her.

Swing, parry, block, over and over, faster and faster, until individual bolts of pain merged into a constant throbbing misery. Alessa tried to step outside her body. She didn't cry out.

"Break." Chest heaving, Renata strode past Dante without sparing him a glance.

Gripping her weapon for support, Alessa dropped to one knee, her face twisted in agony. Turned away from Dante, with a curtain of sweaty hair to shield her face, she hoped he wouldn't see.

Boots stopped in front of her. "Does she know you're injured?"

"No. And she isn't going to."

"You're hurt, and this isn't helping." Dante scowled.

"Neither is talking about it."

She pulled herself up before Renata returned. When the older woman's bo struck her shoulder a few minutes later, Alessa spun away, mouth open in a silent scream of pain.

Dante stormed out of the room.

So much for impressing him.

When Renata finally put their training materials away, muttering about servants who didn't know how to polish weaponry, Alessa limped out.

Dante was leaning against the wall in the corridor. Sleeping. Upright. Eyes closed, full lips parted, thick eyelashes resting on his cheekbones like the stone wall at his back was a feather bed.

She'd barely convinced her mentors he was a vigilant and dedicated guard, and he was napping on the job.

With a grunt, she kicked the toe of his boot.

Dante's eyes snapped open, and his knives flashed toward her.

Fifteen

L'uomo propone, Dio dispone.
What man proposes, god disposes.

Alessa stumbled back, yelping as the door handle jabbed her side.

Dante jerked away, and his snarl faded. Looking anywhere but directly at her, he sheathed his blades.

"Sorry." For the first time, he sounded like he meant it.

"You're supposed to *protect* me, not attack me," Alessa said.

"I warned you not to sneak up on me."

"You were *asleep!* In a *hallway!* You can't stab everyone who walks by." She rubbed her chest as her heart fought to escape her ribs. "Do you always carry those?"

"Yes."

"Why?"

His lips twisted in a sardonic smile. "In case someone sneaks up on me."

She rolled her eyes, which somehow managed to hurt.

She'd already been losing hold of the broken pieces of herself before her bodyguard had nearly killed her, and now her bruises throbbed, and every breath burned. By the time they reached the fourth floor, Alessa had to stop and clutch the wall, silently begging the darkness in the periphery of her vision to retreat.

"You okay?" Dante asked.

She nodded, lips pressed together for one steadying breath so she didn't vomit on his shoes. "I need to visit the salt baths."

"Can you do that without drowning?"

"A risk I'm willing to take."

He made a noncommittal sound.

Dante followed her down the narrow staircase off her suite. The air grew warm and thick with salt as they descended, pink crystal lanterns diffusing a rosy glow across the white stone. Droplets condensed on the tips of her hair, already wet with sweat, curling the ends into tight coils.

"See? It's perfectly safe." She gestured to the rippling surface of the pool. A constant current carried the hot spring's fresh water in and stale water out.

Dante sat on the stairs. "I won't look."

Heat climbed her neck, but she didn't have the energy to argue. She'd have to trust him to keep his word.

The warm pool called, offering relief. She'd need it to pull herself together before the Fontes arrived. The high salt content made her so buoyant she doubted she *could* sink, but if it came down to a choice between having Dante haul her naked body out or drowning, she'd stay quiet.

Besides, she wouldn't have to endure the mortification if she was dead, and, bonus, she wouldn't have to welcome a pack of terrified Fontes in a few hours.

Casting furtive glances over her shoulder, she shed her clothes and stepped into the water. The stonemasons who'd shaped the pool centuries ago had recognized bodies weren't made of right angles and the surfaces below the water were carved in a pleasing mix of slopes and curves. She settled herself in a curved hollow with a sound that would have been a moan if she hadn't caught sight of Dante's boots as he stretched his legs. He couldn't be comfortable, but he didn't complain.

From a covered ceramic jar by the side of the pool, Alessa scooped a palmful of the aromatic oil that floated atop a mixture of lemon juice and coarse sea salt, gingerly massaging it between her neck and shoulders.

"What *is* that?"

Alessa jumped, covering her chest with crossed arms, but he was still out of sight.

"Smells like a damned orchard in here."

"What do you have against lemons?" Alessa retorted.

His only response was to radiate curmudgeonly gloom through the wall.

She opened the jar of body scrub again, aggressively wafting it in his direction. "You know, some people think there's healing power left in these waters." If she kept him talking, it would serve as an early warning if he moved.

Dante probably would have preferred to shrug, but the lack of visibility forced a "Hmm" out of him.

"My Nonna says it cured her rheumatic knees."

"Miraculous." Dante's tone was so dry it drew a smile from her.

"Either way, it feels glorious." She waved her hands through the water to create small waves. "La fonte di guarigione."

"La *fonte* della *guarigione*," he said, emphasizing every syllable she hadn't and none she had. "And your accent is terrible."

"Well, *excuse* me," she said, a bit indignant. "I didn't begin studying the old language until I came to the Cittadella, and pronunciation wasn't my priority. Are you fluent?"

"Yes."

"Who taught you?"

Silence.

That's what she got for trying to be nice.

She twirled her hand through the water to create a funnel. "Do you believe any of the old lore?"

"Some."

"How about the ghiotte? Some people think they're still out there."

A pause. "You ever met one?"

"Of course not."

"But you believe they're lurking in the forests, waiting to attack the good people of Saverio."

"No," she said, drawing the word out. "They were banished to the continent, so they were either killed in the first Divorando or died out since. No one could survive that long without a community."

"Maybe they had their own. Maybe they still do."

"You're awfully crabby for someone who doesn't have an opinion. I thought you didn't believe in them."

This time, she was left to picture his shrug.

"You're probably right," Alessa said. "If it was true, Dea would have just taken the power back. Why let someone keep a stolen gift?"

"Who knows why the gods do anything?"

"We know plenty. They created Finestra and Fonte to protect the island. Obviously."

"From the attack *they* send. Why doesn't Dea tell Crollo to knock it off?"

"She's trying to make us better. To remind us about community, kindness, and connection. Two souls joined in partnership, creating a window to the divine and a physical reminder that all mortals can, and must, be a stitch in the tapestry of the world."

"They make you memorize that speech?"

"No."

Yes.

Alessa flicked the water, creating angry ripples. "If our soldiers could drink from the fountain, thousands more might survive every Divorando. It's appalling that anyone could be so selfish."

"*People* are selfish," Dante said. "Everyone just pretends to care about others, hoping they don't get found out."

"How delightfully cynical. All the more reason to have the ghiotte as a cautionary tale."

He scoffed. "Against what? Healing?"

"Selfishness. I always assumed the Finestra was naturally selfless. But I'm not." She couldn't keep the tremor from her voice. "I think that's why it keeps happening. I'm being punished."

Dante seemed to have used up his capacity for conversation.

Alessa stared at the water, wishing she could pull the confession back and wipe it from his memory. What was it about speaking to someone you couldn't see that made one want to overshare?

Right when she thought the conversation was dead and buried, he spoke. "If you even try, you're better than most."

Her lips twitched into a grateful smile. "Why, Dante, are you being nice to me?"

"Not intentionally." A long silence. "You staying in there all day?"

"Do you have somewhere to be?"

She was tempted to stay in longer, simply to aggravate him, but if she stayed another minute, he might have to fish her out after all. Besides, the Fontes would arrive soon. By evening, they'd be alone together for the first time. Well, their first time alone with *her*. For all she knew, they met weekly to discuss how much they loathed her.

Alessa stood, watching the water drip down her legs before reaching for a fluffy robe. Bundling up, with a few pats to be extra sure everything was covered, she walked over to where Dante reclined on the stairs, hands behind his head.

He looked up at her through a fringe of dark lashes. "You didn't drown."

"Maybe next time."

Sixteen

Tristo è quel barbiere che ha un sol pettine.
Do not risk all your eggs in one basket.

A n hour later, Alessa paced before her favorite bench in
the farthest corner of the gardens. Hidden by the tangled branches of a lemon tree, she couldn't see the Cittadella, only leaves and flowers. Sometimes, tucked away there, in a
world so green and lush it felt like paradise, serenaded by bees and
birdsong, she could almost forget her captivity. Not today.

She must have looked like a chicken trying to fly, hands
fluttering by her sides, but she didn't care. She'd killed three
Fontes—*three*—and her brilliant plan to avoid killing another
was to bring them *all* to the Cittadella? The phrase "all your eggs
in one basket" wasn't ominous enough for the occasion.

"Looking for something, Finestra?" Dante said from his position propping up a nearby tree.

Courage. Conviction.

She should have arranged to greet the Fontes one at a time,

each a separate drop of poison on her tongue, rather than swallowing the whole bottle at once.

Dante stepped back from the tree and turned to eye it, drawing one of his knives.

Alessa's heart hitched, even though he wasn't aiming at her when he threw. It stuck in the smooth bark, vibrating.

"I feel ridiculous calling you 'Finestra.' Window."

"Don't you know? I am a *window* to the *divine*." She laughed darkly. "I offer humanity a glimpse of perfection and shine holy light down upon all. You should really be taking advantage of my proximity and basking in it."

His eyes crinkled with a suppressed smile. "Is *that* why it's so bright?"

"Indeed. I'm starting to think this window might have a few cracks in it, though."

He snorted. "All the better to let in that holy light, luce mia."

She gazed longingly at the pale blue sky above the wall.

"If you're planning your escape, that's not the easiest route," Dante said.

Alessa tapped the wall. "If I climb over, will you pretend you didn't see?"

"I'm sure it won't be that bad."

"And I'm sure it will be *awful*," she said. "They hate me."

"Do they even know you?"

"They don't need to. I killed their friends." She waved in his direction. "Quick. Get me a ladder."

Dante turned at the low rumble of the gate. "Too late."

Renata and Tomo were waiting just inside the courtyard. On the other end, framed within the tunnel, a small group huddled like fish caught in a net, shoulders curved with misery.

Kaleb embraced an older man, thumping him with violent affection while a middle-aged woman wept beside them. Josef and Nina clutched each other's hands. Saida stood beside her solemn parents.

They said their goodbyes like heroes entering the jaws of a monster. They were there, but not willingly. They would serve their duty, but they had no faith in her.

Kamaria stood apart from the others, glaring at everyone and everything.

"The other twin fled last night," Renata said with a disapproving *tsk*.

The Consiglio wouldn't like that. It might not be fair to hold her brother's treachery against her, but Alessa had no doubt they would. Hard to say whether it would be enough for them to veto Kamaria if she became a top choice, but she could worry about crossing that bridge later.

Alessa's feet itched to run, but she settled for picking at a thread inside one of the pockets artfully hidden within her full mauve skirt. "Should we wait for the rest?"

"There are no more."

Alessa's heart dropped like a stone. When she'd risen to power, the island had two dozen Fontes, more than enough to choose from, even accounting for those who were unfit for health reasons, age, pregnancy, and the like. She'd killed three. The rest had chosen to abandon their home forever. She could only assume they'd gone to Altari, the closest of the two sanctuary islands still inhabited.

Other people had fled in recent years, too, but *they'd* be permitted to return after the siege . . . if the island was worth returning to. For the god-touched, however, lack of faith was treasonous, and treason meant banishment.

The remaining five stood before her. Well. Five was—slightly—better than none.

Renata stepped forward. "Greetings, and welcome. We're honored by your presence. Please, come into the atrium where the Finestra has planned a lovely reception for you."

Alessa hid her surprise. She had?

Renata waved them inside, waiting until the first round of servers emerged from the kitchens with trays, then made a show of following the servants carrying bags upstairs, to oversee the delivery of the Fontes' belongings.

Tomo conspicuously ducked out next, saying he was going to check on preparations for the evening's banquet, leaving Alessa alone with the Fontes. And enough stilted silence to fill every bit of the four-story atrium.

They'd come dressed for comfort, as she'd requested, but no one looked comfortable.

Kamaria, who'd shed her defensive posture when Renata and Tomo left, did the best at faking it, thumbs hooked in the pockets of her buckskin breeches, wide mouth curled in a smile that said she hadn't a care in the world. Her loose blouse, worn leather boots, and the touch of color in her coppery cheeks gave the impression she'd just leapt off a horse after an invigorating ride. Still, she twitched at sudden movements.

Nina, in a simple cotton dress, clutched her skirts with one hand, and with the other clung to Josef's arm.

Kaleb pounced on a plate of hors d'oeuvres, startling the server, and ate in furious silence.

Alessa cleared her throat. "I apologize for all the secrecy, but we didn't want to unsettle anyone." Anyone *else. They* were clearly unsettled. "The Consiglio has granted me permission to try a new strategy. I'd like to get a deeper understanding of your gifts and your strengths, before we begin training—"

She stepped aside as a line of servers approached with trays of chilled lemonade and limoncello.

Josef accepted a glass, accidentally freezing it so nothing came out when he tried to take a sip.

"Excuse me," said Saida. "How can we teach you about our gifts when you can't touch us?"

"Ah. Well, we may have to bend a few rules."

Saida and Kamaria exchanged looks.

Nina's glass bulged above and below her fingers. "Sorry. Sometimes I slip up when I'm nervous." She loosened her grasp, and the solid crystal goblet regained its shape.

"Wait." Kaleb sounded slightly breathless. "Are you saying you're going to use our gifts *before* choosing a Fonte?"

"I. Um."

"Let's not worry about that today." Renata came to the rescue, descending the stairs. "We'll give you time to get acquainted first, then Fonte Tomohiro Miyamoto will be—" Renata stopped, brow furrowed. A percussion of heavy boots echoed through the tunnel.

A regiment of soldiers filed into the courtyard, led by Captain Papatonis, whose face was white as bone. "Finestra, the Watch is here to see you."

Chills prickled up Alessa's neck.

Soldiers carried in a stretcher with a piece of stained fabric concealing something large. As they set their burden before her, something flopped out from beneath the tarp.

A claw, twisted and underdeveloped.

It twitched.

A nearby soldier raised her bayonet and stabbed the fabric. The twitching stopped, and a trickle of midnight blue snaked out.

Captain Papatonis cleared his throat. "The esteemed Fifth Regiment is here to present the First Warning."

Josef's glass slipped from his hand, shattering in a spray of golden shards.

For better or worse, Alessa finally knew how long she had left.

One month.

One month to choose her Fonte.

One month until they faced a swarm of those . . . things.

One month, and it would all be over.

Seventeen

La morte e la sorte stanno dietro la porta.
Death and fate are behind the door.

DAYS BEFORE DIVORANDO: 28

At Renata's subtle cough, Alessa dragged her gaze away from the creature and forced her lips to move.

"Thank you for your service and your vigilance."

Renata was right, practice *did* make perfect. The ceremonial response had slipped out so smoothly she might have been receiving a bouquet of flowers rather than the mangled corpse of a massive, demonic insect.

The soldiers saluted, armor clanking in the stunned silence of the courtyard, and banged their staffs on the ground, making everyone else flinch.

Visibly steeling himself, Captain Papatonis grabbed the corner of the tarp and yanked it off, exposing a smooth, beetle-black exoskeleton and bulging, liquid red eyes. So intact, so perfect in its horribleness, the scarabeo could have been sleeping.

"I'll have it put in storage once you've had a chance to look it over," he said, before marching away at a clip, mumbling about making preparations.

The soldiers, stone-faced beneath their helmets, bowed and left, abandoning the dead scarabeo in the middle of what had been a cocktail hour moments before.

Alessa took a slug of limoncello.

Was she expected to move it herself? To hang it above her bed like a baby's mobile, perhaps? Something to stare at during the long nights while she lay awake, frozen with dread?

"Someone will remove it later," came Renata's low voice. "Time to lead."

"Ugly, aren't they?" Tomo broke the stillness.

The Fontes wore matching expressions of nauseated horror as Tomo and Renata casually examined the hell-sent creature lying before them in a growing puddle of its own ichor.

"Small, though." Renata walked around the creature, eying it from all sides.

"The First always are."

"Still. Could be a sign of a weak year."

They were restating what Alessa already knew, making idle talk while she worked up the courage to approach a monster larger than a fully grown person. The creature's mandibles curled instead of stabbing out from its jaw, but they were still wide and sharp enough to snap a person in half.

"It does look a bit . . . soft," Alessa said, trying to sound unimpressed.

Saida made a sound between a cough and a sob.

Kamaria and Kaleb had their eyes closed, and it wasn't clear if Josef was holding Nina up or the opposite, as they both looked at risk of keeling over.

Alessa swallowed a bubble of hysterical laughter. Either her years of preparation were finally paying off and she'd been toughened up by the many hours she'd spent in the cold storage room examining mummified scarabeo from past Divorando . . . or she'd finally snapped.

Hors d'oeuvres and a deceased scarabeo. A fitting welcome to the Cittadella of Doom.

Dea, your comedic timing is impeccable.

"The pincers are, uh, more curved than the last batch, wouldn't you say? Closer to those from the Divorando in 431?"

Renata nodded as if Alessa had made a very good point, which was especially impressive since there hadn't *been* a Divorando in 431. It had been 43 . . . 5? 437? It was definitely an odd-numbered year.

It didn't matter. The Fontes didn't look as though they were hearing much of anything.

She muddled her way through a few more derisive comments before Renata clapped her hands together and cheerily announced she'd show the Fontes their new quarters.

Like a train of miserable ducklings, they followed Renata up the stairs, seeming as defeated at the prospect of moving in as they were at remaining near the monster.

"Well, you were right," Dante said, strolling over. "That did not go well."

"You don't think so?" Alessa nudged the scarabeo's claw with the toe of her boot. "I thought the demon corpse lightened the mood a bit."

"Still dead?" Dante gave it a kick and nodded at the wet crack- ing sound. "Still dead."

"I should probably tell Renata to lock the windows, so they don't try to escape."

Alessa stared down at the claw an arm's length from the toe of her shiny black boots. Two identical curves, glossy and smooth, dark and deadly.

They matched.

She didn't check the windows, but she put on a vapid hostess smile and peeked inside the Fonte suite to be sure her new pros- pects weren't making ropes out of bedsheets.

They stopped unpacking at the sight of her in the doorway, and no one seemed inclined to speak, so she mumbled something about staying close by and scurried toward the library, Dante fol- lowing like a surly shadow.

Inside the vaulted room, she stopped, breathing deeply of leather, old paper, sandalwood, and a hint of something strangely enticing she'd never noticed before.

Her favorite room in the Cittadella, the library was also the closest thing she had to an escape, with books and maps of ev- ery kind. As far as she knew, it held a copy of every important book printed on Saverio, and many from before Dea created the sanctuary islands. Even better, the rows of shelves held plenty of less pompous books as well, and she'd already worked her way through hundreds of stories that her mother would certainly dis- approve of.

Dante looked frozen in place. Unblinking, jaw hanging open, utterly gobsmacked.

She'd had a similar reaction the first time she saw the opulent room. The sheer magnitude of books and priceless art pieces were enough to leave anyone speechless, and this time of day, with everything speckled in rainbows from the sunlight streaming through the tall, stained-glass windows, it was downright magical.

She gave him a minute to take it all in, pretending to study an enormous map of Saverio on the nearest wall. Every town on the island was labeled, as well as the intricate system of underground tunnels, and it was so large the mapmaker had included every major street in the city. She raised her hand to trace the many beaches on the farthest shoreline, resting her finger on a tiny cove with no name. It had been named once, but the words were so faded they got lost in the background. Someday she'd visit them all.

Dante shook himself and sprung into motion, striding the length of the room to check behind the shelves for lurkers. No bogeymen leapt from the shadows, and when he was satisfied they were alone, he began peering at titles and pulling books off the shelves. Within minutes, he had a tall stack.

"What?" He glanced over as though he sensed her curious gaze. "Didn't think I could read?"

She must have looked as surprised as she felt.

"No," she answered. "I just didn't peg you as someone who *would*. What sort of books do you like?" A straightforward enough topic, even for someone who seemed allergic to speaking.

He shrugged and returned to the shelves.

"If you have no preference, how do you choose?"

"You ask a lot of questions."

"You give insufficient answers." She crossed her arms. "Fine. I don't need to know anything about you."

"No, you don't."

After carrying his book haul to an end table, Dante sprawled in a leather armchair. His pose was as relaxed as a sunbathing cat, but he flipped through book after book with feverish intensity, putting one down only to grab another, as if hunting for something.

"You won't be here long enough to read all of those," Alessa said, annoyed at her peevishness.

"Watch me."

She was. Too closely.

Between the soft snick of turning pages, silence beat against her eardrums. She'd never realized quiet had weight to it, a pulse that somehow, paradoxically, made it difficult to hear anything else.

Occasionally, the Fontes' voices sounded through the walls, making her twitch.

She wandered toward the door, ears pricked.

"Come la cosa indugia . . ." Dante muttered.

She finished it for him. "—piglia vizio. I *know*. But I wasn't eavesdropping, just making sure they hadn't left without me."

"Uh-huh. Sure you were."

Alessa perched on the armrest of the nearest chair, tapping her heels against the leather. Her soft dress shoes didn't make much noise. She swung her feet harder, each impact making a soft thump.

Dante didn't look up.

He *would* avoid an argument the one time she wanted one.

She reached for a small globe on the end table, spinning it with a flick of her finger. The continents were shaded gray, indicating their destruction, while the islands were painted in vivid color.

Altari's reclusive population was content to be left alone on their snowy island, buying little and selling less. She could only imagine how they'd reacted to the recent flood of Fonte refugees. If *she* could hop a ship and flee, she'd risk the long and treacherous voyage to Tanp, a tropical paradise on the far side of the world. Returning ship crews spoke of water clear as glass, and fruit that tasted like joy itself, but while many a captain returned with saplings, they never grew when replanted on Saverio.

"Do you ever think about leaving?" she asked.

"Saverio?" he said without looking up. "Every damn day."

"There's still time. I'm sure there are captains who'd prefer to weather Divorando under another Finestra's protection. I've heard Tanp is beautiful. A better climate than Saverio and probably a better savior, too."

His eyebrows furrowed. "I'd rather go to the continent and fend for myself."

"That's a *terrible* idea. The scarabeo strip it bare every Divorando."

"Not true. They usually head our way before they eat everything. No point wasting time on grass when there's a whole island full of tasty people offshore."

"You think you'd survive without Saverio's protection?"

"Hasn't done much for me, yet."

"What's stopping you, then?"

"I haven't the coin. Besides, I said I'd keep you alive so you can save Saverio."

She blew out a breath. "Right. Save Saverio."

Her nerves vibrated hard enough to shatter her bones while she composed an elaborate mental fantasy of ripping the book out of his hands and throwing it, just to hear it hit the wall. Anything to break the silence.

Oblivious to her piercing stare, Dante sank deeper into his seat.

"I can leave, if you'd like privacy," she said.

"I'm reading, not bathing."

She slid back until her legs draped over the arm and pulled a throw pillow out from behind her, hugging it to her chest. "Enjoying yourself?" she asked.

"Chair's comfortable. Company isn't terrible."

She dropped her chin to the pillow. "That might be the nicest thing anyone's said to me in years."

Her stomach rumbled loudly, and she slapped a hand over it.

Dante lowered his book. "Can't you ring a little bell for food or something? Isn't that what fancy people do?"

She gave him an arch look. "Yes, we fancy people *love* bells. But I'm hosting a formal banquet for the Fontes tonight and shouldn't spoil my appetite. You're welcome to dine in the mess hall with the soldiers if you'd prefer not to witness the social carnage."

Dante sniffed. "And gouge my eyes out with a rusty spoon?"

"*That* is entirely up to you." She should probably discourage him from speaking ill of them, but if he felt like judging someone else for a change, she wouldn't object. "What have they done to make rusty-spoon-eyeball-gouging so tempting?"

"They complain. Constantly."

Oh. Still her fault, then. "Yes, well, they expected exalted positions serving their illustrious Finestra and Fonte and instead are stuck with the greatest failure in the history of Saverio. It's not exactly what they signed up for."

"They signed up. It's their job."

She sighed. "The last time I ventured into the city, children jeered at them and ran away, screaming at the sight of me."

"They don't treat you with respect, they can't expect anyone else to."

Heat burned the back of her throat. "I haven't exactly earned anyone's respect."

"I don't know about that. Your mentor—the lady—"

"*Signora Renata*. The dowager Finestra. You *know* her name."

"Whatever. Anyway, she looked impressed when you were barking at her earlier, like a puppy yapping at a bulldog."

"Now *that's* the confidence builder I needed."

"Finestra?" Kamaria stood in the doorway, watching them with a strange look on her face.

Alessa tossed the pillow aside and scrambled to her feet, cursing herself for being caught in such an undignified pose. "Yes? Do you need something?"

"We're heading downstairs."

"Wonderful. I'll be right down."

Kamaria left and Alessa rolled her shoulders back, feeling like she should be wearing armor.

"È meglio cader dalla finestra che dal tetto," Dante said softly.

It's better to fall from the window than from the roof. One of Mama's favorites.

"Very clever. Are they falling through me or pushing me out of one?"

He stood, sliding a small leather-bound book into his back pocket. "Only one way to find out."

Eighteen

Chi vive tra lupi, impara ad ululare.
Live with wolves, learn to howl.

Alessa had the place of honor at the head of the table, so she couldn't miss a single miserable glance or flinch as the Fontes took their seats.

To Alessa's right, Nina bowed her head, whispering a soft prayer.

Alessa picked up her fork and the movement startled Nina, who knocked her water glass into her lap.

Across the table, Saida grimaced. Kaleb groaned.

Nina's lip trembled as a servant hustled in with a stack of napkins.

Alessa grasped for old memories, anything to talk about. "Kamaria, do you still play guitar?"

Kamaria idly toyed with her fork. "Yeah. Why?"

"Just wondering. Nina, how are you enjoying the temple choir these days? Your solo at last week's service was lovely."

Nina mumbled, "You're kind to say so."

Josef's voice was soft and gentle. "I keep telling her she has the voice of an angel, but she doesn't believe me."

Alessa tried again. "Saida, how is your project coming along?"

"Going as well as it can, I suppose. I'm focusing on desserts for now."

Alessa tried to keep the conversation going over a starting course of melone e prosciutto, but the stilted responses she pried from the Fontes made Dante seem like a chatterbox in comparison.

The kitchen staff had prepared a feast worthy of divine saviors, probably thinking the Fontes deserved a generous last meal, but Alessa was the only one who did more than pick at it. Aside from Dante, who sat in a chair by the doors to the kitchen, plowing through his third serving with no sign of slowing.

As they waited for dessert to arrive, Dante stretched his legs, clasping his fingers behind his head. His easy movement cut through the tension like a fit of giggles during temple.

Alessa wasn't the only one who shot him a sidelong glare.

Kaleb snapped his fingers at Dante. "Make yourself useful and bring us another bottle, will you?"

Alessa grimaced. "Please?"

Dante snatched a bottle from the sideboard and thumped it onto the table, rattling the dishes, and stalked back to his corner.

"Can't find good help anywhere," Kaleb muttered, poking at his plate of freshly made gnocchi dripping with garlic butter.

"He's a guard, not a servant," Alessa said.

"So, how's this going to go?" Kaleb said. "You torture us until there's only one left, and the *winner's* the last one standing?"

Nina looked on the verge of tears and she didn't seem to notice that her powers were causing the spoon in her grasp to bend in half. "Don't say that."

"Why not?" Kaleb said. "Should I pretend we're thrilled to be here? Overjoyed to become the next sacrificial lambs?"

"Enough, Kaleb." Josef's cheeks flushed darker. "You're being blasphemous."

"And a bigger ass than usual." Kamaria mimed a stabbing motion with her butter knife.

"So." Saida let out a gust of air. "I read this great book about the power of positive thinking, and I highly recommend it."

Kaleb cut her off. "Positive thinking didn't save Emer, Ilsi, or Hugo, and it won't keep her from killing you, too."

"I have no intention of killing *anyone*," Alessa said. "My previous Fontes did not die with one brief touch. We ... persisted, because they'd accepted their role and were committed to the task. I'm not asking that of you. I think—I mean, I'm *confident*—with time and practice I can modify my strength."

"See?" Saida smiled with ferocious optimism "She's been working on it. Positive thinking and practice. It'll all work out."

"And if that cult comes for our heads before then?" Kaleb asked.

Alessa abandoned the last echo of her smile. "They won't come for you—they'll come for me. And if I thought it would save Saverio, I'd let them." She paused to let her words sink in. "But there's no proof for their theories."

Nina's head jerked between them. "What are you talking about?"

Kamaria pressed her temples. "Do they keep you locked in a tower, Nina? Some crackpots are saying she's not a real Finestra, and the only way to raise the real one is to ... you know." She grimaced an apology toward Alessa.

"Are you talking about Padre Ivini?" Nina frowned. "He visited my youth group last week and he didn't seem like a crackpot to me. Every individual communes with Dea in their own way and he is entitled to his interpretation, even if we disagree."

"Not when his interpretation means assassinating Dea's chosen savior," Kamaria said.

"I'm sure he's never *told* anyone to do that."

Josef coughed loudly, saving Nina from wedging her foot any farther into her mouth.

Alessa held in a groan. Somehow, in all the worst-case scenarios she'd imagined, she hadn't expected her first meal with the Fontes to start with a casual chat about her death.

"Yes, well," she said. "There's no proof a Finestra dying would cause another to rise, so you're stuck with me."

Kaleb's eyes narrowed. "No proof it wouldn't."

Kamaria tipped her glass to Kaleb. "If you're trying to get eliminated by being insufferable, truly excellent work."

"I aim to please," Kaleb said, admiring a tiny spark he'd generated between his thumb and pointer finger. "How's your brother, Kamaria? Oh, wait. He ran away, didn't he? I knew my appetite was off. Must be the lingering stink of treason."

Kamaria looked murderous.

"Well, *I* have faith in the gods." Saida pasted a smile on her face. "And in our Finestra."

At least *someone* was willing to pretend.

"Dea doesn't make mistakes," Nina said softly, but it sounded more like a question than a statement.

This was a disaster.

"I wish I could spare you all," Alessa said. "But Saverio needs me, and I need a Fonte. I intend to prove myself so that when the time comes for a final decision, one of you will volunteer."

"And if no one does?" Nina asked.

"The Consiglio will have to choose. But I won't. I know what it's like to be thrust into a role you didn't ask for, and I won't do that to anyone again."

"A toast, then," Kaleb said, pouring himself a nearly overflowing glass and raising it high. "Cheers. To whoever dies first."

Nineteen

Non è prudente aprire vecchie ferite.
It is unwise to open old wounds.

DAYS BEFORE DIVORANDO: 28

Alessa folded her gloves beside her plate and stared blankly at the table cluttered with barely touched plates and empty glasses. The Fontes declined, pleading exhaustion, when a server entered with tiny frosted glasses of limoncello. Their chairs practically left grooves in the floor.

Dante turned the nearest chair backward to straddle it and propped his chin on one hand. "They really *are* scared of you, huh?"

"Of course they are." Alessa curled her fingers into a fist. "I'm the monster who haunts their nightmares."

His eyes softened. She wouldn't have noticed the change a day before, but it was there.

Dante picked up a bottle of wine and squinted through the cobalt glass.

"I watched them open it," she said. "It's not poisoned. Unfortunately."

Dante tipped it to catch the remaining drops and reached for another. Spearing the cork with a knife, he gave a deft twist, popping it out. He tipped the bottle her way, and she shook her head.

She didn't realize she was staring at the knives inked on his wrist until he raised his eyebrows.

"Do you regret it?" Alessa gestured to his tattoo.

"Always."

She had no grounds to judge or pry into his past. She was a killer who'd hired a killer, and he was marked, not banished, so whatever he'd done, it hadn't been cold-blooded murder—probably a street brawl gone wrong. But it struck her that Dante might be the only person she'd ever spoken to who knew what it felt like to end a life.

"It must be terrible to have a reminder of your worst mistake etched onto your skin forever."

He absently rubbed his thumb over the mark. "If I forgot, it would be like they died all over again. They don't deserve that."

Guilt and sadness had always been a weight she couldn't shake off, but he spoke of regret like a gift, like he cared enough to want to keep their memory alive.

"Well," she said, trying to smile and failing spectacularly. "I'm glad I don't have to get marked. I'd run out of space." Her smile collapsed.

"You want to talk about it?"

Only her ghosts breathed in the long silence. She'd carried Emer's story alone for so long, with no one willing to listen.

"The first time, I was so . . . excited." The words came unbidden, like blood welling from a wound. "After waiting so long, I was hungry for any kind of connection, even a simple touch."

"Hungry?"

Heat flared in her cheeks. "It's the best word I could think of."

"You wanted him."

"No." She shook her head. "I don't know. Maybe. But that's not what I meant. I simply wanted to be a part of society again, to be a normal girl who wasn't set apart from everyone else. He was sweet and kind, and I knew he'd be patient with me as I learned how to control his—our—power. I sensed he could be a friend and maybe something more, eventually."

"Was it quick?"

She swallowed. "No. And I only made it worse. I'd been warned I might feel a shock, so when he kissed my hand, I was waiting. I didn't notice he hadn't moved. Until he collapsed. I should have left him and run for help, but I didn't realize it was my fault. It was so obvious, of course. The same thing happened to the child I was playing tag with on the day I became Finestra, but *that* boy wasn't a Fonte. He was just a boy who had the bad luck to be touching me when the gift came. So, I tried to comfort Emer. I yelled for help." She hiccupped a watery laugh. "I wanted him to know I was there, that he wasn't alone."

Her knuckles were white as bone around her glass.

"Because that's what I would have wanted. No one should suffer or die alone. By the time help came, when I started to understand what was happening, he was already dead."

"What did you do?" Dante asked softly.

The dishes before her blurred into a watercolor still life. "I held his hand."

Dante was still asleep when Alessa padded into the sitting area in the morning, wrung out and hollow.

Dea must have known he'd spend his life trying to be surly, so she'd crafted a face that would draw people to him anyway. Or maybe she'd meant to bless him with perfect features *and* charm, but he'd rebelled with sarcasm and a prickly demeanor.

His eyes opened, and her heart skipped a beat.

"Morning, sunshine," she said with a brittle smile. "Our mission awaits."

For Renata, "bonding" had to involve weaponry, so the first item on the Fontes' agenda was whacking each other with blunt swords. Alessa doubted it would do much to build camaraderie. They weren't a team. They were miserable quasi strangers trying not to look at each other.

They took their positions in one long row, eyes forward. Renata strode up and down the line, correcting form, instructing them to picture an invisible opponent, but Alessa visualized each step and flick of the blade as a dance. She'd never *actually* danced with anyone, but her foil became her partner, responsive to her touch, cutting a silver trail through the air. Her muscles grew pleasantly fatigued, and everything fell away.

Renata's loud clap was as startling as being pushed into a cold lake, and Alessa's foil clattered to the ground.

They all watched it roll across the floor.

"Well, that's reassuring," Kaleb said under his breath.

With a pained smile, Renata declared Alessa in charge. Her

absence left a strange and unpleasant intimacy in the room, and Alessa polished her foil with unnecessary vigor.

Kaleb threw his sword on the ground with a clang. "Can someone tell me why we're practicing fighting skills when we have magic?"

Kamaria shot him a death glare. "Not everyone lives in a walled villa, and anyone less privileged than yourself—in other words, *everyone*—knows it's worth learning how to defend yourself."

Kaleb rolled his eyes. "How many times have *you* fought off an attacker?"

"Ask him." She pointed at Dante. "I bet *he'll* tell you."

Dante straightened at the sudden shift of attention his way. "Tell him what?"

"That it's important to know self-defense."

"Oh, sure. If that's what you call it." Dante's lips quirked.

"What's so funny?" Kaleb demanded. "If you have a problem, say it to my face."

Dante stood. "You think a scarabeo will say *en garde* before it eats you?"

Kaleb glared. "Whatever. We have real power."

"You won't last long enough to use it."

Kaleb gestured to the wall. "Hence the weapons—"

Dante scanned Kaleb with a dismissive sniff. "A weapon's only as good as the fighter holding it."

"Dante," Alessa warned. Bodyguards were supposed to fade into the background, not indulge in sword-measuring contests.

Kaleb's hands clenched. "Whoever was chosen as Fonte should have had years to prepare, but we're all playing catch-up because of *her*."

"Watch it," Dante said, but Kaleb didn't heed his steely glare.

"No uniform. You aren't even a soldier. What do you know about anything?" Puffing himself up like an affronted goose, Kaleb strolled over until he was nose to nose with Dante.

Alessa only had time to sigh before Kaleb's chin snapped up, Dante's knife at his throat.

"I know how to find an opponent's weakness."

Kaleb's eyes went wide with fear as Dante nudged his head higher.

"Enough," Alessa said. She didn't mind seeing Kaleb humbled, but she shouldn't have let it get this far.

Dante didn't move.

"Stand down." Slowly, Dante lowered his knife, and Alessa hung her foil on the wall. "Thank you, Dante. Helpful, as always."

Nina chewed on the end of her braid. "Do—do scarabeo even *have* weaknesses?"

Dante flexed his fingers. "Everything has a weakness."

Alessa walked over to one of the painted scarabeo on the wall, trying to remember the details of the corpses she'd dissected. "I never paid much attention to their individual vulnerabilities, but let's find out."

Alessa spotted the thin, worn book she was looking for on the highest shelf of the library, in the section devoted to scarabeo. Her fingertips barely brushed it, even when she hopped. She turned to locate one of the step stools scattered about and found Dante's warmth right behind her, trapping her between him and the shelves. She inhaled sharply and pressed back into the books, sending a few tumbling off the far side.

Dante dropped the book into her hands, then stalked around

the other side to return the displaced tomes to their rightful places, scowling at her through the gaps. He'd let strangers batter him bloody, but looked mortally offended at the possibility of damaging some musty old books.

Gathering her scattered thoughts, Alessa flipped pages as she walked back toward the Fontes. Diagrams blurred into jerky motion, line-drawn scarabeo scuttling across the page so vividly that she shivered.

"There. See where their armor plates meet?" Using a table as a barrier between herself and the Fontes, she placed the book down, open to the page. They craned their necks to see, but made no move to approach, so she nudged it closer and pulled her hands away. "Dante, could you tell us which moves you would use to strike those areas of vulnerability?"

Dante emerged from the stacks. "I'm here to keep you alive, not play teacher."

"Fighting off scarabeo would *help* keep me alive."

He shrugged. "My job's over by then."

She would have thrown the book at his head if she hadn't needed it. She'd probably miss, but it would be worth it to watch his horror on behalf of the poor book.

Josef cleared his throat. "Sir, I apologize for Kaleb's abysmal behavior, but the rest of us appreciate any advice you have."

"I'm a street fighter, not a soldier."

"The scarabeo aren't soldiers, either," Kamaria said. "I doubt they'll follow the rules of engagement. We might as well learn something useful. And I wouldn't mind watching you do that knife trick again."

Neither would Alessa, but she suspected for different reasons. Dante was nice enough to look at under normal circumstances, and primed to fight, he was glorious, but as far as she knew, Kamaria preferred girls.

"What weapons do you get to choose from?" Dante asked.

"Bayonets and long swords, I think?" Kamaria said.

"Exactly. So why are you fencing?"

"Tradition?" Nina ventured.

Dante's expression lost its edge as he turned to her. "On the day of Divorando—"

"On the day of Divorando, we're supposed to use our powers to ward off the invasion." Kaleb was sullen, but less confrontational. "The gods gave us the gifts for defense, so that is what we use. Any weaponry we carry will be ceremonial."

"No wonder so many Finestre and Fonti get wounded." Dante's brows drew together. "If it were me, I'd rather not wait around to be gored."

"Finestre and Fonti?" Kaleb sneered.

"Si, stronzo," Dante said. "*Fonte* is from the old language, and the plural is *Fonti*, not *Fontes*. *Finestre, Fonti, Scarabei*. I wouldn't expect un somaro like you to know that, though."

"Congratulations, Dante," Alessa said with a wide grin. "You've just been promoted. In addition to bodyguard, you are now the Cittadella's premier fighting coach."

If his glares were as deadly as his knives, she'd have bled to death.

"Could you *at least try* not to threaten anyone this afternoon?" Alessa said to Dante as they waited in the training room for the others to return for the afternoon session. "This is difficult enough without them scared of you, too."

"Kaleb's an ass."

She fought to keep her expression severe. "Everyone is under a lot of pressure. I'm sure he'll improve eventually."

"Doubt it," Dante said. "People don't change."

"That's not true."

"It's completely true. Kaleb was born an ass and he'll die an ass."

"Well, he's also a Fonte, so if you hurt him, they'll send you to the continent, and he'll continue living as an ass while scarabeo gnaw on your bones, so cut it out."

Dante looked thoughtful. "Free transport. Might be worth it."

Alessa pointed to a chair in the corner.

Kamaria arrived first, gaze flicking around the nearly empty room until she found Dante, who pulled out a cloth to polish his knives, appearing to ignore everything else.

"Finestra," Kamaria said by way of greeting.

"Kamaria. Good to see you."

"Yeah, sure. What Kaleb said about my brother last night." Her expression held a challenge. "He didn't—I mean, I don't think—" She sighed. "He's never been one to turn down a dare, and his friends . . . It's just, I'm sure he regretted it as soon as he woke up."

"I won't hold your brother's decision against you, if that's what you're worried about."

"It's not."

Renata entered the room in a whirl of motion, and Kamaria turned away, leaving the rest unsaid, as Tomo and the other Fontes strode in.

"Ah, Kamaria, join us," Tomo said, ushering them to one side of the room while Renata turned her attention to Alessa with the intensity of a general on the eve of battle.

Alessa struggled to focus, her attention sliding back to where Tomo sat, surrounded by a ring of Fontes.

Renata climbed onto a stone ledge against the wall. Above her, a large spider scurried on a half-completed web, glistening fibers stretched in an intricate design. Renata pointed to the lower edge of the web. "What happens if I tug this string?"

"It will break," Alessa said dutifully.

"Precisely. Get up here."

Alessa stole a glance at the Fontes. Nina quickly looked away.

On the ledge, Alessa followed Renata's directions and lightly pinched one strand.

"Pull. Gently."

The web shifted shape but remained intact as Alessa drew the string down.

From the corner of her eye, Alessa caught Dante watching as the indignant spider stopped working and scurried into the corner.

"Now, return it and release without damaging anything."

This part was more difficult, requiring Alessa to roll her fingers to detach without snapping the thread, but soon the web was back in its original condition.

"There, you see?" Renata smiled. "A Fonte's power is intertwined with their soul, and if you try to pull it free, you damage the connective fibers. You need to draw just enough of their gift to meet the part of you that controls your own power, then release. It isn't a fight, it's a give and take."

Alessa frowned. "I think I understand." Maybe.

"I know you're nervous. I've been in your position."

Not exactly.

"Finestra?" Tomo called out. "I told the Fontes that I will demonstrate first."

Renata stepped down with a thump.

Alessa had assumed they'd draw straws to decide which of the Fontes would go first. Not Tomo. He hadn't said anything about volunteering until they had a room full of witnesses, and now Alessa and Renata couldn't argue without revealing their fear. They had no choice but to follow his lead.

Renata gave a jerky nod and turned to Alessa. "Strategy?"

Renata might never have truly understood Alessa before, but now someone *she* loved was threatened. Her fear was palpable.

Alessa recited from memory. "Steady hands, slow breathing, light touch, inner calm."

"How?"

"Fingertips only."

"When you sense the power?"

"Control and contain."

Tomo extended his hands, palms up, as Alessa walked over to him.

Every eye in the room followed the movement as Alessa removed her gloves. Her palms were slick with sweat.

She lifted her gaze but didn't quite meet Tomo's eyes. She couldn't. The thought of watching his light go dark—

No. She wouldn't even think it.

He was waiting.

Everyone was waiting.

With a deep breath, Alessa reached her fingertips toward his.

Twenty

Chi semina spine, non vada scalzo.
If you scatter thorns, don't go barefoot.

DAYS BEFORE DIVORANDO: 27

The wind whistled outside as night fell, but the air in Tomo's room tasted as stale as the crypt.

Propped up in bed on a pile of pillows, his eyes were black pools of shadow against his ashen skin.

From his bedside, Renata turned as Alessa entered on whisper-soft feet. "He's resting," Renata said in warning.

"I won't stay. I just needed to see . . ."

"Come in, child." A wan smile spread across Tomo's face and he released Renata's hand. "Put on some tea, won't you, love?"

Renata shot Alessa a sharp look as she left the room.

"Sit, sit. Leave your guilt outside," Tomo said. "I'm a weak old man, and I was overdue for one of my spells. A bit too much excitement, that's all." He patted the bed beside him, but she perched in a brocade chair instead. He might want to show that he wasn't afraid of her, but she was afraid of herself.

"You aren't old, Tomo."

He smiled. "Age is relative. When I was your age, I saw a man of forty as a day shy of a hundred."

"I'm just thankful you're okay. I thought—" She squeezed her eyes shut against the memory of the color leaching from his face. "You were very brave to volunteer."

He tutted. "I only made it worse. Renata said you had to call off the remainder of the lesson."

"Everyone was worried about you. We'll start fresh in the morning."

"I'm sorry."

"Don't be. Get some rest. I can manage without you."

His eyes drifted shut. "I know you can. You're meant to bring people together, Alessa."

With the echo of her name in her ears, Alessa slipped out of the room, wiping her eyes.

"Will he be okay?" Dante asked.

"I don't know, but if the Fontes weren't terrified before, they are now."

"Did you even touch him? It happened so fast I couldn't tell."

"Barely. It doesn't matter. Today was supposed to reassure them. Instead they saw the last Fonte suffer a heart spasm the moment we touched. I'll be fortunate if they show up for tomorrow's training at all."

As they made their way upstairs, sobs, faint but unmistakable, echoed from the library. Alessa held up a hand to warn Dante.

"I'll volunteer," came Josef's voice from inside. "You go home with your family."

Alessa tried to retreat, inching backward, but ran into a Dante-shaped wall.

"And what about *your* family?" Nina asked. "Haven't they lost enough?"

"I'm sure whoever she chooses will be . . . fine," Josef said, his tone soothing.

"Fine? Ending up like Tomo, or worse?" Nina sniffed loudly. "Renata was a *good* Finestra and she still broke him. Can you imagine what *this one* will do?"

This one. Alessa hugged herself.

"I'm older and stronger than you. I can take it."

"Kaleb should do it. No one would miss him." From her tone, Nina knew Kaleb would never volunteer. He'd be gone before Alessa finished thanking those who *did*. "I'll do it." Nina's voice trembled, and Alessa could easily picture her raising her pointed little chin, tears glistening on her copper-colored lashes. A portrait of a martyr.

Dante let out a sympathetic breath.

Alessa couldn't fight the thread of envy that came with the guilt. Poor, delicate Nina, whose brave sacrifice made people want to protect her.

But not Alessa. People only helped *her* when she bribed them with coin or because the gods demanded they do so. Sympathy, kindness, love, and friendship—all those precious human experiences that made for a full life—those were for other people, not her.

She tried to hustle away as their footsteps neared, but there wasn't time to make it to her suite before the couple stepped out of the room.

They faltered at the sight of Alessa and Dante.

"Oh, hello there," Alessa said. "Didn't realize the library was being used."

Josef gripped Nina's hand. "Finestra. How is Signor Miyamoto doing?"

"Good." She nodded. "He's good. Awake, feeling much better. He has these spells often, I'm afraid, and with the excitement . . ." She bit her lip. "Anyway, please tell the others he sends his best, but he won't be able to attend our training in the morning. I've asked the kitchen staff to send something up so there's no need to dress for dinner."

Nina wouldn't meet her eye, but Josef thanked Alessa, then cleared his throat. "We know it's not your fault," he said. "All of this. I just want you to know that we don't blame you. I—I don't blame you."

Alessa swallowed hard. "Thank you."

Josef bowed and ushered Nina toward the Fonte suite.

If she could have walked down the stairs and out the front gate, Alessa would have kept going until she reached the farthest edge of Saverio, but the library would have to do.

Josef didn't blame her. For Tomo? Or for Ilsi? Either way, she blamed herself enough for the both of them.

Alessa stepped inside the dim library, lost in thought, and nearly collided with Kaleb.

He jumped back, the whites of his eyes stark in his face. "Shit, you had to listen to that, too?"

Alessa massaged her chest above her pounding heart. "Were you spying on them?"

"No. I was looking for something to drink." Kaleb held up a crystal decanter he must have swiped from the credenza. "But the star-crossed lovers showed up, and I got stuck listening to their whining. Were *you* spying on them?"

"Of course not." Alessa gritted her teeth. "I forbid you to mock them about this."

"Oh, don't get your gloves twisted." Kaleb's sneer didn't reach his eyes. "I'll finish this bottle and burn it from my brain."

He bumped Dante on his way out.

Alessa clenched her fists. "Do you think he'll tease them?"

"Probably. He's been a pain in the ass since he got here. Doubt he'll change now."

"Oh, right, I forgot." Alessa rolled her eyes. "People can't change."

"I said people *don't* change."

"Same thing."

"Not really." Dante tapped the credenza. "You didn't tell me there was a stash of the good stuff in here."

"Most of it is ancient rather than aged."

"Chi ha bisogno s'arrenda," he said with a wink.

She shook her head with a faint smile, making a note to look that one up. Too restless to sit, she grasped the rungs of a rolling ladder mounted against a wall of bookshelves and began to climb.

At a rustle of movement below, she peered down at Dante. "Are you trying to look up my skirts?"

"Don't flatter yourself. I'm making sure it doesn't take off and drop you on your ass. I don't feel like catching you."

"Oh, Dante," she crooned. "You *do* know how to make a girl's heart flutter."

He smirked. "If I was trying to make you flutter, you'd know it."

She dropped the book, aiming for his aggravatingly gorgeous face, but she knew he'd catch it regardless.

"*The Siege of Avalin*," he read, holding the ladder in place with his foot so he could open the book.

She wrinkled her nose. "Well, if that doesn't capture the mood of the evening." Of all the books in the Cittadella, she'd pulled out an account of the one Divorando that Saverio almost didn't survive.

"The Finestra who panicked, right?"

"Yep. Ran back to the city and tried to hide. The Fortezza was breached, rivers of blood ran through the streets, hundreds were massacred before his Fonte coaxed him back to the peak. Oh, take my advice and skip chapter seven."

Dante promptly flipped to chapter seven, because of course he did. "'The Orphans Left Behind.' Nothing compared to waterfalls of blood or whatever you said. *Orphans* means they were lucky enough to survive, at least."

"And is surviving always better?"

"Point taken."

"It's not the worst chapter, just the saddest. They put the babies in group homes, and within months, most stopped crying and refused to eat." She blinked away tears. "Only one group thrived."

She climbed down, turning to lean against the ladder, but Dante was too close and too tall, so she found the lowest rung of the ladder and pushed up on her toes, as if he wouldn't notice she'd suddenly grown six inches.

Dante's eyes twinkled at her sudden height and he stepped back. "And?"

Alessa hopped to the ground. "And? . . . Oh, the babies. Right. The girl caring for them had lost her entire family in the siege, so she held them all the time. Singing to them, rocking them, talking to them. Mostly just holding them. That was all it took. Everyone thought they needed food and shelter, but touch was what they needed most. Without it, the other babies simply gave up."

Dante bit his lip. "And you know how they felt."

She flushed. "Not entirely, but I can relate. That's all."

He tapped the book against his palm. "Does it happen when you touch *anyone?*"

"As far as I can tell." She laughed, sharp and bitter. "Ironic, isn't it? I would *kill* to hold someone's hand, but if I do, I kill them."

"And all this isolation is supposed to make you appreciate the holiness of connection or something?"

"Yes. A Finestra's earthly relationships are severed so we can avoid distractions, remain pure of heart, and be fully committed to the quest at hand. I'm supposed to appreciate connection more by not having any."

"Seems contradictory."

"It worked. Made me quite eager to have a Fonte."

His eyebrows drew together. "You got a real shitty deal, Finestra."

"Alessa," she said softly. The words tasted strange, awkward and unfamiliar on her lips. "My name is Alessandra Diletta Paladino."

"Thought you weren't supposed to have a name."

"I'm also not supposed to kill my Fontes or have a man in my suite."

He gestured to the wall. "You going to tell *them?*"

"Maybe I should. At least they'd know what name to curse. But no."

"Why are you telling me?"

"I don't know." She sank into a chair and pulled a pillow to her chest. "I'm tired of being a title rather than a person, I guess. Just don't say it where anyone might hear you."

He studied her, thoughtful. "Alessandra. The gods' chosen protector."

"How do you know that?"

"Too much religion in my childhood."

She knew what *that* was like. "Your parents were devout?"

"No." His expression darkened.

"Well, my full name roughly translates to *the gods' beloved, brave protector of humanity*. Dea must have felt she had no choice but to pick me after my parents set me up like that."

"Does your family ever visit?" he asked.

"Finestra, remember? I have no family."

"Yes, *Alessa*, I remember." Her name on his lips sent a strange thrill through her body. "So. Your family. You had one."

She sighed. "Yes, I had a family. I suppose I still do, depending on how pious you are."

"Are *they* pious?"

"My parents are. They haven't spoken to me since the day I left. They're faithful believers."

"And shitty parents."

"That's not fair."

He didn't look convinced. "Siblings?"

"I have—*had*—oh, forget it, I *have* a twin brother named Adrick. Sometimes he delivers things or sits on the other side of the garden walls to speak with me, even though it's against the rules."

"So, was your life . . . good? I mean, you seem so . . ." He struggled for the words, twirling his hand through the air as though flipping through a mental stack of vocabulary words. "Lonely. Like you miss it."

"I do. I miss them so much it's like something's been carved out of my middle." She dropped her gaze. "My father used to call me his little cat, because I couldn't resist an available lap." She gave a sad laugh. "I was *too* affectionate at times. I used to embarrass Adrick by trying to hold his hand around his friends."

"It must have been a shock."

"Becoming Finestra was like drowning. You go every day of your life without noticing the air in your lungs, and suddenly you're plunged into deep water, and air becomes the most precious gift you never knew you'd been given and never thought would be taken away."

"Not sure I'd notice."

"That's sad."

He shrugged.

"I wish you were the Finestra, then. All the personal space one could ever want, an epic battle, and plenty of isolation. Clearly the gods missed their perfect candidate."

He huffed a humorless laugh. "The gods don't want me."

She didn't know what to say to that. "So. You know my full name, and I still don't know your *last* name."

"*Last* name?" Dante said with a twinkle in his eye. "Luce mia, you don't even know my *first* name."

"Wait." Alessa stood. "Dante isn't your *real name?*"

"It's my name, just not my first name." A smile teased at his lips as Alessa prowled closer.

"What's your first name, then?"

His smile deepened. "I'm not telling."

"Why not?" Alessa's voice rose with indignation. "Just to annoy me?"

"'Course not. Annoying you is a perk, though."

"I bet it's something terrible, like Eustice. Maybe I'll call you that until you tell me."

He snorted. "Call me whatever you want. But don't expect me to answer."

"How do you say *jackass* in the old language?"

"Stronzo."

"Bastard?"

"Bastardo." Dante sauntered toward the door. "Should I write these down for you?"

"I'm sure they'll come in handy."

Dante held the door for her to go first. A bastardo, but a gentleman.

Twenty-One

Chi pecora si fa, il lupo se la mangia.
Become a sheep and the wolves will eat you.

DAYS BEFORE DIVORANDO: 26

The island began trembling during breakfast, as though it, too, shook with dread. The second quake sent Alessa back upstairs, dripping with spilled orange juice and grumbling about deities who *could have* sent messages composed of clouds or rainbows, but oh, no, they simply *had* to use natural disasters as a countdown clock.

The shaking subsided by the time she stood in the training room in clean clothes, but Crollo seemed determined to dump an ocean from the sky. She set to work arranging the pillows she'd brought to make it feel less threatening—and break any potential falls—but she couldn't do anything about the ominous rumble of the storm.

Kamaria leaned against the wall, projecting rakish ennui in snug, fawn-colored breeches, but she kept fiddling with the laces of her untucked blouse. Nina stood behind Josef, subtly mirroring his movements like the tide responding to the moon. The pale pink of her dress was a change from her usual white attire, but not by much.

Kaleb's usual scorn had melted into sullen gloom, and in case anyone wasn't entirely certain how he felt about being there, he'd chosen to wear uninterrupted black from head to toe. Feet planted wide, arms crossed, he glowered at anyone foolish enough to glance his way.

Saida was the first one to meet Alessa's questioning gaze, and she stepped forward. Dressed as if bright colors could banish the oppressive air of pessimism, each layer of her skirt was brighter than the last, and her eyes were highlighted with blue eyeshadow. The color coordinated perfectly with the scarf she'd tied around her hair, presumably to keep it from whipping around when she used her powers.

"We can sit, if you'd like," Alessa said, gesturing toward the scattered pillows.

Saida pulled her shoulders back and looked Alessa directly in the eyes. "Thank you, but I prefer having room to move."

To escape.

Working her fingers, Alessa tried to coax her blood to circulate, even though cold fingers were the least of anyone's concerns.

In one corner, Renata watched intently, lips moving in a silent litany of "gentle, easy, careful" that matched the refrain in Alessa's head.

Her hands were so clammy she wasn't sure she'd be able to hold on, so at Saida's jerky nod, Alessa curved her thumb and pointer finger around Saida's wrists like a bracelet.

Her power woke with a surge, a current racing through her,

greedy, yearning for something long denied. It was too much, too fast.

Saida whimpered, and Alessa let go. She needed a second. "Thank you, Saida. I'll come back to you. Josef?"

He'd brought a glass of water for Alessa to try and freeze and had the foresight to place it on the ground so they didn't end up with shattered glass everywhere.

Alessa took Josef's smooth, cool hands in hers and stared at the water glass. Nothing changed. A chill hit her breastbone, spreading toward her limbs. It might have been Josef's gift, or merely her growing panic.

He held on longer than Saida, insisting he was fine through gritted teeth, as though afraid he'd be sick if he opened his mouth.

It was only the first day. They had time.

A little.

Not enough.

Kamaria sauntered over, carrying a candle in a metal stand. "I brought props." Her voice was light, but the flame shook. She put it on the floor and grabbed Alessa's hands.

Alessa couldn't get her hands free. She was going to hurt Kamaria, or worse—

Focus. She gave herself a mental slap. Breathing deeply, she reined herself in until the greedy need abated. Then—only then—she tried to reach for the flicker of Kamaria's power. It brushed against her mind, dancing like a flame in a breeze, but she couldn't grasp it.

Renata had told Alessa to think of a singer—frankly, she was starting to lose track of the metaphors—but her attempts to use her power felt like straining to remember a forgotten melody or having a word at the tip of her tongue. It was there, inside her, and a part of her *knew* how it was supposed to go, but the more she strained, the harder it was to grab hold.

Kamaria's grip loosened enough for Alessa to pull away, and they let out matching sighs of relief. Trembling slightly, Kamaria bowed with a flourish and a cocky grin.

The candle hadn't done anything.

Three Fontes, no results.

Icy fingers of panic walked up Alessa's spine. She'd been so worried about *killing* Fontes she'd never considered the horrible possibility of keeping them alive but being unable to channel their power.

Kaleb skulked over, looking so stiff he might snap in half if she made a sudden move. His hands were cold, and large—a ridiculous observation but the first thing she noticed before she opened her mind completely. A jolt went up her arms, and she let go with a gasp.

Kaleb bent over, clutching his hand. "Dammit, that *hurt!*"

"I'm sorry," Alessa said. Lightning danced between her fingers. "I didn't mean to—"

"Your turn, Freckles," Kaleb sneered at Nina, who was cowering behind Josef, whispering a prayer to Dea. "Get on with it. Evil monster bugs a comin'."

"You're such a bully, Kaleb." Nina lowered her hands, eyes shining with angry tears. She cried through her turn, sobs shaking them both until Alessa struggled to maintain a light touch. She didn't even try to use Nina's gift for warping matter. One step at a time. Nina needed reassurance before she could stand a chance of being a useful Fonte.

After one more round where "no one died" was the best anyone could say about it, Kaleb declared the session over and stalked out, glaring at anyone who dared look his way.

Alessa let him go. He might light the Cittadella on fire if she attempted a pep talk.

The others filed out behind him, but Kamaria hung back. "Can I ask you something?"

"Of course."

"Do the Finestra and Fonte have the power to pardon someone of a high crime?"

Alessa cut a glance at her.

"Don't worry, I'm not a serial killer or anything. I'm talking about my brother. I know what everyone thinks, but Shomari's not a deserter, I swear. Like I said, he's just a sucker for a dare, and his friends challenged him to sneak onto a ship. The little jerks ran away when the crew woke up, and I bet you anything Sho tried to hide so he wouldn't get in trouble, then panicked when the ship left the dock, and he officially became a deserter. He didn't even take anything with him."

Alessa blew out a breath. "I've always been told desertion was an unforgivable crime, but I don't know, maybe under the right circumstances."

"Like if his sister became Fonte?"

It was tempting to say yes, to lock in one strong contender, but she couldn't use Kamaria's brother as coercion, and she truly didn't know. "Maybe. I can't make any promises."

"I get it. Sorry we're not making this easy for you."

Alessa tried to wipe her eyes discreetly as Kamaria left the room.

"Don't say anything," she said to Dante, who was watching her far too closely.

"Wasn't going to."

She sniffed. "They're all alive."

"They are."

"Saida has a good attitude. Josef was a good sport. Kamaria was strong and she seems motivated. Kaleb was ... well, Kaleb was Kaleb."

"I enjoyed watching him squirm."

She gave him a scolding look. "Be nice."

"I'm not nice."

"I think you might be, actually."

Dante looked mortally offended, which struck her as so funny she began laughing, then couldn't stop, until the tears she'd been fighting broke free and she wasn't sure if she was laughing or crying.

Dante looked increasingly horrified, but she couldn't have stopped herself for anything in the world.

"Uh, are you okay?" he asked.

"Never better," she wheezed. "Inigo?"

"Wrong."

"Alberto?"

"Still wrong." He held the door open for her.

"Ranieri?"

"Not even close."

"Julian? Amadeo?"

"All right, piccola, that's enough for today."

The rain had become a deluge during their training session. Water coursed from the eaves of the courtyard, ferocious gusts of wind sending sheets of rain sideways, so the covered walkway offered no protection.

Alessa and Dante sloshed through the courtyard to the stairs, and she heard a huddle of servants arguing about the fastest way to bail out the kitchens. If the Cittadella, perched at the top of the city, was this inundated, she hated to think of everywhere else.

"Shall we make a run for it?" Alessa asked Dante.

Rainwater dripped from the tips of his hair as he looked at the sky. They were going to be drenched no matter what.

"Come on." Alessa grabbed her skirts and dashed into the pouring rain. She could barely see past the water coursing down her face, but she stuck her tongue out at the statue of Crollo as she passed anyway.

A loud rumble, and someone slammed into her.

"What—"

Dante propelled her forward as something crashed to the ground behind them. The statue. Shards of marble skittered across the waterlogged courtyard.

She stumbled but didn't fall. Dante had her arm in a vise grip, hauling her toward the stairs.

"It's not going to fall *again*." She struggled, but his hand might as well have been an iron shackle. "You can't touch the Finestra, you dolt. The earthquake is over."

"There was no earthquake, and that wasn't an accident."

She tried to turn around. "Did you see someone?"

"I could barely see anything."

He let her go when they reached the stairs, pushing aside wet hair plastered to his forehead.

Dante flicked the drops from his fingers and gestured at the side of her face. "You're bleeding."

"What?" She touched her cheek.

Dante gripped her elbow again, urging her along, but her waterlogged skirts kept tangling her legs, binding them together.

"Oh, for Dea's sake, hold *on*." She yanked her arm free and found the clasp, unwrapping herself and bundling the wet fabric into her arms. The forest green tights she wore beneath were nearly as thick as pants, and her leather boots—which were probably ruined—went above her knees.

Dante's gaze flicked down, then immediately up and away.

"Oh, please," she said. "Like you've never seen a woman's legs before."

"Just keep moving," he said gruffly.

When they made it to her rooms, Alessa hurried to the bathroom to examine her injury. The cut on her temple, courtesy of a stray piece of marble, was straight, as long as her finger, and relatively shallow. Nothing that required stitches, thank the gods, because she would've had to do it herself and she'd probably faint. First her ear, now her face. At this rate, she'd look like a battle-worn Finestra before Divorando even began.

Dante came up beside her. "I found salve. Hold still." He raised a finger, and Alessa stumbled back, tripping over the commode and falling into the tub.

"Have you lost all sense?" she said. "You can't *touch my skin*, or you'll *die*."

Dante blinked. "Oh, right. Here." He tossed the salve into her lap.

Her backside hurt, her temple smarted, and she must have looked ridiculous with her legs draped over the side of a bathtub, feet sticking up. Meanwhile, instead of looking like a drowned rat, Dante looked gorgeous, hair curling, white shirt translucent and plastered to his chest, and his pants—no, she was *not* looking at his pants.

She glared at him while unscrewing the cap. "Are you laughing at me?" she said. "You think someone tried to kill me *again* and you're *laughing?*"

He raised a fist to his mouth. "Someone's been trying to kill you the whole time I've known you."

She hurled the salve at his head.

He caught it. "Can we agree that when I tell you to move your ass from now on, you do it without question?"

"Fine. Can we agree that as long as I do, you won't drag me around? The Finestra isn't supposed to be manhandled."

"Deal." He shook the salve at her. "Done with this?"

Alessa pushed up to her elbows, squinting at the inside of his wrist. At the two crossed blades, the thin circle of minuscule letters around it—the mark that declared him a criminal, a killer. The *faded* mark.

Dante dropped his hand, but she'd already seen the proof.

"It's fake," she said. "You marked *yourself.*"

Twenty-Two

Si dice sempre il lupo più grande che non è.
In a story, little lies make the wolf bigger.

DAYS BEFORE DIVORANDO: 26

The laughter wiped from his face.

"Why?" Alessa clambered out of the tub. "Why would you pretend to be a criminal? An outcast?"

"Why do you care?" He slammed the salve onto the counter and walked out.

Leaving a wet trail behind her, she ran after him. "I'm trying to understand you."

"There's your first mistake."

"If you aren't marked, you don't even need a Fortezza pass, so why did you come to work for me?"

He wouldn't—or couldn't—look at her. "Because men do stupid things when women cry?"

"Not good enough. You lied to me."

He whirled on her, eyes flashing. "You found *me*, remember? And mark or no mark, I *am* an outcast. No home, no family, no friends."

"I told you—" She stopped, suddenly lightheaded. "I thought you understood what it felt like, but you've never killed anyone."

"You say that like it's a bad thing. Maybe I just didn't get caught."

"Which one is it?"

"I didn't save them. Same thing." He stared at the floor, hands gripping the hilts of his knives like they were the only thing tethering him to the ground.

She couldn't stay angry when he looked so lost. "Your parents?"

"To start."

"For what it's worth, I'm a much better listener than I am a Finestra."

"You don't need my ugly history."

"What's one more tragedy?" She gave a delicate shrug, a gamble that paid off when he quirked an almost-smile. "I told you mine," she said, a teasing lilt to her voice.

He turned to the rain-streaked balcony doors, fists clenched, mouth tight. She was about to leave him in peace when he finally spoke. "They were killed by a mob. People we'd known all our lives turned on them, dragged them outside, and beat them to death."

She shivered. "Why? What could they possibly—"

"*Nothing*," he snapped. "They didn't do *anything* to deserve that."

"No, of course not," she said in a hurry. "I didn't mean—"

"They weren't perfect, but no one deserves that."

"Of course not. I just can't fathom why people would do something so terrible for no reason."

"Oh, I'm sure they had *reasons*. People always have reasons. People can justify anything if they want to enough."

"I'm so sorry. How old were you?"

"Old enough." The anger in his voice was for himself, not her, but it made her flinch.

"How old?"

"Twelve. But I was big for my age. Strong. I could've fought, given them a chance to get away. And I didn't." His voice was so hollow it seemed to pull the air out of the room. "I hid. I heard it all and I did nothing."

"It wasn't your fault."

"Of course it was." Dante dragged a hand through his hair.

"You were a *child*."

"And they were my family. I should have died *with* them."

There was nothing to say. Even if she could find the right words, they wouldn't reach him, locked away as he was inside himself. And she knew, without a doubt, that if she said the wrong thing, she'd snap the fragile lifeline he'd given her to hold.

How cruel, that sharing someone else's grief did nothing to alleviate it for them. In physics, there were rules and forces, equal and opposite reactions, a balance. But emotions didn't obey rules, and though sympathy settled over her like a heavy blanket, it did nothing to help him. No matter how much she was willing to bear, she couldn't lighten his load. Even her hands, which stole power, strength, and life itself, were powerless to siphon off any of his suffering.

So she didn't speak, but she didn't leave. Standing close, she offered what little comfort she could with her presence alone.

Dante stared at the rain-drenched city below, but she knew he wasn't seeing anything at all.

There was more wincing than sobbing in the following days, but a week into their training, the Fontes still flinched every time Alessa came near.

Tomo had mostly regained his strength, but he watched from a safe distance as Alessa took turns using everyone's gift, even Nina's. The wrongness of shifting matter made Alessa's stomach churn, though, as if the laws of physics fought such an unnatural force.

At the end of one especially long afternoon, the Fontes and Alessa sat around the formal dining table, wilted like flowers in a drought. Tomo and Renata had joined them for a quiet supper of white fish in a lemon wine sauce—the quality of the Cittadella's food had *definitely* improved since the Fontes arrived—and even they didn't try to make conversation beyond answering Saida's hesitant questions about their family recipes. Tomo perked up a bit, looking charmed as she explained her project. He knew a surpising amount about baking, too. While he listed a number of dishes for Saida to choose from, Renata smiled weakly and promised to think of something later, and everyone else seemed relieved that they didn't have to find the energy to speak for a while.

As Tomo and Saida debated the use of rice flour versus gelatin in a dessert Alessa wasn't familiar with, Kamaria stared blankly at the nearest candelabra. Her powers made the flames grow and shrink in a lazy rhythm as though the fire itself was breathing, swirling smoke toward Kaleb. She either didn't notice or chose to ignore his pointed sighs.

Eventully the conversation lapsed into silence.

"I think it may be time for a break," Tomo said, tapping his new walking stick against his chair.

Alessa nearly cried. A *break?* They were supposed to be finished for the day.

"Is there something in particular you still want them to work on?" Renata asked. "Everyone seems a bit tired."

"I ordered sweets," Saida said tentatively. "Maybe a little sugar would help us power through."

"Very thoughtful of you, dear," Renata said. "But Tomo, I think they've had enough for one day."

"My apologies," Tomo said. "I was unclear. I didn't mean *today*, but rather, a full day of rest tomorrow."

Renata stiffened. "I don't think that's wise."

"Rest is as essential for training as sleep is for learning. A day of rest, prayer, and time with family will rejuvenate us all, and I can think of no better way to give warriors purpose than remembering what we're fighting for. Besides, Mastro Pasquale is coming in the morning, so the Finestra will be occupied sitting for her formal portrait."

Alessa wasn't the only one who stole a glance at the line of portraits on the wall, centuries of Duo Divino captured in oil paints, staring solemnly back at them. At first glance the people in the portraits seemed to have little in common, ranging in size, shape, skin color, and gender. But one thing they *did* all have in common was that every single Finestra was paired with a Fonte.

Well, at least Mastro Pasquale, who'd been Alessa's art tutor in the early years of her time as Finestra, was talented enough to add a Fonte later and make it look as though they'd posed together.

Wouldn't *that* be a fun story for tour guides to share with future visitors to the Cittadella. Assuming, of course, that Alessa managed to find a Fonte and together they triumphed over Divorando so the Cittadella was even standing in a month.

Renata rubbed her forehead. "Might as well get half of it finished now. I suppose you may all take a day of rest." It seemed to pain her to grant it. "But I expect everyone an hour early the following day, prepared to give one hundred percent. And I hope you all make good choices about how to spend your day off."

With a hostile glare at the portraits, Renata stood in a swirl of burgundy skirts and helped Tomo to his feet as he waved off a round of thanks.

"Well," Saida breathed when they'd gone. "This definitely deserves a celebration. I'm glad I splurged for the deluxe assortment with the chocolate-dipped cannoli."

A pastry box appeared from under Saida's chair like a magic trick, and the Fontes eagerly dove in.

Josef, Nina, and Kamaria took their desserts to go. Kaleb ate his in one bite and snagged a second from the box before it made it to the head of the table.

"They're from Il Diletto," Saida said. "That's your family's pasticceria, right?"

Alessa blinked at the familiar logo obscured by her thumb.

"The Finestra doesn't have a family," she said softly.

"Right," Saida stuttered. "Of course. I know that. I just thought—"

"Wait," Kaleb said around a mouthful of pastry. "Your brother's Adrick Paladino?"

Alessa's throat tightened. "Like I said, the Finestra doesn't have—"

"Yeah, yeah." Kaleb waved a hand in annoyance. "The Finestra springs, untouched, from Dea's holy loins. Got it." He licked a smudge of powdered sugar from one manicured fingernail, squinting at her. "You don't look anything like him. Well, maybe the eyes."

There was no point clinging to her divine origin story if they refused to play along. "I wasn't aware you even knew Adrick, much less his eye color."

Kaleb went slightly red. "He's everywhere. Can't avoid him."

Saida looked like she'd start whistling if she could. She handed the box to Dante. "You two can share the rest. Come on, Kaleb. There's bound to be a battle for the shower before cards, and I'm not going last this time."

"Pssht," Kaleb scoffed. "If we aren't training tomorrow, I'm leaving now."

Saida chased him out the door. "We're in the middle of Chiamata!"

Kaleb's voice echoed down the corridor. "Switch to Scopa, then. Josef and Nina are practically sewn together, they can play as a pair."

Dante picked up the box of sweets and held it out, but Alessa demurred, toying with her necklace, a small silver pendant on a delicate chain. "You can go, too, if you want. I know you didn't plan on being stuck with me for so long when you took this job."

Dante gave her a funny look. "It's not a big deal."

Like probing a sore tooth to see if it still hurt, she couldn't resist pressing him. "You sure? I bet parties get pretty wild this close to Divorando."

"Do I *seem* like a party guy?"

"I have no idea what kind of guy you are. All I know is Dante isn't your real name, and that you read a lot of books, punch strangers for money, memorize proverbs in the old language, and claim to be a terrible person without providing a lick of evidence to back it up. *You*, NotDante NoLastName, are a complete mystery to me."

He sat forward. "And you can't stand mysteries, can you?"

"Not at all."

"Well, here's a truth for you. I don't enjoy most people, so I don't enjoy most parties."

"Shocking. I used to love parties. And people. When they weren't scared of me."

On second thought, a mouthful of sugar was exactly what she needed.

Ignoring her outstretched hands, Dante continued his methodical perusal of the assorted pastries. "I'm not scared of you."

She raised a victorious fist. "One down. Victory is mine."

Chuckling, he popped a puff pastry into his mouth.

Twenty-Three

Lupo non mangia lupo.
Wolves don't eat wolves.

DAYS BEFORE DIVORANDO: 20

Back in her suite, Alessa debated aloud what to wear for her portrait session the following day, while Dante ignored the topic entirely, lounging in an armchair with yet another book.

She tore through her closet, pulling down armfuls of ruby silk, silver taffeta, and violet lace, and hung a half dozen gowns she'd worn once or not at all from the privacy screen between her bed and the main room.

After some very loud throat-clearing on her part (and one small but heartfelt foot-stomp), Dante looked up long enough to log his vote by grunting in the general direction of a crimson dress. She didn't bother asking for his input on jewelry or shoes, but arranged her picks beneath the dress so she wouldn't have to rummage in the morning.

Wandering back toward the sitting area, Alessa picked up the small, leather-bound book he'd left open on the side table and ran her finger over the words inside the cover.

Per luce mia.

"Is this for me?"

Dante glanced over and bolted upright. "No."

"Sorry." She jerked her hand away. "I didn't mean to pry."

"No. It's fine." His cheekbones darkened. "You can look at it. It's in the old language, though."

Alessa opened to a page at random. "O mangiar questa minestra o saltar della finestra," she read, stumbling a bit. "Something about ministers . . . jumping out windows?"

"Minestra is soup. Eat the soup or jump out the window. It means *take it or leave it.*"

"Ah," she said, closing it. "I'd begun to wonder if you'd memorized a book of ancient proverbs, and voila, here it is."

"More than one, actually. The *holy* man who took me in after my parents died made me read the Verità every day. It was big enough to hide other books behind it."

"Oh." She chewed her lip. "How long did you live with him?"

"Too long. Took me three years to get away."

"That's awful." She wanted to ask more, to understand what he'd been through, both during his time in captivity and the years after, but instinct told her a true friend would change the subject.

Her fingertips detected grooves on the back of the book, and she flipped it over to see letters carved into the leather.

E. Lucente.

"I knew it!" Alessa crowed. "Your name *is Eustice!*"

Dante shook his head with a crooked smile. "The *E* is for *Emma.* It belonged to my mother."

"Drat," Alessa sulked. "Well, at least I know your last name now. *Lucente. Light.* And *Dante* means . . ."

"Enduring."

"Enduring light," she mused. "I like it. You called me that once: *Luce mia.*"

Dante crossed and uncrossed his arms with a soft throat-clearing. "She used to call me that."

Her heart ached for the little boy he must have once been. "What are you reading now? Anything good?"

He slid a glance her way. "You tell me. I found it by your bed."

The blood drained from her face. "Give it back."

He pulled it close. "I will. I'm just borrowing it. Fair trade."

"You can't. It's *mine.* I mean, it's not *mine.* I found it. It was clearly not meant to be in the library, so I removed it. To discard it."

"Why would you do that?"

"It's . . . inappropriate." The tips of her ears went hot.

"Well, someone's enjoyed it. Half the pages are dog-eared." His lips twitched.

She busied herself by shuffling throw pillows around. "I wouldn't know."

"They marked the best parts, if you ask me."

Best. The most scandalous—that's what he meant—but as she *had not read it* and therefore could *not* have folded pages to mark scenes for future reading, she could neither argue nor agree with his assessment, and the bastard knew it.

"The author is quite, eh, descriptive," he said, all innocence. "Ah, here's a good line. 'When the Prince Regent turned to display his most royal sword, the lady gasped. Such an impressive weapon could—'"

A pillow to his face cut him off. Laughing, he tossed it aside. "Fess up. How many times have you read this?"

"I told you, I didn't—"

"A dozen? A hundred?"

"You're a horrible person, you know that?"

"I do." He sounded far too serious, and she hesitated, wondering if she should apologize, but his expression shifted to wide-eyed sincerity. "But I simply *must* find out if our intrepid heroine chooses the prince or the rogue, so don't you dare spoil it for me."

Alessa pulled herself tall, every bit the haughty Finestra. "I would *never*. Only the worst sort of people spoil book endings."

"True. And you can't. Obviously. Because you haven't read it."

"Because I haven't read it."

"You know, there's nothing to be ashamed of." He stole a glance at her. "It's perfectly normal."

"To read?"

"To enjoy this kind of book. You may be a holy vessel and all that, but you're still human."

"Sort of."

He sat forward. "Entirely. Title or no title, power or none, you're still human. Don't let the holy nonsense mess with your head."

"Holy *nonsense?*"

He waved away her indignant protest. "Keep your gods and goddesses on their pedestals if you want, but the rituals, the rules, the isolation? You know that isn't really from *them*, right? That's written by mortals. Men, mostly. We have a bad habit of locking up people who scare us, and the thing that scares men with power most is a woman with more of it."

She couldn't imagine why anyone would want her power, but

there were a million things she didn't understand about people, so she didn't argue. Even Adrick had sounded jealous the last time they spoke.

Dante gave her a pointed glance. "If parts of this deal don't work for you, ignore them. Take the traditions you need and toss the rest. Be bold."

"Bold, huh?" She snatched the book from the table. "In that case, I'll take this back."

Dante's laughter followed her to a chair on the balcony.

"They were talking about a card game tonight," he said, coming up behind her. "You should go."

"I tortured them all day." Alessa smoothed her skirts. "I'm sure they don't want me there."

"Won't know unless you try," he said. "You want friends, go get them."

"I won't *force* anyone to be my friend."

"Ha! You keep bullying *me* into it." Resting his hands on the back of her chair, he bent close to her ear. "You aren't *scared*, are you?"

Alessa tossed her head with righteous indignation, thwacking Dante in the face with her hair.

Laughing, he brushed a few strands from his cheek. "You smell like an orchard."

"I smell divine, thank you very much. My Nonna makes me soaps and scrubs with homegrown lemons and sea salt. It's good for the complexion."

"I'll keep that in mind. They let you visit your grandparents?"

"No. I'm not even allowed to write to them, but the rules don't specify who I can shop from, so I order a basket every few months, and Nonna writes secret notes on the inside of the wrappings."

"I'm beginning to see where your rebellious streak comes from."

"I'm named after her, too, and I inherited her tendency to take in strays. If she ever met you, she'd force you to eat lots of pasta and scold you for being too handsome."

"You think I'm handsome?"

Alessa went pink. "No. But *she* would. And she wouldn't expect you to speak, so you'd be happy. When she isn't singing to herself, she's talking to herself, and it's impossible to get a word in edgewise. My Nonno is Deaf, and she always forgets that everyone else isn't."

"Sooooo"—he drew the word out—"she's an older version of you?"

"I suspect you didn't mean that as a compliment, but I'm taking it anyway."

"Whatever it takes to build your confidence, luce mia. Come on, let's go."

She didn't move.

"Up and at 'em, soldier."

She gripped the arms and hooked her ankles around the legs, but Dante tipped her chair forward, leaving her no choice but to stand or get dumped on the floor.

"I despise you."

"I can live with that."

Voices grew audible as they crossed the hall, followed by laughter at a joke she hadn't heard. Everything she'd wanted for years was behind a door, and all she had to do was knock.

Dread. Hope. Two sides of the same coin, spinning too fast to tell them apart.

Alessa held her hand up until her arm ached, then lowered it. "I can't."

"How are you going to face a swarm of scarabei if you're too scared to knock on a door?"

"Crashing a social event uninvited is worse than a battle to the death."

"Just say hello."

Alessa cringed at another burst of laughter from the other side.

"Fine, I'll do it."

Alessa moved to block his path.

"Don't you dare." She wagged a very ineffective finger in his face as he towered over her.

"Coward," he said with a grin.

The door swung open, and Alessa whirled to find an equally startled Saida clutching her chest in the doorway.

"Finestra. Is something wrong?"

Behind her in the room, Josef dropped a hand of cards on the floor, and Nina did an awkward dance to save a drink from spilling across the table as she jostled it in her haste to stand. If the girl was half as clumsy outside the Cittadella, Josef must need to use his powers all the time to keep from being drenched.

"No. Nothing's wrong." Alessa smoothed her skirts. "I merely wanted to check if you needed anything."

The Fontes made a horrified tableau, watching her like a family of mice might face a cat who'd unearthed their den.

Saida blinked. "I don't think we need anything. Do we need anything?"

Heads shook.

Alessa nodded. Then realized she'd been doing so for an awkward length of time and stopped abruptly. "Excellent." Another half-nod. "Well. Then. Have a lovely evening."

"You, too."

"Thank you."

Saida closed the door, but she didn't throw the deadbolt. So there was that for a silver lining.

Dante popped his lips. "Okay. Maybe you should have brought something to loosen them up."

"Nina is only fifteen."

"Cookies for her and alcohol for the rest."

"You could have suggested that *before* I stood there like a dunderhead."

Dante stole a look at her as they retreated to her rooms. "Hey, points for effort."

She gave him a mock scowl.

Her pent-up nervous energy had nowhere to go, so when Dante, with a waggle of his eyebrows, held up another romantic novel he'd found, she refused to play along.

"That's a good one," she said. "But I forbid you from getting stuck in a book right now."

"Forbid me? You think you can give me orders?"

"I give you orders all the time. You just don't follow them." She cut a glance his way. "Dante, you're my only friend."

"I think you might be mine, too." Dante pinched the bridge of his nose. "*Dea*, that's pathetic, isn't it?"

"Quality, not quantity. Now, I'm asking *very* nicely, so you have to say yes."

"To?"

She clapped her hands. "Playing with me."

Dante squinted, and she smiled brighter. If he was going to tease her about reading smutty novels, she'd fight back by working innuendo into every conversation.

"Fine," he said, still studying her. "Should I raid the library, or do you have something to drink in here?"

"I'm the *Finestra*. A divinely ordained warrior."

"That a no?"

"I'm just making it very clear that it would be inappropriate—" She hoisted herself up on the counter, reaching to open the highest cabinet and nudge a loaf of stale sourdough aside. "*Highly* inappropriate to keep liquor in my room."

The easiest to reach was a dusty bottle of limoncello she'd forgotten to chill, and she held it up for his consideration. Dante arched an eyebrow. She put it back.

Biting her tongue, Alessa flicked a heavy decanter with her fingertips, her other hand poised to catch it when it tipped over the edge.

Long browned fingers caught it in front of her face, and Alessa snatched her hand away. Pressing back against the cabinets, she turned to berate him.

And forgot how to speak.

Dante stood so near to the counter he was practically between her knees, his dark eyes so close she could count the flecks of gold.

His gaze dropped to her lips.

"Get back," she squeaked. "I don't need another death on my conscience."

Cradling the bottle with more care than he showed for his life, Dante turned to lean against the counter beside her, still too close. "Be my own fault, wouldn't it?" He pulled the cork and took a swig. "Oh, that's good."

"I'd still have to live with the guilt *and* find a new bodyguard." Alessa selected two lowball glasses and hopped off the counter. She gave him a pointed look. "They're called drinking glasses."

"Fascinating." He held out the bottle, sighed when she didn't take it from him, and put it on the table.

Alessa poured a bit for herself, then corked the bottle and held it close to her chest. A hostage. "Let's play a game."

"Eh?"

"A *game*." A distraction from her social failure.

"What kind of game?"

"A drinking game." She took a sip—like a *lady*—and let the challenge dangle.

He dropped into the chair, his elbows hitting the table with a thump. "I'm listening."

"Truth or challenge. When it's your turn, you choose for that round."

Dante tipped his chair back, skepticism etched on his face. One of these days, he was going to fall on his ass, and she dearly hoped she was there to see it.

"If you don't perform the challenge or answer the question, you take a drink."

A slow smile spread across his face. "Works for me."

"You're just going to say no to everything, aren't you?"

"Yep." The front legs of his chair thumped down.

"*No*." She clutched the bottle tighter. "I won't pour unless you participate."

He flicked his fingers for her to proceed. "Fine. But I'm not telling you my name."

"It can't be *that* bad."

"I never said it was."

"I'm going to get it out of you, one way or another. It has become my life's mission. I'll stop at nothing. Thumbscrews, the rack. Coming right up."

"I'd love to see you try."

"Are you ticklish?"

"Not a bit."

"I bet you are. I bet you giggle like a schoolgirl." Alessa gave him an arch look. "I'll double your salary if you tell me."

His eyes crinkled with amusement. "No payment could be more satisfying than besting you. I'll take it to the grave."

"Oh, come on."

He considered. "Fine. I guess I could tell you on my deathbed."

"Two things to look forward to, then."

"Are we playing or not?"

Teasing him was fun, but she couldn't risk him changing his mind. "I'll start with an easy one. Most beautiful place you've ever seen?"

He pursed his lips slightly. "A little beach on the far side of the island."

Her heart twisted. "What does it look like?"

He lifted his glass, let it plunk to the table, then did it again. "A beach."

"What *kind* of beach?"

"The kind where the land meets the sea," he drawled, reveling in her annoyance.

She shook the bottle with a wet slosh. "Humor me. I haven't been on a beach in years."

He cast his eyes to the ceiling. "High cliffs on both sides. A narrow path to get to it, so it's not worth the effort for most. But the water . . ." He trailed off with a wistful smile. "I've never seen that color anywhere else."

"It sounds perfect," she said with a sigh. She rewarded him with a stingy pour and tucked the bottle between her thighs, the most secure place on earth. "What's my question?"

"If you could do anything before Divorando, what would it be?"

"Easy. Control my power and stop killing people."

"No, no. Games are meant to be *fun*. Pick something good." Dante lifted his glass to his lips.

"Lose my virginity."

Dante choked. Red-faced, tears in his eyes, he pounded his chest.

Alessa preened. "Better?"

"Much," he croaked. "Challenge."

"Hmm. Say something nice about Kaleb."

"Nope." He tipped his glass.

"Slow down," she protested with a laugh. "The game will be over in five minutes if you drink that fast."

"Nah. Iron constitution." He patted his firm abdomen. "Ugh, Kaleb. Fitting he makes electricity."

"How's that?"

"Ever been near a lightning strike? Not fun."

"You have *terrible* luck."

"It wasn't a direct strike. I've also broken seven bones, including my nose, been stabbed, burned, and nearly lost a finger."

She grimaced. "The gods must really hate you."

"I'm certain they do."

"That makes two of us, then."

He scoffed. "You're the savior. After Divorando, you'll never work another day in your life. They'll write sonnets about you."

"*Or* I'll kill every remaining Fonte on the island, everyone on Saverio will die, and it will be all my fault." She pressed the cool, sweating glass to her cheek. "I hate hurting people."

"No, really? I couldn't tell."

"I have one job. *One*. Why can't I do it?"

He gave her an appraising look, trapping his lower lip between his teeth. "You said you felt hungry."

"Hmm?" She dragged her gaze from his mouth, but his eyes—warm and dark, like molten chocolate cake flecked with toffee—didn't make it any easier to concentrate.

"When you touched your first Fonte, you said you felt *hungry*. Have you ever really *been* hungry?"

She wrinkled her nose. "Everyone's been hungry."

"Not like when dinner's late—*truly* hungry. So famished you'd choke down dirt to fill the hole in your belly."

"I suppose not."

"Well, when you're that empty, and you get your hands on food, you know you'll be sick if you eat too fast, but you can't help it."

She stared into her glass as though it might hold answers, but all she found was her own warped reflection. "Okay . . ."

"That's why they locked you up in here, right? To remind you about connection and community by taking it away from you?" He waited until she looked up, then held her gaze. "They starved you, and you gorged yourself the first chance you got."

Unease sat heavy in her gut. "Are you trying to say I kill people because I'm so pathetically lonely I gobble them up? Because that doesn't make me feel any better."

"I'm saying it's not your fault."

Her throat constricted. "Books make it sound romantic to die from loneliness, but to kill someone *else* with your loneliness? Now, *that's* a talent."

Dante leaned forward, elbows on the table. "Maybe if you took the edge off, you'd gain some control."

Her lips twitched. "What, like an affection snack?"

"Something like that." Dante drummed his fingers on the table. "Could you get a pet?"

"A *pet?*"

"Small? Furry? Domesticated animals?" He mimed clawing at the air. "Like a cat."

Alessa took a slug of whiskey, coughing at the burn. "You're proposing I get a *cat*. To fill the gaping, empty hole inside my soul. A *cat*."

"Why not? Maybe you'd see better in the dark."

"Or kill a cat."

"You think so?" He looked surprised. "They have fur over their skin."

"I don't know, and I don't want to find out. If I killed a sweet little kitty, I'd never forgive myself."

"For a cat? You've already—"

"Killed three people? Is that what you were about to say?"

He had the decency to look uncomfortable.

"At least they agreed to it. An animal can't."

Dante still looked thoughtful.

She raised a finger in warning. "If I wake up tomorrow and find a cat in my room, you'll both be put out on the street."

He laughed and reached for her glass, as his was empty, but she swatted his hand away.

Was it possible?

She'd always believed she was supposed to embrace her isolation, blamed herself for letting loneliness fill the spaces meant to hold divinity, but Dante's words had her doubting.

Maybe she'd been fighting the current, swimming in the wrong direction, all along.

After cutting herself on the blade of hope so many times, would she be a fool to reach for it again?

Twenty-Four

I frutti proibiti sono i più dolci.
Forbidden fruit is the sweetest.

DAYS BEFORE DIVORANDO: 20

Around midnight, Alessa poked at the front of her blouse. She'd spilled something. At some point. She didn't remember what, exactly. Eyes crossed, she raised a blurry finger to her nose—oops, her cheek. No, that was her chin.

"That's not whiskey." Her words sounded squishy.

Dante, sprawled in an armchair with one leg draped over the side, mouth open and one eye closed, squinted at a carved wooden statue he held in front of his face. "No, that's the water I told you to drink an hour ago. Poured half right down your dress like a river between your breasts."

Alessa scoffed. "I did *not*. And if I *did*—which I *didn't*—you shouldn't discuss a lady's bosoms."

"Bosoms?" He dropped the statue—a priceless heirloom at least two centuries old—on the cushion beside him. "Don't think *bosoms* are plural."

Alessa stood, chin high, and waited for the room to right itself. "Of course, they are. Bosoms almost always come in pairs."

"*Breasts* come in pairs, but I don't think *bosoms*—who even *says* that?—can be plural. Two breasts, one bosom. As in, I have two legs, but one crotch, that sort of thing."

"I wouldn't know."

"About grammar?"

"About your crotch. And *you* shouldn't notice when a girl spills water down her cleavage."

"I *didn't*," Dante said. "But you got all squeaky about how cold it was. Then you drank another glass of whiskey, so I doubt the water will help much." He stared longingly at his glass. "Whose turn is it?"

"Mine, I think."

"Sing something."

"Pass. I'm a terrible singer." Her next sip went down a bit too easily. "*You* sing something."

She didn't think he'd do it, but in a voice as rich as honeyed whiskey, he sang:

"*I took my bonnie lass out on a ship,*"

Oh, dear. The burn of alcohol and the warmth of his voice seemed to be melting something inside her.

"*To give her a taste of the sea,*"

Well. This wasn't fair at all.

"*And when we got back on shore once more,*"

Dante took a breath, a wicked gleam in his eyes.

"My bonnie lass tasted me."

She threw her head back, crowing with laughter. "Oh, bravissimo. Such an angelic voice for a devilish song."

"Grazie." He bowed his head. "Your turn."

"I'm not singing."

"Favorite color, then."

"Green," she said. "You're terrible at this. My turn. How many people have you kissed?"

He scrunched his face in thought. "Seven. No, eight. Wait, do twins count as one or two?"

"Twins are distinct human beings, so two, obviously. And that's disgusting. You shouldn't kiss siblings."

"They weren't *my* siblings. I never turn down a kiss from a pretty girl."

Surprising his tally wasn't higher, then. She'd be first in line if she wasn't so deadly, even with his many personality flaws. Although, with a few drinks in him, Dante was almost charming. Or she was no longer capable of judging. The whiskey had warped everything else, so it was quite possibly blurring him, too. Even her glass was listing to one side. Or maybe that was the floor. Or herself. Hard to tell.

What were they talking about?

She gathered her scattered thoughts. "I guess I wouldn't either, if I knew it wouldn't end in tragedy. My only attempt did *not* go well."

Dante grinned lazily. "Takes practice."

"Then add kissing to the list of things I will never master."

"Eh." He waved a hand. "I'm sure you'll figure out the death-touch thing eventually."

Alessa giggled, batting away a little voice warning her she'd regret all of this when she woke in the morning. "Hype-hyper-hypothetically speaking, if you could get past the high likelihood of a painful death, would you ever want to kiss me?"

"Hypothetically?" He enunciated the word more clearly, but not by much.

"Obviously."

"Hard to get past the painful death part, to be honest." He clinked his glass against hers.

"It's *hypothetical.*" She kicked at him, but barely swiped his leg. "You'd *never* even have to act on it. Is it that hard to pretend you think I'm pretty?"

"That's not what you asked."

"Then I want a do-over." She tucked her hair behind her ears. "Do you think I'm pretty?"

"Yes. Favorite food?"

She fluffed her hair with exaggerated pride. Surely she deserved an extra point for prying a compliment from his stubborn lips. "Still not a real question."

"I'm trying to steer us into safer waters. Greatest fear?"

"Oh, much safer." She frowned. "That we all die."

"Boring."

"That it will be my fault? I think I'm more scared of that than the actual prospect of everyone dying. That must make me a terrible person."

"I'm not one to judge." He rolled his fingers across his glass. "Favorite hobby?"

"Aside from accidentally killing people? None. Perhaps I should learn to knit."

"You're a gloomy drunk, you know that?"

"It was your turn anyway. Is it too late to change my mind about a cat?"

"Ah, so you accept my theory?"

"That I'm so pathetically lonely I pull the life out of my partners? Sure, let's go with that one." Her breath came faster. "I might need more than one cat."

He put his glass down and stood. "I have an idea."

Alessa backed away. "What are you doing?"

"I'm giving you a hug so you can save the world."

She knocked a chair over in her haste to escape. "No. Bad idea."

"You're covered from toe to chin, and I'm a full head taller than you. You'd have to leap into the air and smash your face against mine to hurt me."

Putting the couch between them, she mustered her most stern glare. "It's too dangerous."

"Do you want a damn hug or not?"

Desperately.

She swallowed. "Gloves."

He yanked them from his back pocket, shaking his head with amused exasperation.

At his first step, she skittered backward. "Your face."

Dante rolled his eyes but glanced around the room until he found a display of colorful scarves hanging from pegs by the door. Snatching a bright purple scarf, he tucked one end into the top of his shirt and wound it around his head. His gloved fingers plucked at the folds, trying to pick them apart so he could see. "Dammit, where'd you go?"

Alessa pinched her tongue between her teeth.

One dark eye became visible, and he opened his arms and waited.

Courage, desperation, or pure drunken stupidity drove her into his embrace.

The moment they touched, every muscle in her body pulled so tight she couldn't have moved if she wanted to.

He was warm.

It was all she could think. She'd forgotten that people felt warm.

She tried to rest her hands on his back, but jerked away reflexively. His arms came around her, strong and unafraid, so she tried again, placing her palms on the flat planes of his back.

Bit by bit, muscle by muscle, she eased into him until her cheek rested against his chest.

The steady beat of his heart accelerated.

She tried to find the strength to move—she didn't want him to fear for his safety—but he didn't pull away, and *nothing* had ever felt so good. Nothing. This hug was officially the best thing that had ever happened to her.

Pathetic.

She didn't care. It felt like breathing after being underwater for years. Lulled by warmth and comfort, she let the world fall away, every sense soothed by the strong arms holding her up, the firm heat beneath her cheek—

She jerked her head up.

Dante's voice rumbled through his chest. "Did you just fall asleep?"

Alessa blinked. "Maybe."

"Really?"

"Only for a second."

"Huh. Not what a man usually wants when a woman's in his arms, but I guess that's a good sign?"

The fabric of his shirt rubbed against her skin as she nodded.

"Better?" he asked. "Satisfied?"

Satisfied? Not even close.

Better? Yes.

She mumbled something meant to be meaningless.

"What?" One arm tight around her, Dante fumbled to adjust the absurd scarf with the other.

"Nothing." She burrowed deeper into his embrace. "Don't worry, I'll let go in a minute."

Dante paused. "Take your time."

She only wobbled a little when she stepped back. "Will you *please* tell me your name?"

He rubbed his lip. "Tell you what. You save the world, I'll tell you my name. How's that for motivation?"

"Seems like a very high bar for basic information about an employee."

"Take it or leave it." Dante yawned. "I'm going to take a shower. Drink more water. You'll thank me."

Alessa weaved to the sink to fill a large glass. Sloshing more than a bit on the floor, she made her way to bed and resisted the urge to lie down.

Her nightclothes were in the closet off the bathing room, and she wasn't about to barge in while Dante was showering, so she stripped to her slip and kicked her dress away before climbing into bed. It took some maneuvering, but she kept the sheets pinned to her chest while she reached for the glass again.

She gulped half of it through sheer force of will. The rest would take more motivation. She frowned at the tepid water.

Getting ice would require sprinting across the room—bad idea sober, treacherous in her current state—before Dante returned.

Lukewarm tap water would have to do.

As she steeled herself for one more sip, Dante walked out in nothing but a towel.

Alessa lowered the glass from her still-parted lips.

"Sorry. Forgot a change of clothes." He cocked his head. "You okay?"

Oh. She was staring. And didn't really feel like stopping. She held up a hand. "Don't move."

He scanned the room for trouble, then crossed his arms. "Why am I standing here?"

"You told me to be bold."

"And?"

"And a half-naked man is in my bedroom, so I'm *boldly* looking."

He ran his fingers through his hair, bemused. "That's . . . not what I meant."

"You don't get to dictate what someone does with your advice. I'll work on other kinds of boldness later. For now, I'm ogling. Unless you're shy."

"*Shy?*" He ran his tongue over his teeth, not entirely hiding his smile. "Hardly." Palms out, he spun in a slow circle. "There. Seen enough?"

A dangerous question. "I suppose I'll let you put your clothes on now."

He snorted. "Like you could stop me."

"I could kill you with my pinky."

"I'm shaking."

She threw a pillow and he caught it, tucking it beneath his

arm as he headed for a stack of clean clothing on the couch. "Keep throwing these at me and you'll have none left."

A smile playing on her lips, she sank into a pile of pillows. At least one person treated her like a regular person. It was more than she'd dared to hope for in a very long time.

Twenty-Five

Le bestemmie sono come la processione: escono dal portone e ritornano dallo stesso.

Curses are like parades: They return from whence they came.

She was dying. She *had to* be. Her skull seemed determined to split down the middle, and she was fairly certain heads weren't meant to do that. She swayed, grasping for something to hold herself up, but finding only air.

Dante caught her elbow. "Steady."

"How many times—" She tugged but couldn't get away and gave up as the movement sent the world swooping.

"Relax. I'm wearing gloves, and you have long sleeves *and* gloves."

"Nothing in the history of the world has ever been less effective than telling a person to *relax*." She yanked her arm free. "My head hurts."

"Should've had more water."

She found the wall and pressed her forehead against the stone. "I'm dying."

"You aren't dying. You're hungover."

"Why aren't *you* hungover?"

"Do you *want* me to be?"

"Yes. I do. Very much so."

"And here I thought we were such good friends."

Were they? She hadn't had a friend since she was thirteen, but maybe a night of drunken idiocy was how it worked for adults. She couldn't think over the loud throbbing in her head—because throbbing had a sound all of a sudden—so she set her mind to walking instead. Duty waited, whether she was up for it or not.

"Sometimes the best cure is a bit more poison. There might be a little left in the bottle."

She gagged. "Sounds like advice invented by a greedy pub owner."

"Come on, you need to eat something."

Alessa's stomach performed acrobatics as she took her seat. Sweat beaded her forehead, hot and clammy at the same time. Checking to be sure no one was looking, she pressed a water glass against her cheek, sighing at the cool.

Dante deposited a plain roll on her plate, glared at her to eat, and returned to his post by the door.

Alessa nudged it away and swallowed a few times.

Kaleb had already bolted for the day, and the remaining Fontes scarfed down their pastries and juice, clearly eager to begin their day off.

"Too much fun last night?" Kamaria smirked at her while Nina chattered to Josef about which temple service they should attend, or whether they should attend them all to cover their bases.

Alessa stared at her fork in misery.

"What are your plans for the afternoon, Finestra?" Saida asked. "Do you get to leave after your portrait session?"

Alessa gave up on eating. "I don't really have anywhere to go."

"Oh." Saida chewed her lip. "Sorry."

The one good thing about her itinerary was the fact that the only thing she needed to do to survive the day was sit.

It nearly killed her anyway.

It took an hour before Mastro Pasquale was satisfied with her pose, since she couldn't physically arrange her subject, and Alessa was worse at taking directions than usual.

Silver haired, vaguely androgynous, and with features so striking she could have been one of her own sculptures, the mastro also had such a dry wit Alessa could never be sure if she was joking and had learned long ago that it was always safer not to laugh.

Mastro Pasquale finally moved behind her easel but continued to quiz her former pupil about sfumato and chiaroscuro, ordering her to tilt her head, arch her back, raise and then lower her chin, while she sketched an initial outline.

Long before the artist declared an end to the day's session, Alessa was convinced sitting was the most difficult physical task of them all. Her only consolation was that Dante had looked a bit stunned when she stepped out in the red gown, and he'd barely looked away since.

"Beautiful contrapposto," Mastro Pasquale said to Dante, who'd been watching the ordeal from a safe distance. "Finestra, you see the smooth line of leg there, how the off-axis twist of his torso accentuates both shoulders and hip?"

Dante looked slightly alarmed as Alessa nodded thoughtfully.

Mastro Pasquale snapped her fingers. "You should come to my studio and model for my next sculpture."

"You really should," Alessa said through gritted teeth so she didn't ruin the "curve of her neck" for the third time. "Mastro Pasquale is famous for her attention to anatomical details."

"This is true," the mastro said as she began packing up her supplies. "I pay well, too, but don't bother coming by if you're a wilting violet."

Alessa rubbed her neck. "Oh, Dante assures me he is not shy at all."

"Excellent. Here's my card. Finestra, it's been an honor. I will return when your Fonte is ready." She handed Dante a gilded slip of paper and swept out of the gardens.

Dante flicked the card at Alessa. "Did you just volunteer me as a nude model?"

Alessa plucked the card from where it fell in the grass. "You spend half your time standing around and scowling. Might as well get paid for it."

"You're already paying me for it, and I get to keep my clothes on."

As they reached the fourth floor, Dante stopped. "Is it okay if I run out real quick? You should be safe enough if you lock yourself in. Won't take long."

Alessa's heart and stomach competed to see which could sink faster at the prospect of the rest of the day alone, locked in her rooms while everyone else spent time with family and friends. Even Dante had better things to do on his day off than stay with her. "Visiting someone special?"

"No. Just checking something."

"Left a lantern burning?"

"Something like that."

The day stretched ahead of her, silent and lonely, but she pasted on a smile and told him to go right ahead.

"First, let me show you the barricade I found—" Dante tensed as they entered her suite. "Wait. Someone's been in here."

Her eyes darted in every direction, but the only thing out of place was a platter of lemon verbena cookies on the table. She could smell the zesty tang and see the curls of candied lemon peel on top.

"It's okay," she said, exhaling. "Someone dropped off treats."

"Don't the servants usually leave food in the hall?" he asked. "How many people have keys to your suite?"

She frowned. "I don't know. Someone comes to change the linens and to clean and . . ." She squirmed under his judging gaze.

"We're changing the locks." Dante reached the platter first, snatching it up to sniff it.

She crossed her arms. "Are you going to lick them, too, or do I get one?"

He took a small bite and promptly spit it into his hand. "*Daphne.*"

"Who?"

"*Daphne gnidium.* A poison that tastes terrible, so you probably wouldn't have eaten enough for it to kill you, but even a few bites and you'd wish it had. Be thankful for amateur assassins."

She sat with a gusty exhale. "How do you know what poison tastes like?"

"I was a stupid kid." He dumped the remaining treats into a trash bin, examined the tray, then tossed it, too. "I'll get your food from now on. One of the kitchen maids was eager enough to show me around. I'll talk to her."

Apparently, a rogue poisoning was just another day in the life of the Wolf.

Or not.

Dante tapped a knife against his thigh. "Dammit. I don't like leaving you unprotected."

"Then take me with you."

"The city isn't safe."

"Neither is the Cittadella, apparently. My parents are bakers. They might know who made the cookies. I doubt they're harboring assassins in the storeroom, so you can leave me there while you run your errand."

Dante frowned. "I don't know . . ."

"No one will recognize me. I won't be dressed like the Finestra, and half the guards are busy salvaging supplies in the storage levels that got flooded the other day."

"Do you always break this many rules?"

"Believe it or not, it's a new development." She clasped her hands below her chin. "Please, Dante. Even if they don't know about the cookies, I want to see them. If you're right about why I keep hurting people, maybe closure would help."

"Or make it worse."

"Please?"

She hid her satisfaction when he grumbled assent. If he ever realized how often she got her way by making doll eyes at him, Dante would never agree to anything again.

Alessa hung up the ruby gown and riffled through her closet, settling on a simple blue dress with long sleeves that mostly concealed her gloves, and gold tights so pale her legs appeared bare unless one looked closely. She wanted to return home as herself, not the Finestra, so she cleaned her face and parted her hair, braiding it into a simple plait down her back.

Looking at her reflection, she had the strangest sense it wasn't a mirror at all, but a window to another life, a glimpse of the girl she could have been. She tried on a carefree smile, but it didn't fit. There was no other Alessa, no other life. This was all she had.

The quaint storefront was fancier than it used to be, the lettering redrawn in gold, the windows replaced with beveled panels.

"Nice-looking place," Dante said, probably wondering why Alessa was staring at it instead of entering.

"They've made good use of their stipend." She should probably be glad the monthly payments they received for their sacrifice—for sacrificing *her*—were helping the family business, but she wasn't noble enough to hide her bitterness.

"Want me to come in?" Dante asked.

"No," she said. It would be hard enough without a witness. "Just come back as soon as you're done."

It was almost closing time, and the bakery was empty, the display case lacking its usual goods. Cloaked in the lingering scents of yeast and sugar and her childhood, Alessa locked the door behind her and flipped the sign.

"We're about to close for the day, but there are a few loaves—" Her father walked out from the back room, dusting his flour-coated hands on his apron, and jerked to a stop at the sight of her.

His hair was longer, more salt than pepper, and his face was slightly more drawn, but his expression matched the last one she'd seen on his face—dismay and awe, tempered with melancholy.

"Finestra." His arms lifted, then dropped. "What brings you here?"

She ached for the hug that wouldn't happen. "Hello, Papa. Please, use my name."

He darted a look around the empty kitchen. "Alessa. My little love, you're all grown up."

"I've missed you." Tears slipped down her cheeks.

He came out from behind the counter but stayed out of reach. "We've missed you. I'll never understand why the gods make the choices they do, but I have faith. I know this can't be easy."

An understatement if she'd ever heard one. If she let herself, she'd dissolve into a sobbing puddle, so Alessa allowed herself one sniff and pulled the tainted cookie from her pocket. "Do you know who made this?"

Papa furrowed his brow. "I haven't made a batch in a while, but Adrick was manning the kitchen yesterday. He might have. Why?"

Her heart rate kicked up, escalating at the sound of footsteps on the back stairs.

"Marcel, have you turned the sign?" Her mother stopped mid-step as though the floor had taken hold of her shoes.

"Mama."

"Finestra." Her mother dropped into a low curtsy. "With all due respect, you shouldn't be here."

Her foolish heart sank. "I know what the Verità says, Mama. I won't stay long."

"If you know what it says, then you know what the gods ask of us. You aren't supposed to be here."

"I know, but I needed to—" The words caught in Alessa's throat. Why *was* she there? To unravel a mystery she didn't want the answer to? In search of love she knew she wouldn't find? Or simply to find closure? "Say goodbye."

Her mother was already turning away, so Alessa couldn't see her face when she said a curt, "Goodbye."

Papa moved his fist in the sign for *I'm sorry.*

Alessa didn't respond. It wasn't fair to expect him to take sides, but it hurt that he wouldn't.

Thirteen years. Thirteen years of being the sun in her daughter's sky, and now her mother wouldn't even look her in the eye for one last goodbye.

In that moment, something inside her withered and died.

"Is Adrick here?"

Papa winced at her cold tone. "No, he's at the apothecary. Why—"

She was out the door before he finished.

She should have waited for Dante, but her mother's rejection and the pain in her father's eyes drove her away. She needed to find Adrick, to pull out the sliver of fear that she might have no one left.

Around the final corner, she nearly ran into a group of white-robed Fratellanza members clustered in front of the apothecary.

Shielding her face as if blocking a glare, Alessa darted into the narrow alley between the apothecary and the tailor next door.

For once, Dea was on her side. Adrick was out back, holding an empty crate. The tiny walled yard behind the building was crowded with them, overturned and arranged in a rough semi-circle.

Adrick gaped. "What are you *doing* here?"

"I have to talk to you."

"No. You have to leave. Right now."

Alessa fumbled for the cookie, pulling it out with a scatter of crumbs. "Who ordered these from the bakery yesterday?"

Adrick blanched. "I don't remember."

"Do you remember if you put poison in Papa's lemon verbenas, or did someone add it afterward?"

Adrick pulled at his hair. "I can explain, but not now. You have to leave. This isn't how—" He jerked his head at the sound of voices from inside the shop, his entire body tensing.

"What is wrong with you?"

"I'll come to the Cittadella tonight, I promise. *Please*. Just go."

Adrick's alarm cut through her anger, and Alessa fled, stuffing the crumpled handkerchief back into her pocket.

The Fratellanza members were no longer out front, but every face on the street became an enemy, whether they looked her way or not. People saw what they expected to, and a clean faced girl in simple clothing wasn't worth noting, but in her heightened state, it felt like a massive light shined directly on her, drawing every malicious gaze.

The street was crowded, and as she debated whether to head back to the bakery or try to find Dante near his old stomping grounds of the Barrel, her eyes caught on a figure a block away. It was embarrassing how easily she'd spotted him, how her attention snagged on a brief glimpse of the back of his head as he strode in the opposite direction.

She called his name, but he didn't turn. Too many passersby did.

She'd have to catch up.

As she dodged people, trying to keep him in sight, Dante knocked shoulders with a man passing the other way, and they whirled on each other like alley cats looking for a fight.

Two women stole glances at Alessa as she passed their roadside stand, sizing her up a bit too intently, and she pulled her hood down, losing sight of Dante as she tried to melt into the crowd.

She almost walked right past the narrow alley, but Dante's voice stopped her in her tracks. At the very end of it, he was arguing with a man in a white robe.

Alessa ducked behind a stack of barrels, heart in her throat, and watched them through a gap.

The man was tall and thick-waisted, with a shorn head. Not Ivini. Relief flooded her veins, but it didn't last long.

"And what's in it for me?" The man sneered, and Dante met his vitriol with extra to spare, but most of his response was drowned out by shouts from the street behind her as a cart overturned. She only caught one word.

Kill.

Stars flashed in her vision.

Was it a threat . . . or a promise?

The man clenched his fists.

Dante flipped his daggers, catching them by the hilts.

Alessa held her breath.

The air crackled with tension, as each man seemed poised to strike, but neither spoke or moved for a long time.

At long last, Dante sheathed his blades with a derisive sneer. "Vvai a farti fottere."

The older man spat on the ground and backed away, his attention so fixed on Dante he didn't notice Alessa as he passed.

Anger swelled inside her, cresting like a wave.

Her mother cared so little she'd barely say goodbye, her brother was setting up for a meeting while the Fratellanza gathered nearby, and now *Dante* was making deals with one of Ivini's men in a dark alley? Secrets and more secrets, piling upon each other.

She had nowhere to go. And she was *not* leaving this alley until she got answers from *someone*.

Dante's back was turned when she stepped out into the open. She stared him down, willing him to face her, to cower with shame or explain what in Dea's name was going on.

Unaware of her presence, he drew his arm back and punched the wall hard enough to shatter every bone in his hand.

A violent tremor ran through him, and he punched again. And again. And again. Each blow came faster, harder, bits of plaster falling to the ground with every impact.

Her hand flew to her mouth.

His hand. He was going to destroy it, if he hadn't already.

She stepped forward. To stop him. Or yell at him. She didn't know.

Her foot crunched on a broken bottle.

Dante turned so fast she didn't have time to speak.

His eyes flashed, brilliant and terrifying with rage, and twin fires tore through her abdomen.

Her lips parted on a gasp. She looked down at his fists, clutching the hilts of his knives, pressed against her.

Blood dripped between his fingers.

With a ragged gasp, Dante pulled the knives free. They clattered to the ground.

Her protector. Her killer.

Alessa breathed his name as her legs gave out.

Twenty-Six

Piove sul bagnato.

When it rains, it pours.

DAYS BEFORE DIVORANDO: 19

Dante caught her, sinking to his knees to slow her fall.

Why?

Betrayal and pain reverberated inside her as the world shrank to the cradle of his arms.

She searched his face for answers but found only horror.

Dante's lips worked soundlessly, forming the words, *No, no, no.*

Don't ever sneak up on me.

He'd warned her. More than once.

She hadn't listened.

No glorious, heroic death for her, after all.

Dante lowered her to the ground, bracing her neck so she barely felt her head meet stone.

She needed to warn him to be careful about touching her, but darkness was closing in.

His shadow blocked the sun as he bent over her, and she cried out at new searing pain.

Had he stabbed her again?

No. He was pressing on her wounds, shaking his head as though arguing with himself about how bad the damage was, but the truth was in his eyes. He'd struck to kill, and he never missed.

Some injuries weren't fixable.

Dante abandoned his efforts to stanch the bleeding and took her hands in his, which were coated so thick with her blood it looked like he, too, wore gloves.

She couldn't have escaped his grasp if she tried.

I held his hand.

He'd remembered.

Dante tugged on her gloves, but the sodden leather resisted his attempts. Good. He shouldn't do that. She curled her fingers, but she was too weak to stop him. Rough palms pressed against hers as Dante twined their fingers, stifling a hiss of pain.

Could a heart soar and break at the same time?

She didn't want him to die, but the golden river of warmth seeping through her skin, his spark of life, warmed her from the inside, unfurling in her chest. The euphoric sensation lit her up from within, almost glorious enough to make her forget she was killing him. Even in her death throes, she *took*.

Dante's hands seized, crushing her fingers, and his breath went from ragged to tortured.

Her heart gave a feeble thump.

He collapsed on top of her, their hands locked together.

They were both going to die.

But not alone.

No one should die alone.

Twenty-Seven

Chi è all'inferno non sa ciò che sia cielo.

He who is in hell knows not what heaven is.

The afterlife smelled like piss and sour rye, but Alessa began eternal life with a man in her arms, and if the gods wanted to reward her despite her failures, she wasn't going to fuss at them about the details.

She ran her fingers down the valley of his spine, ridges of muscle on either side, and he moved against her with a low moan, stubble rough against her neck.

If she'd *known* about the perks, she might not have dreaded death quite so much.

And yet, the ground was hard and unforgiving, her entire body ached, and nearby, someone paused a slurred rendition of a bawdy tavern song to belch.

Which ... didn't seem right.

Forcing her eyes open, she stared into the muted dusk until

shapes and colors coalesced into a view of a brick wall, and closer, a head resting on her chest, face obscured by the angle. Muscles went tight beneath her hands as the mystery man groaned again.

Not the afterlife. Not a faceless man.

Dante.

And he was *not* enjoying being on top of her.

Alessa yanked her hands back and stretched her neck to keep her head away from him, but his forehead was still resting on the skin beneath her collarbone and she couldn't move him without touching him, and—

Her back scraped against cracked cobblestones as she fought to get out from beneath him. It was like dislodging herself from a landslide. With a final heave, she wrenched her torso free, and a dagger clattered to the ground.

Memories rushed back.

Dark eyes, deadly anger, daggers buried in flesh. Something—fear, shock, or blood loss—was dulling her pain, but she didn't need evidence to know the truth.

She was done for.

But he wasn't. Not yet.

As she twisted to one side, her palm met a puddle of blood. Fear spiked through her at the afterimage of Dante's horrified guilt. The kind of guilt that could drive a person to turn his blades on himself.

She covered her mouth and tasted blood, stale and rusty.

Please let it be mine.

She found a soggy glove beside Dante's head and wrestled it on so she could turn his face toward her.

His face was gray, his eyes closed.

She leaned closer, searching for his breath. Dante gasped, surging upward, and his nose cracked against her cheekbone.

Alessa fell back with a yelp, met by Dante's stream of curses.

"Oh, your poor face," she cried out.

"I'm fine." Sitting up, he raised a hand to his clearly broken nose and ducked his head.

"You're not fine."

But when he looked up, his face was bloody but otherwise normal.

What in Dea's name?

"Are you bleeding?" he asked.

Blinking in confusion, Alessa looked down at a body that didn't feel like her own. "I—I don't think so." The front of her dress was stiff and cool, not damp with the pulse of fresh blood.

"Move your blasted hand, will you?"

"I can't. I need to keep pressure on it, so I don't start bleeding again."

Dante took her wrist, protected by the end of her sleeve, and pulled her hand away. She sucked in a sharp inhale as he ripped the tear in her dress wider to reveal a handspan of pale skin, blood-stained, but unbroken.

Impossible.

"I thought it wasn't going to work." Dante sat back and covered his mouth with a shaking hand.

Alessa bent to look at her abdomen. "I don't understand."

"Don't you?" Dante watched her, tense.

There was only one possible explanation.

Blood pounded in her ears.

"You're a ghiotte."

Twenty-Eight

Chi nasce lupo non muore agnello.

Those born as wolves cannot die as lambs. / People don't change.

DAYS BEFORE DIVORANDO: 19

It wasn't every day a girl received a mortal wound, turned around at death's threshold, and discovered her only friend in the world also happened to be one of the creatures from her nightmares. It was . . . a lot.

Ghiotte were evil. It was fact, not opinion. But Dante *wasn't.* He couldn't be.

At first, she thought he wouldn't answer, hoped he'd scoff, and they'd both marvel at the absurdity of what she'd said.

He jerked a nod instead.

"You're a ghiotte," she said again. Her thoughts tangled, impossible to tease apart. She seized the most important thread and tugged. "And you used your gift to heal me."

"No," he said. "*You* used it."

"But *you* chose to hold my hands because you thought I *could*."
Euphoria filled her. "Dante, you saved my life."

His expression darkened at her breathy wonder. "I'm your
bodyguard. That's literally my job." He stood and brushed off his
pants. It was futile. They were thoroughly soiled with blood and
filth and not worth salvaging.

Her mind churned with a tempest of emotion—horror, gratitude, fear, and awe. "Dante, you held my hand, and *you didn't die*."

He looked uncomfortable. "For a minute, I thought I might."

"But—"

"Don't get excited. I don't have any *useful* powers." Dante
scanned the alley, practically twitching with nerves. "You need to
get back to the Cittadella, and I have to get out of here."

Alessa was prodding her miraculously intact belly.

With an impatient huff, Dante hauled her to her feet.

She swayed drunkenly and held out her bloody hands, one
glove on and one off, as though to show him some fascinating
treasure.

Dante gave her the long-suffering look of a sober patron at
a bar past midnight and tucked her under his arm to hustle her
along.

He was alive.

She was alive.

How in Dea's name were they both alive?

She giggled, loopy from relief—and blood loss, if she was
honest—and wrapped her fingers around his waist. Heat curled
at the press of his body against her, the shift of firm muscles with
every step.

They probably looked like lovers, clinging to each other, in search of a private alley. She giggled again. Except for the blood. She didn't have much experience for reference, but in books at least, clandestine romantic encounters didn't *usually* involve quite so much of that.

Ever the grumpy chaperone, Dante did not steer them into a darkened alley, but half carried her, with an insider's knowledge of the winding, unnamed streets, until the harbor cave loomed before them.

Inside, Dante maneuvered her down the path. The brisk walk had not cleared her head, but done the opposite, and stars burst in her vision as he leaned her against the wall. Vaguely aware she was sliding down, Alessa couldn't stop herself. Dante caught her, propping her up with a knee between her legs.

"Oh, dear. You haven't even bought me dinner," she said with a snort.

He sighed, all taut muscles and jerky movement as he fished beneath her cloak for the key in her dress pockets.

Pressing her face into Dante's shirt, she breathed him in. It seemed like a perfectly normal thing to do, but on second thought, probably wasn't. Hard to blame her, though. Whatever magic had healed her wounds had not replenished the blood she'd lost, and the deficit was taking a toll on her already subpar impulse control.

"Whoops," she mumbled, lifting her head. "Little dizzy."

Dante didn't respond, his eyes darting everywhere as he unlocked the gate, his breath fast and shallow. This wasn't the boy who'd teased her about racy novels or offered to hug her to save the world. *This* was the trapped animal she'd seen on her balcony the night she brought him home.

He was frightened of her. Of course. Everyone was. And now

that he'd experienced the excruciating pain she caused everyone who got too close, he'd forever be scared of her, too.

"I'm sorry." She stuffed her hands in her pockets. "I won't touch you again."

"Huh?" He blinked, focused on her. "No. It's not—That's not—Do I need to carry you?"

"Relax," she said with what she hoped looked like a confident wave of her hand. "I can walk." She wasn't steady, but she kept herself moving forward.

There was something else bothering her. Something she had been angry about or wanted to understand. Her thoughts were sluggish and disjointed, but she seized on it at last as Dante closed the gate behind them. "Who was that man? And why were you arguing with him?"

Dante tensed. "It doesn't matter."

"It most certainly does. You met with one of Ivini's suppli-cants, who wants me dead, and then you almost killed me. I de-serve to know what's going on."

He'd also healed her, which somewhat negated her argument, but Dante must have wanted to avoid that subject.

"He's the guy who took me in after my parents died. Told the mob that a child could be reformed, and he would take care of it. You know, save my immortal soul." He urged her forward with a hand on her lower back. "I saw him in the crowd the night I met you. It's been years, so I wasn't sure if he recognized me, but I figured I should make sure he was keeping his mouth shut, so no one would find out. So much for that plan." Dante opened the last gate and put the key in her hand. "Lock the gate behind you."

Why did it sound like goodbye?

"You aren't coming?"

"I—" He raked his fingers through his hair. "I have to—I can't—"

The man who fought opponents twice his size without flinching, who stared down angry Fontes, who never shied away from a girl whose hands brought pain and death, was trembling because she knew his secret.

"Dante, I would *never* tell anyone."

He let out a ragged breath. "You know what'll happen if this gets out?"

A ghiotte in the Cittadella. A rat in the kitchen. Angry mobs, torches blazing and pitchforks at the ready. She'd be lucky if they didn't toss her on the pyre with him.

His eyes flashed. "Pick your damn Fonte, stay in the Cittadella, and forget you ever knew me."

"At least come in for your things," she said, her voice soft.

"I'll buy new things."

"Please. Let's talk about this."

"There's nothing to talk about."

It was too much, too fast. He was slipping away, and she hadn't even processed what had just happened and who he was. *She needed a moment, dammit.*

"Then my blood will be on your hands again," she said. "I give myself a seventy percent chance of collapsing on my way up the stairs, tumbling all the way down, breaking half my bones and cracking my skull, and you won't be there to heal me, so I'll die for the *second* time today in a puddle of my own blood. What a tragic end to the day's story of survival."

He kept glaring, but there was a hint of something else behind the anger and fear.

It might have been hope.

"Please?" She raised a shaky hand to her face, sagging against the gate. It really wasn't fair to use his weakness against him, but desperate times demanded desperate measures.

Dante washed his blades in the sink, dried them with clean towels, then washed and dried them again before returning them to their sheaths.

He was pacing when Alessa left to bathe, and he was pacing when she peered around the screen before getting dressed.

He was a ghiotte.

A person considered barely human.

Demon-touched, selfish, and cruel to the core.

She was supposed to fear him. Hate him. It should have changed everything.

But it didn't.

A ghiotte had taken her hands in that alley, not knowing if he'd survive his desperate gamble to save her. A ghiotte had risked his pride *and* safety to wrap a ridiculous scarf around his head and hug her when she needed it more than anything in the world.

From the day they'd met, Dante had tried to convince her he was cruel, unkind, and cold, but his actions made his words ring hollow. He was a ghiotte, but he was still Dante. And he hadn't chosen his fate any more than she had.

She found him trying to scrub her blood from his white linen shirt. At the sound of her footsteps behind him, Dante threw the shirt into the sink and braced his hands on the counter.

"I promise I won't tell," she said, with the steady calm of a person soothing a growling dog. "But I have to know something."

He didn't turn around.

"The stories say ghiotte are demons disguised as men." She swallowed. "Is it true? Are you . . . something else? Underneath?"

"Are you asking if I have horns?"

That was exactly what she was asking, but it seemed best to neither confirm nor deny it.

"No," he sighed. "No horns. No tail. No claws. This is me."

The breath whooshed out of her. Not a monster, at least no more than she was. In that instant, she made up her mind.

"No one else has to know."

Dante looked irritated rather than grateful. "Someone already does. Why do you think I was threatening him? It's bad enough he knows I'm in the city. All the money in the world won't keep him quiet if he finds out I'm in the Cittadella. It's one thing to have your runaway ghiotte wandering free, another to let him sleep on the Finestra's couch."

"Then we'll make sure he doesn't find out. Dante, please. You can't go. Not now, when I finally know how much we have in common—"

"*Common?*" Dante spat out. "What do we have in *common?*"

"A lot. For one, we both understand what it's like to be hated and feared. We both have gifts we didn't ask for."

"Gift," he scoffed. "Some gift."

"You can heal yourself. My gift only kills people."

His fingers flexed against the porcelain. "Mine has killed plenty."

She squeezed her eyes shut. "That's why they killed your parents."

"Yeah. And yours are getting paid extra for birthing the blessed Finestra. Like I said, we have nothing in common. You're a savior. I'm an abomination. You got a castle, and I got locked in a shed by a man who tried to beat the evil out of me."

Her stomach roiled.

No, their lives *weren't* the same. Not in the obvious ways, but in the hidden, broken, jagged spaces inside them . . . why couldn't he see how they *were*?

"I'm sorry for what happened to you. You didn't deserve that, and neither did your parents. But . . ." Alessa clenched her fists, stunned at a possibility. "Maybe your power *can* help others."

Dante scoffed. "What? Like being your Fonte? Good luck with that. The only gift you'd get from me is a slower death to watch the world end."

"No, of course not. But I could practice on you."

"You mean torture me."

She flinched. "But not kill you."

"I'm not *invincible*. I'll die if you try hard enough."

"But you're closer than anyone else. You keep saying you don't care about your safety. Is it so different from fighting for money? You could help me save Saverio."

"What's Saverio ever done for me?"

"There are *children* who will die horrible deaths."

"Children grow up and become cruel like everyone else."

"I didn't want this duty either, but at least I'm trying."

"You're the savior, not me. I'm the selfish one, remember? This is *your* problem."

She wanted to rake her nails down his face, to rip the cold disdain away by force. "Nice try, Dante, but it's too late. I *know* you. There's no way you're fine with letting thousands of children die when you couldn't even ignore one kid in trouble."

"What are you talking about?"

"I saw you with that beggar girl getting pushed around by one of Ivini's goons. You stopped him."

Dante threw his head back. "Don't make me into some kind of hero because I hate bullies. I am *exactly* what everyone says I am."

"I don't care what the stories say. You're a good person—"

He threw his hands up. "*Stop!* You don't know what kind of person I am. You have no idea what I've done, who I've hurt."

"Then tell me. Convince me. Prove you're evil. I dare you."

He tore at his hair. "Fine! There was *one* person who tried to help me after I ran away. Just one. *Ever.* And I killed her."

Twenty-Nine

Quando l'amico chiede, non v'è domani.
When a friend asks, there is no tomorrow.

DAYS BEFORE DIVORANDO: 19

Alessa's blood went cold. "I don't believe you." Her words didn't sound convincing, even to herself.

"Believe it." His voice was flat. "This kid found me after I ran away. Couldn't have been more than ten. Trips over a bloody, barely conscious stranger on the beach, and instead of running, decides to nurse me back to health." He laughed bitterly. "She saw me heal. I couldn't hide it."

Alessa hid a shiver. The Dante she knew—or thought she knew—would never kill an innocent child to keep them quiet. But maybe she didn't know him at all.

"So, I lied. Said I'd found the Fonte della Guarigione high on a cliff. She wanted to know where, kept asking, so I kept lying, moving it higher, making it too hard to get to. But she wouldn't let it go."

A curious child. A fearful secret. And Dante, on the run and desperate to hide the truth.

Alessa was going to be sick.

His eyes burned like embers. "I found her body the next morning, shattered on the rocks below."

She swallowed back tears, even as her knees went weak with relief. "An accident. You didn't mean for her to get hurt."

"It doesn't *matter*."

"Yes, it does. I, of all people, know what that's like."

"Stop!" Dante shouted. "We *aren't* the same. You touch people and they die, but it's not your choice and it's not your fault. *Everyone* who cares about me dies, and it's *always* my fault. You give. I *take*."

"Then change."

"People don't change."

"*I* have." Her voice shook with anger. "I've changed so many times I've lost count. When I became Finestra, I was a naive girl who believed what anyone told me, followed the rules without question, even when it felt wrong. Even when I thought I'd shrivel up and blow away. I became a husk of a person, all pain and bitterness. Then you came. And you didn't revere me *or* pity me. You noticed when I made myself small, and I hated it. I wanted to prove you wrong, so I *changed*." Alessa drew herself up and looked him in the eyes. "I don't care what anyone says—your gift is a part of you, but it doesn't define you. You can choose to be better."

His eyes were hard. "Well, I choose not to. And *this*"—he pointed from himself to her and back—"is not a thing. We aren't the same. We aren't friends. We aren't *anything*. I'll finish this damn job because we made a deal, but that's it."

"You are such an ass."

"Now you're catching on."

Fury spiked through her. She wanted to dig her fingers into his stubborn face until she stole his soul from his body, once and for all. Ghiotte or no, he wouldn't stand a chance.

She stormed out instead. Any would-be assassin who chose this moment to attack her would lose.

For five lonely years she'd told herself it was only her gift and her position that kept everyone away. That if anyone spent time with her, then, surely, they would care about her. Not the Finestra or the savior. Her. Alessa.

But Dante had heard it all, and he didn't care. He was only there because she paid him to be, and she was so pathetic she couldn't tell the difference between a friend and an employee.

She needed air. She needed to escape.

At the sound of voices ahead, she ducked inside the darkened kitchens.

From the thickest shadows, someone hissed her name. Not her title. Her *name*.

A dark figure stalked toward her.

She backed away, feeling behind herself for the open door. Instead, her hands met the hard muscle of Dante's thigh.

"For Crollo's sake, there you—" he started to say, before swiftly lunging around her to shove the shadowy form against the wall. A blade flashed in the dim light from the hall, and the intruder yelped.

Alessa knew that yelp. "Stop!" she cried out. "It's my brother!"

For a second, she thought Dante would slice his throat anyway, but he stepped back, knife pointed at Adrick's chest.

"Adrick, what are you doing here?" Alessa demanded.

"What is *he* doing?" Adrick retorted. "He's not a Fonte."

"He's my guard."

Adrick raked Dante with a skeptical look. "Half dressed?"

Dante had grabbed a shirt before following her, but only a few of the buttons were fastened.

Dante's eyebrows lowered. "It's the middle of the night."

"Yeah, it is." Adrick's eyes narrowed.

"Dante, could you give us a minute?"

Dante's glare deepened. "Yell if you need me."

Adrick stepped forward, the faint light from the French doors to the gardens illuminating his face as he cast a furtive glance around the dark, quiet kitchen.

"Adrick, how did you get inside?"

He rubbed his hands on his pants. "I know someone. Who is that guy? Didn't he fight at the docks at one point?"

Alessa sighed loudly. "I told you, Dante is my guard. And yes, he used to fight at the Barrel. Enough stalling. What was going on today? Who tried to poison me? And why?"

"I don't know."

"Bullshit."

"Look, it doesn't matter right now."

"Doesn't matter? Because it looks to me like you made Papa's special cookies and gave them to someone who *added poison to them* and delivered them here so I would get sick or die. And you aren't even slightly surprised. *Why?*"

Adrick seemed to steel himself. "I'll explain after you tell me if you have a Fonte. Is it working?"

She jerked back. "Yes. Sort of. It's complicated."

"It's a simple question."

She crossed her arms. "It's a complicated answer."

"So, no, then. And everyone here knows it, so you had to hire a thug from the docks to be your hired muscle." His face twisted like he was fighting a laugh, and Alessa waited for the punch line, but he choked on a sob. "You've tried, but there's no time left."

"You're giving up on me? Really? Adrick, I am trying so damn hard—"

"I know. I *know* you're trying." Adrick's hoarse whisper faded into defeat. "You always are. *Trying* to cook dinner and burning everything, so we have to eat watered down soup instead. *Trying* to write the perfect essay for homework, then forgetting it at home so I have to retrieve it for you and get in trouble. *Trying* to be Finestra and killing your Fontes instead, leaving me to do the work of two people and jeopardizing all our lives."

Every word sliced another wound that would never heal. A lifetime of guilt and embarrassment thrown in her face, and it only hurt more that it seemed to pain him to say it.

She was a burden. A screwup. And Adrick knew better than anyone, because he'd been there, cleaning up after her.

"I'm sorry." Adrick's face had never looked so drawn and serious. "But there aren't points for effort in this. I don't want this any more than you do, but I . . . I think, maybe, that's why I'm here. Maybe the whole reason I was born." Tears glittered in his eyes as he pulled a small bottle from his pocket.

Alessa backed away, her skin going cold. "What is that, Adrick?"

If she had to endure his betrayal, he needed to live with the guilt of saying it.

"You had your calling, sister. Now I understand mine. You know I'd never want to hurt you."

"Then don't."

Adrick flinched. "Why do you think I told you to leave today?

Do you think they would have been as careful as I would? No one else would take every precaution to make sure you didn't suffer. Don't you see? This is your way out. You'll be a hero, and we'll be saved." Tears streamed down his face. "I made it special. For you."

She wanted to scream, to pound his chest with her fists. She wanted to cling to him and beg him to take it back. Instead, she remained perfectly still, barely breathing.

Adrick placed the small blue bottle into her palm and wrapped her gloved fingers around it.

She stood there, staring at her closed fist between his hands. It was the most contact they'd had in years.

"Are you going to force it down my throat?" she whispered.

His eyes closed. "No. I know you'll do the right thing."

Dante darkened the doorway. "Time's up."

"Goodbye, little sister." Adrick swiped at his eyes. "I'll make sure no one ever forgets your sacrifice."

Adrick left, and Dante approached, brows knit. "What was that about?"

Oh, *now* he was concerned? After he'd thrown their friendship in her face, he expected her to rip her wounds wide open for him? "Like you care."

"I didn't mean the stuff I said."

"Save it. I don't want to talk to you."

She ran to the French doors at the end of the kitchens and threw them open.

A frigid wind whipped her skirts around her legs, and icy rain pelted her face. Despite her gloves, her fingertips stung as soon as she stepped outside.

"Bad night for a stroll," Dante said behind her.

"I need to think."

"Unpleasant spot for it."

"Unpleasant company isn't helping. If you want to finish this job, do it. But be a shadow." If he didn't want to be her friend, he could be her enemy. That seemed to be all she had left anyway.

"Can I say something?"

"No." It felt delicious to shoot him down.

Ice coated the branches, encasing the trees like glass sculptures. Shivers shook her, but she kept walking.

Dante dogged her footsteps. "I'm *trying* to apologize."

"Don't bother."

He sighed heavily. "Look. People usually try to kill me when they find out. I panicked." He blocked her path, his gaze intent beneath eyelashes glittering with ice. "Will you please come inside?"

"No."

He growled in frustration. "I'll do it, okay? I'll let you practice on me."

"Why? You don't care about Saverio."

"I'm not offering to help Saverio. I'm offering to help *you*."

She closed her eyes. "Forget it. It was a ridiculous idea. You don't even have a gift I can use."

"What do you *want*?" Dante demanded.

The frigid rain dripped down her cheeks like tears. "To be left alone."

"Not now. In general. You say you want to be a hero, but you're real quick to play the victim. You say you want friends, but you won't forgive me. You say you want my help, but you won't take it. So, what is it?"

She gestured to the high wall around the garden, at everything it kept her from. "To save Saverio. That's what the Finestra is meant to do."

"I didn't ask what everyone wants from *you*. I asked what *you* want."

"It doesn't matter."

"I think you're scared."

She rolled her eyes. "A swarm of demons is coming, and *I* have to protect us. Who wouldn't be scared?"

"No, that's not it. You're scared of losing yourself."

"I'm *supposed* to lose myself. My name, my family, my life."

"Exactly. And you don't want to. Can't blame you, but you need to decide what *you* get out of this, if you're going to pull it off. So, what do *you* want?"

"I want it all to go away!" She whirled away from him. "I want to stop being brave and alone. I want a hug when I'm sad, like a normal girl with a home and a family. I want to hold hands and kiss in dark alleys and swim naked in the ocean and do every other silly little thing I never realized I might never get to do."

"There are better places for kissing than alleys."

She laughed, dangerously close to hysteria. "Thanks for the tip. Doubt I'll need it."

"If you want to control your power so you can live a normal life and kiss in every alley in the city after Divorando, then grab onto that." He shivered. "Now, can we *please* go inside?"

She tried to retort with something witty and sharp, but her teeth chattered too fiercely for her to speak.

"Dammit, I'm claiming bodyguard prerogative. Come on." Grabbing her wrist, Dante towed her behind him.

The warmth of the kitchen wasn't enough. Every shudder sent ice rattling to the floor from her wet skirts.

Dante attacked them, swatting at the layer of caked-on ice.

"Hate to break it to you, but dying of hypothermia won't help Saverio."

She swallowed a sudden lump in her throat. "It might."

He looked up at her. "You don't really believe that."

"Other people do."

Dante's gaze fell on the bottle in her hands. "What is that?"

She hesitated. "My mother's perfume."

Dante snatched it from her numb fingers, uncorking it to wipe the rim with a finger and raise it to his lips.

"No!" She tried to grab it back.

He hid the bottle behind his back. "What's in it?"

She clenched her teeth, but her lower lip trembled.

Dante dumped the contents into a potted miniature lemon tree and hurled the empty bottle into the soil. He was gearing up to rail at her, though how it was her fault her brother wanted her to poison herself, she didn't know. But his expression said he wanted to hurt *someone*, and she was the only one there to take it.

She managed a weak, "I like that tree," and burst into tears.

Muttering profanities that somehow sounded sympathetic, he crushed her to his chest, and she clutched at him, desperate for his body heat seeping through their layers of cold, wet clothing. The truth poured out in a torrent—how a thousand mistakes in her life had piled on top of each other, how Adrick had counted them up, tallying the proof that she couldn't do the one thing she must. How every minor embarrassment and childhood error was now evidence used against her by the person she'd trusted to stand by her no matter what. Ivini had stolen the last member of her family, but it was her failings that made it possible for him to do so.

She could feel Dante's struggle for control in the taut muscles of his back as he fought the urge to chase Adrick down, but she fisted her hands in his shirt and held on for dear life. If he left her now, she'd crumble into nothing.

"What if he's right?" she asked. "Maybe I was never meant to do this. Dea had faith in me, but I didn't deserve it. Everyone's figured it out but me. You said it yourself. The gods have given up on us—or at least me."

"*Now* you start listening to me?" Dante said. "People like Ivini make a living convincing scared people they know the answers, but the loudest people rarely know the most."

"That doesn't mean he's wrong."

"It doesn't mean he's right, either. Come on, let me try."

Did she even have a choice? Did she *ever* have a choice?

"You think too much." He tipped her chin up with a gloved finger. "All talk, huh? Brave enough to suggest it, but not to make a move."

Her breath caught. "Don't tempt me."

"I'm *trying* to tempt you. You said I can be better, so let me try."

"And *you* keep saying you aren't a hero." Something fluttered to life in Alessa's heart—hope, fear, or something else entirely.

"I'm not." The corner of his mouth kicked up in a smile. "*You're* the hero. I'm just asking a girl to hold my hand."

Chapter Thirty

Come la cosa indugia, piglia vizio.

Wait at your own peril.

Alessa muddled her way through training the next day, which went about as well as the sessions before their day off—if one could call a near-death experience and attempted sororicide a "day off"—and she wasn't the only one who only emerged from a stupor at the sight of a parade of wheeled icebox carts in the courtyard.

Josef had planned the surprise, a fact he took a bit too long explaining as they eyed the alluring treats.

Alessa held back as the others perused the selection from Josef's family's gelateria. To be polite. And because her dread about the coming evening, when Dante would take his turn being tormented, was quickly overtaking her hopes that he could help her.

He'd dodged death at her hand once. That didn't mean he would again.

Beside her, Josef puffed with pride as he watched his fellow Fontes make their selections. "I've always thought you can learn a lot about a person by their favorite flavor."

"Oh?" Alessa said.

"I usually choose vanilla." He looked at her expectantly.

"Because vanilla is . . ." *Boring* felt like the wrong answer.

He smiled as if offering her the solution to a puzzle. "Subtle, but complex."

"Of course." Alessa called out a request for dark chocolate and raspberry and waited for Josef to take a bowl from an alarmed-looking gelato scooper and hand it to her. "Tell me more." She'd never really had a chance to speak with him one-on-one, and if the topic of frozen desserts was her best chance to get him to open up, so be it.

"Most people act like vanilla lacks flavor, but it's actually quite nuanced. The notes vary depending on where you source the beans and how you prepare them before blending." Josef smiled at his bowl, which was still half full, and thanks to his gift, showed no sign of melting. "I know I'm a man of few words, but I like to think that I, too, am more complex than people assume."

Alessa nodded pensively. "What does mine say about me?"

Josef flushed. "I couldn't presume, Finestra."

Alessa sighed. "Nina, then. Stracciatella? Let me guess, sweet but inconsistent?"

Josef blinked, befuddled. "I know her too well. It wouldn't be fair."

"You can't propose a gelato theory of personality, and then hold out on me, Josef." She eyed Dante across the room, but while Josef might be the stuffiest boy she'd ever met, even he would notice her pathetic curiosity if she wasn't careful. She settled on a safer option. "What did Kamaria get?"

"Half mint and half cafe latte, but she orders something different every time she comes into the shop."

Alessa thought. "Hmm. Let me try. I'd say she craves excitement and adventure, and she hates being bored."

Josef's eyes twinkled. "I concur."

"This is fun. Do Kaleb."

"Strawberries and cream. I haven't figured him out yet."

"You and me both. Pink. And sweet." Alessa shrugged. "Yeah, I've got nothing."

They let the subject drop for a bit, each absorbed in their dessert.

"Limone," Josef said, out of nowhere.

"Excuse me?"

"That's what Signor Dante chose. If you were wondering. You may not have been."

"I wasn't." *Methinks I doth protest too much.* "What does limone say about a person? A sour disposition?"

Josef looked mildly offended. "Lemon is not *sour*, it's *tart*. Not the same at all. The culinary section of the paper called our limone a 'near-perfect blend of tart and sweet: appealing, layered, and complex. The heart of Saverio in every scoop. A classic.' Our family has spent years perfecting it. It's our most beloved flavor."

Alessa licked a bit of gelato off her spoon. "Of course. The perfect flavor. My mistake."

Dante eyed them as if he knew he was the topic of conversation.

With an obnoxiously cheerful grin, Alessa spooned another

scoop into her mouth and promptly got her first taste of the dark chocolate, which entirely ruined the effect. Her eyes slipped closed to fully appreciate the melding of hedonistic chocolate and fruity tartness melting on her tongue.

When she returned to the mortal plane, Josef had moved on to analyzing Saida, and Dante was jabbing at his limone as though it had offended him.

"Quit stalling," Dante said. Elbows propped on his knees, he watched Alessa pace.

She'd put it off as long as she could, chewing each bite of dinner as slowly as possible.

"We almost died yesterday," she said, yawning dramatically. "Doesn't that warrant an early bedtime?"

Dante glared at her through his lashes. "That was your excuse last night. Are we doing this or not?"

She'd already left him unconscious once. A second touch might be too much.

"I've changed my mind," she said. "This was a terrible idea."

"If we wait for a better one, we'll all be dead. Look, as someone older than you—"

"Pfft. Not by much, if at all. Do you even know how old I am?"

He dragged out the question like it was sucking years from his life. "How old are you?"

Alessa smiled because she knew it would irritate him. "I am eighteen."

"Like I said. As someone older than you—"

"How old are *you*?"

"Nineteen. Or twenty. Stop interrupting."

"How can you not know how old you are?"

"I don't carry a pocket calendar and I lost track of the date a few weeks ago. Do you *always* ask so many questions?"

"I don't know, do I?"

"Har har. Now, let me finish. As someone older than you . . ." He paused, anticipating an interruption, but she clasped her hands innocently in her lap instead. "I can tell you, it's always better to get something unpleasant over with quickly. Drawing out the wait only makes it worse."

A truth she knew quite well at eighteen, but it was easier said than done.

"First, tell me how this works. Can a ghiotte heal from anything?"

Dante picked at a loose thread on his chair. "No, not anything, or my parents would still be alive. If you cut my head off or drop a wall on me, I'm done for. Regular injuries, I'll recover. If it's a repeat injury, it's easier. The first time I broke my arm, it hurt like a beast. By the third, I barely noticed. Healed faster, too. I think that's part of the . . . gift, but I don't know."

"Is it like that for all of you?"

"If I ever find another ghiotte, I'll ask."

"You don't know how it worked for your parents?"

"I was a kid. I didn't take notes. It was just a thing I knew to keep quiet about. All I know is that for me, the worse the damage is, or if I'm tired or hungry, it takes longer."

She blew a stream of air through pursed lips. "Are you hungry now? Tired? Thirsty?"

"I'm fine. Let's start with the basics. I know about your first Fonte, but how'd it end with the others?"

Rubbing her arms, Alessa tried to recall. "Ilsi's heart stopped on our fourth try. Hugo tried for a few seconds, collapsed, and cracked his skull on the table. I don't know if I killed him or the fall did."

Dante pursed his lips like she'd detailed a mundane grocery list rather than a series of gruesome deaths. "We'll stay seated, then. Get over here."

Her thighs barely touched the chair before she sprang back up. "My hands are cold."

"Well, in *that* case." Dante slapped his thighs as though to leave. "Sit down."

"It's too dangerous. With the Fontes, there's a reason to risk it, because I need their gifts. But you're . . ."

"Worthless?" His tone was light, but his hands curled into fists. "I have nothing to offer, nothing to defend Saverio with, so it's not worth adding another tally to your guilt list?"

Alessa pressed her fingers to her temples. "No. That's not—"

"Well, you're right. No one would miss me."

"I would." Her lower lip trembled, but she wouldn't cry. Her tears had roped him into this mess in the first place.

"I'm not going to die."

"You don't know that."

He shrugged. "Nothing's killed me yet."

"That's a ridiculous argument. *Anyone* could say the same, and it would be true."

He winked. "Have a little *faith*, Finestra."

She'd been gloveless around him before, but she'd never taken them off *for* him, and as he watched the fabric slide down her forearms, she saw her skin like it belonged to someone else. The faint blue veins on the inside of her wrists, the pale palms and slender fingers. Her heart thumped viciously against her ribs. "I'm letting go if you so much as twitch."

She shrank back as he reached for her.

"Hands on the table, palms up. *No* grabbing."

He sighed but did as he was told.

"You still feel pain, though, right?" she asked.

He raised his eyebrows. "Yes."

"Then why are you so damn calm?"

"Worrying about pain doesn't stop it from happening," he said. "If you don't breathe soon, I'll poke you in the belly like a stubborn mule."

"You're an ass."

"Yup. Now, do it already."

She hovered her palms above his, lowering until their fingertips brushed with every heartbeat. With a shaky breath, she pressed her hands against his. His hands, like the rest of him, were strong and deft, rough but graceful.

Dante grunted softly, but she was lost to the sudden surge of power. *Yes more want need take yes.* Her gift demanded, like the ocean dragging a sinking ship under. Tethering herself, she focused on his face, fighting the craving until the tide receded.

His jaw went rigid, but he didn't pull away.

When she lifted her hands, they exhaled.

"Well," she said. "How bad was it?"

"Bearable." He cracked his knuckles. "Again."

"Not yet." Shaking her hands out, she left to fetch water and crackers. If hunger and thirst were risk factors, she'd shove both in his face at the first sign of trouble.

Out of habit, she put both glasses in the center of the table and sat, stunned by the realization that, even without gloves, she could have simply handed it to him.

Dante ignored the crackers, but downed half his glass. "You go palms up this time. I'll pull back if I need to."

She hated relinquishing control, but she couldn't gauge his pain, and he could. This time when they touched, the voracious *need* was less insistent, and she was able to pay attention to everything else. She counted silently, noting the texture of his skin, the steady beat of his pulse against her fingertips, how very *alive* he felt.

He let go as she reached fifty-two.

"Well?" she asked, breathless.

"Better. The first time hurt. This was . . . uncomfortable, but not unpleasant."

"Those words mean the same thing."

"No, they don't."

"Of course they do. If something is uncomfortable, it's unpleasant."

"Not always."

"Give me one example of an experience that's uncomfortable and *pleasant*."

"A massage. Amazing after a fight, but *ouch*."

"A *what?*"

"A body rub for sore muscles. You've never had one? Oh, right. 'Course not."

"You *pay* someone to rub your body?" Who was she kidding, she'd pay *to* rub his body.

"For a good massage I'd beg, borrow, or steal. There's this girl who lives above the Barrel—" He shook his head with a small smile. "Scented oils, clean sheets, and her hands are magic."

"I don't need the details, thanks." But the image he'd painted was already there, and her face went hot.

Dante narrowed his eyes. "What is going on in your head right now?"

She lifted her chin. "I was struck by the memory of you in that fighting ring. I was quite sad that something so pretty was about to be destroyed."

Whatever he'd expected, it wasn't that. "Uh. Thanks?" He pointed to her eyes, then turned his fingers to his own. "Focus. I'm trying to explain how something can hurt in a good way."

"And I'm trying to explain why the words *good* and *hurt* don't go together."

"They can, though. I just need the right example." He grasped in the air for some elusive example, until his gaze fell on a stack of novels. "Arousal!"

Her cheeks burned so hot her hair might light on fire. "I said I *don't* need the details."

He bit his lip against a laugh. "Unrelated. Bear with me. I know you've been locked up here for a while, but I'm guessing you've still thought . . . thoughts." He aimed a pointed look at the books. "So. Like I said, *uncomfortable* but not *unpleasant.*"

She wiped her expression blank. She was thinking all kinds of thoughts at that very moment, but she would *not* react.

He snapped his fingers. "Exercise. I should have said that first."

"You *really* should have."

He laughed far longer than he deserved to. "You know what I mean, that good ache in your muscles after a hard workout. Uncomfortable, but pleasant."

"Fine," she said through gritted teeth. "Does it feel like *any* of those things?"

"Well, no." He frowned. Of course it didn't. It felt like pain, and she'd never wanted to know more specifics than that, but she had to understand if she wanted any hope of taming it. "It's more like a . . . buzzing. Or a vibration. It only hurts when it's too . . . fast? Intense? It knocked the wind out of me at first, but it got less noticeable each time—more like a purr."

"What is it with you and cats?"

He grinned. "Guess you remind me of one."

"Because I'm so sweet and lovable?"

"No, that's not it."

"Mysterious and graceful?"

"Definitely not. It's probably because you never sit correctly, and you get visibly annoyed when anyone reads a book in your presence."

She *humph*ed, uncurling her legs so her feet dangled, toes barely touching the floor. "Most chairs are too tall for me. It's uncomfortable."

"Excuses, excuses. Anyway, when you touch me, think like a cat."

There was no excuse for the vivid mental image of herself in dramatic eyeliner, slinking toward him, hips swaying in a feline prowl, that popped into her head, but there it was.

Dante absently tapped his knee. "It's like stretching. If you yank someone's arm back, you could dislocate it. You have to ease in, stopping at the point of good pain. Speed and force make a difference. Like, touching foreheads is fine, but do it fast enough and it'll get you thrown out of a fight. See what I mean?"

She raised her eyebrows. "I've been head-butting people?"

"In a way. Don't think about power, just focus on touching. You aren't hurt right now, so you don't need anything from me."

Had a sentence ever been so untrue?

She took a deep breath. "Promise me you'll stop if it's too much."

"Cross my heart and hope to die." He slid his hands across the table.

"You aren't allowed to."

Two of her Fontes had made it past two touches, but no one had endured more than four.

Alessa closed her eyes, gathered herself. No taking, no using, no stealing. *Just touching.*

Alessa leaned over the back of the couch, her cheek a handspan from Dante's parted lips, and held her breath until a reassuring gust of air warmed her skin.

Skin to soul, she was wrung out like a wet rag. They'd spent hours practicing, and she needed rest, but every time she got into bed, she panicked and ran back to make sure he was only sleeping.

The whole time, she'd been so scared the next touch would be the one that proved too much. But while her anxiety mounted, Dante had only grown calmer as the hours slipped by and the touches stretched longer.

By the time he'd agreed to stop, she was thrumming with more strains of nervous energy than she could label, and each brush of hands was branded on her memory, her skin tingling and hypersensitive as if she had a fever.

During the last few attempts, he'd claimed it didn't even bother him anymore, but it had clearly taken a toll, because he'd fallen asleep where he sat, fully clothed.

She checked his breath one more time. Still alive.

This time she managed to get in bed and stay there, to stare at the ceiling in stunned disbelief.

Dante—dark-eyed, tousled hair, sarcastic, stubborn, beautiful Dante—who'd been sleeping in her room for days, could *hold her hands* without suffering. And if she could touch his hands, she could touch his lips—

Focus, Alessa.

This wasn't the right time, but after Divorando? The thrill racing through her at the possibility wasn't going to make sleep any easier to find.

Her eyes were sandy from exhaustion, but each aftershock of excitement jolted her fully awake again, leaving her with too much time to remember the slide of his palms against hers, the gentle strength of his fingers around her wrists, his pulse throbbing against her fingertips.

The most wonderful night of her life. And one of the most heartbreaking.

Finally, she could touch someone without hurting him, but his gift was the only kind that couldn't save Saverio.

Thirty-One

Un diavolo scaccia l'altro.
One devil drives out another.

DAYS BEFORE DIVORANDO: 17

Dante took his new duty as seriously as he did the rest, and they touched a half dozen times before breakfast. He fastened her necklace for her, passed her a muffin, ruffled her hair. She was getting better at sensing the difference between "purring" touches and those that made him wince. She couldn't describe it, but there *was* a difference, and the painful moments were already becoming infrequent.

With an hour to kill before training began, and because Dante said he was afraid she'd wear a hole in the floor with her pacing if she didn't find a productive use for her nervous energy, they returned to the library.

"Do you have a reading compulsion? Should I be concerned?" she asked while he arranged his second armful of books on a table. "Why do you read as though books are about to go extinct?"

"Research."

She eyed the titles, half in the old language. A few historical, others religious, and a handful appeared to be fairy tales. "On what?"

He cast a wary glance over his shoulder. "People like me. I don't know much besides the stories, and those aren't all true—horns and all that—but there must be more. And plenty were banished, not killed, so they might still be out there. Somewhere."

Alessa sank into a chair. Beside him. Because she could do that now without her pulse spiking at his proximity. Well. Without her pulse spiking in a bad way.

It sat like a heavy meal, the thought of ghiotte roaming free. Unfair, maybe—if one ghiotte wasn't evil, it was reasonable to assume the rest weren't either—but it was difficult to shake years of conditioning.

Still, she took a book off the pile closest to her and began trying to flip pages. Gloves made it difficult, so with a brief pause to savor the novelty, she took them off and continued.

A thud from the wall between the library and Fonte suite made her jump.

Twenty minutes until she had to torture them again.

Dante was unique, or at least rare, and she might be getting better at reining in the destructive power of her gift with him, but that didn't mean it would translate to anyone else.

"What are you doing?" Dante asked as she took a lungful of air and held it for a count of three.

"Deep breathing. I can control my power better when I'm calm, so I'm practicing calming strategies." She exhaled, pushing out the breath until her chest went concave.

"You're never calm."

Another deep inhale. "Hence my problem."

Keeping one hand on his book, Dante extended his other without looking over. "Give it here."

Her body didn't seem to understand that it was just for *practice*, especially when he grew tired of holding their clasped hands up and lowered them to rest on his knee.

Only Dante's focus on his task saved Alessa from having to explain why her neck was turning red.

Resuming her hunt for the word *ghiotte*, she found one example, bookmarked it, and moved on to the next.

Idly, Dante curled his fingers and unfurled them in her palm, sending lightning bolts up her arm.

Was this a joke? A test? How was she supposed to read under these circumstances?

Dante leaned closer to the page, brows drawn in concentration, and his thumb began tracing lazy circles on her wrist.

Alessa's book might have burst into flames for how well she could read it now.

"Careful," Dante said, only half paying attention. "You're putting out surges over there."

She snatched her hand back and stood, fumbling to catch her chair before it tipped backward. "We should get going. Can't be the last ones there."

In the training room, Dante watched from his usual spot on the wall. Checking his knives, shifting his gaze away when the Fontes reacted from pain. She recognized his tells now. He was more uncomfortable as a witness than he'd been when he was on the receiving end.

Kaleb skulked over, and Alessa touched his palms, searching

his face for any sign it was different this time. His expression cycled between dread, confusion, and skepticism, but he didn't yank his hands away.

Dante dipped his chin in a subtle nod of encouragement.

"What's the deal?" Kaleb asked. "Why is it better this time?"

Only Kaleb would be equally annoyed when she didn't hurt him.

Alessa shrugged. "Practice?"

Now came the hard part.

"I'm going to try to tap into your power this time."

A deep inhale, breathing life into her gift, and Alessa's hair drifted up in an electrified cloud, crackling with Kaleb's power.

He yanked free.

"Sorry," Alessa said, but she couldn't hide her delight. Kaleb was frowning, not screaming. Progress.

She refrained from celebrating, but by the final round, she was sure of it. She was getting better. She could harness the urge faster and more completely, until she felt more like a ship's captain and less like a prisoner roped to the mast.

"Today went well, right?" Alessa said when the lesson was over, standing on one foot to put her shoes on outside the training room.

Dante grunted an affirmative.

Glancing up at him, she lost her balance. With her finger hooked on the back of the slipper, she couldn't put her foot down, so she threw her free hand out to catch herself but misjudged the distance and smacked it against the wall instead. Wincing, she examined her throbbing knuckle.

Dante dropped to a crouch with an exasperated sigh and curled her fingers over his hand. Discomfort flickered across his face, but his expression cleared as the last of her pain vanished.

"There. *Try* to be careful," he said. "And don't scowl at me for *fixing* you."

"You said it didn't hurt anymore!"

"It *doesn't*. Unless you're injured. When you use my power, I feel *that*." He seemed to realize he was still holding her hand and dropped it.

"Oh. Right. That makes sense. In that case, help me up." She raised her arms, and Dante hauled her to her feet. "Touching is a start, but I need to *use* their gifts, too. You saw what happened with Kaleb."

Dante smirked.

She wagged a finger at him. "Not nice."

"I keep telling you I'm not a nice person."

"And I keep telling *you* I don't believe that. Didn't you take this job because I *cried?*"

"That makes me a sucker, not a saint." Dante rubbed his stubbled chin. "And it wasn't the only reason. If there's anywhere to find the information I'm looking for, it's here."

"Is *that* why you were creeping around the night of the gala?"

Sheepishly, Dante tugged his ear. "Guilty."

He no longer trusted anyone to bring food without poisoning it, so they stopped by the kitchen on their way up. Covered dishes wafting steam behind him, Dante took the lead, and Alessa hurried after, her mouth watering at the aroma of garlic and pancetta.

"How am I supposed to practice the next part, though?" Alessa said as she unlocked her door. "It's like trying to draw something I've never seen."

Dante put the tray on the table, brows drawn together in thought.

"What's that old saying?" Alessa continued. "About blind men and elephants? That's me, trying to sort through a dozen sensations in the half second I experience them without killing someone at the same time."

"It feels different when you're trying to *use* someone's power, though, right?"

"Sort of. It's like absorbing a gift is my default—with them, at least—and I have to actively *stop* myself. With you, it's not as . . . insistent? Wait, that's not true. In the alley, it hit hard."

"Because you were dying. You needed my power." Dante divided up the plates and arranged silverware as Alessa fetched a chilled bottle of limoncello. "Not sure how to work on that, since you aren't hurt."

The first taste of pasta distracted her momentarily, but she was a dog with a bone, and even the most enticing meal couldn't deter her for long.

"If I broke my thumb—"

"Do *not* injure yourself. Eat."

"I can only practice with a *healing* gift if I'm hurt."

"No. I'm not enabling this."

She kicked the table leg, but only scuffed the toe of her slipper.

"Broken toe?" Dante said in a monotone.

"Unfortunately not." She narrowed her eyes before lunging for his belt.

"What are you—" Dante danced out of her reach. "Do *not* stab yourself!"

"I'll just prick my finger."

He scorched her with a glare. "I'll let you bleed to death."

"No, you won't. Give it to me."

He slapped her hand away and stepped behind the table. She feinted left, jumped right, and her skirt caught on the corner of the end table. Dante stopped it from tipping, but a small statue tumbled over the edge and landed directly on her foot, its sharp corner breaking the skin.

Half laughing, half crying, Alessa pressed her other foot on top of the injured one. "There," she said through gritted teeth. "I'm hurt anyway. I win."

He gave her a flat stare. "Congratulations."

"Like it or not, we're doing this."

For once, he accepted defeat. "Remember, ease—"

Distracted by the blood dripping onto the carpet, she took his hands.

The pain blinked out, the wound sealed, and Alessa was left open-mouthed and breathless while Dante rubbed his temples.

"Are you okay?" she asked. "Sit down so you don't fall."

Dante waved a hand as though to protest, took a halting step forward, and reached out to steady himself. Careful not to touch his bare skin, Alessa guided him to the settee. Dante sat and blinked repeatedly, his eyes unfocused. "I'm fine. Just dizzy."

"I'm sorry."

"Stop being sorry. Just ease into it next time."

"Are you sure you're all right?"

He was, apparently, because he spotted her hand inching toward his knife and trapped her wrist. "I'm not letting you injure yourself."

"Then how am I supposed to practice?"

"I'll think of something."

"A paper cut?"

He dropped his head in his hands.

After a few rounds of what Alessa dubbed "touch training," Dante sprawled in his go-to armchair with a history of ghiotte hunting while Alessa tried her best not to disturb him with her pacing.

Dante's eyes flicked to her, heavy-lidded with annoyance. "Go to sleep."

"I'm not tired." Her body, her business. Sleeping was the last thing she wanted to do. She wanted to celebrate. Or something. There'd been no paper cuts or other injuries in the past few hours, since Dante swore he'd quit if she even thought about injuring herself again, so she'd focused on fine-tuning the flow of power instead. Less effective than using his gift, but it meant hours studying his reactions until she could read his comfort by the tension in his hands, the size of his pupils. She was learning about her power by studying him. And she wanted more.

More of *Dante*.

His friendship. His secrets. His feelings. His touch.

"Read a book or something, will you?" Dante rolled his shoulders back.

"I can't. I'm too wound up." For the first time in years, she could *touch* without hurting someone, and every moment she didn't, she thought about doing so. Any kind of touch. All kinds. The brush of a hand, a hug, a shoulder to rest her head on. And other touches, the kind she had no memories of, but wanted.

Like an animal emerging from hibernation, ravenous and focused on one overriding need, she couldn't stop craving what she'd been denied for so long.

"I give up." Dante marked his page with a dagger bookmark. "I can't concentrate with you flapping around the room."

"I'm not *flapping*." Alessa pressed her hands to her side to stop them from—*dammit*—flapping. She wouldn't be greedy. She could live with a platonic friendship—maybe—if she could curl up in his arms and be reminded she was still a person beneath the Finestra. He'd be gone in a few days, and she was a coward.

Even a normal girl couldn't casually ask a boy to—what? Cuddle? Hold hands for reasons less pure than saving the world?

"I've never heard anyone sigh so loud in my life," Dante groaned.

She flushed. "I'm sorry. It's become a bad habit."

"Sighing?"

"Pacing. I've never been good at settling myself."

"How hard can it be? Stop moving, fall asleep."

"Maybe for you. My father used to have to pin me in a full-body bind to get me to stop wiggling so I'd sleep."

"That checks out." Dante rubbed his temples. "Just come here, already, and put me out of my misery."

"Very funny. I *can't* kill you, remember?"

"I'm not asking you to *kill* me. I'm not good for much, but I *am* a warm body. I have a book I wanted to finish anyway."

Her heart leapt, but her feet didn't move.

Dante dropped his chin with a look of eternal suffering. "Offer expires in ten seconds."

She hurried over.

He was so big, there wasn't much room left on the oversized chair. Dante waved at the triangle of open space between his thighs and made a spinning motion with his finger, like she was the world's hardest to train puppy.

Alessa perched on the edge of the chair, hands folded in her lap. "Stop *thinking* so loud," she said, glad she couldn't see his face. "I can hear you laughing at me in your head."

"You look like you're sitting on a bed of nails."

Alessa crossed her arms. "I haven't done this in a while."

"Done what?"

"*Snuggled. Cuddled.* Whichever word you use."

"I don't use *either* of those words."

"Wolves don't cuddle?"

"Not when the lady wolf's all stiff and cranky. That'll get you bitten."

He hooked her waist and hauled her back to lean against his chest, shifting her until she was where he wanted her. His other arm came around her. To hold his book.

"Will you relax? I can't see over your head when you're so stiff."

She forced herself to unclench so he could tuck her head beneath his chin, but she was too distracted by the rise and fall of his chest to see anything but squiggles on the page.

"Will you read for a bit?" she asked.

"I *am* reading."

"Out loud. I like your voice, and it's been a long time since someone read me a bedtime story."

His arms tightened around her as he flipped back to the first page. "On a faraway island, in a long-lost sea, the moon and the sun refused to share . . ."

He tensed as she arched her back slightly and found a more comfortable position. He probably wished she'd go away. But his next exhalation was deeper, more relaxed, so she didn't offer to leave.

A muscular chest wasn't the softest surface she'd ever lounged on, but she could get used to it. Lulled by the whiskey-warmth of his voice, her eyes fluttered shut as the story unfolded behind her eyelids. A star-crossed pair of lovers, a tragic war in the heavens.

His heat seeped through her nightclothes, warming her to the core, and she drifted into the sweetness of half-sleep.

"Did you just melt?" Dante asked in a droll tone.

"Don't flatter yourself."

He coughed a laugh. "Not like *that*. Just didn't know a person could go so limp."

"Yeah, well, it's been a while."

"Sorry you're stuck with me, then. I'm new to this whole . . . cuddling . . . thing."

She patted his arm with a perky, "You're doing fine."

"You're desperate, and I'm here, eh?"

"Exactly." She paused. "Thank you."

"At your service, Finestra." He yawned in her ear. "Now, *please* go to bed."

Thirty-Two

Per piccola cagione pigliasi il lupo il montone.
With a small excuse, the wolf seizes the sheep.

DAYS BEFORE DIVORANDO: 16

Alessa had never truly appreciated Renata as a warrior, but when the former Finestra tapped Dante to be her sparring partner for demonstrations, Alessa and the Fontes were spellbound with awe.

Round they went, trading thrusts and parries, both agile and light on their feet, unflinching despite the clang of steel on steel. They were breathtaking.

"Truce!" Renata called out with a laugh. Hair falling loose from its bun, she grinned with exhilaration at having a worthy opponent at last, and Alessa felt a pang of affection and camaraderie for the woman who'd once been a girl facing a Divorando of her own. "Dante, I'm leaving you in charge. They need to work on—well, everything."

Dante forgot to maintain his grumpy detachment when Josef

mastered a knife thrust, and Nina blocked a swing with her bo. He even cracked a smile when Saida pranced around the room in celebration of hitting a bull's-eye.

"Hey, cut it out, Nina!" Kaleb shouted, his sword drooping like a wilted flower under Nina's sweetly innocent gaze.

Alessa couldn't participate in hand-to-hand combat, but she took mental notes while Dante coached Kamaria and Saida. And everyone stopped what they were doing when Dante called on Kaleb to be his sparring partner.

"No weapons," Dante said. "No boots. No groin, no eyes. I don't want to kill you today, but I will if you try something dirty."

Evenly matched in height and weight if not skill, Dante and Kaleb circled each other, looking more relaxed than either had in days. For all his spoiled laziness, Kaleb had paid attention, and he blocked a few of Dante's maneuvers before Dante turned up the heat.

He hooked Kaleb's leg, and Kaleb hit the ground, hard.

Alessa leapt out of the way as they rolled across the floor in a sweaty tangle of limbs.

"Get him, get him, get him," Saida muttered.

Josef nudged Nina with his elbow, looking a bit miffed about how intently she watched the match.

"What?" Nina gave an innocent shrug, her bright eyes fixed on the two men grappling with each other. "It's educational."

With a laugh, Kaleb tapped out, and the combatants sprawled on their backs, chests heaving.

"Good fight, man." Kaleb punched Dante on the shoulder.

The others left, sweaty and laughing, as Alessa and Dante hung back, gathering their discarded training weapons.

Settling a sabre in its mount, she wiped her forehead. "How

did you learn sword fighting, hand-to-hand-combat, knife skills, *and* spear-throwing if you read all day?"

"You can learn a lot from books." Dante scooped a discarded bo from the floor. "After I ran away, I worked for anyone willing to teach me. I learn fast. It's a gift, I guess."

A smile spread across Alessa's face. "I have an idea."

Dante stilled. "I don't like it."

"You don't know what it is."

"Based on your last idea, I'm *confident* I won't like it." Dante held his saber behind his back as she stepped closer. "Step away from the saber."

"I'm not going to hurt myself," Alessa said. "Fight me. Hand-to-hand combat."

"You're half my size."

She poked him in the gut. "I am a *warrior*."

"A *magical* warrior. You don't know how to wrestle, much less against someone bigger and stronger."

Alessa smiled. "But *you* do. You even called it a *gift*."

"You want to use *my* talents against me?"

"No. I want to *magnify* them and *destroy* you."

He dropped to a crouch and beckoned her forward. "Come and get me."

Alessa gave an excited hop, then stripped off her gloves and raised her fists.

"Good grief," he said. "Completely wrong."

He unwrapped her fingers, positioning her thumb correctly.

The moment stretched as they stood there, face to face, her fists in his, until her entire body seemed to vibrate at some inaudible frequency that she didn't know if he could sense, too.

"Do you feel anything?" she asked. Someone had to speak. She felt all sorts of things, but most had nothing to do with fighting.

"Maybe?" He appeared so calm, so cool, she could have screamed. "But I don't know what you're getting from me."

Time to channel her pent-up energy for good use. "Let's find out." Bracing her feet, she brought her fists up.

Dante swung at half speed.

She blocked it without a thought, reflexes that weren't her own taking charge of her body.

"Oh, this is fun!" Alessa bared her teeth.

Dante danced back with an exaggerated look of fear. Round and round, they circled. She sized him up with impunity, taking stock of his balance, weight, unprotected parts.

Hopping on the balls of his feet, Dante waited with the patience of someone watching a toddler attempt their first steps. Cocky. Sure of his superiority. Underestimating her. Underestimating *himself*, really. It was his gift, after all.

She darted forward and jabbed him in the gut.

He coughed. "I'm not sure I like this."

"I do." She swung again and clipped his side. "Ugh. It's fading."

"Not so fun now, huh?"

Her next punch was so weak he caught her fist midair. She grinned. How quickly he forgot.

"Thanks," she said, and in one fluid motion, twisted free, grasped his wrist, and spun around, wrenching his arm behind him.

Dante dropped to his knees with a sound somewhere between a grunt and a laugh. "This isn't fair."

"Life isn't fair." As long as she had regular contact with his skin, she was skilled, but a minute or two without, and it faded, leaving her woefully outmatched.

Better to win a short fight than lose a long one. Forcing him facedown on the mat, she put one knee on his back and the other on the ground.

"I win!" She raised her arms in triumph and then tumbled forward as he rolled over, throwing her off balance. She landed on top of him, chest to chest, legs tangled.

"Not over yet." He pinned her arms, avoiding her bare hands, and grinned as she squirmed. The last glimmer of his gift faded to nothing, and she stopped fighting, breathing heavy. Every inhale pressed her chest into his.

She could count his eyelashes, see the flare of awareness as he realized what she already had about their position.

She panicked.

Dante startled as she planted a quick kiss on his cheek. The brief touch of her lips to his skin revived her gift, and she neatly rolled out of his grasp. A total failure as far as flirtation went, but an effective gambit in a fight.

Flinging himself sideways, Dante grabbed her ankle and tugged her toward him.

She slapped at his hands, making him laugh, but it was enough contact to revive her.

"I'm not even using"—he grunted as they rolled around— "Ow! Half the things I know—" He caught her knee before it reached its target. "Because I don't want to hurt—urggg."

She got him in a headlock—or at least she was pretty sure that's what it was called—and squeezed until he turned an alarming shade of red and smacked the ground repeatedly, then slapped her arm.

"Oh, sorry!" She let go with a chipper smile. "I forgot the signal."

His head in her lap, Dante wheezed. "Congratulations. You win. With my skills. So really, I win."

She opened her mouth to refute his claim, but the sneaky bastard sprang into action, getting her on her back with an absurdly complicated maneuver she'd have to ask him to demonstrate later.

Straddling her hips, he pinned her arms above her head and smiled down at her. "Gotcha."

Someone shrieked.

They snapped their heads toward the doorway where the Fontes stood, slack-jawed and horrified at the sight of their divine savior pinned beneath her bodyguard.

Kaleb grabbed a four-hundred-year-old sword from the wall and pointed it at Dante. "Release the Finestra or I'll kill you."

Thirty-Three

Bocca chiusa non prende mosche.
A closed mouth catches no flies.

DAYS BEFORE DIVORANDO: 16

Dante let go of Alessa's wrists—as if *that* was the biggest issue with their current position—and they scrambled to their feet.

"I—he—we tripped," she said.

Kaleb lowered the sword a fraction. "He's not trying to kill you?"

"No. Definitely not," she said. Kaleb's protectiveness would have warmed her heart if he wasn't about to murder Dante. "We just, um, fell."

"Really?" Kamaria said. "You *tripped*. And landed like that."

Saida slapped a hand over her mouth, but couldn't stop a high-pitched squeak.

Kamaria rolled her eyes. "You've been living without parents for too long if you think anyone would believe that."

"You were *touching him*," Nina said. "And he was *smiling*."

Well, that sounded worse than she probably meant it to.

Saida wiped tears of laughter from her eyes, but she was the only one amused. Nina looked like she'd been slapped, Josef wore the outrage of a Temple monk who'd wandered into the women's baths by accident, and Kaleb still looked furious.

"Why were you touching him?" Kaleb said. "And why did he like it?"

Alessa's mouth worked, but no brilliance came to mind. "It was a grimace of pain."

"That's not what *I* saw," Nina said.

"He's a fighter. He's tough." A half-truth.

It didn't seem to appease them. Time for something slightly closer to the truth.

"Dante's been helping me practice with my power."

"Why?" Kaleb demanded.

Dante cleared his throat. "Any sacrifice for the good of Saverio. Dea calls, I answer."

Alessa subtly stepped on his foot.

Nina's eyes narrowed. "I didn't realize you were devout."

"More importantly, how?" Kamaria said, studying Dante in a way that made Alessa uncomfortable. "He doesn't have a gift."

"No, of course not." Alessa knew she was protesting too vehemently, but she couldn't rein it in. "But I *can* absorb other talents while he gives feedback on . . . pain levels. Like a, um, a pain gauge."

Nina cocked her head. "I would have thought a Finestra's touch would be even worse for a regular person. That's a really generous sacrifice to make."

"Decent of you." Kaleb rested the sword on the ground. "But you're still an ass."

Dante muttered something in the old language, and Alessa smiled brightly. "Well, now that we've settled that, I hope we can all agree to keep this quiet. I mean, it's a little unorthodox, but hey, anything that helps, right?"

She bit her cheek as she waited, but the grudging acceptance on their faces didn't slide back into anger.

"We came to invite you to join our game." Nina said, sounding more confrontational than usual.

"Oh," Alessa said, momentarily thrown. "And you've changed your mind?"

Kamaria rolled her eyes. "No. I mean, who here *hasn't* been caught while . . . eh, practicing . . . before, hmm?"

Alessa's cheeks flamed. "I—Thank you. We'd love to."

Josef was a brilliant card player, but a terrible loser. With a near-mystical ability to remember who held every card and strategize accordingly, he'd won the first three rounds, sitting straighter with every victory, unable to hide his utter delight, but he'd been sulking since Kaleb swiped his best card. Nina, on the other hand, was terrible at the game but cheered for everyone, regardless of which team they were on or whether their victory came at her expense.

Kaleb rolled the dice. "Stop being so *happy* every time I beat you, Nina. It really takes the fun out of it."

Nina fluffed her skirts with an impish grin. "That's why I do it."

"I fold," said Saida with a heavy sigh. "Josef stole all my best cards. Again."

Alessa selected a card with Crollo on it from the top of the pile and added it to her hand, then looked over her shoulder at Dante, who'd opted out of the game, insisting he was on the job.

He craned his neck to see her hand, scratched his nose with two fingers, and pointedly looked at Kaleb.

Alessa cleared her throat with a delicate cough. "I believe it is *my* turn, Kaleb. Not yours. And before I roll, I would like to steal a card."

Kaleb grumbled as he flicked the card in question across the table. "You said you'd never played before. How are you so good already?"

Alessa bit her lip, placing a pair of Dea and Crollo cards on the table. "Blessed by the gods, I suppose."

Dante shifted from one foot to the other.

Kaleb's eyes narrowed. "Wait a minute. Are you two conspiring?"

Saida groaned. "You can't accuse everyone of cheating because you're losing, Kaleb."

"I'm not accusing *everyone*, just the Finestra."

"Maybe you should write down a recipe instead of being a poor loser. I'm still waiting on your contribution to my project."

Kaleb made a face. "I told you, I don't know how to bake. Desserts show up in my house and I don't ask questions."

A young woman in an apron rapped on the door. "Beg your pardon, but the lady's timer went off."

"Oh," Saida said. "My rosogolla is finished cooling!"

Apparently, Saida had charmed her way into the kitchens earlier to make dessert. She returned a minute later with a large pan, and the room filled with the scent of milk and sugar as she began spooning fluffy white balls onto small plates. "I thought we could use a treat."

Kaleb grumbled. "A clever distraction so you can peek at our cards."

"Whose recipe is this, Saida?" Josef bumped Kaleb's chair, looking a bit *too* innocent, on his way to help Saida pass out plates.

Saida grinned. "This one is from my own family. Good, isn't it?"

It was. Sweet and slightly sticky, with the faintest hint of something floral. "Is there rosewater in this?" Alessa asked.

"Nice catch." Saida looked impressed. "Dante, do you have any special family recipes you'd be willing to share?"

A series of emotions flickered across Dante's face before he shook his head.

"Get up." Kamaria gestured for Kaleb to swap seats with her, so she could sit beside Alessa.

"I swear, Kamaria," Kaleb said. "If you touch my cards, I'm claiming your winnings."

"Man-child," Kamaria shot back.

As Josef explained the mechanics of card counting, while swearing he'd never actually cheat because he had morals, Kamaria leaned close to Alessa. "Nina may be as gullible as a goldfish, but I'm not."

Alessa coughed. "Huh?"

Kamaria licked her finger. "Your little wrestling match with Signor Crankypants. I mean, you *are* getting better, so I believe that he's helping you with your power—but he was *enjoying* your hands on him, and he shouldn't have been. Sorry. That came out harsh. Not your fault you pack a punch. But . . . why is he different?"

Alessa held her gaze. "He's helping us. Does it matter?"

Kamaria seemed to consider. "Fair enough. But be careful. If I'm wondering, someone else might, too."

After an hour in Dante's arms the night before, Alessa was addicted. She stalled on her way to bed, watching Dante fold his shirt and stretch out on the couch, hands behind his head.

At her sigh, his eyelashes fluttered as though she'd ruffled them from afar.

Alessa walked toward her bed. Stopped. Turned back. Sighed again.

"Will you get over here already?" Dante said, his voice thick with sleep.

She popped back out. "I thought you were going to sleep. Did you change your mind?"

"No. But if the only way *you'll* go to sleep is near a warm body, then cut to the chase and come here. Don't worry. I'll keep my hands to myself."

Of course. He'd scoff at every other rule of polite society, but when it came to touching her, he'd be a saint. She wasn't about to give him a chance to change his mind, though.

"Sheesh, you really don't know how to do this—" Dante made a show of grumbling as he arranged her in front of him, but soon they were snuggled together like spoons in a drawer.

She shivered as his breath tickled the nape of her neck.

"Cold?"

"A little," she said, hoping he didn't notice her voice squeak.

He snagged a blanket draped over the back of the couch and draped it over her.

She could have offered her bed, but inviting Dante there felt like an entirely different proposition than lying beside him on a couch, so she kept quiet. Plus, the couch was narrow, which meant she had to be close to him or she'd fall off. A perfect excuse to get closer. She shifted, wiggling her hips, and her bottom snuggled up—

Oh. Maybe wiggling was dangerous. She would *not* wiggle. No wiggling. Not even a little wiggle. She wouldn't move at all. She'd stay still and try not to feel anything. Or . . . try to feel everything. *Without* wiggling.

She stared into the darkness, wondering if he was as aware of her as she was of him. Or if he was regretting the invitation. But eventually, his warmth and the steady beat of his heart dragged her under.

She floated, mired in the space between light and dark, thoughts and dreams. A blanket on the sand, a calloused palm brushing across her rib cage. With lips like his, Dante had to know a thing or two about kissing.

He made a low sound deep in his throat, and her eyes flew open.

She was either asleep and having the best dream ever, or he was asleep and—his hips moved, pressing against her, and her cheeks flamed—*he* was asleep and having a *very* nice dream. Or . . . they were both awake, and he wanted to see if she was interested in *not* sleeping. Which she was, but she hadn't responded, so he might think she was saying no.

His breath tickled her ear, and she lost track of her thoughts. *Breathe*, she reminded herself.

His lips brushed the sensitive spot just below her ear, kindling a fire below her navel. Her thoughts scrambled as his fingers grazed the underside of her breast. This felt so right—nothing had *ever* felt more right—but Dante had made it clear he planned to keep his hands to himself. Which he most certainly wasn't.

Speak. She opened her mouth, and a whimper slipped out.

Dante wasn't a liar. Which meant he probably wasn't awake.

"Dante?" It came out barely more than a breath.

Try harder, Alessa.

She said his name again. Louder.

Dante tensed like she'd dumped a bucket of ice on him, then vanished, vaulting over the back of the couch.

"I'm sorry," he gasped. "I don't know what happened. How long—I mean, how many—No, don't answer that. My fault. Not yours. This is my fault."

Something crumbled inside her at the horror on his face.

Why had she expected anything else?

"Dante, it's fine."

He raked a hand through his hair. "It is *not fine.*"

"You were asleep." She hugged her knees to her chest.

He let out a string of curses. "It doesn't matter. It's *not* okay. I'll leave right now, and you'll never see me again." He began gathering his things, leaving a trail of dropped items behind him.

She clenched her fingers. "It was my fault."

"It's *your* fault I groped you?" He shook his head. "No."

"I didn't wake you. Not right away." A mortified heat crept up her neck. She'd melted under his touch, while he'd been dreaming of someone else, and she couldn't even salvage her pride by denying it, or he'd leave, consumed by guilt.

He bent to retrieve a dropped sock. "You can't blame yourself for panicking, waking up with someone pawing at you—"

"Dante, I wasn't asleep!"

He froze so long she thought the silence might shatter.

"I—I thought, maybe you were awake, too." Alessa hugged her arms to her chest, which felt about to cave in. "I'm sorry. It was wrong. *I* was wrong."

Dante sighed so deeply his lungs had to be completely empty. "I told you I'd keep my hands to myself."

"You were *asleep.* I wasn't. Blame *me.*"

"It was *my*—"

"Can we just agree we both screwed up and promise never to touch each other again without making sure it's okay first?"

He looked at the door.

"Dante, if you disappear, I'll have to tell them why you left. *Please* don't make me do that."

He didn't want her, but she didn't want him to go.

He bit his lip. "I'm still sorry."

Not as sorry as she was.

Thirty-Four

Molti che vogliono l'albero fingono di rifiutare il frutto.
Many desire the tree who pretend to refuse the fruit.

DAYS BEFORE DIVORANDO: 15

Dante and Alessa ignored each other as much as two people could while trapped in close proximity, but the morning was so tense she was eager to start training. Nothing like a day of torturing friends to get a girl's mind off the sting of rejection.

For their last day of training before Carnevale, however, Crollo blessed Saverio with a blistering heat wave, and the temperature plus the looming deadline meant tempers were short when she arrived in the training room.

The room grew stifling as the temperature ticked higher by the minute. Alessa and Josef teamed up to cool the room, but he couldn't withstand her efforts long enough to provide much relief, and Saida's attempt to cool everyone merely buffeted them with air so thick it felt like being thumped by a hot blanket.

"I can't take a whole day of this." Kaleb groaned. "It's like try-ing to breathe boiling water."

"There's nowhere to go," Kamaria said. "The whole island is scorching."

"There's the *ocean*," Kaleb said.

"We can't go to the beach," Alessa said. "We need to practice, and they're all crowded."

"Not *every* beach," Dante said. He shrugged. "I know a place."

Alessa should have objected, or at least hesitated, before agree-ing, but the thought of spending their final training session together on a beach instead of the stuffy training room was too tempting.

An hour later, a train of lanterns bobbed through a tunnel growing dustier the farther they went.

Kamaria hung back with Alessa as they neared the far side of the island and got their first taste of fresh air. "So, did that wrestling match continue in your room last night? Tell me ev-erything."

Alessa laughed nervously.

"Not *everything*. I'm not asking why he's different. But since he *is* . . . did he kiss you?"

Alessa bit the inside of her cheek. "No."

"But he wants to." Kamaria lowered her voice as they caught up to the others.

"That's the problem. He doesn't."

"Oh, please," Kamaria said. "That boy wants you so bad his pants might catch fire."

Alessa shielded her face against a sudden glare of sunlight as Kaleb and Dante wrenched open the rusted gate at the end of the tunnel. "I mean, if that's the only way to get them off."

At Kamaria's burst of laughter, Dante turned back, glowering.

Alessa blushed as Kamaria leaned so close her lips nearly brushed her ear. "And *that*, kid, is what jealousy looks like."

Alessa stifled a laugh, hoping the sudden change in lighting was enough to disguise her fluster.

"Watch your step," Dante called back. He kicked a rock to prop the gate open, then another for good measure.

By the time Alessa and Kamaria stepped onto the narrow ledge beyond the gate, Kaleb was half-running, half-tumbling down the narrow steps carved into the cliffside, sending rocks clattering ahead, while Josef, Nina, and Saida followed more carefully.

When Alessa had asked Dante to name the most beautiful place he'd ever seen, this had been his answer. Now, it was hers, too. The beach below was a natural harbor, a triangular slice carved from the coastline, framed by high cliffs. Cerulean water kissed white sand in a spray of prosecco bubble waves below a few determined trees and shrubs hugging the cliffside. Where the cliffs notched, grass carpeted a small clearing, perfect for a cozy beach cottage where a girl could watch for a rowboat silhouetted against the sunset.

Dante glanced back at Alessa walking beside Kamaria. "Need help?"

"We're fine," Alessa said. "Help Saida."

Saida's diaphanous skirts kept catching on the rocks, and her efforts to save them put her a little too close to the edge. Dante gave Saida his arm to help her the rest of the way down.

"If Dante's jealous," Alessa asked Kamaria when he was out of earshot, "why did he jump off the couch last night when we were finally getting somewhere?"

"Oh ho," Kamaria chortled. "Now *we're* getting somewhere. Details? No? Ugh, you're no fun."

Alessa removed her shoes when they reached the sand and sat in a patch of shade beneath a withered lemon tree, while Kaleb ran straight into the ocean, fully dressed, sending arcs of water flying. Nina gleefully dragged Josef, hopping on one leg as he tried to roll up his pants, toward the water.

Kamaria took her time, disrobing without a hint of self-consciousness, as she continued their conversation.

"Broken and angry isn't for everyone," she said, pulling her shirt over her head. Alessa tried to focus on the girl's face, fiercely aware that hers was going pink. "If you aren't willing to wait for him to sort his shit out,"—her belt hit the sand—"there are easier relationships out there for a sweet, innocent thing like you."

Alessa scrunched her nose. "It's not innocence so much as lack of opportunity."

Kamaria shimmied out of her pants. "Well, if grumpy boy doesn't work out—"

"Hey," Dante hollered. "Are you two coming in?"

Alessa lifted her chin. "A Finestra doesn't get to run around half-naked."

"Suit yourself." He pulled his shirt over his head, muscles rippling across his back as he bent to remove his shoes.

Alessa snapped her mouth shut when she realized it was hanging open.

Kamaria exhaled loudly. "Did it just get hotter out here?"

"I can't tell." Alessa dropped her head to her knees. "I hit my melting point a while ago."

"I bet you did." The bronze curve of Kamaria's hips swayed with every step as she strutted toward the waves, calling over her shoulder, "We might not be alive in a month, so whatever you want, get it now."

Alone on the sand, sweat dripping down her spine, Alessa watched the others frolic.

Saida gathered her skirts to her knees, only to get stuck in the crossfire of a furious splash fight between Kamaria and Kaleb.

As Saida chased them through the shallows, Alessa peeled off her leggings. She'd had most of her skirts altered to cross higher in the front, because she looked frumpy wearing tights while everyone else had bare legs. Without them, her dress was borderline scandalous. Or it would be in the city. Here, with Kamaria leaping from rocks in her undergarments and Nina frolicking in a shift, Alessa felt like the prudiest of prudes.

It was already the hottest, most awkward day of her life, so with a shrug, Alessa unfastened her skirt and used it as a package for her leggings, blouse, and gloves. In only a silk slip, she stood to bask in the sunlight, skin tingling with the promise of a future sunburn, hot sand shifting beneath the tender soles of her feet.

Like all Saverian children, Alessa had spent much of her childhood bare-bottomed on the shore with salt-stiffened hair and sand in every crevice. She'd never been on this particular beach, but it felt like coming home.

Dante quickly looked away and dove under when she turned in his direction, pulling himself through the water toward an enormous boulder sticking out in the center of the cove.

Gathering her courage, Alessa paddled out to Dante and pulled herself onto the rock. "How long are we giving each other the silent treatment?"

He kept his gaze on the horizon. "I think I can keep it up for two more days."

"I'm sure you can." She hugged her knees to her chest. "I can tell you're upset."

"Yeah. I am."

Right. Excellent. Glad she'd brought it up, then. "Well, I'm sorry. I'm sure it was disappointing to wake up and find me, when you were probably hoping for the girl with the magic hands."

"What?" He dragged a hand through his hair. "I never said I was disappointed. You thought I was thinking of *someone else?*"

Wait. "You were dreaming about *me?*" He didn't deny it. "And you were *enjoying* that dream?" Her mind flashed back to the feel of his body pressed against hers.

His cheekbones darkened. "Think the evidence was pretty clear."

"Then why did you flip out when I told you I wanted you?"

"Because you *don't*. You're desperate, and I'm your only option. That's what you said, remember?"

"Dante, that was a *joke*."

"Doesn't mean it's not true. Pretty soon you'll be the most beloved person in Saverio, and I'll be back on the docks with the rest of the trash. I know stale bread's better than nothing when you're starving, but you'll be much happier if you hold out for a real meal."

"You are not *stale bread*," she said. "And I can make my own decisions."

"Yeah, well, you hired me to look out for you until you get a Fonte. I'm not going to let you do something you'll regret."

"You patronizing son of a . . . Get up," she said through gritted teeth.

Dante stood and crossed his arms, staring down his nose at her.

"Do I have permission to touch your chest?" she asked.

He frowned. "Why?"

"So I can shove your stubborn ass into the ocean."

"You're asking permission to drown me?"

"No. I'm asking permission to *touch* you. If I kill you, it will be entirely without your consent."

"You know," Dante said, in the tone of a patient teacher. "Someday you'll thank me—"

He hit the water with a splash she hoped left his backside stinging for hours.

When the brutal sun went down and the air cooled to a tolerable temperature, they settled in a circle around a fire Kamaria had made with driftwood. Using her gift, she coaxed the lavender flames to dance while Saida sent a targeted breeze to fan them, and Nina passed out a picnic dinner.

Kaleb jutted his chin at Dante. "What happens if you touch us *while* touching him?"

Kamaria snickered. "I didn't sign up for that kind of thing, but hey, two for the price of one."

Kaleb made a gagging face at Kamaria before turning back to Alessa. "You said he's like a gauge or whatever. So, grab on and use your handy-dandy power detector to dampen the power while we're practicing. Makes more sense than doing it when you're alone."

"Depends on your goals," Kamaria muttered.

Alessa kicked sand at her foot.

Any other day, she'd jump at the excuse to take Dante's hand, but he could barely look at her.

"Might as well," Saida said. "Anything's worth a try if it might help, right?"

Nina hugged her knees. "I'll do anything that will lower the odds of people dying."

"Dante?" Alessa asked tightly.

Grumbling, he walked to the center of their circle.

Staring past Alessa's shoulder instead of directly at her, he extended one hand to her and raised his other hand, thumb out to the side. His meter, she assumed.

Her heart lurched as his palm slid across hers, and his thumb turned to the ceiling.

Saida giggled, and Alessa couldn't help but smile.

Dante's thumb arced down.

"I guess laughter is good." Josef said. "It *is* sort of funny."

In a *tragic* way.

Pretending both hands she held were Josef's, Alessa focused on sensing her power. Dante was a meter, nothing else. A weather vane with long eyelashes. A rain gauge with a tumble of dark hair over chocolate-brown eyes with tiny flecks of gold around the irises. A thermometer with—

Her thermometer hissed. "Damn, that's cold."

"I'm okay," Josef said, a bit strained.

Alessa gathered the strands of power, turning her sights on the waves lapping at the shore. She held while the power built, then released.

Nina shrieked with delight as the closest waves froze into a crystalline sculpture.

"That was good!" Kamaria looked around at everyone. "Right? That seemed good."

By the time night fell, Alessa was ready to head back, but the others wanted one last swim, so she and Dante entered the tunnels alone.

She didn't want to be angry at him. She wanted to drink him in, to memorize his face.

But it was dark, and she could barely see him anyway.

Dante stared at the gate from the Fortezza to the Cittadella. "If we lock it behind us, they can't get back in."

"Then don't lock it," Alessa said.

"I'm not leaving an open gate below the Cittadella. That's, like, bodyguard rule number one." He scowled at her through his hair.

"Okay, then we'll stay close by and let them in when they return." She studied him. "I could give you a trim while we wait. I used to cut my brother's hair and I've been doing mine for years. You want to look nice for my wedding, don't you?"

His lips twisted. "Go ahead, Finestra. *Try* to make me presentable."

Alessa led Dante to the empty kitchens, where she found a pair of shears, and ordered Dante to sit. Standing behind him, she mused about studying the texture as an excuse to run her fingers through his hair, the sheer indulgent pleasure striking like the rush of a double espresso hitting her bloodstream.

Thick, tousled strands curled around her fingers, as though they wanted to hold on. With a slow drag, she lightly scraped her nails down to his nape, and he shivered.

"I used to love having my hair played with." She let the smile color her voice. "Don't you find it so relaxing?"

Dante cleared his throat and said roughly, "Sure. Relaxing."

She took her time, starting in the back and working her way around to the front, where he watched her tug the long curls straight to be sure they were even. The heel of her palm rested on his cheek as she bent closer to get a better look.

His eyes flicked down to her loose neckline, and he swallowed. He probably had a view clear down to her navel with the loose blouse she'd chosen. He might insist on punishing them both by keeping his hands to himself, but she didn't have to make it easy for him.

Pursing her lips, she leaned in for another snip. If the only part of him she could claim was his attention, she wasn't about to let go.

He shifted in his seat. "Are you finished?"

"Not quite," she said. "I enjoy having you at my mercy."

Desperation flashed in his eyes. "Do you have to make this so hard?"

She bit her lip. "I'm *trying* to make it hard."

A muscle ticked in his jaw. "I can never decide if you're trying to sound crude or if it's unintentional."

"Oh, it's *always* intentional. That's the *only* thing I learned from all those romantic novels that I actually get to put into practice." She put down the shears. "There. You're gorgeous, damn you."

Golden brown eyes searched hers, but she didn't look away.

"You know," she said, choosing her words carefully, "the first time I saw you in that ring, I thought you were the most terrifyingly beautiful person I'd ever seen, and I didn't even *like* you at that point. I wanted you long before I knew you were an option, and I know this isn't the right time, but after Divorando—"

"After Divorando, you'll have your pick." He looked unhappy but resigned.

"And what if I picked you?" She held her breath.

"You won't. You'll find someone like your first Fonte, and that's not me."

"No. You're nothing like Emer. He was sweet and kind and

gentle and the girl who chose him wanted all those things. She never thought she'd go through what I have, but that girl didn't stand a chance of surviving. Maybe she wouldn't have fallen for someone like you, but I'm not *her* anymore—"

Boom.

Dante stood. "What was that?"

Alessa put the shears in her pocket. "I don't know, but it doesn't sound good."

Dante grabbed the first soldier who ran past. "What's happening?"

The soldier swallowed, throat bobbing. "A mob, at the gates. Demanding to see the Finestra."

Thirty-Five

Le rose cascano, le spine restano.
The roses fall, and the thorns remain.

DAYS BEFORE DIVORANDO: 15

They couldn't wait one more day?" Dante said.

The soldier flinched at his anger.

"Let him go, Dante. It's not his fault." With salt-stiffened hair and sand in every fold of her skirt, Alessa was a mess and in no state to speak to a crowd, but there wasn't time to change.

The booms grew louder the closer they got to the front gates, but she didn't stop until she reached the steps before the Cittadella.

"Where is her Fonte?" Padre Ivini, his silver hair slicked back, blue eyes gleaming with an unholy light, stood in the center of a roiling crowd in the piazza. "Why the secrecy?"

The crowd parted as people shied away from Alessa's approach.

Ivini stopped. "Ah, *Finestra.*"

Adrick stood in the group behind Ivini in one of those ridiculous robes, and she shot him a venomous glare. Emotion passed across his features—anger, disappointment . . . relief?

"You dare question Dea's choice?" Her voice shook with what she hoped came across as righteous anger.

"No, my lady," Ivini said. "I know exactly what *Crollo* meant in choosing you. His final trick will doom us all if we let it stand. Admit it. Your touch cannot save, only kill."

Panic rose in Alessa's chest as the crowd rustled around them. "Guards, remove this man from the piazza at once."

Captain Papatonis and his guards traded uncertain looks.

"The people are afraid, Finestra," the Captain said. "No one has seen you perform. It might reassure them."

Ivini smiled with satisfaction. "See? Call your Fonte out here and show us, then we'll sleep peacefully in our beds."

Easier said than done. It didn't even matter that she hadn't chosen one yet, because none of the candidates were there.

"The connection between a Finestra and Fonte is sacred." Alessa fumbled for the tenets she'd read a thousand times. "You can't honestly expect me to perform an act of divine intimacy in front of strangers?"

"It's for a good cause," Ivini said with a sly smile.

"Captain." Alessa turned to Papatonis. "You're married. If I gave the order, would you summon your wife here, take off your clothes, and perform your marital duties for all to see?"

Papatonis's face went red. "Of course not."

"Ah, so *you* wouldn't perform an intimate act in public. Interesting. But *I* should?"

Ivini's eyes narrowed. "Lay hands on someone *else*, then. *That's* not sacred."

"Are you volunteering?" It might be worth it to watch him scream, but she struggled enough to control her power when she was calm and prepared. Now, it raged, unpredictable and angry like the rest of her. If she touched Ivini, she'd hurt him or worse, and while she'd love to watch the light dim in his eyes, it might be the last thing she ever saw if the crowd combusted.

"I'll do it." Dante stepped forward.

She forced herself to sneer, as if he and the whole situation were beneath her.

People were watching. Waiting. Her heart thudded.

"Here's a brave soul." Ivini glowed with anticipation. "If your words are true, Finestra, prove it."

Alessa drew the moment out, making sure everyone had a chance to see her examine him, curling her lip in disgust. Then, as though deigning to touch something revolting, she extended her hand toward Dante's.

"Where we can see," Ivini said sweetly.

She rolled her eyes, gratified to earn a few chuckles. With a sigh of feigned irritation, she held up her hands so the crowd could see they were bare, then placed them on both sides of his face.

The crowd held its collective breath. A second passed, and another. With languid boredom, Dante slid his hands in his pockets.

Alessa turned to Ivini. "How long must I stand here before you admit you were wrong?"

Scattered chuckles. Ivini fumed.

Alessa flicked her fingers at Dante in a haughty dismissal. "If we're finished here, I have more important things to do than appease your theories, *Padre*. And I imagine the good people of

Saverio would like to get on with preparations so we can enjoy Carnevale. I look forward to presenting my Fonte to you all tomorrow evening."

The cheer that rose was weak, but they weren't jeering, and Alessa marched back to the Cittadella with her head high.

Dante looked ready to haul her up the stairs when they were safely inside, but she shook her head. "The Fontes. They're still locked out."

As they reached the bottom of the stairs, her legs gave out. Alessa sank against the wall, breath shuddering out of her. She would have slid all the way down, but Dante yanked her into his arms.

"*Dea,*" he breathed into her hair. "I thought they were going to kill you, and I couldn't fight them all—"

But he had.

She dragged his head down and stopped his litany of what-ifs with a kiss.

Dante stilled.

Parting her lips, she traced his lips with her tongue, and his control snapped. His hands were everywhere at once—cupping her face, running through her hair, gripping her waist. He pressed her against the door, pressed his mouth to hers, pressed his hips into her, as if trying to meld his storm of desperation with the tempest raging inside her.

They'd taken a risk, and it had paid off, but Dante's ragged breath said he knew how close they'd come to losing it all.

"Knock, knock," called Kaleb. The gate rattled. "Anybody home?"

Dante dropped his head to Alessa's shoulder with a groan.

He didn't say a word as she let the others in, but Kamaria

eyed Alessa's pink cheeks with a knowing look as they traipsed up the stairs, chattering and laughing. No one else noticed that Dante and Alessa were silent.

At the top, Alessa realized she had to say something. Tomorrow was the last day for all but one.

"I'm so glad I got to know you all," she said with a smile. "The Consiglio will see you in the morning to interview you and make recommendations. I hope—" She swallowed. "I hope someone will volunteer, because I don't want to leave such an important decision to a random drawing or have the Consiglio choose. But no matter what, I'm truly thankful for your hard work, and ... and for your friendship. I can't tell you how much it's meant to me."

Saida sniffed loudly, which set off a round of laughter, and they wished each other a good night.

When the door of her suite clicked closed, Alessa and Dante were alone. Her lips tingled, still swollen from his kiss, as their eyes met.

He pointed at her bed. "Go."

She flushed, her heart pounding.

"Alone." He sat on the couch. "You're so close. Don't let me distract you now."

"I can't change how I feel about you."

"It doesn't matter how we *feel*. Some things aren't possible."

Tomorrow evening, she'd stand on the balcony with her chosen Fonte.

The next day, she'd be wed. And he'd be gone.

Thirty-Six

Al povero mancano tante cose, all'avaro tutte.
A poor man lacks many things, but a greedy man lacks them all.

DAYS BEFORE DIVORANDO: 14

The following day dawned too beautiful to trust. No icy rain or brutal heat, no ominous clouds. In fact, no clouds at all. No breeze, for that matter, but the temperature was too perfect to complain about the stillness, and the world outside Alessa's balcony rang with the sweet twittering of birds beneath an azure sky.

She'd slept alone, in her bed, heart aching to be near him, to cling to their last hours together, but Dante was more cool than usual.

She decided to work innuendo into as many sentences as possible, hoping the challenge of making him laugh would tamp down her anxiety and dread about saying goodbye.

The Fontes would be sequestered with the Consiglio for a grueling series of final interviews. Their strengths and weaknesses would be weighed and measured, and they'd be ranked. After, she'd see who was left and who—if anyone—would volunteer.

She had nothing to do but worry until then. She'd worn her loose white Consiglio gown, in case they called her in, so at least she was comfortable while her insides twisted into knots.

Alessa opted to worry in the gardens, which worked out nicely as Dante had plenty of room to pace. She picked a tiny white flower from a nearby bush and pushed the stem into her high bun, then another.

Kamaria was the most likely to volunteer, and if Alessa was choosing, she'd be her top choice. But the whiff of treason left by Shomari's defection was a variable she couldn't dismiss.

Kaleb wasn't likely to volunteer. Nina was so fragile. Saida's gift was tricky to use. Josef would be a strong battle partner, but in his time at the Cittadella, she'd barely seen him smile. It shouldn't matter, but the thought of facing Divorando without a few laughs was rather depressing.

By the second hour, Alessa had an entire halo of lacy petals around the base of her topknot and had moved on to gathering a bouquet.

"How long is this going to take?" Dante grumbled. "You have pollen in your hair, by the way."

Alessa brushed at it, but she couldn't see the top of her head. "Emer and Ilsi were approved within a half hour, but it took an entire day before the Consiglio cleared Hugo. I thought for sure they were going to send him home and make me choose again."

Dante stopped pacing. "You never talk about him."

"He wasn't the most interesting person. He was so bland that he might as well have been a bowl of vanilla pudding. I chose him because I was tired of killing people I liked."

"Oh. Is today worse or better, then?"

"Both?" she admitted. "I *like* them. All of them. Even Kaleb. I have more control over my power now, but I'm still asking someone to face Armageddon."

A line formed between Dante's eyebrows as he walked over to tilt her chin—down, not up, alas—and blew on her hair, gently de-pollinating her.

"Did you know that *Finestra* is a base word for other words?" She couldn't help herself. "Like *defenestration*."

Dante stopped blowing. "Yes." He sounded wary. Smart of him. "It means to throw someone out of a window."

She snickered. "Or to *break* a window. It's a metaphor for—"

"Don't you dare finish that sentence."

She fluttered her eyelashes in mock innocence. "Deflowering a virgin."

Dante couldn't stop the laugh that burst free. "I want it on the record that I didn't even *touch* your flowers."

"There's still time."

"Is this a side effect of forced purity and years with nothing but novels for entertainment?" He tugged his ear. "All these pent-up naughty thoughts finally taking over?"

"Maybe," she said with a cheeky grin. "Or maybe it reined me in, and I would have been even worse. Can you imagine?"

"Dea help me, I cannot," Dante said, pushing a lock of hair off his forehead. It promptly slipped back, and Alessa reached to brush it away. His jaw went tight. "I need some exercise."

With a sigh, Alessa trudged after him to the outdoor training yard around the side of the building. Dante started raising and lowering himself from a bar, and she strolled closer for a better view.

"Can I help you?" Dante asked.

"I'm sure you *could*."

With a huff, he dropped to the ground for push-ups.

"Ever since you called yourself stale bread, I've had a wicked craving."

He paused, shook his head, then pushed back up.

"I *adore* bread. Especially baguettes. Long, thick, hot and slathered with—"

He hit the ground, shaking with laughter. "Enough. Mercy. You're a champion of lewd baking metaphors."

"I haven't even begun. I grew up in a bakery, you know. Should I detail my obsession with pastries?"

He got to his feet and dusted his palms. "I am *not* a pastry."

"Sure you are. One of those mystery pies that could be savory, but actually has a sweet filling under all those layers of crispy dough."

He squinted at her. "Are you calling me *doughy?*"

"You started it."

Someone coughed discreetly. A servant hovering nearby. "Excuse me, miss. Interviews are over and the Fontes are waiting for you."

Alessa wasn't sure what she expected when she entered the library, but she didn't expect to find Nina sobbing and clinging to Josef, Saida with her head in her hands, Kamaria shouting at everyone to shut up, and Kaleb chugging the contents of a glass decanter that had been half full of vodka the last time Alessa checked.

"Hey!" Dante shouted. When they kept at it, he kicked the door shut with a loud bang that cut through the noise.

"What is going on?" Alessa said.

Everyone began yelling at once. Nina's wails drowned out whatever Josef was trying to say in his calm, precise way, and Kaleb seemed to be yelling nonsense sounds from pure annoyance while Saida berated him for being immature at a "time like this."

"Will you shut up already?" Kamaria hollered. "For Dea's sake. Bunch of headless chickens."

Alessa took advantage of the decreased volume to ask again.

Kamaria held up a hand to stop anyone from interrupting. "Everyone volunteered. Including me, obviously the best choice." Alessa's surge of relief didn't last long. "But the esteemed old farts of the Consiglio aren't too thrilled about my brother's recent decisions—shut *up*, Kaleb!—so, despite the fact that I *am obviously the best choice*"—she shouted the last part in Kaleb's direction— "they unanimously recommended Josef. So Kaleb's sulking about his wounded pride, Saida's convinced you need a more supportive Fonte, Nina's flipping out about Josef being picked, and like I said, I'm *obviously the correct choice* no matter what a bunch of stuffy old people think, so they all need to cut it out already!"

Alessa blinked once. Twice.

Kamaria crossed her arms. "But. Obviously, the final decision is yours, and when you pick me, I'll fight the Consiglio myself if they don't put their stamp on it. So. Choose."

Of all the scenarios she'd mentally prepared for, Alessa hadn't made it this far into the realm of the impossible.

Kamaria wasn't wrong about who she'd prefer, but she'd made a promise. While she hadn't expected more than one Fonte to vie for the position, the fact remained: she'd promised she wouldn't choose. They'd done their part by volunteering, and the Consiglio had done theirs. The only way to keep her word was to accept the official verdict.

"I'm sorry, Nina," Alessa said. "But I have to accept the—"

"No! You can't have him!" Nina's gift exploded with her rage, and the nearest window shattered.

The world erupted into a deadly rainbow of flying glass.

Dante shielded Alessa, but her ears rang in the silence that followed.

Still, she couldn't mistake what Nina said next.

"I should have dropped a *hundred* statues on you."

Alessa dug her fingernails into her palms, but a glass-fronted cabinet bowed and wavered like a bubble about to pop, and another wave of glass burst across the room.

"Stop it, Nina!" Josef shouted. "What have you done?"

Nina's anger dissolved into pitiful sobs.

Kamaria lay curled on the floor, clutching her leg as blood spread across her buff-colored pants.

Dante took Alessa's chin, turning her face to him. "Are you hurt?"

"I'm fine," she said, ducking away. "Kaleb, how bad is it?"

Kaleb pressed on Kamaria's leg. "Bleeding's slowing. She'll be okay, but she'll have a wicked scar."

Alessa turned to see Dante pulling a massive shard of glass from his shoulder. He sagged against the wall, sliding down it to sit. Cursing at herself, Alessa hurried to give him cover. She hadn't even asked if he was hurt. He'd heal, but the sight of exposed muscle and bone turned her stomach, and the remnants of his tattered sleeve weren't enough to hide the damage.

"Help Kamaria. I'll be fine," Dante said to Alessa.

"I know you will, but they don't." She looked around desperately for something to cover his torn flesh as it began to knit to-gether.

The door flew open. Guards stared, open-mouthed, at the room dusted with glass and blood.

"There was an accident," Alessa said. "Get bandages. Go!"

It took them a moment, but the Cittadella guards were tasked with protecting the Finestra and Fonte, not arguing, and their training kicked in.

"Saida and Kaleb, help Kamaria to the couch. Elevate her leg."

Kaleb gaped at Dante. "What about—"

"Just do it." Alessa bent farther, blocking Kaleb's view.

"I'm sorry," Nina cried. "I never *wanted* to hurt anyone. *This* was an accident."

Unlike the statue.

Alessa clenched her teeth. First, she had to take care of Kamaria and protect Dante's secret. Then, she'd deal with Nina's betrayal.

Saida rushed inside with an armful of bandages, colliding with Nina, who seemed struck by the need to make amends and tried to wrestle them from her. Rolling her eyes, Saida shoved a handful into Nina's hands and took the rest to where Kamaria lay on the couch, forearm over her eyes.

Alessa held up a hand to stop Nina, but she kept coming, her red-rimmed eyes fixed on Dante's shoulder, where he was trying, unsuccessfully, to cover what was left of his injury with his free hand.

Nina stopped mid-stride and shrieked.

"What?" Saida said. "What's wrong?"

Heaving for breath, Nina pointed. "Ghiotte!"

Kamaria groaned.

"Oh," said Saida. "Yeah. I had a hunch."

Teeth bared in a snarl, Dante struggled to his feet as Kaleb stalked over. He'd never looked more like a cornered animal, and it made Alessa ache.

Kaleb stopped a safe distance away. "No wonder you win every fight. I should have known."

"What is wrong with all of you?" Nina cried. "*He's* the reason she killed Emer and Ilsi and Hugo."

"Dante wasn't even here when my previous Fontes died," Alessa said. "He's done *nothing* but help us."

Nina shook her head. "No, he's evil. A killer."

"Like you almost became today?" Alessa said. "Or when you used your *gift* to knock a statue on me?"

Nina began to sob. "I didn't *want* to. I was scared."

"For Dea's sake, Nina, you tried to *kill* the Finestra," Kaleb said. "Take it down a notch with the righteous indignation. Dante had more than enough opportunity to kill us all, but so far, you're the only one who's tried to."

"Nina." Josef said, jaw tight. "If word gets out about this, it won't be good for anyone."

An understatement. If the public suspected a ghiotte had infiltrated the Cittadella, they'd blame him for every death she'd caused. Few would listen to reason.

"I'll leave." Dante said.

"No!" Alessa couldn't tell who'd yelled louder—her, Saida, or Kamaria.

"I say he stays," Saida said. "And Nina leaves."

Kaleb shrugged one shoulder. "I'm not telling anyone. But Nina talks more than she prays, and she prays plenty. I don't think she can keep this to herself."

"Nina," Alessa said. "I don't want to banish you, but I will if

I have to. If you'd rather be safe inside the Fortezza, protected *by me*, you'll give me your word you'll take this secret to your grave."

Josef pulled himself up to his full height. "I give you *my* word. If she tells a soul, you can banish me, too."

"Nina?" Alessa waited.

Nina glared through her tears. "I'll stay quiet, but *only* if you don't choose Josef."

A love for a love.

Alessa nodded. "Josef, take her home."

Still sobbing, Nina let Josef lead her toward the door. His stone face slipped as they reached it, and he cast one last apologetic look behind him.

"So, what's the deal?" Kaleb asked Alessa. "You can't hurt Dante at all?"

"I *can*, and I have," Alessa said. "But he's a lot harder to kill than other people, so he's been helping me control my power. He's been helping me exactly as I told you, and more. And I think, maybe, his gift almost works like a . . . release valve?"

Saida snorted loudly. "Sorry. Can't help myself."

Alessa ignored her. "All I know is that I can control myself better with him—Saida, *stop* laughing—than the rest of you. It's been extremely helpful, and without him, you'd all be in much worse shape."

Kaleb circled Dante. "A real live ghiotte, huh? I always thought you'd have horns. Disappointing."

"Finestra," Saida said, "I don't think Kamaria will be in fighting shape, so it has to be me or Kaleb. Who do you choose?"

• • •

Hours later, the library was scrubbed clean, and only one Fonte remained in the Cittadella. The others had said tearful farewells, promising to return for the ceremony the following day.

In the end, it hadn't really been a choice. She'd never been able to use Saida's gift very well, and with Kamaria unable to stand, Kaleb was the only one left. He'd gone pale, but accepted graciously, bowing and saying something about honor and duty. Saida had burst into tears while Kamaria gnawed on her lip, glowering in the way of a person trying not to cry.

Alessa and her partner stepped out to wave at the crowd below.

Thousands of people, clad in their brightest garb, flowed through the streets like a multi-hued river, down from the Cittadella, all the way to the city gates and beyond. *Everyone* was invited to Carnevale, even the Marked. One last day for every Saverian to enjoy the best life had to offer before the gates and the Fortezza were locked, and they were left outside. Every face glowed with a fierce determination to enjoy the night. There was no celebration like the last hurrah before a battle.

Alessa waved until her arm grew tired, until the cheers faded enough for the Grand Master to announce the start of the festivities and dismiss the crowd. A new roar erupted as the people of Saverio donned their masks and turned away from their saviors, moving on to more important matters, like living.

The next day, after the confetti and detritus of Carnevale was swept away, Alessa and Kaleb would be joined before Dea and the eyes of the Church, forever bound by shared duty and responsibility. He'd be her constant companion until Divorando, her partner in every way that mattered, until they faced death together and, hopefully, saved their home from annihilation.

"Excellent," said Renata from just inside the doors. "That went beautifully. Now, I'll leave you two alone. But first . . ." She looked decidedly uncomfortable. "I should probably remind you that while Dea had the good sense to make sure regular use of a Finestra's gift is effective for preventing pregnancy, when Divorando is over, you will have to find, erm, other methods."

Kaleb shot a frantic glance at Alessa. She bit her knuckles to stop from laughing and gave him a quick eye roll, which seemed to calm him a bit, but his palpable relief that the magical side-effect of her power would be irrelevant for their relationship only made it harder not to laugh. As a battle partner, Kaleb checked most of the boxes. As a *lover?* Not so much.

Besides, her heart was already taken.

Dante waited inside, his face colored by a spray of fireworks, as musicians outside took up their instruments and a vigorous tune joined the sounds of laughter, sparklers, and exclamations of joy.

The awkward trio surveyed each other as Renata left the suite.

"Was she saying—" Kaleb started.

Alessa snorted a laugh. "Yes, Kaleb. Any Finestra and Fonte are temporarily infertile as long as they regularly use their gifts. Dea's no fool, and battling morning sickness *and* scarabeo at the same time would be a bit difficult, don't you think?"

Dante studied the floor.

"Huh," Kaleb said. Bobbing his head nervously, he tapped his leg along with the rhythm. "Well, that's good to know, but also, I didn't need to know that. Kinda wish I could forget that happened, actually."

Alessa giggled. "You should go to Carnevale, Kaleb."

"What?" Kaleb spluttered. "I can't."

"Why not?" she asked. "Most people wear masks or face paint.

No one has to know. It may not be a regular wedding, but every bachelor should have one last night on the town before settling down."

And every bride deserved an evening with the man she loved before promising herself to someone else.

Kaleb wavered briefly, then ran out the door, calling out his thanks over his shoulder.

Dante gazed out at the purple sky. "They're going to burn the city down if they set off any more of the big ones."

"Way to focus on the positive." Alessa came up behind him and took a chance, resting her forehead between his shoulder blades, her hands sliding around his waist.

Dante covered her hands with his and nodded to the wall, where a dozen glittering Carnevale masks hung. "What's the point of the masks, anyway?"

"My mother said it was so people could kiss other people's partners and pretend it was an accident."

He laughed. "Pick one. I want to see how you look."

"They're *priceless*. They were ordination gifts from past Carnevale Masters."

"Who better to wear one, then?" He stepped out of her arms and took down a red mask with curved black horns, dusted with gold. Turning back, he held it to his face. "How do I look?"

"Like a vengeful demon."

He made his next selection—pale blue and silver, with edges curved like wings—and cradled it in his hands. "Then I guess you're the blessed savior."

Something hung in the air, a finality she couldn't ignore. Tomorrow, he would leave. She hadn't asked him again if he'd seek refuge in the Fortezza or not, afraid she already knew his answer.

Even if she did save Saverio, there was no promise they'd both be alive when it was over.

Dante's eyes shone as he held out the mask. "What do you say, Finestra? One reckless night before you save the world?"

Thirty-Seven

Contro l'amore e la morte non vale essere forti.
Against love and death, there is no point fighting.

DAYS BEFORE DIVORANDO: 14

Garlic and wine flavored the air thick enough to taste as Alessa and Dante wove their way down a wide street lined with bistros and bars. Crowds of people laughed and grinned beneath lopsided masks, embracing old friends and new. On one street corner, an opera singer belted an aria, while flamboyant salsa dancers spun nearby, and a mariachi band played an old favorite a block away. The cacophony should have clashed, but somehow it was the perfect blend of jubilant noise. Alessa basked in the ferocious joy and desperate love all around.

Dante strolled by her side in the same clothes he'd been in the first time she saw him—tawny, worn-in trousers and a slightly frayed white shirt—and she'd tried to match him as best she could, in a simple, rose-colored skirt, leather-soled slippers, and an ivory blouse with flowing sleeves. A pair of men in robes passed them without a glance for the young couple in masks. There was no reason for anyone to suspect she was the stiff, buttoned-up Finestra who wore glittering finery at lavish galas.

Dante snagged a piece of chiacchiere from a passing tray, shouting his thanks to the bearer, who was already pressing his treats upon the next lucky recipient. Breaking it in half, Dante held it out so Alessa could take a bite.

Even before the tang of lemon zest and mandarinetto touched her tongue, her mouth watered. Her lips brushed his fingertips, tempting her to linger, but a puff of powdered sugar tickled her nose, and she pulled back to sneeze.

Adjusting her mask, she beckoned him to follow her to a picked-over chocolate stand across the street where three half-melted lumps were on their way to becoming puddles. She took them all.

"Silk isn't cheap." Dante pulled one of her gloves off and trans-ferred the chocolates into her empty palm. "Which one's mine?"

She popped one in her mouth. "Who said any are for you?"

With a mask over half his face, she could hardly be blamed that her gaze kept slipping to his mouth.

Dante pulled her back before she ran into a loudly intoxicated man, grasping her wrist to steady her—or so she thought—but instead, lips met her palm with a heat she felt in her toes. Then again, and both chocolates were gone. He grinned like the Wolf he used to be.

A pair of dancers clipped her before she could scold him for his thievery, and the impact sent her into his arms.

Eyes met, breath caught, she leaned in, ready to dance, to kiss, to—

Dante set her at arm's length. "You okay?"

No, because you threw away a chance to kiss me and you're leaving tomorrow so I can marry someone else, she wailed inside her head.

Aloud, she went with, "You're a horrible tease," and sucked a smudge of chocolate off one finger with a pout.

"Who's teasing now?" At the heat in his gaze, Alessa understood the word *smolder* for the first time.

She peeked up at him through her lashes. "Ask nicely, and I'm all yours."

He coughed on nothing.

"It *is* you!" a loud voice slurred.

Dante shoved the tall boy careening toward them—not to hurt him, just to stop him—but he took a minute to regain his balance anyway.

"Sorry." Kaleb's white teeth flashed beneath his jade mask. "Didn't suspect—aspect—" He stopped. "Expect! Didn't *expect* to see you here, but I won't tell anyone. Do I look heroic?" He draped a strip of scarlet fabric over his shoulders and struck a pose. "Just needed the right outfit." He bit off the consonants in his attempt to enunciate clearly, and the effect of his slurred speech paired with the ridiculous pose sent Alessa into a fit of giggles.

"Absolutely," she said. "I am in awe." She wanted to shoo him away, to forget that *this* was the boy she'd be marrying in the morning, not the one on her arm, but Kaleb looked so sheepish as he dropped the pose that she didn't have the heart to hint for him to leave.

"Doubtful," he said. "I've been a real tool, but I'll do better."

Dante turned away, pretending to be absorbed in the festivities.

"It's never too late to become who you want to be, Kaleb," Alessa said. "I should know."

"Maybe you can teach me," he said. "Partners, right?"

"Right."

"Way more fun out here, though." Kaleb's hand swept through the air, and Dante caught a statuette he knocked over.

"Enjoy yourself tonight, Kaleb," Alessa said. "But try to sober up before the morning. I'd like you to remember it later. And drink some water."

Kaleb gave her a wobbly salute and yanked her into a loose, awkward hug, his head cocked at an angle so their faces didn't touch.

"Your friends have left you behind," Dante said, prying Kaleb off and guiding him with a firm hand on his shoulder. "How about you catch up with them, eh?"

Kaleb loped off, and Dante and Alessa continued down the street alone, pausing to watch dancers twirl and dip, tossing coins into a mandolin player's case, and laughing at a puppet show where a miniature Finestra pounded a stuffed scarabeo to death while a crowd cheered.

"If only it were that easy," she whispered.

"Maybe it will be."

"I hope so," she said, trying to soak in the sight of every joyful face.

The streets were so densely packed they could hardly move through the riotous mass of Saverians. Polished city residents passed drinks to roughnecks from the docks, and wide-eyed villagers rubbed elbows with rowdy sailors, listening raptly to stories told by settlers returned from the continent, easily identified by their out-of-style, homespun clothes and universal air of bravado. It took a special kind of person to voluntarily leave Saverio's comforts for the battered continent. Alessa slowed as she passed a small crowd crying tears of mirth as a woman in a sleeveless tunic, her skin burnished by long days under the sun, shouted a tale that ended with an imitation of her partner falling into an ancient canal in the ruins after too many ghost stories.

Dante chuckled, but Alessa's laughter faded quickly. The longer the battle, the more of these people would die. Soldiers, the Marked, and their children who were too young to enter the Fortezza without them. The colorful, vibrant streets would soon become a battlefield, and she was their last line of defense.

"This way," Dante said.

Twining his fingers with hers, he towed her along as he cut a path through the revelers. Her view was nothing but backs and chests, and in the center of it all, Dante's sure grip and confident stride, parting the crowd with his broad shoulders and effortless air of command. They broke free from the mass of humanity when he led her into an alley so narrow he had to release her hand.

She couldn't resist.

As she stopped, Dante turned back, and she made a show of examining the alley and wiggling her eyebrow.

"I promise," he said with a laugh. "There are better places than alleys."

Soon, the ocean rolled out before them, so glorious in the dying sunset that she could hardly believe anything cruel and ugly could exist in the same world.

They weren't the only Carnevale-goers who'd had the same idea, and she averted her eyes from the scattered couples dotting the sand, an ache growing in her chest.

The shape of him, the way he moved, stirred a hundred wants she wasn't allowed to have, and she knew, no matter what happened in the morning or on the day of Divorando, that she'd never forget the rasp in his voice when he was tired, the way his eyes crinkled when he was trying not to laugh, or his ridiculous proverbs for every occasion.

Was there any use in dreaming of a life beyond the battle, where Dea's Finestra and Crollo's ghiotte found a happily ever after?

The rocks became pebbles, pebbles became sand, and Dante waited as she slipped off her shoes, toes sinking into the slowly fading warmth of the sand. The ocean shushed them while the city sang above as she stretched her legs to match his stride, shoes dangling from her fingertips like earrings.

They slowed in unison, walking closer, until the backs of their hands brushed with every step.

Almost touching, but not quite, they stopped to stare out at the sea. It fractured in the center, the jagged outline of a distant shore breaking the horizon, one peak higher than the rest. There, at that very moment, demons were making their inexorable way to the surface.

"It's hard to believe something so beautiful can be so deadly, isn't it?" she asked.

She turned and found him watching her instead of the ocean.

"Yes," he said softly. "Hard to believe."

She held onto his gaze. No teasing tip of the head or challenging stare. No jokes. Just a girl waiting for a boy to kiss her.

And he did.

The ocean sighed with them, as though it, too, had been waiting. Dante brushed his lips against hers, lightly, questioning. As though she was just a girl and he just a boy, and the world wasn't about to end, and she wasn't marrying someone else in the morning.

Heat simmered, but it waited patiently, because this moment wasn't for heat, but warmth. Not for haste, but a slow sweetness. An introduction of sorts. She knew him, and he knew her, but they didn't know each other like this.

When he rested his forehead against hers, neither spoke. The soft thud of her heart and the brush of his thumb over her palm said everything words couldn't.

I'm sorry.

I'll miss you.

I hope.

I want.

"Take me home," she said. "I want to fall asleep with you one last time."

He dropped a lingering kiss on her lips before taking her hand.

One last night.

Her room had never seemed so small or her bed so large. Alessa gnawed on her lip while Dante kicked off his shoes, then frowned at the floor, shoeless but otherwise fully dressed.

Wonderful. Neither of them knew what to do next. Well, she assumed Dante knew *something* about what was to come, but the immediate next step seemed to stump them both.

Dante rubbed the back of his neck. "When you said you wanted to sleep . . ."

"I didn't mean sleep," Alessa said quickly. "I mean, sleep, too, but—"

He stepped closer and ran the pad of one thumb across her cheekbone. "You are *very* pink right now."

"You're not supposed to notice." She pushed onto her toes,

but still couldn't reach him. "Do you *have* to be so tall? How am I supposed to kiss you?"

"Climb?" He bent with a laugh to kiss her.

"Do you still feel it?" she asked, suddenly self-conscious.

Dante cocked his head. "You'll have to be more specific."

"My . . . my gift. What does it feel like now, when I'm not try-ing to use it on you?"

"Let's see." He tipped her chin, and his lips found hers, slowly, as though he could stretch a night into a lifetime. She responded, instantly, and his hands found her waist. His kisses deepened, un-til he kissed her with the urgency of a man who hoped tomorrow would never come. He pulled back, breathless. "What was the question?"

"Hmm?" She blinked, dazed.

He bit his lip, looking quite pleased with his effect on her. "I still feel that . . . purr . . . or whatever you want to call it. But I think I like it."

"You think?"

He answered with another kiss. Unequivocally.

She could have spent a lifetime savoring the slide of his lips, the dance of his tongue, the breath they passed between them as though it was the only air left in the world, and they would both die without it. She wanted to take her time exploring every fascinating part of him, but her hands were impatient, and once they found the strip of bare skin between his pants and shirt, her palms slid beneath. His abdomen was all firm ridges and taut muscles, but his lips were full and soft.

His fingers cupped her bottom, pulling her into him, and she melted, softness yielding to the hard planes of his body. When his hand cupped her breast, she forgot how to breathe. Refusing to let go of each other for the time it would take to walk to the couch, they tumbled onto it in a tangle of arms and legs instead.

She looked down at him through the fall of her curls, kissing the scruff of his chin, his lips, his neck, reveling in the husky rasp to his breath. After the third time he caught her halfway through falling off, Dante rolled with her, catching their fall. She wrapped her arms and legs around him, so he hauled her up with him as he stood, laughing into her neck as he carried her to the bed.

"I know they say these skirts were designed for Saverio's stairs," Dante murmured, trailing kisses across her belly. "But I have to believe *someone* was thinking of this."

He nuzzled her through fabric, his breath warming the bare skin of her thigh, and the world faded away into velvet darkness and yearning, her hands tangling in his hair as she begged Dea silently to let it last an eternity, then not so silently.

But Dante the lover, like Dante the fighter, was determined to find her every weakness, and he did, until she arched against him and the breath shuddered out of her.

She was limp, spent, soft and drowsy, as he found his way beside her and pulled her to him, kissing her forehead, her eyelids, her neck—anything he could reach. She snuggled close, whispering against his neck.

"Are you sure?" he asked.

She was. As sure as she'd ever been about anything. Pushing up to kneeling, she pulled her blouse over her head. The moon gilded her body until it didn't look like hers at all, and Dante was stunned into immobility. Her skirt was more difficult, but that seemed to snap him out of his reverent trance. He unhooked it with a flick of his wrist, threw it on the floor, and she was naked and only a little self-conscious as he gazed at her.

Up to her, then. A smile played on her lips as she nudged him to lift his arms and she fought to remove his shirt. It hit the floor and she squinted, fumbling with the buttons of his pants. Her hand slipped inside but she jerked it back out at his strangled sound. "No," he said with a ragged laugh. "Good pain."

Like unwrapping a long-awaited present, she took her time undressing him, daring him to be self-conscious, but he wasn't. His confidence was warranted. The sculpted muscles she'd admired when he was a stranger were even more captivating up close, now that he was anything but.

Even as her thoughts dissolved, Alessa decided Dea had surely spent extra time and effort crafting Dante, because she couldn't find a single flaw. Although, if he *had* one, it wouldn't be a flaw to her. Still, every line and plane, ridge of bone and lean muscle, was more perfect than the last. To her eyes, to her hands.

Dante let her explore until it seemed he couldn't take it any longer. Then, moving with a feline grace, he rolled her beneath him.

Somehow, every second of her life seemed to have led to the moment he settled himself above her. In the short time she'd known him, she'd learned to stand on her own, to take up space, and love herself, but she still had so much to learn, starting with what it meant to be one with another, even temporarily. She made a soft sound at the first bite of pain, and he stopped, soothing her with slow kisses until she begged him to continue. He moaned, and her breath hitched. Her eyes flew open. "Did I hurt you?"

"That's—" He stopped to breathe. "That's *my* question."

It didn't seem appropriate to laugh, but his eyes were smiling, so maybe it wasn't so strange to laugh in a moment like that, or maybe it was, but she didn't care—before she could decide, his hips flexed, and she forgot all about laughing.

She could feel the strain of his control, but his lips were soft and coaxing, and bit by bit, she relaxed. And then there was no more pain, or only brief flashes, but the tiny hurts were banished almost immediately by his shared gift. "I can't—"

She silenced him with a kiss, wordlessly urging him on. She wouldn't—couldn't—reach the peak again, but it didn't matter. She wanted to watch him, to memorize his expression.

When he relaxed, so boneless and heavy she thought he might be asleep, she ran her fingernails up and down his back, rubbing her smooth cheek against his rough one.

She'd given him that. For once, her body—her touch—had shared pleasure, not pain. Power had been a bad thing for so long, something she needed to suppress, control, and fear. But this . . . *this* was power, too. The power to give, to connect, to convey the thoughts and feelings she had no words for.

For five years, she'd been told she was a window to the divine, and for the first time, watching Dante's face, she'd believed it.

His muscles bunched as he gathered himself to move away. She whimpered a protest and clutched him to her.

Lifting his head, he kissed her nose. "I'll crush you."

"I'll die happy."

Rolling to the side, he pulled her with him and laid her head on his chest. "You can't die tonight. You have to save the world."

The moment was too precious to darken with doubts and fears, so she wiggled deeper into his arms as he murmured soft sweetness against her forehead in the old language. Some things didn't require translation.

She woke to utter darkness and a cool draft instead of Dante's warmth. Reaching, her fingertips found his back. He was sitting on the edge of the bed.

"Come back to me," she whispered.

The clouds had rolled in while she slept, so their second time was only touch, taste, and sounds. Kisses leaving trails of heat and murmured words that weren't really words but feelings shaped into sighs mingling between parted lips.

Thirty-Eight

A gran salita, gran discesa.
The higher the rise, the greater the fall.

Alessa would've made the night last forever if she could, but she expected the sun to rise in the morning.

It didn't.

The sky outside was dark, and her bed empty when she woke with nothing but tangled sheets beside her. She scrambled for the lamp, pulled the string too hard, and had to grab it before it tipped.

Dante was sitting on the couch.

"Come back to bed," she said. "It's still dark."

"It's morning," he said. "Technically. Happy wedding day."

The wall clock confirmed it was long past time for the sun to rise. Crollo had sent her a full day of darkness as a wedding gift.

Dante ran a bath for her, and she coaxed him into joining her. Lying back on his chest, Alessa watched as bubbles popped on the surface of the bath water, ripples distorting the lines of her bare legs. Dante's were too long for the tub and his knees jutted from the surface like golden islands on either side of her bare hips. He bathed her with the reverence of the faithful, and for once, she accepted it as her due.

"Tip your head," he said, hands cupped above her.

Alessa closed her eyes and let him rinse the suds away. With lazy fingers, she moved her fingertips over his muscular thighs, swirling the dark hair. His breath frayed, but in true Dante fashion he refused to be distracted from his task. After soaping up again, he took her hands in his, massaging her palms with his thumbs, his fingers sliding slick and smooth between hers.

"My family had an orchard," Dante said. "Right by the beach. It bothered me, at first. That you were a complete stranger but smelled like home."

He worked his way up her arms to her shoulders, gently at first, then with more pressure, kneading the taut muscles.

"And now?"

Dante's hands slid forward to trace her collarbone, and she tipped her head to one side.

His lips brushed the flushed skin of her temple. "It's perfect."

Only when her fingers were prunes and the water was cold did Alessa drag herself from his arms.

Three weddings. But this time was different.

Once, as a girl, she'd been asked to serve as flower girl in a neighbor's wedding. Marveling at the flock of attendants who fussed over the bride's hair and adjusted her jewelry, telling her how beautiful she looked, Alessa had dreamed of the day she'd be in the center of it all, surrounded by love and excitement.

Instead, she'd dressed for three weddings alone.

Now, on a day the sun wouldn't shine, Dante fastened the buttons of her cream-colored dress, studded with diamonds. The first time she'd worn it, on the night of the gala, she'd faced off with a surly stranger who'd looked at her with scorn. Now he stood behind her, gathering her loose curls with achingly familiar hands to brush a kiss on the nape of her neck. He didn't fuss, and he didn't tell her she was beautiful. He didn't have to.

The moon hung like a silent sentinel watching over the city. She wouldn't have to worry about tripping over the detritus of Carnevale, despite the dark, because this ceremony wouldn't be on the Peak.

This one was different in other ways, too. Less fear, more hope. Not the naive hope of a young girl, but a hope borne from trial and failure and overcoming.

Kaleb wasn't a stranger. He'd survived her touch, and she knew how to use his power. This time, she *would* fulfill her destiny.

Together, they'd face the darkness. And afterward, her dream lay just out of reach.

Dante sat on the bed, watching as she dawdled over her makeup brushes, dusting her cheeks for the third time.

The clock chimed.

"It's time for me to go," Dante said.

She dropped the brush to go to him. "You're not staying for my wedding?"

He hooked an arm around her waist and pulled her onto his lap. "Please don't ask me to."

Nestling her face into the crook of his neck, she breathed him in. "You know it's not that kind of marriage."

"You don't have to be in someone's bed to belong to them,"

Dante said. "My job here's done. Besides, I'm still a liability. If the truth about me gets out, you'll both be guilty by association."

Swallowing a lump in her throat, she brushed a curl behind his ear. "Where will you go?"

"Planning to track me down?"

"If you'll let me."

"Alessa." He sighed. "We weren't meant to have this, and we definitely aren't meant to have more. Not now. Not ever."

"I'm not meant to be widowed. You're not meant to exist. Maybe this time things are *supposed* to be different. What if Dea's trying to tell us something, and we just aren't brave enough to listen?"

"And what would she be telling us? That a ghiotte and a Finestra are supposed to defy every law of nature *and* the heavens for their own selfishness?"

"It's not selfish."

"I promise you, my feelings for you are *entirely* selfish." He nuzzled her cheek. "You told me to be better, and I'm trying, but I don't want to share you. I've never felt so selfish in my life." He reached for something and placed it in her hands.

A book.

Small, leather bound, full of his proverbs, and engraved with his mother's name.

"For you." He wrapped her fingers around it. "To remember me by."

She wanted to speak all the thoughts in her head and feelings in her heart, but she couldn't without crying. And she wouldn't trap him with tears again.

So, Alessa accepted a final kiss and didn't resist as he set her on her feet and pulled her close for one last hug.

She didn't watch as he let himself out.

The book was still warm from him, a piece of paper marking the last page he'd read. Inside the cover, beneath the original inscription, he'd written:

> Luce mia,
> My mother called me her light, because I was hers.
> And you are mine.
> Being with you has been a gift and an honor.
> —G. D. Lucente

She covered her mouth to hold in a sob as his words warped every remembered kiss into a silent farewell. She wasn't ready to let go. She'd never be ready. Why had she let him leave?

Her heart cried out to run after him for another kiss, one last glimpse, to make him promise that this goodbye wasn't for good.

But when she flung open the door, Kaleb was already there.

Time was up.

"Let's get this over with," Kaleb muttered, looking bleary-eyed and miserable enough for them both.

She offered him a wobbly smile. "Tactful, as always."

"Sorry. Old habits die hard."

She told him to wait and trudged back to place the book on her pillow. Dante couldn't have meant *forever*. She had to believe that. She opened it for one last look, to his last page, and the scrap of paper she'd taken for a bookmark slipped free.

On it was a postscript written in spare lettering:

> P.S. If you still want to know my name, consider it your
> prize for a successful battle.

She hugged it to her chest, dizzy with relief. Not goodbye. Not forever. As long as she saved the world and survived a war with the gods. As far as motivation went, she couldn't think of anything better.

She and Kaleb didn't speak on their way to the temple. Bless him, he looked terrified. And hungover. A stereotypical groom despite the odd circumstances.

Renata and Tomo watched from the front row, along with the entire Consiglio, as they entered. To Alessa's surprise, Kamaria was seated by the altar, guitar in hand, and she began playing the Canto della Dea to accompany their walk.

It was a struggle to keep her eyes on Kaleb during the ceremony with Saida sniffing loudly beside Josef, and Kamaria clearly trying not to laugh about it, but Alessa stood when told, bowed her head during the prayers, recited the words she needed to, and even laughed—a little—when Kamaria's snickering earned a scowl from the Padre.

Soon enough, it was over, and Kaleb smiled. A small, nervous smile, but a smile nonetheless.

Before, Alessa had been the Finestra in name only. Now she was in truth. Kaleb was her Fonte, and he would be her partner in battle.

Tomo and Renata came up to congratulate them, heaping praise on the Padre and the other members of the Consiglio about how smoothly the plan had gone and how the island would be well protected because of their brilliance.

"Go on," Renata said in an aside. "We'll keep them busy for a while so you two can get away."

The sooner they could return to training and change into

their normal clothing, the sooner Alessa could pretend it was just another day, so she took the opening.

"Now what?" Kaleb asked, as they walked back down the aisle.

"I don't know," Alessa said. "I guess we keep practicing until Divorando."

The others were waiting in the foyer outside the temple, Kamaria on crutches, Saida mopping her eyes with her sleeve, and Josef waiting to clap Kaleb on the shoulder like a stern, elderly man trapped in a seventeen-year-old's body.

They raised a cheer, and Kaleb sniffed loudly. "Dusty down here."

Alessa removed her gloves to wipe her eyes, and Kamaria nodded at them. "One last time, together?"

The world went blurry as they all reached out, stacking their hands together.

Their powers tingled through her skin, melding into something she'd never experienced before, expanding inside her chest into something buoyant and electric.

The foyer lit up as tendrils of lightning snaked through swirls of snowflakes amidst fiery tornados ringed with clouds of mist. A magical ecosphere expanded and contracted around them in time with Alessa's breath, illuminating their awestruck faces. Glittering ice crystals danced and chimed in a strange and beautiful song as though her power—their powers—rejoiced. Alessa's gift purred with satisfaction.

Almost simultaneously, Kamaria, Josef, and Saida let go. Everyone but Kaleb. The magic remained for a moment, then their gifts winked out. Her power expanded to fill the space left behind. What had been enough was no more, her gift no longer sated, like a sudden thirst.

Kaleb's grip went lax. His eyes flew wide, and his fingers curled like paper lit on fire. He hit the floor with a sickening thud.

No. Not again. Alessa's ribs were iron bars, locked around her lungs.

Her fault. Always her fault.

"No. No. No." Alessa backed down the aisle, shaking her head, away from yet another dying Fonte.

Failure. Murderer.

There it was. Her answer. The verdict. Dea had spoken.

She wasn't meant to save. She was created to kill. That's all she'd ever do.

Across the corridor from the temple, the stairs led back to the Cittadella.

To her right, the corridor to the city.

To her left, darkness.

The darkness won. She ran.

Thirty-Nine

A torto si lagna del mare chi due volte ci vuol tornare.
He ought not complain of the sea who
returns to it a second time.

DAYS BEFORE DIVORANDO: 13

There were worse places to die.

The moon hovering just above the horizon seemed twice as large as it had in the city. Alessa sat on a large piece of driftwood, running her palms over the rough bark until something caught. She pulled the splinter free and tossed it into the grass, then squeezed her finger until a trickle of blood dripped into her palm.

If she'd been another girl, in another life, perhaps she'd be sprawled on a beach blanket with someone she loved, counting stars, trading kisses, and watching the ripple of moonlight on the waves. But that life was not for her.

Dante once described this beach as the most beautiful place

he'd ever seen, and now it would be the last place she'd ever see. That would have to be enough.

All she'd asked in return for years of her life, her family, her name, was to not be alone when the monsters came. To face death on that cliff with a partner by her side.

If she'd died, she'd have died a hero.

If she'd suffered, at least she wouldn't have suffered alone.

That was the deal. That was the promise.

Lies. All of it.

The gods had given their verdict.

Either humans were a loose thread to be snipped, or humanity wasn't the problem, *she* was. Either way, she had no choice.

Her heart was still beating, but she *was* death. Not created by Dea, to save. But by Crollo, to usher in the end.

She couldn't connect. Couldn't save Saverio.

Would she be welcomed to the heavens for trying, or had her soul blackened the day her hands became weapons?

Smearing tears across her face with a hasty swipe of her arm, she tore off her dress. The last mark she'd leave on the world, a stained wedding gown in the dirt.

Clad in a thin slip, she walked into the ocean.

When it grew too deep to stand, she swam.

She couldn't force herself to drown, but if she kept swimming, her arms would eventually grow too weak to carry her back. The water would close over her head, a new Finestra would rise, and her family, her friends, Dante—everyone except her—might have a chance to live.

Ivini said the only way to save the island was to sacrifice *her*, but sacrifice demanded loss. It required a choice. *Her choice.*

She'd die if she had to, but not as a victim.

If anyone was going to get a shrine for killing the False Finestra, it would be her.

A poorly timed sob left her choking on a mouthful of water as she passed the rock in the center of the cove. She ordered her body to accept it, to allow the water to flood her lungs, but panic sent her arms thrashing, grasping.

Her hands met stone and she hauled herself onto the flat surface, gasping and coughing.

So selfish, she couldn't even drown herself to save the world.

Hugging her knees to her chest, she stared across the quiet ocean. Time and space had no meaning on the day of endless night.

At a distant splashing, her numbness flared into anger. All those years hating her loneliness, and when she needed it, she was denied. She didn't want to see anyone.

"I've been searching for hours."

Even him. Especially him. Dante pulled himself onto the rock.

"You found me," she said, sounding dead to her own ears. "Now leave."

The night concealed him, but she didn't have to see to know what he looked like. Memories were more vivid than anything she could make out in the darkness.

"It wasn't your fault." His hand found the base of her neck, kneading gently, but she didn't lean into his touch.

"It's *always* my fault."

Her island—her people—were doomed, and there was only one way to save them: by sacrificing herself. And she didn't want to. She wanted to pretend she was just a girl, to forget everything beyond the beach and stay there forever with the beautiful, stubborn man who didn't flinch at her touch or shy away from her like the rest of the world.

He was the ghiotte, but she was the monster.

"Did you hear me?" he said, low and insistent. "Kaleb's *alive*. Unconscious, but alive."

"How do you know? You weren't there."

"I came back, but you were already gone. The doctors said he'll pull through."

"Fine. Kaleb's alive." Maybe if she emerged from the bone-deep numbness, she'd be relieved, happy even. She hoped not. Feelings would only make it harder to do what she had to. "If I can't keep a Fonte conscious through a wedding, I can't keep one alive through a battle. I can't save us."

She didn't realize she was shaking her head until he took her face between his hands.

No matter how far she ran, she would always be dragged back to that wretched peak where she would fail and watch her whole world end. Her fault. Dante's love was just one more tie binding her to the life she never wanted.

Hot tears rolled down her cheeks. "I'm so tired of trying and failing and hurting people. I don't want to do this anymore."

"Then don't."

"I have no choice." She wanted to rip down the sky and shred it with her fingernails, to pluck every star from the fabric of the heavens until the fathomless darkness matched the void inside her.

"You always have a choice." He held her face, forcing her to look in his eyes. "If you don't want to go back, we won't. We'll find a cave, fill it with supplies. Barricade ourselves inside until the scarabei die out."

"I'd be a traitor. A pariah. Even if Saverio somehow survived, I'd be an outcast for the rest of my life."

He shrugged. "You make that sound like a bad thing."

A sound escaped her lips somewhere between a wet laugh and a strangled breath. "Thousands of people would die."

"True." He pointed at a patch of grass beyond the sand. "We could build a little house right over there."

"Amidst the barren land decimated by a swarm of voracious demons."

"Plants grow back."

"Before we starve?"

"I'd fish for our dinners."

She sighed. "And I'd raise chickens."

"You'd probably name them and talk to them constantly."

"I'd have to, or I'd drive you up the wall with my chatter."

Dante ran his thumb over her cheek. "We could get a cat."

He was offering her everything she'd ever wanted. But there would be no friends visiting for supper. No family. No strangers, even. Only her and Dante and a little house on a perfect beach. Her dream, broken and warped.

She crashed into him, kissing him so fiercely he fell back. Her knees scraped the stone on either side of him, and he caught a breath, but instead of talking sense into her, his hands found her waist.

Hot, insistent, demanding, she dared him to try and soothe her, but instead of dousing her fire, he met it with his own. She burned hotter and brighter until she was sure she'd flame out like a dying star and destroy everything around her.

Then, shuddering breaths became shuddering sobs and he held her as she cried.

Running his fingers through her hair, he whispered dreams that would never come true and sunny days they'd never see, in the whiskey-sweet voice she loved so much, his words slow and languorous, as though they had forever.

When her body was wrung out and she'd run out of tears, Alessa let Dante help her into a sitting position. "If we don't die, can we come back here?"

Dante looked up at the moon, vulnerability in his expression. "You really think you'll want to be with a ghiotte when you're everyone's favorite savior?"

"I haven't saved anyone yet."

He lifted her hand to his lips. "I don't know about that."

Forty

L'armi dei poltroni non tagliano, né forano.
Cowards' weapons neither cut nor pierce.

DAYS BEFORE DIVORANDO: 12

I t was after midnight when they returned to the Cittadella, but Alessa had to see for herself.

A woman dressed in medical whites dropped a quick curtsy as Alessa entered the Fonte suite. The Cittadella's attending doctor, bent over the large, four-poster bed, didn't immediately look up, busy with whatever task she was performing.

Kaleb lay motionless beneath crisp white sheets, his eyelids blue and his lips pale.

The walls closed in around Alessa.

They lied.

She groped behind her for a hand to hold, but Dante was waiting in the hall. She had to face this alone.

"How is he?" she asked, holding her breath for the answer. Surely, a corpse wouldn't need medical care.

"Stable." The doctor's clipped response and her expression held Alessa fully responsible. "He was quite dehydrated and overtired. I would have advised him against any strenuous activity, if I'd been consulted. Which, obviously, I was not."

"So, you don't think . . . I mean, he'd been fine previous times."

"In my professional opinion, his collapse was a result of multiple factors. Divine or not, your profession is physically taxing, and Mr. Toporovsky should have taken better care of himself. I do hope when you are called to train the next Duo, you prevail upon the Consiglio to assemble a team of medical consultants. Despite what some may say, it is *not* an insult to Dea to use the wisdom she granted us."

Alessa bowed her head like a guilty child, though she'd never objected in the first place. The Consiglio were the ones who got their robes in a bunch when Tomo had suggested seeking outside opinions about Alessa's little problem.

"I expect he'll make a full recovery, but until then, he needs rest. *Complete* rest."

"Yes, Dottoressa. Of course."

The nurse gave a sorrowful look at Kaleb's angelic profile, as though she suspected Alessa was there to finish him off.

Alessa closed the door too fast, and the sound rang out in the quiet.

Dante, leaning against the stone banisters, raised his eyebrows as if to say, "See? I told you."

She wanted to laugh. Or cry. Or both.

Dante held out his arms, and Alessa walked in. Her harbor in stormy seas, warm and solid and hard to kill.

Kaleb was alive. And he'd remain that way as long as she stayed away from him. She still had a Fonte. Technically. He might not be strong enough to fight, and they'd have to replace him with one of the others for the actual battle, but she hadn't killed him.

Startled by a sudden shout, they leapt apart, Dante's face mirroring Alessa's alarm.

Afraid to look, but needing to know who'd spotted their ill-timed embrace, Alessa peered over the railing.

Renata stood in the courtyard below, her hand pressed over her mouth.

Behind her, Tomo stared up at Alessa, looking more disheveled than she'd ever seen him before.

Dante whispered, "They were frantic when I left."

Alessa let that fact sink in as her mentors hurried up the stairs.

"*Blessed Dea*, we thought you were dead!" Renata said, breathless, when she reached the top.

"Not quite," Alessa said with a rueful smile.

"We thought we'd lost you," Tomo said.

Renata cast her eyes to the ceiling in silent prayer. "Child, you scared a decade off my life."

Tears trembled on Alessa's lashes. They were relieved to see her alive—*her*, Alessa, not the Finestra. She hadn't realized how much she needed that. "I'm sorry. I thought I'd killed Kaleb, and the gods were telling me to sacrifice myself."

"Dear girl." Tomo shook his head ruefully, too choked up to continue.

"While I admire your decisiveness, this would have been a *very* good time to ask for a second opinion." Renata exhaled a shaky breath. "But I must say, I am proud of you for your willingness to make difficult choices. You've grown up."

The tide of guilt retreated at Renata's gentle tone, and Alessa pulled herself together. "What will we tell people?"

"Nothing," Renata said firmly, brushing her sleeves as though trying to smooth the wrinkles in their plans. "You'll pick someone else, and we'll keep it quiet until after Divorando. I don't like lying to the public, but all will be forgiven once you've saved us."

"We're just thankful *you're* safe," Tomo said fervently.

Renata's face softened. "Dea have mercy, I might sleep tonight after all."

"Come on, then." Tomo tugged on Renata's arm. "You need sleep, and I need a drink."

Alessa backed away from the railing as they left, and the Cittadella fell silent once more.

Brushing her hair aside, Dante dropped a kiss on the back of her neck. "I should go," he said, but his arms tightened around her.

She turned to face him. "Nina swore she wouldn't tell, and that man has no idea you're here. Stay until Divorando, so I can drag you to the Fortezza myself and face battle knowing you're safe and not doing something reckless like trying to protect the docks single-handedly."

"Always with the hero stuff," he murmured against her lips. "I keep telling you it's not my thing."

She slid her hands into his back pockets and pulled him closer. "You can lie to yourself, but you can't fool me."

At the sound of a harsh throat-clearing, they leapt apart again.

Poised at the top of the stairs, Renata's face was studiously blank. "I forgot to mention, your armor is in your room."

"Armor?" They were still two weeks away from battle.

"For the Blessing of the Troops."

Of course. When the sun rose, she'd stand before the assembled army and most of Saverio to bestow Dea's grace upon the army.

Carnivale celebrations were over, she had wed Kaleb on the day of Rest and Repentance, and now the final stage of preparation began. Soldiers would bid farewell to their families, march to their posts, and camp out on every hillside, cliff, and stretch of shore around Saverio, weapons at the ready and eyes on the sky. Saverians with Fortezza passes would begin to move inside in shifts, and those who were marked would nail up every window, erect makeshift barricades, and pray with newfound desperation.

"If we're lucky, it will be so blinding, no one will notice your Fonte isn't with you." Renata speared them with a loaded glance. "Until then, might I suggest you move this reunion *behind* a closed door?"

Dying a thousand deaths by mortification, Alessa managed to nod regally. She'd never asked what the punishment was for a Finestra who violated the rules about touching someone who wasn't a Fonte before Divorando, but not tattling was probably one of those unspoken courtesies each Finestra offered to the next.

Alessa followed Dante inside her suite as Renata's prim footsteps ended with the slam of a door on the level below, and covered her face. "Please tell me that didn't just happen."

Dante was trying too hard not to laugh to answer.

"How can you *laugh?* That was mortifying."

"Consider it a rite of passage." Dante kissed the margins of her face around her splayed fingers. "You *know* those two were getting handsy before *their* big battle."

"*Why* would you put that image in my head?" Alessa wailed. "Besides, they were wed and blessed, so they were allowed." She nudged him with an elbow. "*I'm* the terrible person who left her unconscious partner's bedside and got caught groping my bodyguard."

"You call *that* groping?" Dante pried her hands away from her face. His smile died as they stared at each other, and she knew he was going to bring up leaving, to offer her what little safety he could with his absence in case Nina didn't hold her tongue. As long as he was gone, Alessa would be able to dismiss any rumors as hysterical fabrication.

But once he was gone . . . he'd be gone.

Two suits of armor lay on her bed like stiff metal bodies. One, constructed for Alessa's precise measurements; the other, one of the many usually mounted in the Fonte suite, chosen because it was the closest to Kaleb's measurements.

"You and Kaleb are almost the same height, you know. Similar build, too. Under a suit of armor, no one would know the difference."

Dante tucked her hair behind her ears. "I can't be your Fonte. What would I do, heal myself until the scarabeo gave up and flew away?"

"I'm not asking you to stay for the *battle*." She kissed the hollow at the base of his neck. "Only for the Blessing of the Troops. It's my last public event, and people will talk if my Fonte isn't there."

Alessa twined her fingers together behind Dante's back.

"Please?" she said. "Stay a little longer and save me one last time?"

The metal was cold and unforgiving, even atop a thin, sleeveless tunic and leggings, as Dante eased a chain-mail tunic over her shoulders, then helped her don the breastplate, and strapped panels to her thighs and calves.

She'd wear gloves for the Blessing, but not for the real battle.

Her hands, feet, and legs would be bare beneath the armor when it came time to fight, so her Fonte could hold on, even if he or she became too injured to stand.

When she'd gotten her first armor tutorial, she'd asked why the Fonte and Finestra helmets left the back of their necks exposed, but Tomo had explained how looking up was essential in a war when your enemies attacked from above. And, hopefully, the Finestra and Fonte would do their jobs well enough that very few scarabeo got within range of them anyway. The troops, densely packed together on the hillside, were a much more tempting feeding ground than two lone figures atop a peak, protected by magic. She hoped.

"I didn't think he could even sit up," Renata said as Dante descended the stairs to the courtyard. "How'd you get him into his armor?"

Dante flipped up the visor.

"Oh," Renata said. "Brilliant."

Dante flipped it back down as Captain Papatonis marched in to escort them to the piazza.

Alessa had to admit it was impressive—the thousands of armored soldiers in perfect lines, standing at attention in the piazza. And if she let out an *ooh* of admiration when they began their first series of drills, it was drowned out by the watching crowd's awe.

As they moved into the second series, her gaze caught on a flutter of white. Icy fingers crawled up Alessa's spine as Ivini led a line of robed figures into the piazza.

He'd never brought anything good into her life before, and she doubted he was here to make amends, but the *Fratellanza* made no move to disrupt anything, merely filling in the little bit of empty space on one side. She couldn't exactly have him expelled because her neck prickled with warning.

Renata wasn't pleased either and said something to Captain Papatonis that sent him toward Ivini, a cold look of determination on his face.

Alessa sent Ivini one last glare, poking him full of eye-daggers, then returned her attention to the troops. Ivini had tried his best and failed. He wasn't worth another moment of her time.

The Captain rejoined them as the exercises concluded, and Alessa stepped forward to take her place for the Blessing. Dante stood slightly behind her on one side, Renata and Tomo on the other.

"Dea, blessed Goddess of Creation," Alessa began. "We ask you to guide our weapons—"

With a hiss of metal, a guard in the front row drew his.

"Creature of Crollo!" he yelled and sprinted toward them.

Heart in her throat, Alessa fumbled for her ceremonial sword, but Dante drew first, stepping in front of her. To protect her.

"Get back, Finestra," the Captain yelled, running forward to join Dante as a human shield.

Or so she thought.

But when Captain Papatonis raised his sword, it wasn't to ward off the mutinous soldier. And Dante was bracing for an attack from the front, not behind.

Alessa screamed a warning, but it was too late.

Forty-One

Chi ha un cattivo nome è mezzo impiccato.
He who has a bad name is half hanged.

The hilt of the Captain's sword smashed into the base of Dante's skull, and he crumpled to the ground.

Five years of training and every lick of sense flew out the window as Alessa tried to lunge for him, but Renata, who'd never, not once, touched her, held her back with a vise grip around her arm.

"At ease, Captain." The ice in Renata's voice stalled Alessa's fight. "Explain yourself."

"I assure you, I will," Captain Papatonis said gravely.

Two soldiers hauled Dante upright by his arms, and the Captain roughly removed his helmet.

"That's not her Fonte." With a vicious yank of Dante's hair, he forced his head up. "It's an imposter."

The crowd gasped, recoiling in horror, as if they were witnessing some grotesque specter and not a beautiful man who'd been felled by a cowardly attack from behind.

In that moment, Alessa hated them all.

Tomo laughed uncomfortably. "Oh, dear. Given the circumstances, we decided studying was a better use of Kaleb Toporovsky's time, so we brought a stand-in, Captain. A harmless little maneuver."

"You see, Captain? You've disarmed him and knocked him unconscious, when you simply could have asked us." Renata raised her voice. "Dearest, why don't you send Signor Toporovsky to the balcony?"

Tomo's cane tapped a frantic beat on the stairs as he hurried away.

Alessa couldn't breathe for the hundred years it took before Kaleb stepped onto the balcony. Tomo was probably bracing him up from behind, and there was a decent chance he was about to keel over, but Kaleb waved and blew kisses, grinning like the guest of honor at a birthday party. The air rushed back into Alessa's lungs as thousands of troops and a thousand more civilians looked up to see their Fonte, alive.

"Begging your pardon, Signora," said the Captain. "But that's not the only problem."

Dante opened his eyes with a low groan.

"Allow me." Ivini stepped forward, half-turned so the crowd could hear his every word. "My apologies for the spectacle, but I had to act when a member of my flock informed me that evil had infiltrated the Cittadella."

"No," Alessa said. "That's not—"

"Quiet," Renata hissed. "For his sake and yours."

Without warning, the Captain slashed Dante's face with his dagger.

Alessa leapt, but Renata was faster. "Enough!"

Blood dripped down Dante's cheek, puddling on the white stone, but he couldn't hide his face with his arms pinned and a knife at his throat.

Dea, help me, Alessa begged silently. *I don't know what to do.*

She opened her mouth to speak, but he shook his head in the tiniest no.

"As you'll see, that *thing*," Ivini continued, "is a ghiotte."

Dante's eyes bored into Ivini's as the wicked gash across his cheek began to knit back together, and the crowd rumbled like the first warnings of a storm.

"Using his wicked wiles, he secured a spot by our Finestra's side, tainting her magic and weakening our Fontes." Ivini motioned as though shielding his eyes against Dante's wickedness. "A formal execution is too good for the creature, but my flock will dispose of it."

"No," Alessa gasped. "That's not—We cannot—"

Tomo coughed, his look pleading with her. "Finestra, you are a compassionate soul, but perhaps we should let cooler heads prevail."

Renata gripped her tighter. "Hold. Your. Tongue."

There was nothing she could say. Nothing she could do. If she showed mercy—if anyone realized she'd known and allowed Dante to stay—or worse, that she'd welcomed him into her arms . . .

"There will be no killing here today." Tomo's calm demeanor was a splash of cool water on the fires raging all around. "The Blessing of the Troops should not be tainted by such ugliness."

Ivini, the picture of indignant horror, seemed to realize his plan to become Saverio's avenging angel, executioner of demons, was crumbling. "But Signor. He brought evil into this holy place. Tainted her purity with his sin. He deserves to be punished."

"And I expect the Consiglio will agree, but that decision is up to them, not *you*," Renata said.

Alessa shook with rage and fear. They were trying, but they could only do so much.

Ivini pivoted to don the role of guilt-stricken martyr. "La Finestra sul Divino. Your benevolence is inspiring. I beg you, let me transport the creature to the continent, then. Even if it means my own death. My final act of penance for how I have wronged my savior." A gratified smile toyed at his lips as scattered voices from the crowd cried out in protest.

"We would not have you risk yourself, Padre," Renata said with a benign smile. "We'll let the Consiglio decide what the appropriate punishment should be. Now, Captain, take the prisoner inside and wait for further orders."

Alessa tensed, half afraid, half hoping Dante would fight his way free from the guards.

His eyes were lifeless as they turned him toward the Cittadella.

A third soldier followed, prodding him in the back with her sword. "You try to run, we'll kill you."

Alessa's heart squeezed. She had no leverage but to refuse to fight if they didn't release him. And no one would believe her. If she didn't fight, Dante would die along with everyone else.

All she could do was to make sure he wasn't executed. At least, inside the Cittadella, he'd be protected until she figured out how to release him or convince the Consiglio to show mercy. When

Divorando was over, he could flee to the continent, change his appearance, hide out for a few years until people forgot.

"Shall we finish?" Renata stepped into the space where Dante had been moments before.

"I'd like to say something to the Finestra first," Ivini said.

"Haven't you said enough?" Alessa said.

Renata squeezed, hard.

He'd won. What else could he want? To accuse her *again*? Demand Kaleb dance for them to prove he was truly alive?

Ivini's face sagged with anguish, and he dropped to his knees. Behind him, robed figures followed suit, heads bowed. "Finestra. Can you ever forgive me for casting aspersions on you? Truly, I only hoped to serve Dea. It's clear now that Crollo saw your incredible potential, the gift that is your strength, and he cowered in fear. Sending one of his minions to hobble you only proves your worthiness. I should have had faith. I should have known. I am so deeply sorry. If you banish me, I will go tonight."

Renata spoke before Alessa could tell him to leap from the nearest cliff. "That won't be necessary, Padre. After all, to err is human."

"To forgive, divine," Ivini breathed. "Finestra, can you ever forgive me?"

The answer was no. Definitely not. But Renata was clever, and she had a plan. Alessa didn't know what it was, but she wouldn't risk ruining it.

Alessa gave her nemesis the widest, most painful smile of her life. "Crollo has made fools of many *better* men than you. What kind of Finestra would I be to punish a holy man trying to protect his people?"

Damn him, Ivini wept.

Every fake tear that rolled down his face stoked her fury higher, but she had to credit his acting skills.

Ivini didn't want forgiveness. He wanted power. He'd positioned himself against her when she was failing, kicked her when she was down, conspired against her and stolen her own guards' loyalty. Now that she had a Fonte, alive, Ivini had found a scapegoat. And so, her greatest foe stepped into his new role as her staunch defender and humble supplicant. Whatever it took.

No more assassinations. No more poison. She had a way out, and Ivini realigned himself with a new cause to rally his sheep.

The drill sergeant shouted a command, and the troops snapped to attention with a deafening clamor. In perfect, regimented symmetry, Alessa's army took a knee, fists thumping against their chests.

This time, everyone looked directly at her.

"Congratulations, Finestra." Renata spoke for Alessa's ears alone. "They love you. They'll fight to the death for you. And *that* is how you win a war."

At what cost?

"Win the battle, and all is forgiven. You've never been more powerful," Renata said. "Your people will do anything you ask of them."

"I want him freed."

Renata released her arm. "Anything but that."

Forty-Two

Ciò che Dio fa è ben fatto.
Each day brings its own bread.

DAYS BEFORE DIVORANDO: 11

"I demand to see him," Alessa said the moment they were inside.

Renata shushed her viciously, but she wouldn't be silenced, not with Dante's life on the line.

"Will you stop and think, for once?" Renata had never looked so old. "Your Fonte is bedridden, and the people need to believe everything is going according to plan. Ivini plays this city like a fiddle and he's publicly declared himself on your side. Don't squander that gift."

"She's right," said Tomo. "You can't be suspected of sympathizing with him."

"You know he wasn't responsible for my dead Fontes. You know he isn't evil. Without him, I'd be dead a half dozen times over. This isn't fair."

"You've made it this far without realizing life never is?" Renata's eyes softened.

"At least let me see him." Alessa choked on her words. "Please."

"Dearest . . ." Tomo said softly.

Renata sucked her teeth. "No weeping. Chin up. Eyes blazing. Walk in there like you're about to rip his limbs off."

Luckily for them all, Alessa had more than enough pent-up anger to fake it.

Tears dried, regal mask in place, she followed Tomo and Renata to a small holding room reserved for drunken or unruly soldiers in need of cooling down.

The Captain bowed at their approach. "Finestra, Signor, Signora, I failed to see the threat inside our own walls. If it's your wish, I'll resign immediately."

What Alessa wished for was to slash *him* across the face with one of Dante's knives.

"Do you still doubt your Finestra?" Renata demanded.

"No," the Captain said breathlessly. "Never again. Crollo must be mighty afraid. Our Finestra will be the greatest in history."

Renata gave Alessa a pointed look.

Alessa held out a gloved hand, palm up, toward the Captain. "The daggers."

"Oh, of course." The Captain retrieved them and handed them over.

Alessa examined them, then slipped the dagger painted with Dante's blood into the hidden pocket of her dress. The other, she flipped, catching it by the hilt as Dante taught her.

Without signaling her intent, she stepped forward and thrust the dagger up toward the Captain's chin.

His head snapped up, eyes darting to Tomo and Renata, who

said nothing as Alessa tapped the knife against the lump bobbing in the Captain's throat. He could have disarmed her. They both knew it. But she was his Finestra, and if she wanted to kill him, he would let her.

"I will forgive you, Captain," Alessa said, her words clipped. "If you swear from this point forward you will report directly to *me* about any concerns regarding my safety."

Captain Papatonis croaked his assent.

"And if you ever attempt another stunt like that without my approval," she said, "I'll feed you to a scarabeo myself."

"Wonderful. Now that we've settled that," Tomo said, "we'd like to speak with the prisoner before we make our recommendations to the Consiglio."

The Captain ran a finger beneath his collar as Alessa lowered the dagger. "I'm not sure that's safe."

"If the three of us can't protect ourselves against one chained ghiotte, we'd be pretty pathetic saviors, don't you think?" Renata said.

"And, besides," Tomo said with a bland smile, "the Finestra is armed."

The captain had no rebuttal.

Inside the room, Dante sat against the wall, ankles bound, hands tied behind his back. He could have looked ferocious—monstrous, even—but Alessa only saw fear in his coiled muscles, desperation in his sneering bravado. His gaze locked on her as if he was drowning and she held the only rope.

"Leave us, Captain," Tomo said.

Alessa managed to wait for the door to close before kneeling to wrap her arms around Dante's neck. His body was rigid as iron, brittle as glass.

"I hate to intrude, but we need some answers," Tomo said. "What do you have to say for yourself, boy? Why did you come to the Cittadella? For money? Power?"

Dante scuffed a toe on the ground. "She asked me to."

"Any other reasons?"

Alessa took a long breath. "He wanted to find information about other ghiotte. Where they might have gone. And we've been looking for clues about where the Fonte di Guarigione might be, if it still exists."

"Why?" Renata asked Dante. "You already have its power."

"I thought if I found it, maybe we'd be forgiven." Every word he said seemed to hurt, as though he had to carve the truth out of himself. "Or at least left alone."

"And you, Finestra?" Tomo said. "How long have you known?"

Alessa pressed her forehead to the tight tendons of Dante's neck for several breaths before standing to face her mentors.

"A while. He's been helping me learn to manage my power. That's why it was going so well . . . until it wasn't."

"Has he ever tried to hurt you?" Tomo said.

Hurt, yes. Tried? "No. And he had plenty of opportunity. He was kind to me when no one else was. Dante has a million reasons to be cruel and heartless—" She laughed sadly. "But he's absolutely terrible at being evil."

Dante's breath shuddered out of him. "I was already planning to leave after Divorando, so you don't have to worry about me tarnishing her further."

A hole tore open in Alessa's chest. "Once people see—"

He shook his head. "If you let me out, everyone will think they were right about you. I'm not worth it."

"You're worth it to me."

Renata's brows drew together. "You think they'll stand by you if you ally yourself with a ghiotte? You're too smart for that, Alessa. When Divorando is over, you two can run away with each other, for all I care. I'll commission a ship for you, and . . . I'll train the next Finestra. Right now, you need to focus on saving Saverio. If you don't, he'll be dead anyway."

"I'm afraid she's right." Tomo took Renata's hand. "We've asked far too much of you, dear girl, but right now, Saverio needs you more than you need him. No offense, young man."

"He's imprisoned, not dead," Renata said firmly. "Now, Tomo and I will take what we've learned from our *interrogation* and persuade the Consiglio to *keep it* that way. In the meantime, you will visit your bedridden Fonte and make sure our little stunt didn't kill him once and for all."

The Cittadella buzzed with soldiers whispering about the monster in their midst and servants breathlessly relaying the news to every person who crossed their path, as though anyone in Saverio hadn't already heard it ten times over.

Alessa saw more concern on their faces during her walk through the building than she had while grieving all her dead Fontes combined.

Their fear and anger had a new target now, a shared enemy, and everyone swelled with righteous fury that a monster had tricked their *beloved* savior.

One young soldier blocked her path to the stairs, blubbering and taking a knee.

Alessa fumbled her way through absolving the young man, acutely aware how many people were watching to see if she'd offer mercy.

After so many years wishing for a bit of sympathy, she finally had it—because the man she loved was taking the blame for every harm she'd ever done.

Kaleb's eyes fluttered open as she cracked the door to the Fonte suite.

"You're awake," she said, coming in. "I'm so sorry. I don't know what happened. Everything was fine. Good, even, but . . . it fell apart."

"Yuck. Apologies are so awkward." Kaleb wrinkled his nose. "Besides, it looks like I might have a heart thing. Doctor says it wouldn't usually be a big deal, but that power flare-up of yours set it off."

A heart condition. Not her fault. But he'd endured her touch so many times before without collapsing.

"Sorry," she said. "I mean, *not* sorry."

"The secret's out, huh?"

She nodded miserably.

"Please stop crying. I can't take it."

"All this time thinking Dea's gift was my greatest weapon, and tears are even more effective at destroying men."

"You have quite the arsenal," Kaleb said. "Where is he?"

Alessa plucked at the sheets on the side of the bed. "They're moving him to an empty crypt while the Consiglio deliberates."

Kaleb shuddered. "How very gothic. Pour me a glass, will you?"

Alessa reached for the pitcher of water beside his bed, but hesitated before handing it to him.

"Oh, stop. I'm not scared of you," Kaleb said. "What happens now?"

"I don't know. I haven't decided who's going to take your place, yet."

"Why choose?" Kaleb asked. "Bring them all."

"That would be a sight, wouldn't it? A whole passel of Fontes on the Peak. We'd run out of room."

"Nah, one group hug and you'd vanquish the scarabeo with a bigger version of that snowflake tornado you nearly killed me with. Other than backfiring on *me*, it was pretty awesome."

Backfiring. Something prodded the back of her mind, disconnected thoughts trying to fit together, but they were interrupted by Tomo and Renata before she'd finished assembling the entire picture.

"It was unanimous," Tomo said, grave faced. "We persuaded them to wait until after Divorando, but they intend to hold a trial."

Alessa leapt to her feet. "You said—"

"I said we'd *try*. And we will. This isn't over."

A week earlier, Alessa would have been mortified to weep in front of Kaleb, Tomo, and Renata, but no one seemed disgusted or disappointed, not even Kaleb with his aversion to crying.

Kaleb struggled to sit up. "After all he did for us, they're going to leave him moldering in a crypt through Divorando, with no way to escape if things go south? And then what? A public stoning?"

"Hopefully not, but for now, we have no choice." Renata looked at Alessa. "He'll be given food and water through the bars, but the guards won't have keys. We made it clear we won't tolerate any mysterious disappearances or 'accidental' deaths. Justice will be served."

Justice. There was no justice in putting someone on trial for what they were, not what they'd done.

Alessa tried to hold on to the smallest bit of hope. For now,

Dante was safe. But he'd be alone through the siege, surrounded by marble tombs and people who hated him.

"Go ahead," Renata said, taking Alessa by the shoulders. "Cry. Rage. You deserve to. You're angry, and you should be, but you get to choose whether it will make you bitter or make you better."

The siren call was strong, but Renata was right. Railing at unfairness wouldn't help anyone.

"Your people have never truly listened to you before, but they will now." Renata squeezed Alessa's shoulders. "Win the battle, and we can find a way to save him. But first, you must win. Don't waste his sacrifice. Take the power it gives you and *use it*. He's not the only one who needs saving."

Forty-Three

Belle parole non pascono i gatti.
Fine words don't feed cats.

As the sun went down, Alessa stood before another gathered crowd in the piazza. The hush of anticipation was so profound, the acoustics so perfect, she didn't have to yell.

"Today is a day of mercy," Alessa began. "The Consiglio has decreed that the ghiotte will be given a trial after Divorando, and I—" She took a deep breath. "I have agreed. As Dea bid us, Saverians *must* be a people of mercy, forgiveness, and welcome, who protect each other from the forces of evil and chaos."

Her gaze fell on a sharp face beneath slicked-back silver hair.

"There is no divine grace like forgiveness, is there, Padre Ivini?" she asked.

Ivini nodded, his keen eyes assessing. "Your benevolence toward the wicked is like seeing the face of Dea."

Her smile was so saccharine she hoped it gave him a tooth-ache. "It is, isn't it?"

Alessa took a long moment to find the grubbiest faces in the crowd, the hollowed cheeks and fearful eyes of the Marked. Soon, the city gates would close for good, and they would be on the other side. They watched her for reassurance that she was strong enough to defeat the swarm before it descended on their ramshackle homes and devoured them.

As they stood there, the last far-flung villagers were trickling into the city, passing huddles of Marked and baring their wrists at the city gates to receive their Fortezza assignments.

When Divorando came, she'd have an army at her back and magic in her grip. The Marked would board up their windows and doors and huddle inside, praying and hoping they lived to see the morning.

"Five years ago, I was chosen by Dea to protect you, and I didn't understand why. I wasn't the smartest or the bravest. I wasn't always kind, and I often said the worst thing at the worst times. Signor Miyamoto and Signora Ortiz have had their work cut out for them."

A few laughs broke out, cut off by shushing.

"Dea made me powerful. At first, I thought, too powerful. I no longer think that. My gift was a challenge to become more than I thought I was. And today, I'm going to challenge you. I used to have a brother who believed I'd always do the right thing. Ironic, as he was asking me to do the wrong thing at the time, but like most sisters, I didn't listen."

She paused, with an indulgent smile for the scattered nervous chuckles.

"I once asked someone to be better, and I was told that people don't change, that they're selfish and cruel and only pretend to be good. I disagreed then. And I disagree now. Today I ask you to prove me right. We are flawed, imperfect, and often broken, but we all contain the potential to be more. Those who bear the mark of crimes have made mistakes. Some grievous. They have stolen, hurt, and at times, taken lives. I am your Finestra. I have taken lives, too."

A few concerned murmers fluttered between groups, but she pressed on.

"Not intentionally, and not out of anger, impulse, or revenge, but knowingly. I'm not so different from those who've stolen to eat or killed to live. I suspect many of you feel the same about mistakes you've made, but I believe in you as Dea believed in me, and if I've learned anything, it's that we're strongest when we love more, forgive more. Not less."

She was stronger for loving Dante, who grew up steeped in the conviction he was evil. He'd watched his parents die at the hands of people he knew and trusted, believed it was his fault that fear and hatred drove people to cruelty. He might be the only remaining ghiotte, but he wasn't the only person who'd grown up believing sin flowed in his veins, that his legacy was his destiny.

"Dea created a Finestra because connection *is* our salvation. Today, I'm asking you to prove her right. Will we barricade our doors and cover our ears against the screams of those who deliver our milk and brew our ale, or will we try and save every soul we can?"

Silence.

A lone cough echoed in the stillness, and her stomach sank as she wondered how long to stand there.

A finely dressed man stepped forward, hat in his hands. "It

isn't a fortress, but our family home can hold a dozen or more, and stone walls are better than none." He gestured at a ragged-looking woman with a baby on one hip and a toddler clinging to her leg, her marked wrists visible as she clutched her children to her. She burst into tears.

"I'm too old to be a soldier, but I have a good arm," said a swarthy man with thick muscles. "One of the Marked can have my spot in the Fortezza. I'd rather throw rocks at the bugs, anyway."

One by one, then in pairs and groups, people stepped forward. Some volunteering to fight, others to give their spots to those in need, yet more to welcome the overflow into their homes.

Hundreds of people, volunteering to face an army of demons armed with nothing but sticks and bats, knives and rusted pipes, choosing to fight so others might live.

If only Dante could see it. Dea's faith in them had not been wrong. And by sharing their sacrifice, no one had to bear it alone.

Together, we protect. Divided, we unravel.

And suddenly, she understood.

The key to her power had been right there the entire time.

Forty-Four

Nessuna nuova, buona nuova.

No news is good news.

DAYS BEFORE DIVORANDO: 11

S till reeling from her revelation, Alessa didn't notice the
door to her suite was open and nearly leapt out of her
boots when a figure popped out of nowhere.

"Oh, sorry!" Saida squeaked.

Kamaria awkwardly stood from the couch, favoring her
wounded leg. "Kaleb's awake and in a beast of a mood, but he doesn't
know anything about what's been happening, so we told him to go
back to sleep. What *happened* out there? Is Dante going to be okay?"

The sympathy on their faces was too much, and Alessa
crumpled.

"Oh, no." Kamaria limped over and gave Alessa a rib-
crunching hug, while Saida patted her back.

It wasn't the first time she'd wept that day, but this time she
cried with her friends' arms around her.

When the worst of her sobs were over, Saida ordered her to sit and bustled off to gather ingredients for something she swore cured heartache.

Alessa had no appetite, but any baker's daughter knew how food soothed the baker as much as the recipient, so she let Saida have at it.

Kamaria seemed relieved they'd moved past emotions and began ticking off a list of non-terrible aspects of the current situation on her fingers. "One, he's inside the Fortezza, so he won't get chewed up by scarabeo. Two, sounds like a lot of other people will be safe, too. We can figure something out after Divorando, but first, we need to get through it."

"Seriously?" came an indignant male voice from the doorway. Kaleb, clutching the doorframe. "You're having a party without me? Almost dying wasn't enough to earn me an invitation?"

"We're planning, Kaleb," Kamaria said.

"And baking!" Saida called from the kitchen.

"Using our brains and our skills." Kamaria smiled like a cat about to pounce. "What could you possibly contribute?"

"Ha ha ha," Kaleb said. He turned to look at someone in the hall. "Couldn't stay away, huh? Help me in, will you?"

Alessa stood as Josef helped Kaleb totter inside. "You aren't supposed to be here. I promised Nina I'd scratch you off the list."

"In exchange for a secret," Josef said. "The secret's out, so the deal is off."

"Was it her?" Kamaria asked. "Did *she* tell Ivini?"

"She says she didn't." Josef stopped, forcing Kaleb to stop with him. "She was scared and trying to protect me before, but she's not evil. Dante in prison doesn't help anyone."

"Then, if she kept her side of the deal . . ." Alessa said, a question in her voice.

"I've made my choice." Josef helped Kaleb sit on the couch. "Whether she likes it or not, I'm here to help."

Saida brushed flour from her hands and came over with a tray of teacups. Kaleb sniffed his, grumbling about adding something stronger.

"Any more distractions before we get on with it?" Kamaria asked. "Anyone need to use the restroom? Everybody got a snack? Your beverage of choice?"

"No," Kaleb grumbled, eying his tea.

"Aww, does baby need a nap?"

Kaleb stuck his tongue out at her.

"If we're all settled, then it's time to decide who's taking Kaleb's place. I may not be in the best shape of my life, but you find me a better pair of crutches, and I'll be there."

"Any of us would," Saida said. "It's up to you."

Alessa's idea came fully into focus as they all volunteered once again. For days, the pieces had been just out of reach, but watching so many people step up to give their safety away forged the final connection. "I think the texts are wrong."

"Care to be more specific?" Kamaria said.

"Sorry," Alessa said. "I'm still sorting through it. Okay, so, out of everyone on Saverio she could have chosen, Dea gave this gift to *me*, knowing who I am. How much I hate to be alone. How badly I wanted to be a part of a community. To make connections and have friends."

"Aw, group hug." Saida stepped forward, arms outstretched.

Kamaria hauled her back by her skirt. "Let her finish."

"The holy doctrine says I needed to lose my identity and be

isolated to form the kind of connection a Finestra and Fonte need, but I think, maybe that's bullshit."

"*Finestra,*" Kaleb gasped in faux horror. "Such *language.*"

"Shut up, Kaleb," Kamaria said.

"Shut up, Kamaria," Kaleb retorted, mimicking her tone so perfectly Saida got a case of the giggles.

"While we're on the topic," Alessa said, "can you all please use my name? I know there are rules, but I think some have gone off track over the past few hundred years."

"Screw rules," Kamaria said. "They're overrated."

Alessa smiled. "Well, um, hi. I'm Alessa Paladino. Nice to officially meet you."

"Alessa?" Kaleb said. "Really? I would have pegged you as a Mary, or maybe Marie."

"This is a fun little theological lesson," Kamaria said, earning an elbow from Kaleb. "But you still haven't told us who's going to hold your hand when the bugs come."

"That's what I'm trying to say." Alessa took a deep breath. "I was sort of hoping it would be . . . all of you."

Four pairs of eyes stared blankly at her.

"I think Kaleb collapsed because you were each absorbing part of my power, so no one was overloaded, but when you let go, Kaleb got the full force, and it was too much."

"Meaning?" Josef said.

"Meaning I'm *supposed* to have more than one Fonte. Simultaneously."

"Whoa," Saida said. "None of the texts ever mentioned such an idea."

"Didn't they, though?" Alessa smiled sadly. "*Together, we protect.* It's in every song. On every mural. Maybe it's what Dea wanted from the beginning. She told us to find safety in connection. In community. We—the *people*—wrote it down and turned it into a million rules regulating everything a Finestra could wear, touch, love, or speak to. The gods didn't make those rules. That was *us*."

"The apocalypse is coming in—" Kaleb pretended to check his watch. "Ten days? Eleven? Who can keep track? And we're throwing out the rulebook. Nice. What about the part that says ghiotte are evil?"

Alessa couldn't smile. "That one might take longer to fix, but we'll figure it out after we save the world."

Josef still looked dazed. "A *team* of Fontes?"

Kaleb cleared his throat. "Ahem. I have it on good authority that the correct pluralization of the word is *Fonti*."

Kamaria punched him on the arm, and they broke into a childish slapping fight.

Alessa watched them bicker with fierce affection. The Verità may have said loving no one was the only way to love everyone, but she'd fallen in love with Dante, and now her heart could burst with love for her friends.

Love didn't demand perfection. The people—human, flawed, imperfect—who'd begun writing the Verità hundreds of years ago might have started on the right path, but they'd gotten lost along the way, a pendulum swung so far it had snapped. And if they were wrong about that, they might be wrong about other things.

She'd tried to be like Renata, strong and stoic, hiding her emotions beneath a layer of cold detachment, and it had never fit. She'd tried to be what she thought the gods wanted her to be, what she was told the people needed her to be, and it had gotten her three dead partners, and a shell around her heart. She'd been stunted until she threw off the rules, shut the holy books, and let herself be the emotional, stubborn, distracted mess she was.

Her mistake was playacting at being someone *else*.

She *was* still Alessa. She was a person, a daughter, a sister, a lover, a friend. She didn't have to shed those roles to become Finestra. She only had to rearrange the parts she already had. She might be but one stitch in the tapestry, but every stitch had a purpose, and threads couldn't become art without them.

To become one of many, she had to be *one*.

And to win the battle, she needed her friends.

Forty-Five

Tardi si vien con l'acqua quando la casa è arsa.
It is too late for water when the house is burnt down.

One week before Divorando, Alessa couldn't take it any longer.

Saida and Kamaria were asleep in her bed after she'd made a big show of falling "asleep" on the couch hours earlier, and Josef and Kaleb were staying in the Fonte suite, so when she stole out of her room and eased the door closed, the coast should have been clear. But Kaleb, as always, was a pain in the ass.

"Leaving without me?" he wheezed, hanging onto the railing.

"What are you doing out of bed?"

"I couldn't sleep, and I heard you stomping around out here. I'm going with you."

"Going where?" she asked, innocently.

He gave her a look of utter exasperation. "If you say you took me to see the monster with my own eyes, maybe you won't get accused of treason. I wanted to scold the mongrel who dared to soil my angel, or something like that." He waved a dismissive hand. "Come on, help me down the stairs."

Alessa didn't want company and she didn't want to share the few stolen moments she got with Dante, but Kaleb had a point.

They paused midway across the courtyard so Kaleb could catch his breath. "Has no one wondered why I haven't been out and about? Truly?"

"We told everyone you're taking your duties so seriously you've become a recluse. The waving was very helpful, though." He'd waved magnanimously down to the servants from the hallway railing the day before.

"You're going to let him out, right?" Kaleb winced with every step, his fingers digging into her arm, his free hand white on the railing.

"I can't. Ivini's told his supporters to back us instead of fighting us, and it would all fall apart if I align myself with a ghiotte. I can't take that chance, especially after everyone agreed to let the Marked in. We're finally united."

"Yeah," Kaleb said. "Against someone who doesn't deserve it."

"Shocking, I know, but it turns out this whole divine savior thing isn't *quite* as fun as they made it sound."

"Not *fun?* What part of this isn't fun?" Kaleb snorted with laughter. "I'm having the time of my life, aren't you?"

"It's a party every day."

"Carnevale from morning to midnight."

"A birthday that never ends."

As they slowly made their way down through the Fortezza, they left the smooth walls of the main corridor for older, rougher tunnels, and finally, the catacombs. Kaleb was trembling and sweaty despite the damp cold, and the echoes of his wheezing made it seem as though the thousands of skulls lining the walls were breathing.

Two half-asleep guards stood outside the crypt where every deceased Fonte and Finestra lay in state.

"We're here to pray for the..." Alessa struggled to get the words out.

"Revoltingly hideous monster," Kaleb finished for her, speaking far louder than necessary. He grimaced and waved the guards away. "Shoo, will you? It's bad enough without being gawked at."

The guards traded irritated glances, but let them pass.

The mausoleum was entirely made of stone, with individual tombs on either side, gated to keep their occupants' eternal slumber from being disturbed.

When they reached the first empty crypt, which Alessa realized with a lurch might someday be hers, she could make out the lone figure in the dark.

The day she'd met him, Dante had been in a cage, but he'd been magnificent, dominating the space with grace and power. Now he slumped in a corner, his eyes dull and lifeless. And it was her fault.

She might have thrown herself at the bars in a sobbing mess if Kaleb hadn't shattered the moment.

"You're not dead," Kaleb said cheerfully.

Dante stood slowly, as if it took too much effort to move. "Neither are you."

Kaleb bent close to the bars and spoke in a stage whisper. "Don't know if you heard, but she tried her *very* best."

Dante's lip curled in a half smile. "She tried to kill me a few times, too."

"First torture, then she locks you up?" Kaleb shook his head. "Women."

Alessa rolled her eyes. "Yes, this is obviously a *woman* thing."

She could have kissed Kaleb for making light of the situation, though. Dante couldn't disguise his misery, his every movement jerky with tension, from the unconscious clench of his fingers to the tic in his jaw. It nearly broke her.

"She told you her theory?" Kaleb asked Dante.

After she finished explaining, Dante said nothing at first, merely stared at the wall. Then, "All of them, huh? You couldn't have figured that out a few weeks ago?"

They laughed for too long, sitting in the dark, with bars between them and marble tombs all around, amidst the scurrying of rats and insects, a few days away from Armageddon.

Kaleb gave them a sheepish grin. "Well, I'm sure you'd like some privacy, but I don't think I can make it up the stairs without help." He turned to Alessa. "And you shouldn't be here alone."

Dante tensed.

"Relax," said Kaleb. "I'm not accusing you of anything. Well, I mean—eh, not my business. Actually, I guess it is my business? But I don't really want it to be, so anyway, there are appearances to keep up, and it needs to *look* like she hates you, so I'll just . . . turn around for a few minutes."

It was as close as they'd get to being alone, so Alessa put Kaleb from her mind and pressed her face to the bars. Dante met her there, warm skin framed by cold metal. She worked her hands into the stained fabric of his shirt, pulling him as close as she could.

The only sound was his rasping breath.

"Not much longer," she whispered. "I'll never let this happen to you again."

"Don't make promises you can't keep, luce mia." Dante kissed her forehead through the bars. "And don't worry about me. I've been through worse. Probably will again."

Her cheeks grew wet with tears. "How did you survive it for all those years?"

Dante made a low, exhausted sound. "You don't want to hear about that."

"I want to know everything you're willing to share with me." She lifted his hand to trace the lines on his dirt-creased palm, seeking to memorize the feel of every calloused fingertip and taut tendon. Raising it to her mouth, she pressed a kiss to the dark smudge inside his wrist, all that remained of the false tattoo, in silent apology. "You don't have to tell me anything. Especially now. It's not the time."

"I'm in a jail cell. Seems like the perfect time for confessions." Dante drew her hand through the bars and held it to his rough cheek. "He used to taunt me."

Alessa swallowed. She'd come to recognize the inflection on the word *he* when Dante discussed his abuser. He never said the man's name, and she suspected he never would. Names had power, as Dante knew.

"He liked to remind me that I was the last ghiotte. 'You're all alone and you'll die alone, and when you do, there will be no more.' Like he knew that would break me."

"The scarabeo had better eat him slowly."

Dante huffed a laugh. "He was wrong, though. And I held on to that for three years."

She resented the involuntary tremor her body conjured at the thought of other ghiotte, prowling the forests of Saverio like she'd always imagined in her nightmares, but a lifetime of tales were hard to forget. "There *are* others? On Saverio?"

"Not anymore." Dante's grip eased, tacit permission for her to pull away, but she didn't. "By the time I got free and went to find them, they were dead. Burned in their beds. Nothing left of their house but ash and ruins."

Alessa closed her eyes against the sting of tears.

"I refused to believe it at first. Went to the nearest village, certain they'd be there, and I saw my aunt. She'd barely look at me, told me to get as far away as possible, change my name, and never come back. She's not ghiotte, so they spared her, but Uncle Matteo and Talia . . . Gone."

No wonder he cursed the gods. Crollo might have made his body impervious to injury, but not his heart. She refused to believe Dante *was* cursed, but she couldn't deny his life had been. Yet, somehow, he'd kept swimming against an ocean of grief, fighting the current that fought to drag him down, to shape him into Crollo's monster.

She twined their fingers together. "It's almost over. Soon, it'll be nothing but clear skies, cats, and beaches forever more."

He smiled sadly. "You're going to do great, you know."

She rubbed the back of his hand with her thumb. "I'd fight better if I had Saverio's best bodyguard looking out for me."

Dante's sigh was so heavy with regret she felt it in her toes.

The final days sped past in a dizzying blur of preparations as the Fortezza prepared to become a hospital and the army readied their battle stations, while the ragged militia practiced with their ugly but effective-looking homemade weaponry in the piazza.

Alessa and the Fontes trained unceasingly.

They worked out a system, a rotation of sorts, to be sure everyone had a chance to breathe and restore their strength, while ensuring no one was left alone to bear the brunt of her power. Even now, the few times their timing was off left the Fontes in agony.

With every day, her power grew, as though it, too, could sense the looming darkness on the horizon.

Dante loomed, too, his face appearing in her mind at all times, no matter how inopportune, and every time, her power ran away with her.

Kaleb didn't participate in the training, though he'd offered, but they let him sit in a chair, covered with blankets, despite his irritated protests that he looked like a sad, old man.

Three days before Divorando, their training was interrupted by a kitchen maid nervously twisting her hands in a flour-covered apron.

Apparently, a certain delivery boy had barricaded himself inside the pantry, refusing to leave unless Alessa spoke with him. The girl would have called the guards to knock down the door and drag him out, but it seemed the kitchen staff was rather fond of the charming boy from the bakery, and they were hoping Alessa wouldn't insist on that option.

"Traitors," Alessa muttered. After sending the girl to relay a carefully worded message laden with swear words, Alessa gave a terse summary of her last run-in with her brainwashed brother, before leading Saida, Josef, and Kamaria downstairs.

Kaleb stayed behind, sulking at missing out on the fun.

The kitchen staff cleared out when Alessa arrived.

"Go home, Adrick," she said, glaring through the cracked pantry door.

"Not until you listen to me."

"The last time I listened to you, you tried to get me to kill myself."

Josef stepped toward the pantry. "Would you like us to make him leave, Finestra? I'm happy to freeze him out, or Kamaria could light the door on fire."

Kamaria cracked her knuckles loudly. Adrick's hair blew around his face as Saida joined in.

"I was an ass and I'm sorry," Adrick said. "If you'd rather light me on fire than listen, so be it, but I'm not leaving."

Alessa groaned. "Give us a minute, but if I shout, come running."

Kamaria, Josef, and Saida retreated to the far side of the kitchen wearing matching glares as Adrick slunk out of the pantry.

"I'm sorry," Adrick said, his shoulders hunched. "I've felt terrible ever since—well, you know. But I really thought I was doing the right thing. How could I have known you were being sabotaged? I didn't even think ghiotte still existed!"

Alessa flexed her fingers. This was the point, wasn't it? To let Dante take the fall so she was absolved from blame? Still, it was infuriating to hear it from Adrick's lips.

"I got so stinking drunk that night, because I was all torn up, and the brother I was drinking with kept rambling on about this kid he'd tried to save from damnation, swore he was a ghiotte, and he'd tracked him down to the city where the kid was fighting for money—anyway, it took me a few days to figure out why the name sounded familiar, but eventually it clicked."

Alessa cursed.

"I told Ivini as soon as I found out," Adrick went on, oblivious. "And he saved you, so we're even, right?"

Alessa's hands itched to wrap around her brother's neck. "*You* told Ivini? Because you thought it would make me *forgive* you? If you weren't my brother, I'd kill you."

Adrick's mouth moved in silent confusion. "I—I thought— Alessa, he's a ghiotte!"

"I'm aware," she said. "A ghiotte who saved my life more than once, including the time my own brother tried to convince me to *kill myself*. So, that's why you're here? To claim credit for saving me from the ghiotte? Dante *helped* me. He *believed* in me. *He* never betrayed me. Sorry to break it to you, Adrick, but you can't lay the blame on him. Still wish I'd taken that poison?"

Adrick exhaled shakily. "No. No, I'm really glad you didn't. You're my sister. I love you."

She rolled her eyes.

"And—" He cringed. "And because a ship arrived from Altari an hour ago, crammed with people."

"Altari? Why?" Alessa asked. "Is their Finestra even worse than I am?"

Adrick swallowed. "Their Finestra is dead."

The air beat against her eardrums.

"A new one didn't rise. Their island is completely defenseless."

"Are you saying I have *two* islands counting on me now?" Alessa said.

Just when she thought the weight of responsibility couldn't possibly get heavier.

"So, what, you heard their story and realized *you* could have been responsible for two islands being in their position?"

Adrick seemed to shrink in on himself.

"Doesn't feel good, does it? Welcome to my life, Adrick. It's a lot easier to blame someone else when things go wrong than it is when *your* decisions have terrible consequences. If I'd taken that poison, two islands' worth of people would be waiting to die."

"Go ahead," Adrick said flatly. "Let them turn me into an icicle or a torch or whatever."

"Did you see my brother, Shomari?" Kamaria interrupted, unable to pretend she wasn't eavesdropping for another moment. "Or are other ships still on the way?"

Adrick made a face. "They put the most vulnerable people on the fastest ships and sent them first. Their gifted folk took the last and slowest, because they'll have a better chance of defending themselves if they don't make it in time."

Kamaria deflated. "There's still time, though. We could have a whole army of Fontes on the peak!"

"Um," Adrick said, looking a bit gray. "The wind hasn't blown all day, though. This ship barely made it."

Alessa's vision of an army of Fontes vanished in a puff, but the disappointment paled in comparison to her horror at the thought of a ship stranded at sea when the scarabeo came.

"My gift is wind," Saida said. "Is this my cue to run to the docks?"

And so, with Kaleb weakened, Kamaria injured, and Saida setting off on a desperate rescue mission, Alessa's newfound team of Fontes dwindled once more.

Forty-Six

Le leggi sono fatte pei tristi.
Laws were made for rogues.

DAYS BEFORE DIVORANDO: 2

Alessa's final training session with her remaining Fontes was falling apart. The next day was reserved for prayer and rest, as the Finestra and Fonte asked for Dea's blessings, the soldiers readied their weapons, and the last of Saverio settled into their assigned quarters inside the Fortezza, which would be locked at midnight. She needed every minute of practice, but it was impossible to focus.

Saida still hadn't returned, so somewhere beyond the horizon, an entire ship of Fontes was lost at sea, unprotected. The weather had turned chaotic—frigid rain one hour, scorching sun the next, sudden windstorms ripping shingles from rooftops and sending them skittering across the piazza like autumn leaves—and every climatic shift was punctuated by shudders from the island itself.

Meanwhile, Dante was moldering away in a crypt, and Alessa couldn't close her eyes without envisioning marble walls cracking, metal bars screaming under a ceiling collapsing into a crush of rubble. The Cittadella had weathered every Divorando before, and Dea would hold it together through this one as well, but Alessa's gut twisted every time she thought of Dante, caged and alone in the darkness.

She had one job, one responsibility—to use Dea's gift to save them—but this last practice, when she should have been at her peak, she kept slipping, losing control, and overwhelming her training partners.

She kept insisting it was only nerves, but it wasn't.

She'd visited Dante twice before Renata caught her returning and banned her from doing so again. Each time, he'd seemed more faded than the last. They might both be dead soon, and his last breaths would be spent in the exact type of misery he'd been running from for years.

Kaleb threw his blankets on the ground and stood. "Enough."

"Enough what?" Kamaria snapped. Her injured leg had given out an hour earlier, and she sat on the floor, looking mutinous.

"She's falling apart."

"I'm sorry." Alessa folded in on herself. "It won't happen during battle, I promise."

Kaleb made a face. "Just let me do it already."

Kamaria glared. "Do *what?*"

"Take his place. Obviously. We all know why she's a mess. I'll take a snooze behind bars, and you'll be able to keep your mind on the fight."

Alessa wrinkled her brow. "I don't think the people of Saverio will trade their Fonte for a ghiotte."

"They don't have to know," Kaleb said grimly. "One man in a crypt is as good as another if you're afraid to get too close."

"If people found out—"

"They lock the Fortezza until the battle is over, and anyone who tries to open the gates after midnight tonight gets kicked out. All I have to do is avoid turning around until the gates are shut, and it's done. It's a win-win, really. For everyone but me."

"Why would you do that?"

Kaleb picked at his fingernails. "He'll be a lot more useful than me on that peak. I can't say I was looking forward to fighting, but it turns out I'm even less excited to sit around and hide under blankets like a worthless lump. So, give him a sword and shove me in with the dead. At least I'll be helping in *some* way."

"And how do you suggest we switch you without anyone noticing?" Kamaria asked.

Kaleb collapsed into his chair. "Do you expect me to do all the work here?"

"I have an idea." Alessa lit up with hope. "I happen to have a brother who owes me a favor."

"Well?" Kaleb asked, stepping out from behind Alessa's screen. "How do I look?" In Dante's clothing, with his hair darkened by grease, Kaleb could have tricked most people into thinking he was Dante. Not Alessa, though. Maybe, if she didn't look straight at him. No, not even then. But his disguise would have to be good enough.

As far as Renata and Tomo knew, Alessa, Kaleb, Kamaria, and Josef were holed up in her suite, strategizing and exchanging last-minute advice. It wasn't *entirely* false. They just had another victory to secure first.

Kaleb leaned against the wall, crossed his arms, and glared at Josef and Kamaria. "Not bad, eh?"

"Spot on," Alessa said. It felt wrong to laugh at a time like this, but they were all nervous, and laughter might be the best release.

Kamaria jabbed Kaleb in the side. "You just have to lie down and not move. This isn't the time to get cocky."

Kaleb looked down his nose at Kamaria and picked up a large, hunter green cloak with a magenta lining, swooping it over his shoulders. "Kammy, I was *born* cocky."

"Gross." Kamaria made a gagging face. In tan-colored pants tied at the waist with twine, her hair covered by a plaid cap, Kamaria looked like the world's prettiest delivery boy. With any luck, no one would recognize her and wonder why so many Fontes were wandering around the crypts hours before the Cittadella was locked in preparation for Divorando.

"Can we please stay on task?" Alessa asked. "Josef, you'll be waiting. Kamaria?"

"Ready." Kamaria pulled a matchbox from her pocket and struck a match. With a flare, she made the flickering spot of fire hop from the match to a lantern waiting on the table nearby, growing and shrinking the flame until it was precisely as she wanted it. "This will be fun."

"If we don't get caught," Alessa said.

"What are they going to do?" Kaleb said. "Banish us? Too late now. They lock up at midnight. No one in, no one out until the war is won. Or lost. Please don't lose, though. I'm going to be so mad if I spend my last days in some nasty jail cell."

Alessa blew out a breath. "I guess we're ready, then."

Kamaria gave Alessa a saucy wink and tipped her cap.

Below the Cittadella, the main tunnel rumbled with voices.

The air was thick with shared breath and the constant noise of people. People, everywhere.

Alessa and Kaleb stopped frequently to accept words of encouragement and share sympathetic smiles with the Altarians, who were mixed in with Saverians.

On Alessa's arm, Kaleb flashed grins and blew kisses, making a spectacle of waving his cloak around to be sure everyone saw him in it.

The gates were open for one more hour.

They turned the final corridor to the crypts, and found the entrance blocked by a crowd of civilians and a half dozen robed cult members, including Ivini.

One of the robed people was Adrick. Giving Alessa a pointed look, he raised a hand as though to scratch his ear, signing one-handed, "I tried."

Alessa gritted her teeth. Adrick's only job had been convincing Ivini to let him stand guard over the ghiotte for the night. He was supposed to be *alone*. Instead, it was a veritable party of everyone she didn't want to see.

"Ah, Finestra, Fonte," Ivini said, his eyes glittering at the sight of Alessa and Kaleb. "What brings you down here?"

Alessa smiled with benign grace. "One last visit to pray over the creature, Padre. By blessing him, I hope to mitigate the pall he casts over our Fortezza."

"Wonderful," Ivini breathed. "We came to do the same. You must have heard, as I did, that the brave soldiers who were guarding him had to report for battle duty, but no fear, we promised to take over. We'll make sure the prisoner is watched properly."

"Lovely," Alessa said, twisting her hands inside her pockets. Time for the backup plan.

Alessa led the absurdly large procession into the crypts and knelt before Dante's prison. He was curled in the very back, on the ground, and he didn't move despite the noise of so many people outside.

Her heart thudded in her ears, but she began reciting Dea's blessing as slowly as possible. Dante made no sign he was even alive.

Dea, if you love me at all, it's the perfect time for a miracle.

Instead, she got a rock.

It struck the bars, ricocheting back at her. Alessa whirled to face the crowd.

"Who threw that?"

Blank faces. A little boy raised his hand. "I wasn't aiming for you, miss. I thought I had a shot at the ghiotte."

Alessa saw red. "We are here to pray."

"But I didn't get my chance yet." The boy squawked as a man—presumably his father—hauled him back by his shirt, hissing for him to be quiet.

His chance. He hadn't had *his chance* to throw a rock at the ghiotte.

Dante's stillness was more ominous than ever. It had never been so difficult to act calm and in control.

Just when it couldn't possibly get worse, Nina arrived.

Forty-Seven

In bocca al lupo/ Crepi il lupo.
Into the wolf's mouth/May the wolf die.

P adre, you shouldn't go near that creature." Nina sniffed, thrusting her chin in the air. "Oh, hello, *Josef.* Funny seeing *you* here. Still running errands for the Finestra?"

"Duty called," Josef said, looking proud as a peacock. "And I answered."

"I bet it did." Nina looked up at the ceiling, blinking as if trying not to cry. "I knew you'd run back to her. She's clearly captivated you with her beauty and benevolence. How could a mere mortal *ever* compete?"

Josef puffed himself up even more. "We're facing the end of the world, Nina. The future of every life on Saverio is more important than your silly feelings."

Nina's mouth fell open. *"Silly feelings?"*

"Oh, good grief," Kamaria muttered from somewhere in the crowd, and every lantern sputtered out.

Nina let out an ear-splitting shriek, then it was nothing but scuffling, yelling, and Kaleb whispering in Alessa's ear, "This is going smashingly, isn't it?"

Alessa pulled an ungloved hand from her pocket. A small hand grasped it, and her stomach lurched.

Shouts of dismay echoed through the crypt, calling for someone to re-light the lanterns, but every match struck flared out immediately.

The hand was gone, and silk brushed her arm.

"Doesn't *anyone* have a light?" Alessa said.

A flame burst to life, so bright she had to shield her eyes.

Kamaria, cap pulled down to shade her face, swaggered over, holding out a lantern. "Here, miss," she said, her voice pitched low. "Mine seems to be working."

Ivini snatched the lantern before Alessa could.

Ignoring a flurry of indignant gasps, he hurried to the metal gate of Dante's prison, banging the lantern against the bars in his haste. The same still form lay curled in the back.

Eyes narrowed with suspicion, Ivini lowered the light to study the heavy padlock, intact and untouched.

"Excuse me," Alessa said.

Grumbling under his breath, Ivini handed it over.

Alessa tugged her companion toward the corridor, where a suspicious number of lanterns had gone out. The hooded cloak shadowed his face, but not enough to disguise the bruises at such a close distance. "What did they do to you? I thought they didn't have a key."

Dante spoke through gritted teeth. "Don't need a key when you can throw rocks."

Rage burned through her veins, but it had to wait. She'd planned for a quick march through the crowded levels with an alert Dante playing along. Instead, his arm grew heavier around her shoulders, his steps halting, and as they made painstaking progress toward the more crowded levels, every face turning to watch sent a bolt of fear through her.

She cast a desperate look over her shoulder at Kamaria and Josef, who were hanging back and trying to blend in with the hundreds of other Saverians milling about.

People would panic if they raced to prop up "Kaleb," but it would be worse if he fell. Even worse if everyone realized it wasn't Kaleb at all.

Eventually, they reached the main corridor, and she could make out the Cittadella gate.

"Almost there," she whispered. "Only a little farther."

Two figures stepped into their path. Of all the moments.

"Finestra," her mother said, her hand white-knuckled on Papa's arm. "I'd appreciate a second of your time."

Alessa braced her feet to keep Dante upright. "We're in a bit of a hurry, I'm afraid."

"Please." Her voice faltered. "Your brother told us what he did."

"I don't have a brother," Alessa said, her tone flat. "Or a family." And it still hurt as badly as it had the day she'd left.

"I know you're angry at me, but I was trying to do as I was told. As the gods wanted me to. Adrick—" She raised a hand to her mouth.

"He should have protected you." Her father tugged at his short beard. "Not done . . . what he did."

Dante stumbled, catching himself as though he'd almost passed out, and it sent a bolt of panic through Alessa. "I'm glad you object to your son trying to kill the Finestra, but I really must go."

"We object to our *son* trying to hurt his *sister*." Her mother tugged at a lock of gray-threaded hair come loose from her bun. "I was raised to believe it was my duty to forsake my child if he or she was chosen. But I had a duty to you as well. I knew—" She waved a hand. "I knew he visited, and I never asked. I was afraid of what I'd hear. And now . . ." She pressed a hand to her mouth, her breath hissing. "I should have asked. I should have come."

"Did the ghiotte—did he harm you?" Papa asked.

"No," Alessa said. She didn't know if Dante was fully aware of her words, but she said them for him, too. "He protected me. Always."

"When I think of how lonely you must have been to welcome him into your confidence—"

Adrick jogged up, alarm written across his face as he took in the family reunion. "I already apologized, Papa. Let her go. She's got important stuff to do."

Alessa shot Adrick a desperate look, her knees buckling under Dante's weight.

"At least take these." Her mother held out a bundle of envelopes bound with string.

"Okay, Mama, let them go." Adrick took the parcel and bent to wedge it into the pocket of Dante's cloak, blanching as he peeked beneath the hood.

Mama's brow furrowed as Dante's bowed head lolled forward.

They needed to get him inside. Now.

"Mama, Papa," Alessa whispered, holding them with her gaze. "If you've ever believed me about anything, trust me on this. He's

Dea's child, as much as you or I. Probably more. I know what the Verità says, but—"

"If you say it, we believe you," Mama said.

Desperate relief flooded Alessa's body. "Then help me."

They might not have fully understood, but her parents weren't fools.

"May I pray with you, Finestra?" her mother asked loudly. "My husband and son would like to pray with our good Fonte."

Papa threw his beefy arms wide, and Alessa shoved Dante at him. A Finestra couldn't touch anyone but their Fonte, but a Fonte wasn't limited the same way.

With a jovial grin, Papa dragged Dante's arm around his shoulders, while Adrick gave his arm a hearty squeeze, and together, they walked him toward the gate.

Josef and Kamaria slipped past, while Alessa pretended to listen to her mother's rambling prayer.

When they were nearly to the gate, Mama's prayer trailed off. Her eyes welled with tears. "Be safe, my sweet girl."

Swallowing the lump in her throat, Alessa hurried to catch up with Papa and Dante.

At the gate to the Cittadella, her father clapped Dante on the back, practically knocking him into Josef.

Kamaria's gift again made every lantern in the corridor sputter out, drawing scattered screams from every direction as they tumbled inside. Adrick and Josef shared the load of getting Dante up the stairs, every step seeming higher than the last, until they reached the main floor and Adrick had to turn back. Alessa took over, and together they minced across the courtyard, their odd clothing and stilted movements drawing a confused stare from a passing guard.

Alessa grinned widely. "Too many toasts, but a little espresso will sort him right out!"

The guard shrugged.

Upstairs, Kamaria hobbled around, fetching soap and juice while Josef steadied Dante so Alessa could help him out of his filthy clothes.

Alessa looked up from trying to wrench off Dante's shoes at a gasp from the doorway.

"I wasn't looking, Josef, I wasn't looking!" Nina covered her eyes.

Josef sighed and shook his head.

"Did I do all right?" Nina wiggled with pride. "I know my acting was a *bit* over the top, but I had to commit, or it would never be convincing. Josef, you were so *dashing*! The bars bent back in place beautifully, and I think the scream really helped."

"It did," Alessa said. "Thank you."

Nina's lip trembled. "Least I could do. I'm really—"

"You can apologize after the battle, okay?"

Tears glittered on Nina's coppery lashes. "Or during?"

Alessa smiled. "Sure. We're bound to have a few breaks, right?"

Kamaria deposited a tray of steaming bowls and mugs on the table, and swiped the pile of Dante's filthy, torn clothing from the floor. "I'll toss these."

Alessa didn't even bother taking off her own clothes when she and Josef got Dante down to the salt baths, wading into the water fully dressed. "I'll yell if I need you."

Josef nodded. "I'll bring down the broth."

One arm around his chest, Alessa cradled Dante in the water, using her other hand to wet his hair and stroke it back from his face.

Her heart tightened at the memory of when *she* was the injured one soaking while Dante lounged on the stairs, scoffing at her theories about ghiotte. She couldn't remember what she'd said, but her words must have stung, adding another layer of cuts on top of a lifetime of scars. How many times had Dante bit his tongue while people like her discussed how evil he was, how selfish and horrible his parents had been?

She'd spent years wondering if there was something wrong with her, if she was a mistake, a flaw in the divine tapestry of the world, and it had nearly killed her. He'd lived with it his entire life.

Despite a lifetime of misery, Dante had helped a little girl in an alley being bullied by someone stronger and more powerful. He'd chosen to say yes when a scared young woman asked for help.

He'd stayed when he could've left, loved when he could have hated, and he'd let himself be locked up to protect people who had no qualms about making him suffer.

They didn't deserve him.

Josef tiptoed into the bathing room with the tray, nudging it close to the edge so Alessa could reach.

Dante's eyes were closed, but he drifted in and out of consciousness, occasionally wincing as she dabbed his wounds with a wet cloth.

"Don't bother. I'll heal soon enough," he said.

She reached for a spoon, determined to get some sustenance into him so his powers could work unhindered. "Will you let me take care of you, for once?"

"No one takes care of me," he slurred.

Tears pricked her eyes. "I do. Now shush."

The broth, or his powers, revived him enough for a smile to

curl his lips. "Aren't you supposed to kiss injuries to make them better?"

She pressed a kiss to his temple.

"That doesn't count."

"If I kiss you like I *want* to," she scolded, "you'd drop dead from exertion. Heal yourself, and I'll make it worth your while."

His eyes opened. "When is Divorando?"

"Not for another day. Don't worry about it right now. You need to rest."

Josef must have been waiting with his ears cocked at the top of the stairs, because he clattered down the moment she called for help. Together, they hauled Dante from the water, wrapped him in towels, and maneuvered him up the stairs.

Josef was adorably mortified about tucking a sleeping ghiotte into his Finestra's bed.

"Go and be with Nina. She did great."

Josef beamed at her. "She did, didn't she? She really is very sorry—"

Alessa stopped him with a hand. "We've all made mistakes. She was scared and trying to protect someone she loved. I've had enough revenge fantasies tonight to understand that. Besides, I'm going to need all of you on the peak."

Josef bowed low. "It will be my honor, Finestra."

Alessa laughed. "After tonight, don't you think you can bring yourself to use my name?"

"It would be an honor, Miss Paladino."

She nudged his shoulder. "Good enough for now. We'll work on it."

When Josef was gone, she crawled into bed beside Dante.

He groaned and opened one eye. "I feel like shit."

"You look like shit."

He wheezed a laugh. "Aw, luce mia. You do know how to make a man's heart flutter." He groaned. "Is this what it feels like to die? Should I tell you my name now?"

"You're not dying. You're malnourished and not healing at your usual rate. But you *can* tell me your name."

"Ha," he said with a wince. "Nice try. If I'm *not* dying, you don't get it until after you save the world."

"Well, you're too feeble to run away, so I'll get it out of you eventually. Now, sleep."

At some point, his breathing settled, and with it, her last reserves of energy abandoned her.

She clung to him through the night, legs threaded with his, face pressed to his shoulder, counting the hours in the metronome of his heartbeat.

She woke to Dante's sleep-roughened voice. "Aren't you supposed to spend this time in worship?"

Alessa threw the covers back, sighing in relief at his lack of bruises. "What does it look like I'm doing?"

He made a low sound of approval as she ran a hand down his chest. "Gotta remember what you're fighting for, eh? Didn't you say you'd kiss all my injuries?"

"You had *a lot* of injuries, but I'll do my best."

When hunger finally drove them from bed, Alessa and Dante raided the stash of food left by the kitchen staff before they'd retreated to the safety of the Fortezza. The morning slid by in a flurry of kissing, strategizing, eating—Dante insisted they "fuel for battle," which apparently meant snacking every hour—and the occasional stretch of stillness when the full impact of what they were about to face knocked the breath from Alessa. In those moments, Dante seemed to sense the shift in her mood before she did, and he'd pull her onto his lap to quiet her fluttering fingers with a squeeze of his hands, holding her until it passed.

During one bout of nervous shivers, he pulled a cloak from the back of the couch and draped it over them.

"What's this?" He pulled out a bundle of papers, and she took it, untying the string in silence.

"Letters," she said. "From my mother." She flipped through the stack, noting the dates written on the top of each, but not reading any further.

"You going to read them?"

She closed her eyes. "I don't know. I'm overwhelmed just knowing she wrote them at all."

Dante gave her a peck on the cheek. "I'll give you a minute to think about it."

He left to take a shower, and she dared to open the first letter, dated on her fourteenth birthday, weeks after she'd left home for the Cittadella.

> *My dear girl,*
> *I know I'm not supposed to, but I can't help missing you*
> *more than words can say. They held a parade for you*
> *today. Adrick says you looked beautiful, but I couldn't*
> *bring myself to go. How could I, when it would break my*
> *heart even more to see you and have to pretend you aren't*
> *my daughter?*

"Knock, knock. Had enough prayer yet?"

Alessa scrubbed her face of tears and tucked the letter into Dante's book of proverbs, holding it close as she went to open the door.

"Everyone dressed and decent after all that praying?" Kamaria peeked through a gap in her fingers. "Can't have my virgin eyes sullied on the eve of battle."

Nina blushed, and Josef looked scandalized.

"We didn't want to interrupt your prayer—" Nina shot Kamaria a scolding look for her snorted laugh. "But we wanted to check on Dante, and the sun is setting, so the *day* of prayer is technically over. Besides, we have nothing to do but rest, and it's too early to sleep."

"We could spend some more time worrying," Kamaria said. "That's still on my to-do list."

There was another knock on the door.

"Dea help us," Alessa said. "It's the day before the apocalypse, and we're throwing a party."

Adrick stood outside, looking sheepish.

"What are you *doing* here?" Alessa demanded. "You're supposed to be inside the Fortezza."

"I knew you'd fuss, so I hid until the gates were locked. Too late now! I'm going to fight with the militia and help tend the wounded. Warrior medic, at your service."

Alessa sagged against the doorframe. "*Now* you decide to be heroic? I swear, you'll be the death of me."

Adrick smiled hesitantly. "At least this time it's not intentional?"

She sighed. "Come in, then. We have enough food to serve the whole army, but nothing's hot, and the beverage selection is lacking, unless you're a fan of room temperature limoncello."

Adrick rubbed his hands together. "My favorite."

"I believe some of you have met my brother." Adrick's assistance with their heist hadn't been enough to outweigh his past offenses, but it appeared they'd tolerate him.

Dante strolled out, half dressed, as she finished the tense introductions. Adrick startled, visibly astonished at the sight of Dante glowing with health, in stark contrast to the broken wretch they'd smuggled out of the crypt the night before.

"Oh, hey. Gang's all here," Dante said, bicep flexing as he dragged a hand through his damp hair.

Adrick made a soft noise of approval and elbowed Alessa, which she pointedly ignored.

"They came to check on you," she said. "And my jackass brother decided to become a medic at the eleventh hour, so we're stuck with him, too. I'm kicking them out after we eat, because everyone needs a good night's sleep."

"Yeah, yeah," Kamaria said, waving her off. "Any last minute instructions? Pep talks? Battle cries?"

"Yes," Josef said. "We need a team motto."

Dante eyed the book of proverbs in Alessa's hands. "In bocca al lupo. *In the mouth of the wolf.* It means 'good luck.'"

"The wolf's mouth?" Kamaria said. "I don't get it."

"Some say it means to face danger—the wolf—and hope for victory. Others think it refers to how a mother wolf carries her babies, safe from harm despite her sharp teeth. The correct response is, 'Crepi il lupo' or 'Crepi.' *May the wolf die.'*"

Alessa flinched.

"It's just an expression," Dante said to her alone.

"I like it," said Josef. "In bocca al lupo!"

"Crepi!" Kamaria shouted back, fist raised, but it sounded more like *crappy*, and everyone laughed, except for Dante, and it seemed to cost him immense effort not to.

"When this battle is over, I'm giving you all pronunciation lessons."

"All right," Alessa said. "Now that we have our rallying cry, dig in."

"Eat, drink, and be merry." Nina passed a basket of fresh bread to Josef.

Kamaria raised her baguette like a flute of prosecco. "For tomorrow, we may die."

Forty-Eight

Tutti son bravi quando l'inimico fugge.
All are brave when the enemy flies.

DIVORANDO

Doom had a color. Not quite black, but a dark gray shot with blue that reeked of foreboding.

A distant shadow on the slate sea grew closer and larger, expanding to hide the horizon. Below Finestra's Peak, the surface of the ocean was still, holding its breath.

The low, steady beat of the infantry's drum line was meant to evoke an army of steady heartbeats thumping in time. No fear, no doubt, no individuals. A collective.

Alessa's heart revolted, hammering so fast it seemed to lose its rhythm every few beats.

Windows were boarded and streets swept clean. Her army was a phalanx of gleaming armor, but the wall of metal could not entirely hide the people behind it. The grimy but determined faces of the slapdash militia peered through the gaps, searching for salvation.

Searching for her.

She could almost see herself through their eyes. A girl on a cliff, clad in only a thin shift, a breastplate, and a helmet, her arms and hands, legs and feet bare. Every limb had to be exposed and accessible for her *Fontes*, not Fonte, to easily grasp even if they fell.

They, too, wore minimal armor. Only a tunic of delicate chainmail and a helmet, pants cut off mid-calf.

The Captain of the Guard and his finest fighters manned points around the peak, ready to die if needed to keep Alessa and the Fontes alive to fight. Dante stood between the Fontes and their ranks, a bit closer to Alessa than the rest of the guards because he was still, somewhat, pretending to be Kaleb.

Tomo, Renata, and the members of the Consiglio were barricaded behind the high walls of the Cittadella, coordinating communication between the various battalions stationed around the island to stop any scarabeo who made it past the first defenses, ready and waiting to coordinate the rescue of wounded.

Soon, the hillside would be littered with shredded bodies, the dirt stained with blood.

If she only watched the surface of the ocean, she might have thought a storm was rolling in. A shadow, stretching across the waves, a hum that became a rumble. But the cascade of terror washing over her was not from the weather.

Wings beat, the sound of a runaway cart on a track rolling ever faster down a steep hill. Her heart accelerated. With the ocean still, there was no crash or roar of the waves to muffle the drone of a million wings, the clicking of mandibles.

In every past Divorando, Finestra and Fonte had lived to walk away.

Would they today?

Would anyone?

She held out her hands to Josef and Kamaria.

It was absolutely ridiculous to feel embarrassed while waiting for death, but Alessa shuffled her feet and stared at the ground after letting go for the second time. It was hard to gauge distances over an ocean, and she kept acting too early. And every time she took their hands, holding her power in check, the entire army stomped their feet and banged their weapons together, making it even more awkward when another ten minutes passed without an attack.

As she dropped their hands and kicked her feet to stay limber, Dante broke from the line of Fontes and came over to her. He flipped up his face shield to reveal brown eyes beneath tousled dark hair and smiled his crooked grin.

This close, he blocked her view of everything beyond, and for several breaths, there was no army, no field of weapons and fighters. Only the ocean at her back, wind whipping loose tendrils of hair into her face. Only Dante, who moved carefully so no one would see him clasp her hand between them.

"You can do this."

"I know." Alessa managed to resist hurling herself into his arms.

She would, because she had to. And sometimes that was all there was—necessity. She loved her home. She loved the people of Saverio. She would protect them at *any* cost. It seemed so simple now. It hadn't, not so long ago, but the past month had reminded her about love, and she'd never forget again.

Saverio did not have to love her, or protect her, or give her anything. She loved the island like a mother loved a child, without weighing the costs or benefits. The way she loved Dante. If he hadn't come, or hadn't loved her, she still would have loved him until her dying breath.

Love was not conditional. It simply was.

"I'll be right behind you," he said and kissed her hand.

A shout rose from below, but the swarm was still a way off.

Confused, Alessa turned to see a man wading through the crowd. The soldiers let him pass.

They shouldn't have.

Forty-Nine

A chi dici il tuo segreto, doni la tua liberta.
Do not put a sword into your enemy's hands.

Ivini marched a sheepish Kaleb through the ranks of soldiers.

"Hello there, Finestra," Kaleb called up with a cheery wave. "This chap just can't let it go. Made them open the gates and everything, but I want it noted in every history book that I told him it is a banishable offense. More than once. He's not the best listener."

Ivini's eyes flashed from below. "She brought the *creature* to stand beside her. I was right all along."

"And I was right about *you*," Alessa shot back. "So determined to win at all costs that you've thrown away your chance to be sheltered. They're coming, *Padre* Ivini. If you aren't ready to fight, I hope you're ready to die."

Ivini glanced back at the troops. "I had to warn the armies. A ghiotte on the peak? Unacceptable."

"Are you volunteering to take his place?" she asked. "We do have the best view."

Kaleb pulled himself up onto a nearby armory wagon, stocked with extra weaponry for anyone who lost theirs in the chaos.

After a prolonged rummaging, Kaleb pulled out a broadsword, then, with a laugh, a fencing foil.

He pulled the cork from its tip and tossed it at Ivini's feet. "They locked up behind you, Padre. Better grab a weapon or find a house to shelter in. If anyone will let you in, that is. You weren't a big fan of harboring others, though, were you?"

Ivini began yelling at the soldiers, demanding they climb the peak and drag Dante off, but Alessa strode to the edge. It was time to see where their loyalties truly lay.

"Is this the line? Have we reached it yet?" She spoke to the army. "Will you make us weaker so you can kill a man—a ghiotte, but still a man—who came, willingly, to fight for Saverio, even though he wasn't required to? Will you risk your friends and families by striking down a warrior blessed with healing abilities, who climbed the peak today to protect your Finestra and Fontes?"

They stared at her, uncertain.

"Why are we here, if not to fight? Why are we fighting, if not to live? Dante can fight. He's hard to kill. I chose him to be my guard, and he's here to protect me. I ask you now—will you fight *me*? Because I won't let you take him. Not again."

A clang of metal made her flinch. Captain Papatonis, scowling ominously, struck his chest with the flat of his sword, then took a knee.

For a breathless minute, Alessa thought he would be the only one, then a handful of soldiers echoed the movement, more and more, until nearly every metal-clad warrior bowed their heads in salute. Behind them, the ragged militia in their makeshift armor and helmets raised fists in solidarity, and if their roar of approval was a bit too fierce with pride at seeing a fellow outcast standing before the thousands of elite soldiers, she didn't begrudge them.

Padre Ivini blanched, realizing he'd made a terrible mistake.

Alessa smiled grimly at her soldiers. "Today, we fight together."

The soldiers rose to stand at attention, a rolling wave of silver up the hillside. Trebuchets and archers stood at the ready, swords and scythes were drawn, and everyone looked to the enemy in the sky.

Fifty

La morte mi troverà vivo.
Death will find me alive.

The scarabeo did not attack like an army. One minute, they were a dark cloud roiling across the ocean, and the next they were everywhere, wings and claws and gaping mouths framed with glistening mandibles. There was a system to their coordinated movements, but it didn't rely on formations or pre-planned strategy.

The soldiers roared, and Kaleb clasped Alessa's shoulder, adding his spark to Kamaria's fire and Josef's cold. Alessa drew on their power, slow and gentle, trusting Dante to keep the space around them clear while Nina's power threaded with Kaleb's lightning, moving through her muscles and deep into her bones, until her entire body prickled.

Even Nina's eyes were closed and her face serene. Trusting. No sign of doubt in Alessa's ability.

"Time to kill that wolf," Kamaria muttered.

Kaleb gave her a baffled look, but there wasn't time to explain.

Alessa gathered the power they offered, held it, then turned her palm to the sky.

A hundred scarabeo met their end in a burst of fire and ice, and she bared her teeth in a victorious grin.

Another surge of power and a scarabeo shattered directly above them, raining glittering black shards. Alessa didn't flinch or brush the fragments from her bare arms. Let the detritus of demons dust her skin. Let her sparkle with it. Let it be a warning to the rest:

Here she stands, slayer of demons.

Her power purred with satisfaction. Dante had been right all along. Alessa bared her teeth in a grin, savoring the rush of adrenaline through her veins. She had her team, and her power rejoiced. Together, they fought to win.

The Fontes took turns letting go of Alessa, picking up weapons when they weren't *being* weapons. No rest for the weary, but a different kind of effort.

War was deafening. Rattling metal, the twang of bows, booming cannons, shouts and screams, and everywhere, the bone-deep vibration of thousands of wings.

Pacing. Control.

If she pushed too hard, or they weren't careful to keep at least two Fontes in contact at all times, any one of them might snap.

The scarabeo screamed, a thousand fingernails screeching across slate, and the next wave fell, frozen.

Alessa tried to pace herself, gathering and holding their gifts, trying new combinations. Nina's gift still left her queasy, but everyone whooped with glee when Alessa used it to burst scarabeo into grotesquely beautiful sprays of blue ichor.

The guards protecting them were fierce and willing to die for their saviors. Alessa loved them for it, forgave them for every time they'd flinched away from her. Now, when she needed them most, they did their duty.

Wings, sharp as knives, slashed the air before her, and for a second, Alessa saw her own reflection multiplied in the facets of gleaming red eyes.

She *was* terrifying. And for the first time, she reveled in it.

Soldiers shouted, dodging frozen scarabeo, which crashed down as solid and brittle as glass. Soon, their shattered remains made the entire hillside resemble the black rock beach.

Dante swung and slashed, keeping the air around them open. He didn't fight out of duty. He fought for her. And he was spectacular.

Kaleb and Josef made a formidable pairing, Alessa discovered when she tried to throw electrified water at the swarm. Dozens of scarabeo fell toward the sea, writhing in agony as electricity raced through bands of water wrapped around them, lightning dancing across their carapace.

"Mama always said to stay out of the water when it's storming," Kaleb said. Despite his forced humor, he was white as snow, his grip so tight she wondered if her power would suffer from the lack of blood flow to her hands.

Every few minutes, the Fontes moved in tandem, swapping places whenever someone grew fatigued, coordinating their movements so no one was ever left to bear the full brunt of Alessa's power.

The army was besieged, but a growing segment of the swarm ignored the ripe pickings of a field littered with casualties, circling the peak instead, closer and closer. Darting in and zipping by, they whizzed past as if taunting her.

The creatures had begun to realize that the small group on the cliff, especially the girl in the middle, was the main source of their problems.

The wind buffeted her from every side. Warm surges from the shore met cold gusts from the sea, churned by wings into torrents. Each breath she took was wet and sharp with salt.

A scarabeo shattered above her. She dodged its frozen wing-tip, but it sliced the end of her braid. A few inches of hair seemed a fair sacrifice to battle, but now her hair was loose, whipping around her face, obscuring her vision, and she didn't have a hand free.

Tossing her head like an irritated horse, she struggled to see past the tangled strands.

Aim. Fire. Breathe.

Something brushed her neck, and she jumped, but it was only Kamaria, gathering the damp tresses, pulling loose tendrils off her face to tie back.

"I always carry extra," Kamaria shouted over the whine of wings and clatter of weapons.

Alessa laughed. "You don't even have enough hair to tie back."

Kamaria nudged Nina aside to take her spot at Alessa's side. "No, but my friends do."

As the battle raged on, the Fontes began to falter, their power waning and stuttering, but the scarabeo didn't stop.

Her mouth went dry, her eyes gritty with sea salt. Only a faded gleam behind the leaden cloud cover told her it hadn't been days, and for all she knew, it wasn't the sun but the moon.

Someone—she didn't see who—gave the Fontes canteens, and Nina poured a bit into Alessa's mouth so she wouldn't have to let go of Kaleb and Josef.

Not enough, but it would do. There'd be time for water and food when the war was won.

She switched hands again, gathering the power they gave so freely, and hurled it forth to take down yet another wave of demons.

Breathe. Switch. Adjust to the new source of magic. Gather. Throw.

Over and over. Switch. Again.

The mantra inside her head drowned out the sound of battle. Gather. Throw. Breathe.

With every passing hour, the cold fear in Alessa's gut grew.

The scarabeo kept coming, wave after wave.

The army was drowning. Her Fontes were fading.

No more jokes or flashes of bravado to raise their spirits. No one had the strength to do anything but survive.

They couldn't keep this up forever.

Then, through the demon-choked sky, a flash of white broke through in the distance.

"A ship!" Nina cried.

Hope on the horizon.

Fifty-One

A mali estremi, estremi rimedi.
Desperate evils need desperate remedies.

Thank the gods," Kaleb wheezed.

"Will they make it in time?" Nina asked.

"That depends"—Kamaria tried to pry Kaleb's clenched hand free to take his spot, but he was too out of it to let go—"on how much time we give them."

Josef waved for her to take his spot and bent, hands on his knees, gasping for breath.

A scarabeo buzzed above them, and Kamaria ducked, throwing her hands over her head reflexively.

Kaleb gasped, momentarily left with the full brunt of Alessa's strength. She pulled away before it took him down.

Gathering what leftover power she still possessed, she threw it at the sky. Dozens of creatures lit up, bolts of lightning fracturing around them. Twitching, they lost altitude.

Kaleb was on his knees, face ashen.

"Hold on," Alessa said. "Just hold on."

Dante stepped in front of Kaleb, sword at the ready. A scarabeo swooped past, taunting, just out of reach, and he planted his feet to wait. The next time it dove, Dante's sword sliced a wing free. The creature spun, and he slashed again, rendering the other wing useless and lopping off a limb for good measure.

Kamaria cried out as a disembodied claw sliced her arm to the bone.

Nina crouched, trying to stanch Kamaria's wound.

Wings buzzed, too close, then a spray of something wet and sticky struck Alessa's face.

Dante yelled, stumbled. Blood soaked his shirt, dripping onto the stone. "I'll be okay," he said with a wet cough. "Just need a minute."

A minute they might not get. Alessa turned her fear into rage and fought harder.

The ship had stopped as close to shore as it could get, and one person, then another, dove from the side. Others clambered into a rowboat.

The ocean churned, violently tossing the boat and swimmers. Alessa stopped throwing lightning. Past the bursts of fire and gusting wind, she couldn't make out who was who, but whoever was rowing was also propelling the craft with gusts of wind, and the others kept the swooping, screaming scarabeo at bay.

Kaleb's grip was slick; he kept slipping away. But Josef and Nina grasped Alessa like a lifeline.

Alessa gathered their power once more, flinging a blast of cold that tore a massive chunk from the swarm.

Nina cried out in pain, but Alessa couldn't stop to see what had happened.

She needed to buy them time. Precious minutes for the other Fontes to make it up the peak, for Dante to heal. Time.

She didn't have any.

The rowboat was drifting back out to sea, and figures ran, high-kneed, through the shallows, bursts of light and swirls of ice blossoming above them. Small and ineffective compared to what she could do with their gifts, but it kept the creatures away.

So close. They were so close.

The first swimmer to reach the shore held up her waterlogged skirts to sprint up the beach. The tall figure behind her looked like Kamaria. It had to be Shomari, the traitorous brother she'd sworn would help them.

As they vanished below the peak, Alessa turned to her weak, wounded Fontes. Trying to choose was a deadly game of roulette.

Ignoring his protest, Alessa seized the sword from Dante's weak grip, gathering a bit of his fighting gift as she did so.

She glared at the flying creatures above, watching to see which one was next.

One dove, and she arced the blade through the air. The impact rattled through her body, but she'd barely stunned the monster. It swooped back around, and she swung again.

Dante's fighting skills faded, but the demons kept coming. She screamed in anger and frustration.

A beat without an attack, a moment of reprieve. One breath. That's all she asked.

Grime and sweat blurred her vision, and the sword wavered in her grasp.

Dea, help me.

Saida, wheezing, pulled it free. "I'm sorry we're late."

Shomari slid his fingers through Alessa's, using his other

hand to grip his sister's shoulder in an unspoken apology. Kamaria punched his arm, but there were tears in her eyes.

Alessa couldn't look to see how Dante was managing. Didn't have time. She just had to hope it wasn't too late for him.

A century, a lifetime, a heartbeat, a breath. She wouldn't know until later how much time passed while she fought.

Saida's wind and Shomari's water drew a waterspout from the sea, sucking scarabeo from the sky, and when the creatures closest were consumed, Alessa let the water fall and twisted the wind toward the shore to scramble the demonic flight patterns.

Wings snapped, demons fell, and her soldiers were ready below, waiting with swords and scythes to finish them.

The creatures seemed to smell a whiff of defeat, and their screams intensified.

Every hair on Alessa's body rose.

Nina covered her ears, her face screwed up in agony, but Josef was a statue. "Keep going," he said. "Don't stop."

She had no choice.

Blood squelched with every hand she clasped, but when one hand vanished, another took its place.

The world was nothing but a maelstrom of cold and heat, fire and ice, the swell and flux of Nina's strange gift diverting and warping, ripping swaths through the swarm.

Alessa saw sky, briefly, a glint of sun that told her time was passing, then darkness and wings and claws closed in again. But she'd seen the sky and she'd fight to see it again.

A silver blade slashed past, proof Dante was alive and still fighting.

Across the hillside behind Finestra's Peak and the beach before it, soldiers battled, stumbling through the waves, stabbing half-submerged scarabeo. The orderly rows of warriors following commands had disintegrated, commanders shouting orders to ranks who couldn't hear them over the screams, or were too terrified to listen.

And all the while, the swarm above swooped and regrouped, communicating without words, a hive mind that didn't need directions or plans to work in tandem.

Two scarabeo dove at Dante.

He stabbed and slashed, hidden by a tangle of claws and mandibles, and she sent a burst of flame to assist.

The scarabeo fell, screaming, over the cliff's edge.

Dante dropped to his knees, clutching his bloodied side, his sword abandoned beside him.

Dante could heal himself. He *would* heal himself. He had to.

But while soldiers battled around her and the Fontes, keeping the area around them clear, Dante was unprotected.

The roiling darkness coalesced as another wave of scarabeo saw easy prey.

Alessa snatched a scythe from the ground and ran, slashing it toward the scarabeo bent on reaching Dante. The curved blade at the end of the staff lopped off every leg on one side, and the bulk crashed down on the peak, nearly crushing Dante.

"Help him," she shouted at the nearest soldiers. "Keep them away until he's healed."

Fontes waited, hands at the ready, for Alessa to resume the fight, but everywhere she looked, there was nothing but chaos.

She was doing her best, but it wasn't enough. Too many scarabeo got past her, descending on an army lost to panic. She flinched as two soldiers, fighting beside each other, were ambushed and snapped in half.

If only her army could communicate without words, too.

A desperate idea lodged in her mind.

Time to break all the rules.

Fifty-Two

Alla fine del gioco, re e pedone finiscono nella stessa scatola.
When the game is over, the king and the pawn
go in the same box.

The dying scarabeo twitched violently, legs curling in like a dead spider.

Alessa lunged, her bare hand closing over one smooth claw.

She retched as an oily power flowed into her, but she didn't let go until it reached the core of her gift.

Like falling out of bed mid-dream, something inside her came awake with a lurch.

"Regroup," she ordered, but the word wasn't merely spoken aloud. It was an order, a mental compelling, a dozen thoughts condensed into one, like a brain signaling a body to stand.

The army—her army—snapped to attention, thousands of warriors tuned as one. Through her eyes, through each other's eyes, they saw the fight from every angle, countless minds woven together into one.

The scarabeo gave one last shudder and went still.

"To me!" Alessa shouted at her Fontes, and they found her side. Already, the scarabeo's power—she couldn't think of it as a gift—was fading, the precise symmetry of her fighters falling out of rhythm, but as she sent a storm of ice and lightning to fell a swath of scarabeo, the soldiers below fought with renewed purpose, united once more.

They might actually get through Divorando.

She regretted the thought as soon as it came to her. Never tempt the gods. Never.

Fire tore through her. A fire she'd lived through once before.

Nina screamed.

She'd heard that before, too.

Alessa looked down at the front of her slip of a dress, at the sharp limb, thrust into her belly with a scarabeo's death spasm. The creature curled in on itself.

Blood soaked through the links of her chain mail.

Screams. Clanging blades. Her Fontes and guard burst into motion, fighting to surround her as she stumbled.

Dante couldn't slow her fall this time. He was already on the ground. A wide gash ran from his chin to one ear, and he was covered in so much blood she couldn't be sure if they had matching fatal wounds or different ones. Hands clutched at her, trying to break her fall, but she smelled dirt, tasted it. Dante lay a few feet away, a flicker of sunlight across his face.

The army would have to take care of the rest. She wouldn't be saving them.

Dante's eyes opened, and his pupils shrank as he focused on

her. He lifted his head. Fingers clawing at the dirt, he dragged himself closer, then stopped to cough. He didn't bother wiping the blood from his chin before he began to drag himself again.

One arm's length. Another.

His gift might be enough to save him. It wasn't enough for them both.

So many memories she'd never make. Kisses they'd never share. Sunrises and sunsets they could have watched together.

She focused on him, detaching from the raging battle. She couldn't help them anymore. She couldn't even help herself.

The darkness spread inside her, but she held on. Dante was trying to get to her. She had to stay until he did.

What was one more death, or two, on a day when countless had died already?

Everything.

Somehow, he made it to her. Trembling on one elbow, his eyes fixed on hers, and he brushed her cheek with the back of his fingers.

"Gabriele," he said. "My name is Gabriele."

She raised her hand to find his. "But I haven't won."

He smiled. "You will." He grabbed her hand, and his jaw clenched over a scream of pain.

"No," she said, trying to get free of his grip as she realized what he was doing, but Dante wouldn't let go. Hot tears blurred her vision as life drained from his face.

He was giving his gift to her.

She couldn't get free, and she couldn't stop it from flowing to her. Trying to fight it would only waste the gift he gave so freely.

Something twisted in the place where her power originated, the shift from taking a gift to magnifying. She knew it well by now, but she'd only felt it with the Fontes' power, never with *his*.

She sobbed as her pain blinked out, and a new power, greater than anything she'd experienced before, burst free.

Dante was saving her, so she could save them.

The world vanished in a flash, followed by such a complete absence of sound she thought her eardrums had burst.

A dome of light expanded, obliterating scarabeo as it engulfed them, but leaving people untouched. The ghiotte's power of healing and self-protection bloomed outward and banished the darkness.

Alessa stared up, through the ring of Fontes and guards, their weapons raised against foes who were vanishing into nothingness.

Where light met dark, both blinked out, and the bubble began to look like lace.

"Do you see it?" she whispered to him. "Do you see what you did?"

Enduring light, shone through a divine window, burned the demons to ashes.

Dante's gift had saved them all.

"Dante?" She looked back at him, took his face between her hands.

His eyes were open, but he couldn't see.

He'd never see anything again.

Fifty-Three

La speranza è l'ultima a morire.
Hope is the last thing to die.

Alessa's anguished cry was lost to the clamor of battle.

She still touched Dante's skin, but the space between them was as wide as the ocean. His eyelashes didn't flutter, even when a dead scarabeo crashed against the peak, spattering them with gore.

Alessa shook with violent tremors, but distant voices urged her on, hands pulling her up with bruising grips. They wouldn't let her mourn, wouldn't let her be.

The army was still fighting. Her friends were still fighting.

She wasn't alone.

She couldn't give up.

Letting go was the hardest thing she'd ever done, but the battle wasn't over.

Her friends were all around, infusing her with love and sympathy as well as their magic.

Kaleb dragged himself to his feet. At some point, a scarabeo claw had caught him in the face, leaving a brutal gash down his forehead and through one eye, but he was alive, even with half his face a bloody ruin. Squinting through his good eye, he extended his hand to her. Kamaria clenched the other, so tightly it hurt, but Alessa held on to the pain.

Pain was real. Pain meant she was alive. *They* were alive. The Fortezza was full of people, including her family and thousands of others, alive.

The impenetrable wall of claws and wings that had blocked out the sky before was only scattered scarabeo now. Angry monsters crazed with desperation as they sensed their impending failure. The scarabeo would lose, one way or another, but Alessa could stop them from taking more lives. She could stop more from getting to the city, where people cowered behind dented metal shutters as the walls shook and scarabeo gnawed at their doors.

Alessa built a fortress around the heartbroken girl wailing inside her and turned to the sky.

Instinct guided her fight. Two hands, two more. Alessa moved among her battalion of Fontes, gathering and hoarding their power to use as many gifts as possible with every surge.

The scream of anguish she couldn't release was channeled into a weapon, and her power became a crescendo of fury and grief that burst free in a typhoon of lightning and fire and ice. Even the ocean responded, heaving into towering waves that swallowed scarabeo and dragged them to the depths.

Bit by bit, the sky cleared. Sound returned.

A hand released hers. Another. Kaleb dropped and rolled to his back, chest heaving.

Groans and cries of pain mingled with shouts of victory. Alessa went limp, hollow and wrung out, as their gifts faded away.

She sank to the ground and draped herself over Dante's body, shielding him in death as she hadn't in life. Her hands roamed his neck, searching for a pulse, the faintest breath, any sign of life, but nothing. No flutter against her fingertips, no brush of breath against her palm. Nothing.

The general was bowing to her, his scarred face slick with blood and scarabeo gore, assuring her that the soldiers could finish the cleanup without her.

She blinked, and Nina and Saida had her by the arms, guiding her down Finestra's Peak and up the road toward the city.

Panic surged, and she fought free, turning to search for Dante.

He shouldn't be alone. They couldn't leave him alone.

"They're bringing him," Nina said, and Alessa had the strange sense that it wasn't the first time Nina had reassured her of this. "Right behind us, see?"

Sure enough, two soldiers trailed behind them, bearing a stretcher, with Josef steadying it.

The city gates creaked open, and the first wave of cleanup crews stepped out, spears ready to gore any remaining scarabeo who skittered in the shadows. A man, followed by a woman, then more. They stared at the clear blue sky, at the rest of the landscape. Scarred and soiled as it was, Saverio still stood.

One by one, their eyes turned to her with wonder.

Alessa heard herself declare the battle over, and a cheer rose. A cry of victory she couldn't share. Shouts of joy and relief so distant from the agony tearing her apart.

She kept her eyes forward as people moved aside to let the

weary saviors pass, but she could feel Dante's presence, or lack of it, behind her.

Anger bled into the holes left by grief. They needed to know who had saved them, and it wasn't her.

She stopped in the middle of the crowd. "There is your savior. His name was—" She gathered herself. "His name was Gabriele Dante Lucente."

Gabriele Dante Lucente. *God-granted strength and enduring light.*

She sobbed a laugh. No wonder he hadn't told her.

"He believed he was a monster because we told him he was. He believed he could bring only darkness into the world because we told him darkness was all he had. But he was the light. And he gave *everything* to save you."

He gave everything, and she'd lost him.

A small, tentative hand found Alessa's shoulder. Nina, tears coursing down her blood-streaked face.

Then Kamaria, halting but walking.

Josef paused to bow low.

Farther down the line, a hand saluted from a stretcher. Kaleb.

Alessa had made it through a battle with not one, but many Fontes alive.

Her broken, blood-soaked army of friends.

Sometime soon, she would see her family, and she would be thankful they lived, too. Sometime soon she would remember that the world was more than one person, and one death did not erase a thousand lives saved. Someday soon she would feel as though she had done her duty. But not today.

She instructed the men bearing Dante's stretcher to follow her into the temple.

"You have wounds, Alessa," Nina said softly, as the soldiers placed Dante's body on the altar. "You should come inside and let the doctors examine you."

"She will," Kamaria said. "Give her a minute."

Saida beckoned Nina over. "Come on, help me get Kamaria up the stairs."

They left, followed by the soldiers, and Alessa was alone in the darkness.

Three times she'd knelt before bodies on this altar.

This time, tears came easily, but the tears that brought him to the Cittadella in the first place and kept him there the next couldn't bring him back.

The dank cold reached for her bones, but couldn't chill her, because she was somewhere else. Somewhere warm, with hot sand beneath her toes, and a calloused hand in hers.

Gently, she closed his eyes. He could have been sleeping, if one slept on bare stone.

If one slept in clothing soaked with blood.

She ran her fingers over his, so cold and stiff.

Alone in the silent temple, she kneeled before the man she loved. No jeweled coffin or bed of velvet. No funeral or choir. The same in death as he'd gone through most of life—alone and forgotten.

But never by her.

Hands trembling, she cupped her palms as though in prayer, bowing her head to let the tears fall, unchecked.

Outside, people needed their savior, people injured and dying who deserved to be thanked and blessed, but she couldn't bear to leave him alone with nothing to prove he'd been loved and cherished in life.

A gift.

She spread her fingers across his chest, her heart beating hard enough for them both.

She shouldn't even hope.

It was impossible.

But like she'd done for Hugo the last time she kneeled on the altar, she searched the hollows inside her.

Nothing at first.

Then, a flicker.

An echo of Dante's gift, the fragment she'd stolen—no, the part he'd given her—when he'd died.

Slowly, carefully, she drew the power deeper, closer to the part of her the gods had blessed.

She gathered Dante's gift.

And she gave it back.

Fifty-Four

Piccola favilla gran fiamma seconda.
A little spark kindles a great fire.

R elief.

The pain, the noise, the light—it all ceased. The battle vanished, and Dante felt nothing.

Not because his body went numb, but because he . . . wasn't.

He had no heart, so his pulse didn't pound. He *knew* fear, recognized the mental prickle of warning, but not in any way he'd felt before. He had no eyes, so damned if he knew how he could see a glow in the darkness. But there it was. Everywhere. A warm, rosy light concentrated in one spot, expanding to meet him.

Something about the light was trying to calm him, and it *wasn't* working.

After twenty years expecting death around every damn corner, tempting the gods time and time again, daring them to just *do it already*, he was finally dead. And he was pissed.

He'd chosen to become Alessa's guard. To climb that ugly

peak. To heal her with his gift, knowing it would kill him. And he'd do it again.

But he didn't even get to see if it had worked? If she was okay? If the battle was won? He'd finally decided to become something other than a selfish asshole, and his prize was a light show and a headache without a head?

Fanculo. *Screw that.*

He couldn't turn to find the source of the sound, but it didn't matter, because it wasn't behind him. Or in front. If there was such a thing as direction in this place. The sound was inside him. Maybe the light was, too. Or, it would have been, if there was any *him* to be inside.

The sound wasn't music. There was no word for it. It had *meaning*, though. It was a language, sort of, or maybe it *was* language in its purest form. Miseria ladra, his head would have throbbed if he had one.

Death was supposed to be a relief, an end to mortal suffering. This was bullshit.

Maybe if he had an eternity to listen, he'd understand what the light was trying to tell him, but death hadn't blessed him with patience.

I don't speak colors or music. He aimed the thought at the brightest part of the glowing whatever-the-hell-it-was. *Pick a language I know or cut it out. I've had a long day.*

The thing...laughed? Silently. A bubble of affectionate amusement, popping inside him.

Dante sent a mental scowl. *Please tell me we're not doing this for eternity.*

Something tingled. His...fingers? They materialized in front of his face. His face! He had a face. And a body. *Thank Dea.*

Literally.

"Uh, thanks," he said, to test out his voice. It sounded the same. "Dea?"

The bubble of mirth returned, warmer and brighter, but also not quite a confirmation. At least this time the sensation was in his chest, because he had one. Clothes, too, which were unnecessary, but appreciated. Gods probably didn't give a shit about nudity, but it was a hard habit to shake.

"So . . . you *are* Dea? Or you aren't?"

Correct.

He knew that feeling. Didn't answer the question though. It was Dea *and* not Dea. Fun game. "Listen, I don't mean to sound ungrateful here, but can you tell me if it worked? Is she going to be okay?"

The light wavered, almost but not quite fully taking form, flickering like a candle in an open window.

A mirage of a woman, tall and thin, with light brown hair and the same dark eyes he saw every time he looked in the mirror.

"Mama?"

His mother—or the goddess who looked like his mother—reached out a hand to him, her eyes somehow full of love and regret at the same time.

Nothing could have stopped Dante from reaching back.

His hand found only warmth where hers should have been. The light moved up his arm, tingling over his skin, soaking through to heat him from the inside. The first tide of emotion—pride, love, reassurance—was as welcoming as a hearth fire after a freezing rain, and he could have basked in it forever.

But warmth became heat—scorching, crackling, igniting—tinged with profound regret that there wasn't time to do it any other way. This was the fastest way to show him what he needed to know. And there was no time to wait.

His mother smiled, but it was the saddest thing he'd ever seen.

She vanished, and his mind exploded.

A voracious, murky ocean swallowing the shore, battering the city walls, belching forth scaly, fanged creatures with claws like scythes. Ash clouds choking the skies above rivers of blood, and people, everywhere, burning and burning and burning.

One, darkness made flesh, led the attack, battling an army of—

Recognition jolted through him, and a scream tore from his throat as the inferno consumed him.

Fifty-Five

Chi mora mor, e chi camba cambe.
Those who die die, and those who live live.

Alessa bent her head to Dante's unmoving chest, heed-less of the grime and blood and scarabeo ichor caked to his shirt.

Saving the world was such a hollow victory.

Eyes clenched, she fought to lock in every memory she had of him. The way his dark eyes smiled, even when his mouth didn't. How he'd watched her like he desperately wanted to stop but couldn't tear his eyes away. How safe and cherished she'd felt in his arms. And how she loved it when he'd called her—

"Luce mia."

Alessa jerked up.

Dante's haunted eyes met hers.

She blinked, but the illusion didn't fade. The skin on his face was drawn tight with pain, but he was alive.

"Dante." She touched his cheek, and he gasped.

Yanking her hand back, Alessa stumbled to her feet and sprinted to the corridor, screaming for help.

She hung back as medics rushed into the temple. She'd made it through a war without being sick, but sourness clawed up her throat as Dante cried out, his teeth bared in a rictus of agony.

He was alive. Alive. The word became a chant, then a prayer.

The medics poked, prodded, and bandaged for hours before loading Dante onto a gurney for transport to the triage center in the Cittadella, but he was alive.

He nearly bled out on the way there, but by the time the sun rose—or set, she honestly wasn't sure—they said he was stable.

Stable.

She'd never forget the sounds, or the smells, of soldiers hurt and dying. Her battle would go down in history as one of the shortest, but casualties were high, and the wounded were too lost to pain to care about their place in history.

Alessa tried to sit with Dante, but he kept opening his eyes, muttering about shadows that spoke and memories of futures, and he seemed so distressed at her lack of understanding that when a nurse suggested she leave so he could rest, she did.

Dante wasn't the only one suffering. Alessa walked the rows and rows of wounded soldiers, pausing to thank them, listening to their final words, fetching water and broth and bandages. Summoning medics when it seemed worth trying to save them, listening to their final words when it wasn't.

She'd begun to think she'd forgotten how to pray, but she prayed with hundreds, and she meant every word.

Protect them, Dea, and see them safely home. Be it to their mortal lives or their eternal rest, carry them in your gentle grasp and light their way with love.

She'd done her duty, and they had done theirs.

Despite the shocked faces, Alessa made herself useful in any small way she could as the hours dragged on.

She was dabbing a soldier's forehead with a wet cloth when a small voice called out to her.

"Someone needs you in the critical care section," said a nurse who didn't seem old enough for the responsibility.

Heart in her throat, Alessa hurried back to the area reserved for the most serious cases. Dante's injuries had been *so* terrible, but she'd seen him heal before . . .

"Adrick?" she said, startled by the sight of a curly blond head beside Dante's cot.

Adrick was there, tending the sick. He was an apothecary assistant. He was her brother. Of course he'd come.

Adrick stood. "I brought the best pain treatments we have, but he won't take them until he talks to you."

Dante's eyes were open, but he was staring up at the sky, not at her, face pale, jaw clenched, hands fisted at his side.

He blinked, and she exhaled.

Adrick pulled her into a hug, squeezing tight and hauling her off the ground. "You did it, little sister."

"Put me down, you fool." She slapped him lightly on the back. "I'm still dangerous. And for Dea's sake, you're two minutes older than me. Enough with the little sister nonsense."

Adrick laughed and lowered her to the ground. "Don't want you getting a big head just because you saved us all. Now, tell this handsome demon to take the damn medicine, will you? He's more stubborn than you are."

She sank to her knees, pulling off one glove. "Dante—"

His entire body spasmed as her hand found his.

"I'm sorry," she gasped and pulled away, fumbling to put her glove back on. She cursed silently. Of course, he was still too weak to tolerate her touch.

"You won't take the medicine until you tell me something, huh?" she asked, smiling through her tears. "So speak. Then I'm pouring it down your throat."

"Crollo," Dante wheezed. A tear slid from the corner of his eye, and she had to fight the urge to brush it away. "He's not finished. I saw—I heard—" He stopped to take a short, shuddering breath. "It's all connected. Your power. The end. It's not over."

She shushed him. "But it's over for right now, yes?"

A tight, pained nod.

"Then get some rest, so you can heal. And for Dea's sake, Dante, take the medicine."

Adrick measured out a dosage and helped Dante raise his head enough to swallow. Alessa beckoned to the nearest medic.

"You know what he is, right?" she asked, daring the middle-aged woman in spectacles to have a problem with Dante's identity.

The woman nodded, eyebrows drawn. "I do, and I'd be fascinated to hear about what you've witnessed. But as for right now, he's stable, but not improving. These things take time, though."

"But you've seen some improvement, right?" Alessa said. "Small cuts healing, bruises fading?"

It wasn't unusual for someone to waver on the verge of death for days or even weeks after a grievous injury. It was, however, unusual for a ghiotte.

"I'm afraid not, Finestra. If anything, he's had a bit of back-sliding, but we caught it before it got too bad."

Alessa frowned. It *was* still early. And he *had* come back from the dead. It was a lot to ask of one man. It wasn't much to cling to, but she held on to a sliver of hope.

Fifty-Six

Tutto sapere è niente sapere.
To know everything is to know nothing.

P orca troia," Dante cursed, waking with a start—the only
way he woke these days.

Every time he closed his eyes, he died all over again,
and every time he opened them, it felt like being born from the
fire again.

Asleep, awake, it didn't matter. There was no relief.

The never-ceasing noise plucked at his nerves. Labored
breathing, soft moans, low-pitched voices. One more day on this
cot, inhaling disinfectant and waking to other people's misery,
would kill him.

"Puttana la miseria," he said through gritted teeth.

Dottoressa Agostino shot him a dark look.

"Mi scusi," Dante said, only half sarcastically. He'd heard
worse from other patients in the common tongue every damn
day, but she held this against him?

He didn't *feel* pain, he *was* pain. Every damn hair on his head hurt. But he'd put it off long enough. Choking down another groan, he sat up.

Alessa drew his gaze like a magnet. Sitting on a cot across the room, her face lit with joy when she saw him.

She jumped up, excused herself, and hurried toward him, leaving the soldier she'd been talking to gaping at her back. Dante fought a smile. She did that all the time, and she had no idea, flitting from one person or thought to another with no clue that anyone might not be able to keep up.

"How are you feeling?" She knelt beside him and took his hand, silk gloves against bare skin.

"Take them off," he said softly.

Her eyes, more green than brown today, went wide, long lashes fluttering with nerves. "Later. You're still recovering, and—"

"Please," he begged. "Take them off."

She paled. Her hands shook as she removed her gloves and brushed the back of his hand with her fingers.

His muscles seized. He bit his lip, hard. *Che palle.*

Alessa leapt to her feet, blinking away tears. "It's too soon. You need more time to heal. I'm going to find Adrick and Josef. They promised to help you up the stairs, and the doctor says you're ready—" She hurried away mid-sentence.

Dante dropped his head back against the stone wall and stared up at the metal filigree over the courtyard.

No point denying it.

He wasn't getting worse, but he wasn't getting better. At least, no faster than anyone else.

A nurse strode toward him with a bowl of something steaming, a smile on her face that he couldn't return.

They treated him like a normal person, and at first, he'd assumed they didn't know. But they did. Hell, they fought over who got to tend to the *Ghiotte Fonte*. His lip curled at the phrase.

They knew exactly what he was.

Or at least, what he *had been*.

Fifty-Seven

Traduttore, traditore.
Translator, traitor. All translation is flawed.

A month after Divorando, Alessa watched as Kaleb and Dante helped each other stand, swaying until they found their balance. In bandages and loose-fitting robes, they looked like a pair of drunken pirates who'd lost their pants.

Dante caught Alessa watching, and his gaze slid away a bit too fast.

Inhaling through her nose, she tamped down the frequent urge to shake him.

Her feelings hadn't changed. If anything, she cared even more than she had before, but Dante's pride had taken a hit more brutal than the one to his body, and his demons refused to grant him peace, whispering threats or promises he shared with no one.

Time might not be enough to heal all wounds, but it was the only thing she could offer.

Kaleb tipped, grasping open air for a handhold, and Alessa lurched to her feet, ready to help. Dante steadied him before she could, and the two men steeled themselves to begin walking.

The other Fontes and wounded soldiers had returned to their homes to recuperate, but Kaleb claimed he'd grown too used to the luxury of the Cittadella to give it up, and technically, he *was* Alessa's official Fonte.

Dante had no home.

So, they'd stayed.

Kaleb fashioned hats out of bandages, demanding the nurses tell him he was prettier than Dante. He complained dramatically that the soup was too soupy and the cakes were too sweet until they brought him something else, then he'd eat all of his food and steal bites from Dante's untouched tray until Dante got annoyed and ate something out of spite.

Kaleb didn't perform *despite* Dante's glares, but because of them. Dante needed a distraction, and Kaleb provided it.

More important, Kaleb offered the sort of obnoxious encouragement via insult that Dante needed, baffling as it was. Her chosen Fonte and her chosen love spent their days frustrating the physical therapists and nurses who put them through their exercises and monitored their recovery, while tormenting each other in a bizarre contest to see who could express their suffering with the most creative use of swear words.

Dante, being bilingual, usually came out on top.

Thank Dea she'd barely touched him when his eyes first opened on the altar.

If she had, he might have died all over again.

When he spent the last of his healing power to save her, Dante had taken most of his gift with him as he left the mortal plane.

The final remnant, the echo, transferred to her as he died, and she'd used it—with more than a little help from Dea—to coax his body back to the living. But his power hadn't come with him.

Swallowing a lump in her throat, Alessa shouted a few teasing words of encouragement to Kaleb as he took a tentative step. He groaned and invented a new curse word, sending the nurse into a fit of giggles.

Watching Dante brace himself on the headboard of her bed, alone in his thoughts, Alessa urged the heat in the back of her throat to ease.

He was *alive*.

She couldn't touch him, at least not yet, but he was alive.

That was what mattered.

The nurse said something to Dante, and he shook his head, jaw clenched.

Alessa caught Kaleb's eye, and he covered his forehead with the back of his hand in an exaggerated swoon. "Mercy! Nurse, this ghiotte is trying to murder me! Let me rest, beast!"

Dante hid a half smile as Kaleb accepted the nurse's assistance and hobbled out of the room.

He lowered himself to the couch with a grimace, his head falling back with a sigh of relief.

"Can I get you anything?" Alessa asked.

"Nah, just come here," Dante mumbled. "Promise I'll keep my hands to myself."

Alessa checked to be sure there was no skin visible between her gloves and sleeves before walking over. "I've heard that before."

As she passed the open balcony doors, a cheer rose from the crowd below. They gathered daily in the piazza, hoping for a glimpse of their saviors on the balcony, so Alessa obliged every morning and evening, while Kaleb insisted on being rolled to the window often to wave at his supporters.

Dante always refused. He didn't know how to be celebrated or beloved. Another thing that would take time.

She curled up beside him, noting the dark smudge of exhaustion beneath his eyes. "You've been dreaming again."

A shadow passed behind his eyes. "I'm not sure they *are* dreams."

Alessa frowned. "Meaning?"

"I think she's trying to tell me something."

"She?"

"Dea. My mother? Whoever it was. She was proud, like I was finally being who I was supposed to be, or something. But she needed me to know I wasn't finished." Dante stared at the ceiling. "The more time passes, the less sure I am about what I saw— heard—I don't know what to call it. But she was trying to help us, to give us a clue."

Alessa was still wearing her gloves, so she brushed a dark curl off his temple.

Dante leaned into her palm, his lips moving against the silk. "I think she wants me to find La Fonte di Guarigione."

Alessa sat up. "It still exists? Then I'll go right now and bring water back for you. You'll be healed. Maybe you can go back to—"

"No." He shook his head. "I don't think that's how it works."

"Why not? I don't care how far I have to go, I will. You could be healed, your power restored. And if you're right, and Crollo is planning something worse, we need that water for the troops."

"I think that's what she's trying to tell me. That we need to find it before he sends whatever he's planning."

"Well, where is it, then? Is it on Saverio?"

He closed his eyes. "Not anymore."

"Anymore?" Her scalp prickled. "Dante, how can a spring move?"

"It's not a spring."

She made a face. "I don't know much of the old language, but I do know that part. 'ha dato loro una fonte di guarigione—*she gave them a healing fountain.*'"

"Your accent is *still* terrible." Dante half-smiled. "'E quando arrivò il momento della battaglia, i combattenti sarebbero stati forti, poiché ha dato loro una fonte della guarigione.' It can mean fountain, but another way to translate *una fonte* is *wellspring— source.*"

Alessa whispered it to herself, trying on the words with the new meaning he'd offered.

And when it came time for battle, the fighters would be strong, for she gave them . . . a source of healing.

She stilled. "You're saying that Dea's third gift isn't on Saverio anymore, because . . ."

Dante closed his eyes. "Because we banished them."

Her breath left her body.

To survive the horror Crollo had planned, they needed an army of nearly invincible soldiers.

But first, they had to find them.

Acknowledgments

I've always told myself stories, but it wasn't until a few years ago that I tried to write them down. See, "real" writers always seemed like quiet, solitary souls, and I . . . am not. And yet, since deciding to become a writer—or at least *realizing* I'd decided, because apparently everyone knew but me—my life has been filled with more wonderful people than ever. I could fill a hundred pages with gratitude, and I'd still run out of room, but I'll try to keep it (somewhat) brief.

First, my eternal thanks to my agent, Chelsea Eberly, the greatest champion a writer could ask for. Thank you for believing in this book and in me, and for your enthusiasm, guidance, and all around wonderfulness.

Vicki Lame, editor extraordinaire, working with you has been a dream come true. Thank you for seeing everything this book could be, for working tirelessly to get it across the finish line, and for adding me to your incredible roster of authors.

All my gratitude to everyone at Wednesday Books, both past and present: Jennie Conway, Angelica Chong, and Vanessa Aguirre, for your patience, kindness, and attention to detail that kept me (mostly) on deadline, despite my endless questions and all the times I forgot to hit "reply all." I swear I'll get the hang of it eventually. Michelle McMillian, Melanie Sanders, Lena Shekhter, Anne Newgarden, Meghan Harrington, Alexis Neuville, and Brant Janeway, for your hard work behind the scenes, and Rhys Davies for the beautiful maps. A very special thank-you to Kerri Resnick and Olga Grlic, for designing the incredible cover, and Kemi Mai, for bringing it to life. I am in awe. I couldn't have asked for a better publishing team than St. Martin's Press and Wednesday Books, and I'm so honored to work with all of you.

My deepest thanks to critique partners, friends, experts, and authenticity readers who went above and beyond to help me do justice to this cast of characters, including but not limited to Claudia Giuffrida, Amy Acosta, Anah Tillar, Iori Kusano, Anonymous, and Irtefa Binte-Farid, who gets extra friendship points for reading the whole book in one night. I hope I made you proud.

Ron Harris, Kristie Smeltzer, Megan Manzano, and everyone at Writer House, thank you for seeing potential in me before I knew if I had any. Taylor Harris, my local debut buddy, look at us now! Alice, Naomi, Christine, Jess, Meghann, Chae-Yeon, and all my patient friends and family members, thank you for listening to my bookish rambles. Autumn Ingram, thank you for teaching me (and by extension, Alessa) how to innocently slip innuendo into any conversation.

Eliza, Melody, Ryan, Brook, Jeff, Emily, Kristine, Erin, and the rest of the No Excuses crew, thank you for reading those early drafts despite my *terrible* first pitch, especially Lyla Lawless for dissecting all those synopses. Margie Fuston, you're a lifesaver and the only reason this book has a sequel. Thanks for being the angel (devil? devilish angel?) on my shoulder.

Despite detours, disappointments, and discarded manuscripts, my path to publication glittered with magic thanks to the fairy godmothers of mentorship, Brenda Drake and Alexa Donne, and the Pitch Wars and Author Mentor Match communities, especially my mentors, Molly E. Lee and Jamie Krakover. Pitch Wars Class of 2017, you have my heart forever. Kylie Schachte, Jade Loren, Ipuna Black, Julie Christensen, and so many more, thank you for picking me up when I thought I'd never get here, and for celebrating the loudest when I did. Special shout-out to Shelby Mahurin, for a pep talk when I needed it most and for inspiring me to write the book I wanted to read.

My dear friends, Rajani LaRocca, and Andrea Contos, I'm so grateful that writing led me to you. Anna Rae Mercier, my writerly soulmate, podcast partner, and the most patient critique partner on the planet, thank you, thank you, thank you. For everything.

Ayana Gray, Lauren Blackwood, and Natalie Crown, I never thought I'd make new friends during lockdown, but I'm so glad we found one another. Lyssa Mia Smith and Sophie Clark, it was a joy being your mentor and even better becoming friends.

Tamora Pierce, Elle Cosimano, Sarah Glenn Marsh, Hannah Whitten, Lyndall Clipstone, Lauren Blackwood, Ayana Gray, and Allison Saft, thank you for taking the time to read and for the generous praise I will cherish forever. And every writer, reader, and bookseller who has shared their enthusiasm, thank you from the bottom of my heart for loving Alessa and Dante.

Grazie mille to Monica, Emma, and Diletta, for inspiring me, lending me your names, correcting my Italian when I butchered it accidentally, and forgiving me when I did so on purpose. This book absolutely would not exist without you. Dante is lucky to call you family, and so am I.

None of this would have been possible without my amazing family. My mother, who gave me her love for words and the determination to try to make them perfect, and who still tries valiantly to teach me Italian grammar and comma usage. And my father, who taught me to love rom-coms, speculative fiction, and disaster movies. I am who I am, and this book is what it is, because of you.

To my husband, Brian, the most pragmatic person I know, you choose to have unwavering faith in me and my impossible dream anyway, and that means everything. Being married to an author *should* come with really nice benefits, but alas, all you get is your name in the acknowledgments, a messy house, a lifetime of people asking which character is based on you, and my love. And finally, my children. Thank you for all the hugs and brainstorming ideas, for being my biggest cheerleaders, and most of all, for being your wonderful selves. You are my light.